CW01512131

A Moon in All Things

A NOVEL

With Original Songs By
JENNIFER ELWELL COMEAU

Music and Lyrics Copyright © 2025 Jennifer Elwell Comeau and Michael Farquharson

Interior Formatting and Map Illustration: Mariella Travis | www.alleiram.com
Parchment Illustration: John Forssen

ISBN
978-1-961905-45-0 (Paperback)
978-1-961905-18-4 (eBook)

12 Willows Press
Winterport, Maine
www.12willowspress.com

Praise for *A Moon in All Things*

"Atmospheric, subtle, and captivating"

—Forward Reviews, Clarion

"Tears, sighs, fabulous!"

—Geralyn White Dreyfous, Academy Award-winning film producer

"A writer should be able to 'dance with a pen' according to Nietzsche. If we accept this as a test for a writer, then Jennifer Comeau passes with flying colors her first time out of the gate with *A Moon in All Things*. This work is not formulaic magic realism, but rather reality as magic. This is a generous, warm-hearted, and very well-researched novel and the reader will want more."

—Tom Bancroft, former book critic

"An excellent and thoroughly enjoyable read. I felt fully immersed in Comeau's story world and loved the details of sea life and old Irish culture that are inherent to the piece ... the map of the village was wonderful. ... This is fantastic work."

—Ink & Insights Competition (Score: 246/250)

"Comeau delivers a beautifully crafted historical fantasy infused with lyricism and Celtic magic. [The] heroine's viewpoint is consistently engrossing, allowing readers full access to her internal life, as well as a vicarious connection to the natural world that so informs her character."

—Booklife Prize

"Captivated by lucid prose and an irresistible tale of high stakes and true love, I started reading *A Moon in All Things* in the morning, continued into the afternoon and evening, and finished it in a weekend with a grateful sigh. This book will enthrall any reader who has wrestled with following her path. As a coming-of-age tale that dives deeply into questions of home, tradition, and calling, it will stay with me for a long, long time."

—Jena Schwartz, writing coach and author of, *Why I was Late for Our Meeting. Don't Miss This*

"This book brims with life, magic, and a flow back to the forces of nature we have forsaken. Oh my."

—Ellen Kleiner, former publishing editor

"Jennifer E Comeau has crafted a brilliantly written book of magic and healing that I could barely put down. In a time when we sorely need to wake up to the healing properties of plants and spirits of the land, this book will inspire many to open up to the invisible realms around us who are calling us back Home to the wise ways. I am certain that this novel will become a classic along the lines of *The Mists of Avalon*".

—Mare Cromwell, author of *The Great Mother Bible* and Gaia Mystic

"In this fantasy novel, Comeau uses the Irish setting ... and tales of the Otherworld and Tuatha dé Danann to craft an ethereal, fablelike narrative. Morrigan, ... friends, family, and fellow villagers, come alive ... fitting perfectly into the picturesque village ... Morrigan's frustration with the imposed limits on her gender adds a fascinating dimension to the spooky tale.."

—Kirkus Indie Reviews

The Ancient Parchment

"The world is full of magic things, patiently waiting for our senses to grow sharper."
—W. B. Yeats

"It is a fact strange, but nevertheless true, that as the people are forgetting how to talk Irish, and have taken to reading Bibles and learning English, …so have the animals which used in former days to be excessively communicative, given over holding any discourse with human beings."
—Sir William Wilde

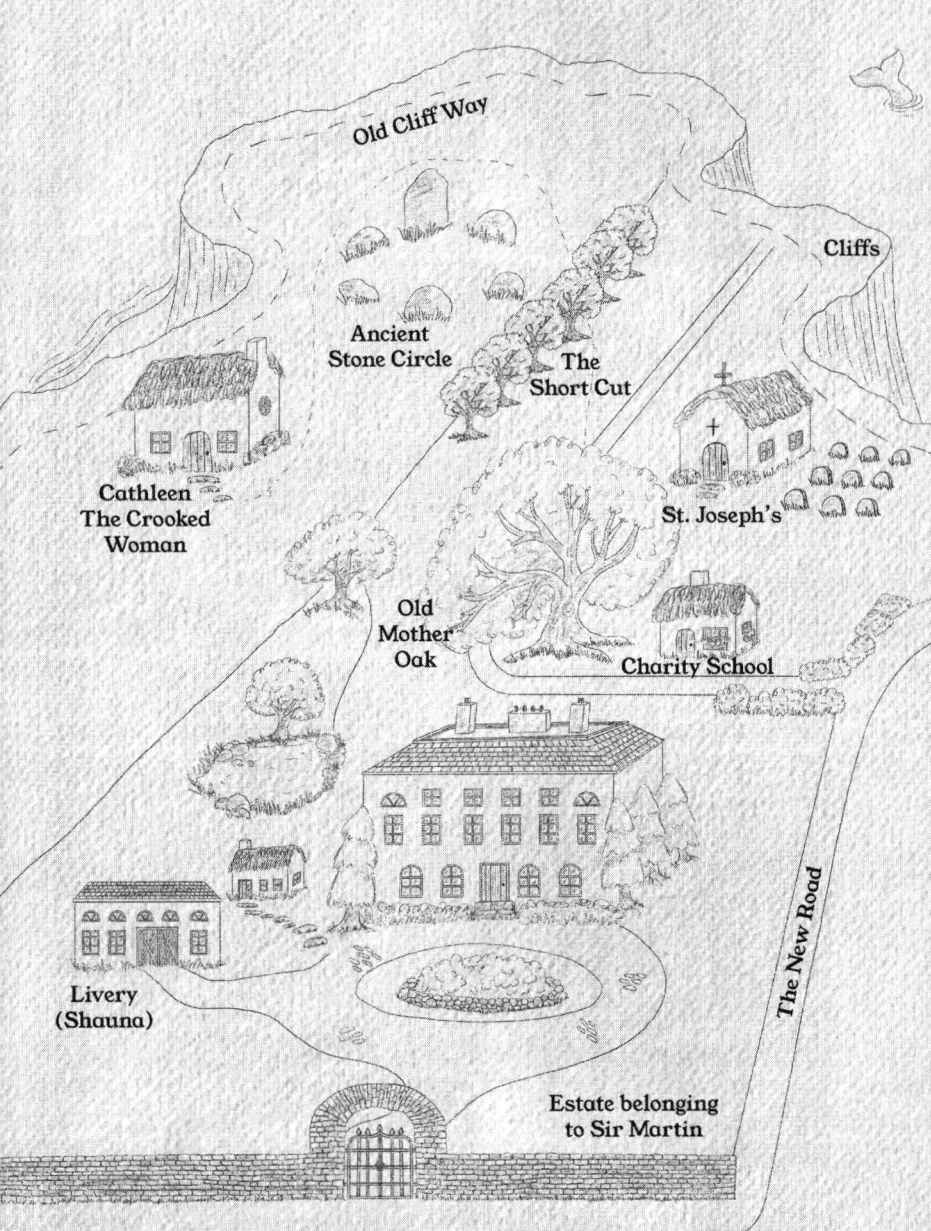

BAILE GHORT NA DARACH
"Village of the Field of the Oak"

Old Cliff Way

Cliffs

Ancient
Stone Circle

The
Short Cut

Cathleen
The Crooked
Woman

St. Joseph's

Old
Mother
Oak

Charity School

Livery
(Shauna)

The New Road

Estate belonging
to Sir Martin

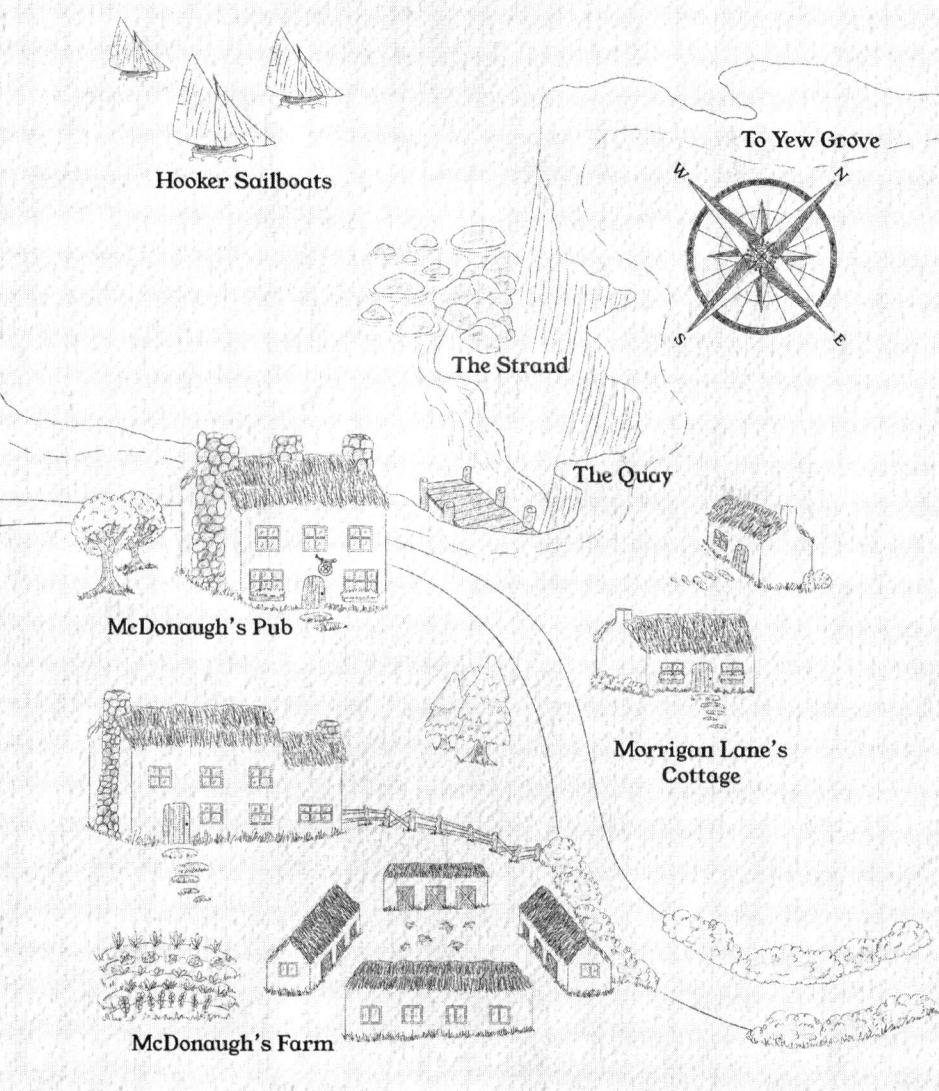

GALWAY BAY

Hooker Sailboats

To Yew Grove

The Strand

The Quay

McDonaugh's Pub

Morrigan Lane's
Cottage

McDonaugh's Farm

Table of Contents

Part One

NEW MOON

1

MORRIGAN

Western Ireland, 1820s

Not that the world had gone from silent to humming, because it had not. Yet it seemed no sounds were of consequence until the bees arrived. Every tree and rock and waterfall noticed their hum as if the land incarnated an ancient melody, the song of the life force. Long ago, nature's overtones had filled the Irish with joy and purpose. Now, under the colonizing forces of England and a growing Catholic Church, to Irish ears, the song of the life force had become a whisper.

Morrigan Lane, however, possessed a deep-rooted connection with the subtle realms of the land, though she herself hadn't fully realized it. Something happened to her when she joined in her people's ceremonies at the stone circle: Her body hummed like a colony of bees, her freckled cheeks flushed with vitality, and she heard leaves rustle a word on the wind. *Believe*. Of course, the ceremonies were much frowned upon these days, and that was the source of Morrigan's unrest.

One dark April night, a night that seemed like any other, Morrigan walked a thousand-year-old footpath high above the North Atlantic. Despite the blackness, she knew the trail as one would the oddities of an old friend. For most of her sixteen years, Morrigan had walked these cliffs when sleeplessness drove her from her pallet under the eaves to the sea. The almond scent of newly flowering broom drifted to her from hardy clumps that

1

clung to thin sandstone soil. Though she could not see them, her mind mapped the great rocks just below the cliff. No doubt having a conversation about weather and waves, she mused.

Letting out a loud sigh, Morrigan put all her longings—to escape the dispiriting burdens of life—into a conjuring spell: *Come, oh trace of new adventure; I'm a daughter of the moon. Shifting shoreline, bring my future; bring it to me very soon.*

Perhaps from nowhere a vast sailing ship would appear to take her away. But she had no wish to leave the land she loved, really. A crescent moon hung across a ridge south of the rocky shore. She stared at it, longing to witness a different kind of crescent—the great sweeping arc of horizon her da had told her about when fishing, surrounded by nothing but ocean. She'd be free if she became a sea captain, the very thing forbidden to her and to all women.

When a sound emerged from beneath the waves, Morrigan jerked, unable to shake the notion of the bay as one great in-breath and she, mere air, pulled into its watery lungs. She tightened her wrap and searched the line of boats anchored in the still waters. Nothing but swells.

Then, a voice thundered, "Come to me. Explore the sea. I shall ferry you to the free." There appeared before her a man in a seaborne chariot just beyond the boats. His arms stretched outward, beckoning. Morrigan froze from where she stood high above the harbor. Had he seen her? Squinting in the darkness, she confirmed that his penetrating gaze was directed at her.

"Christ almighty." Had her spell worked? Morrigan glanced back at the thatch-roofed cottage where her family lay asleep. *Run home!* her mind urged.

"Cast away your life's burdens and join me here upon the waters," said the man. She noticed more details: His long black hair jutted out from underneath a metal helmet, a thick sword hung at his side, and despite what appeared to be a cloak behind him, his arms were bare.

To follow this stranger was madness. As gusts of wind swirled the grasses around her, she caught the lilting sound of her own words, sung by another woman, who appeared like a mirage at the quay, her twilled woolen skirts and red hair wild in the wind. "Come, oh trace of new adventure; I'm a daughter of the moon. Shifting shoreline bring my future; bring it to me very soon." Morrigan felt an urgency from the woman, whose ghostly stare seared her.

Something inside the young woman sprang loose, and before she knew it, her feet were moving, and she was racing down the path toward the quay. When she arrived, the woman had vanished, but the man had not. Heedless of the rules against women on the waters, Morrigan leapt into one of several dories tied to the dock and rowed toward the man shimmering in the moonlight.

He nodded to her and, turning, moved through the swells without a sail.

No sail? Is he real or a specter? The night had become untrustworthy. "What am I doing?" she said aloud. She felt as if she were a marionette, moved by invisible strings. Desperate for some undefined thing, she pushed her doubts away. His distance from her widened, so she made a quick decision to pursue the stranger in her Uncle Colm's púcán fishing vessel, smaller than the other hooker fishing boats and, thus, more manageable. She would try to catch him using only the foresail, for she hadn't the strength to hoist the boat's lugsail.

Morrigan had never skippered a boat before, but her movements were confident because she'd played in the púcán since childhood, mimicking her uncle's routine. She scrambled forward and began to hoist the anchor line, its weight eliciting a groan of effort until finally it clunked to the deck. Then she raised and cleated the foresail as it caught the gusty wind, and the púcán moved in line with the mysterious stranger out into Galway Bay.

"Eeeyooow," Morrigan screamed, for suddenly the vast ocean was an untamed force of wind and waves. Still, deep inside she felt elation at the salt wind in her long curls and the slap of waves against the boat. Gripping the wooden tiller worn smooth by strong hands, Morrigan squared her shoulders and widened her stance. She was captaining a vessel, something she'd only dreamt about.

Keeping the shoreline in view, she glanced at the night sky to spot the constellation Ursus Major and the North Star, essential for nighttime navigation. This her da had taught her during their nocturnal walks home from McDonaugh's Pub.

In the darkness, the moon's light revealed just enough to see the man standing in his boat with his cape streaming behind him like a wake, turning at once from a dark shade to a light one. Morrigan blinked and looked again. She bit the inside of her cheek. "What in all manner?"

When the sea began to churn as if it were a life force unto itself, swirling and growing in size and speed, Morrigan's hand froze on the tiller. She strained her eyes to find the source of the turbulence.

Foolhardy, following this man, she thought. Worse than that: witless and dunderheaded.

Once more she heard the command, "Come to me. Explore the sea. I shall ferry you to the free." Then, the man and his vessel sank without struggle into a chasm made deep by the churning waters.

"Dar fia!" screamed Morrigan in her native tongue. Her boat headed straight for the roiling waves. Heart pounding, she acted by instinct, shoving the tiller to the other side. The boat lurched, and she fell onto the deck grunting as pain shot from wrist to elbow. She scrambled back to the tiller. Now the púcán drifted toward cliffs to the south, nearing a mass of rocks scattered in the waters. She jerked the tiller to the other side, and the vessel came around and back out to sea. How will this end? she thought, realizing how little control she had over the boat.

A voice drifted to her from the shore, "Gadaí!" Thief. A man pointed toward her, running along the strand, bellowing the word over and over.

"No!" shouted Morrigan, waving in protest. Once more she shoved the tiller in a direction that pointed the púcán back toward the quay.

Seeing the boat now approaching land, the man cried, "Ionsaí!" Attack.

From the shallow vessel, Morrigan yelled, "It's me! Morrigan Lane!" She brought a hand to her mouth. The enormity of her transgression sunk in.

"No girl belongs on a boat," Uncle Colm had told her repeatedly, even as her father fed her desire for adventure with tales of Gráinne Ní Mháille—Grace O'Malley to the English. Daughter of the Irish Ó Máille chieftain, she had been a warrior-pirate and ship captain during the reign of Queen Elizabeth. Her courage had become legendary as she sought to protect her native Eire against overwhelming English forces. But Gráinne had suffered for having defied a traditional role. "'Twas said Gráinne had more enemies than lovers, and that was a lot," Tommy had whispered to his daughter with a wink. She'd thrilled at his coarseness, wondering if she could ever be brave enough, like Gráinne, to claim her own freedom on the seas.

Three more men came running down to the quay carrying rakes. Morrigan spoke aloud to calm her nerves. "Uncle's rebuke will be loud and long." Too fast, her boat closed the distance to the other hooker boats. Instinctively, she uncleated the foresail and the boat righted as the sail flapped in the breeze. Throw the anchor! She let go of the tiller and scrambled forward, clinging to the mast to keep from slipping on the wet, wooden deck. Now! Now! her mind screamed. The anchor scraped the bow as she heaved it off the starboard side.

"Thanks be to God!" said Morrigan. As she turned to face the dories bearing down on her, the anchor dug in, the boat hitched, and Morrigan lost her balance, plunging overboard into frigid waters.

The sea stung like a thousand needles. The sea made a lead weight of her shawl. The sea flooded her nostrils, and it burned. Drowning seemed eerily familiar. Morrigan snorted and her arms flailed, but she'd swum in the bay every summer, and thus, she propelled herself toward shore. Her body felt sluggish; it would not obey. Morrigan sputtered just as she glimpsed oars and the prow of a dory.

Hands grabbed her arms and pulled. She fell in a heap into the dory. In the predawn gloom, a man's face peered into hers.

"Who is she?"

"My niece, Morrigan."

Wrapped in her father's coat, Morrigan stood before the stern-faced fishermen.

"What did you think you were doing taking my púcán?" shouted Colm Lane. "Have you lost your senses? My boat could have smashed, my livelihood gone!" His dark eyes glittered.

Morrigan hung her head and said nothing. Her teeth chattered and water dripped from her hair. In her younger years she had learned to say nothing. Thus, while Uncle Colm yelled, Morrigan stared at the horizon, its blue-blackness licked with scarlet, willing herself to escape into a simple song she'd learned from her Grandmother Mamoh: *A baby was sleeping, its mother was weeping; for her husband was far on the wild raging sea.*

"...has had an obsession with my boat since she was a girl, Tommy!"

And the tempest was swelling round the fisherman's dwelling; and she cried Dermot darling, oh! come back to me. Morrigan continued her mental processing.

"… spoiled her with foolish notions!"

With his arms around his daughter, Tommy Lane spoke as though Colm were a bull he'd stumbled upon in a field. "Surely there is a reason she did this, Colm. Never done it before."

Still, Morrigan remained silent, grinding her teeth. A stream of rash words threatened to escape her lips—about how mean it was to keep the sea only for men. Something halted the words she longed to say. When she'd spoken up at other times, she'd been ridiculed or punished. A memory at the hedge school invaded her awareness. She was twelve. To make sense of confusing religious teachings, she had asked, "Schoolmaster Winnett, if Jesus was Jewish, how can the Catholic faith be the only true religion?"

The question had landed like an assault on Schoolmaster Winnett. She did not remember his frosty response, only the pain and shame of kneeling on the punishing triangle-shaped wooden billet. Back then, she'd vowed to stifle her impetuous questions.

Uncle Colm's command startled Morrigan back to the present. "I want an answer from ya, now!"

Morrigan sputtered, "There was a foreigner in a strange vessel. He called for me to follow him. He had a huge, gleaming sword at his side, and he moved straight into the waves on a chariot without a sail."

"A man moved through the waves without a sail?"

"Aye, Uncle Colm. He wore a long cape and said he would ferry me to the free. I didn't know what it meant, but I felt I had no choice in following him." She dared not mention the woman-ghost she'd seen. Nor that at last she'd had an adventure the size of her dreams.

Women who'd gathered began to whisper.

Morrigan added, "And then churning waters swallowed him up, and I was almost sucked into the waves m'self."

Among the women's whispers, she heard the name Manannán mac Lir.

Schoolmaster Winnett, who had been roused by the commotion, waved a dismissive hand. "Preposterous! Manannán mac Lir? 'Tis a pagan notion for simple minds." He glared at Morrigan, folding his arms, and with a quick glance, backed away from the shoreline. Village women had gone silent at his scolding.

Cradling her sore wrist, Morrigan's thoughts spun. She'd heard the women of her village whisper tales at the well, about the immortal souls of the Tuatha dé Danann, once called the gods of the earth and noted for their power to take on the shapes of men or animals when they revealed themselves to human beings. Was Manannán mac Lir one of the Tuatha dé Danann?

Schoolmaster Winnett's voice rang out, "Return to your homes now, and Morrigan, a punishment awaits you. I'll seek out Father Murray to decide a suitable sentence for such blatant disregard for property and position. May God forgive you," he said. Turning, Winnett stumped off, straight-backed and as regal as his diminutive stature allowed. Villagers lingered, hoping for tantalizing snippets about the scandalous behavior of the wild daughter of Betha and Tommy Lane.

Silent and shivering, Morrigan stared at the swells breaking over moored boats, her seafarer's eyes noting the direction of the currents. The stranger's cape *had* changed colors and his sword *had* glinted in the moonlight. Her hands remembered the feel of captaining a vessel as she'd always dreamt of doing. She'd been brave and skillful enough to have saved herself from the swirling waters. I will be a fine sea captain, she thought, and a smile tugged at the corners of her mouth. She hid it.

The mention of Manannán mac Lir had caused Colm to exchange looks with other fishermen. In the emerging light, Morrigan could not discern whether his expression was fierce or fearful. He muttered, "There'll be more to say, Tommy," and he walked away.

"Home you go, Morrigan," said Tommy, giving her a push none too gentle. "As a first punishment, you'll answer to your mum for this." Again, thought Morrigan. Her mum believed Morrigan possessed an unbridled streak that she ought to have outgrown by now. Hurrying home to the warmth of her cottage, Morrigan tried to talk herself into suppressing the things inside her that made her different. She couldn't know those *things*, like a sprung leak in a barrel, would soon be unstoppable.

2

MORRIGAN

Ferry to Freedom

Later that day, a silvery mist skipped over stones and meadows, carrying the scent of the sea into sturdy cottages tucked among small hills and boulders. Morrigan crept toward the well, her empty water buckets swinging in the crook of her arm. She hoped she wouldn't encounter her uncle. She'd avoided making eye contact with anyone during Mass at St. Joseph's and had slipped out of church before Father Murray could stop her. Earlier her mum had given her a strong reprimand and a list of chores to complete in the coming week, including whitewashing the inside of Uncle Colm's cottage. Her older sister, Riona, had treated her with chilly silence.

Morrigan's stomach growled. She'd eaten only a scant bowl of stirabout, the cooked porridge meal meant to sustain her for most of the day. She'd never gotten used to the constant hunger, the burden of being poor. It'd sunk to the bottom of things, a place too deep for tears.

Hearing a bleat, Morrigan slowed her pace. Just over a stone wall lay a baby lamb, born yesterday by the looks of it, and another close by, suckling from a mother who stood, legs splayed, patient. Morrigan neared the wall. "Baaaa, little ones. Welcome to the world. A strange one, it seems." An image arose of the man in his sea chariot. He hadn't acted menacing. His invitation had carried a welcoming magnetism, and something about him seemed familiar.

But that was impossible. She shook off her thoughts and bid the lambs farewell.

The village well had been built centuries ago by local clansmen. A rock wall three feet high surrounded clear artesian water. Here women and girls came to fill their buckets for supper, sometimes pausing to tie a scrap of fabric to a nearby hawthorn—their hopes or worries offered up to the goddess Brigid. Nearing the well, Morrigan overheard her name and snippets of conversation. She crouched alongside bright green rushes, hoping she hadn't been seen.

"—a sea chariot," said Widow O'Rooney, who perched on the rock wall as though overseeing the women. "Morrigan said he had a powerful sword. Could it have been the mythical sword, Fragarach, The Answerer?"

"Ah, The Answerer," replied another woman. "'Tis said the very sight of the sword filled men's hearts with fear. When held against one's throat, no lie could be told."

"Indeed, 'twas certainly Manannán mac Lir, son of Lir, the ancient god of the sea," said Widow O'Rooney.

"Manannán mac Lir is only a mythical being," chided yet another woman, pulling up a full bucket. "The girl said he wanted to ferry her to freedom. Freedom from what?"

"Manannán mac Lir is Guardian of The Otherworld. He ferries the souls of the dead," Widow O'Rooney whispered. She crossed herself. "Could he have come to free Morrigan's soul?"

Morrigan sucked in a breath.

"'Tis said Manannán mac Lir was seen by Isla the healer, just before her mysterious death," said Widow O'Rooney.

Morrigan nearly tumbled from her crouch. How had Great-Grandmother Isla died?

"That Morrigan's an odd girl. Been strange from the moment of her unholy birth. Let's hope she hasn't brought ill fortune upon us through her actions," said the widow. "I've heard the fishermen talk. They're fearful the sea god has put a curse upon their season. Why else would he appear?"

Recoiling, Morrigan looked for a way to melt into the hedges. She'd find water elsewhere, perhaps at a stream on Sir Martin's estate, forbidden though it was.

Young Lettie O'Malley, playing in a nearby streamlet, spied her. "Morrie, was it a sea god you saw?" she asked.

Discovered, Morrigan stood, setting down her buckets. Two bright spots clung to her cheeks. She looked away from the women's stares. With her toes, she rustled a stone from where it was embedded in the trackway. "I don't know. He seemed of a different place and time with his strange metal helmet and streaming cape," she managed.

"What's this about?" asked Cathleen, The Crooked Woman, who'd arrived at the well. The sight of her, hunched over due to a spinal disease in her youth, was disquieting. One could not see Cathleen's face, though she had an uncanny ability to sense moods and situations. Some thought her a fairy woman, capable of applying counter-charms to protect humans from *Them*, The Good People, the sylvan woodland beings who caused bad weather, illness, and all manner of daily nuisances. To others, she was a wise and capable healer and midwife, steadfast in her belief that sea and forest were bursting with curative medicines.

"Good day to you, Cathleen," said the women, respect in their tones.

"Have your superstitions got the best of you then?" asked Cathleen. "And isn't it now the season of Lent?" Many a village woman boasted about her piety during Lent, and any conversation about beings not found in the Christian Bible, like Manannán mac Lir, was strongly censured by the Catholic Church, though Cathleen herself cared little about that. She cared about protecting Morrigan from the women's gossip, seeing something of herself in the unusual girl.

The women mumbled among themselves and then conceded, "Aye, Cathleen, right you are." They gathered their buckets and made their way back to their cottages.

"Fill your buckets, Morrigan," said Cathleen, her voice soft.

"Thank you, Cathleen." A smile bloomed on her face. She watched the women retreat, their pleated skirts of crimson, ochre, and blue swaying from side to side with their careful gait. "Who is Manannán mac Lir?" Morrigan whispered.

"The god that rules the Land-Beneath-the-Waves, a part of The Otherworld. It's where a surging fountain spills forth into five springs to nourish salmon, sea creatures, and us humans. He is of the noble race, the Tuatha dé Danann, who once peaceably inhabited this land. 'Tis said upon hearing of impending marauders, Manannán mac Lir spread his changeable cloak of mists over the ninth wave, turned sideways into the light, and made his people invisible to their enemies."

Turn sideways into the light and disappear. That's what I want to do, thought Morrigan, moving her body this way and that, pondering the how of it. But she knew not to ask Cathleen. The Irish ways. Many things were left unexplained so as not to violate the secret, delicate essence of the thing. A crow's squawk seemed to confirm her silence.

"His cloak, though, Cathleen. It changed colors just as you describe. I think it *was* Manannán mac Lir I saw," said Morrigan.

"If it was," Cathleen whispered, "'tis quite a distinction."

3

BETHA

Isla the Great Healer

Betha Lane was a fetching, blue-eyed, fair-haired fisherman's wife, though fatigue had rounded her shoulders. It was said that a countryman from Clare had once taken an interest in her, despite her lower social status. In those days, Betha's lilting soprano had been sought after by gentle women in their drawing rooms. When it became known that a gentleman of their own class was besotted with Betha, the invitations came to an abrupt halt.

Decades later, she lived in destitute conditions with her husband, mother, and four children. She told herself she was a proud survivor in a cruel land of gnarled hawthorn and voracious seas but worry betrayed her attempt at inner calm. She wore her worry with the same constancy as the crude wooden cross that graced her neck.

The typhus epidemic and harvest shortages of past years had decreased potential suitors, and her elder daughter, Riona, had ambitions to become a proper lady. Though her sons, Liam and Riona's twin, Ruarc, would do fine, her youngest, Morrigan, possessed a distinctive awareness, like Grandmother Isla, although she was blind to it. High-spirited and prone to trouble, Morrigan's escapade on Colm's boat was only the latest. Thus, in the somber light of a drizzly morning, Betha poured herself some tea at the cupboard, adding a decadent teaspoon of sugar before guilt could stop her. Mamoh was already stoking the fire for the watery potato-nettle soup that would be their meager supper. Riona sat on a coarse linen atop the hardened mud floor mending Tommy's favorite pair of wool socks. "Scarlet like sunset at sea," he'd said. "Lucky socks, lucky weather."

At a bench by the fire, Morrigan swirled a spoon in her stirabout, prolonging a soggy walk to the well and more chores to follow. She cast a furtive glance Betha's way and then leaned into her grandmother. A whisper: "Mamoh, Widow O'Rooney said Manannán mac Lir was the man I followed, and I think she's right."

Alerted by Morrigan's low tone, Betha said, "Morrigan, don't pester Mamoh with Widow O'Rooney's nonsense. Such talk is fable, tales for a seanchaí to spin by a chimney corner."

"Mum, Widow O'Rooney said Isla died a mysterious death right after she saw the sea god." She turned back to Mamoh and asked, "What mysterious death? You've never told us how Great-Grandmother Isla died."

"Mamoh, you haven't told us!" added Riona, who moved with grace to join the woman of the house on the bench, her blue eyes expectant.

Mamoh ignored Betha's stern expression, and began, "'Twas the year of our Lord seventeen hundred and eighty four. I was only twenty-six, and you, Betha, had just turned six. An unruly child you were.

"A fearsome thunderstorm struck Inis Mór. That was our home back then. Now, we islanders were well accustomed to the savage gales descending on us from the west—three little islands of Aran like reluctant guardians to Galway Bay. Well as they say, this storm had an intensity we'd never seen before. It came toward us like a claw of black clouds, reaching and gaining. We rushed to bring in our milk cows and sheep and gathered turf. But your great-grandmother had been called out to tend to an illness, though she wouldn't tell me who it was. She said something worrisome: 'I have no dead hand in my possession.' Now the old ones believe a dead hand is a cure for the most harmful of diseases.

"Afterward, none of us reported any illness, though Mrs. O'Flaherty thought she saw a man who looked like young Father Waters heading out into the eerie winds, perhaps to give someone last rites, for he wouldn't have ventured unless the circumstances were dire.

"Mum never returned. I searched for her, as did all the islanders, but we found nothing except a jagged scar on the cliff we'd named The Gregory after Pope Gregory the Great. We could only guess the rock had been struck by lightning and shattered into bits, spilling into the sea. Your great-grandmother walked those cliffs, finding sanctuary there. And so it was said, me own mum, Isla the great healer, must have perished as the lightning struck the massive rock." Mamoh looked away from her granddaughters. They were silent as a steady drumbeat of rain battered the thatch.

"It doesn't make any sense," said Riona. "Why would she have been on the cliffs during a storm? Who would have been ill near those cliffs?" She made a face. Riona seldom ventured to the cliffs; fear kept her away. Morrigan, like Isla, found the verge of stone and sea a haven, sensing ancient conversations there.

"Was Widow O'Rooney right? Did Great-Grandmother see Manannán mac Lir just before the storm?" asked Morrigan.

"'Twould seem so," said Mamoh. "But Isla journeyed to Manannán mac Lir more than once."

Morrigan sat upright. "Where did she go?"

"To the watery vortex known as the Land-Beneath-the-Waves. Isla went only when a person was too ill for her own healing medicines, when she felt it necessary to bargain with Manannán mac Lir on behalf of the soul of the sick. Each time she returned, I'd find her weaker than the last."

Betha tsk'd. "Mum, she was spinning tales for you, just like you're spinning tales for the girls. Manannán mac Lir is a myth."

"I saw a man who seemed not from this world, Mum. What if he was the sea god?"

"There is only one God. Our Father in heaven. You're to dismiss this talk, Morrigan. And you'd best hope Uncle Colm is satisfied with your amends and will forget the incident on his boat." Betha turned her back to them, a signal the conversation was at an end.

Outside they heard the customary Irish greeting, "God bless all in this house!"

"That's Father Murray," said Mamoh. She reached for the cast iron tea kettle, checked the water level, and set it to the coals.

Betha straightened the cross that hung from her neck and ran her fingers down the front of her blouse. Too early to discuss the Easter pageant, she thought. Must be about Morrigan. She opened the door to two visitors, "Father Murray. Schoolmaster Winnett, do come in."

Father Murray made a sign of the cross. "Betha, 'tis a bit of surprise I know. Schoolmaster Winnett seems intent upon discussing Morrigan's, uh, transgressions. Though, of course, I told him the confessional is best for such a thing."

Schoolmaster Winnett waited at the threshold, as though the cottage held a contagion that would infiltrate his body. "Father Murray, we need to know what Morrigan's intentions were in disgracing the fishermen and threatening their livelihood."

The priest cleared his throat and motioned for Morrigan to join him on the narrow bench by the hearth. "Well, I suppose it's necessary to ask you, Morrigan. What has you stealing your uncle's boat in the middle of the night?"

"I'm so sorry, Father Murray. Something in me longs to be on the seas. It's in my bones like it's in Da's."

Winnett made a snarling sound. "Disrupting the peace among us? The seas are not your place, Morrigan."

"I know it's not possible for me," said Morrigan. She spat out the word *possible*. Betha noted her daughter's clenched fists.

"Aye, right you are," said Father Murray. "But why this act now? What really happened?"

Morrigan looked upward, squinting her eyes. Seconds of silence passed. "I suppose I let my fancies get the better of me," she said. Her smile looked like a charm. "'Tis sorry I am that you've had to venture out on my account."

A chuckle arose from the priest. "Venture out. That you did. Schoolmaster, have you ever felt the call to adventure?"

"Never," said Winnett.

Father Murray patted Morrigan's arm. "Ah well, so long as you hadn't the devil's influence to do such a thing."

"No, Father," she said.

Slapping his thighs for attention, Schoolmaster Winnett interrupted their conversation. "Whether intended or not, you have caused great consternation among the fishermen and our village." Turning to the priest, he forced a sentence between his teeth. "And there shall be punishment for this misdeed." To Betha, he added, "Isn't it so, Betha?"

Nodding, she said, "I've added more chores to Morrigan's already. I agree, Schoolmaster Winnett. Rules are to be followed."

At the hearth, Mamoh coughed, and if anyone were listening closely, they'd have heard, *Whose rules?* amid the cough.

"Ah well, I shall think of a suitable punishment," said Father Murray. "Mamoh, thank you kindly, but we have no need for tea at present." With a wink in Morrigan's direction, the priest made for the door.

Still standing at the threshold, Schoolmaster Winnett moved aside to let the priest through. With a stiff nod at the Lane women, he followed him.

4

MORRIGAN

Old Mother Oak

L ater that day, Morrigan wandered toward the wildwood. *Stupid men and their punishments, when all I want is to sail the seas,* she thought. *I need to know about Isla and her travels to Manannán mac Lir in the Land-Beneath-the-Waves.* She'd find the right moment to ask Mamoh whether she knew more about how Isla did it.

The forest, with its muted sounds, felt mysterious and inviting. She slowed as she neared a great sessile oak, walking around its vast trunk, her fingers feeling its contours.

A name came to her, Old Mother Oak, though she couldn't say whether it was from within herself or from outside of herself. She did not know why this tree should have a name when others didn't. All her life she'd felt the aliveness of the natural world in the way a selkie—half human, half seal—does her hidden skin. Now that sense had intensified. Was the sea god responsible for her new awareness?

Lowering herself to a spot where two of the tree's broad roots formed a natural cradle, she sat with her back against the oak and felt the ground beneath her, solid and unmoving, so unlike the relentlessly shifting seas. She placed her palms on the trunk and, in doing so, startled a song thrush who perched on one of the oak's branches some arms' lengths away.

"Oh! I'm sorry little one. I didn't see you there," said Morrigan. Extending her long legs from the base of the oak, her toes reached soft moss. At last she noticed what lay before her: tender cabbage leaves of spring, now deepening to spinach green, a thrush's mating call, gusts of wind like murmurs from a gentle god, the rich smell of forest growth. The oak and glen were a place of refuge from the hectic pace of quay and village. She closed her eyes and slipped into a dream-filled sleep.

A teacher in flowing green robes offered a small square of sheep's cheese and a tin of water, saying, "Sip from the water and eat the cheese, and you will see with new eyes." When she did so, something bloomed in her heart. Morrigan connected to small creatures—a hare, a frog, and a wren. Suddenly, the earth trembled as wolves bounded toward where she sat. Instinct told her she must let them see her eyes. She turned, just as the pack's leader upended her, hurling her into the air as high as a King's Pine. She contorted her body to meet the wolf's eyes, and as she did so, she yielded into the creature's welcoming embrace.

While Morrigan dreamed, an alpha male wolf lay nearby, hidden in shadowy undergrowth. He stared at the young woman he'd searched for, his yellow eyes locked in concentration, his silver head cocked, and his ears—dark at the base and turning silver toward the tips—canted forward as though listening to a silent oratory. With a low rumble of satisfaction, he lowered his head to his paws.

5

MORRIGAN

Shifting Sands at the Quay

Morrigan skipped down the trackway, breathing in the scent of reawakening earth. Rambling blankets of gray-leafed sea purslane crept onto the path. Spring days came quickly, like the running of a hound upon the moor. It was market day, and that meant her advanced charity school was not in session. She made a pained face as she lifted a small, notched stick—a scoreen—hanging by a string around her neck. The notches accounted for one's language transgressions at the school, where only English was tolerated.

Tallying the marks on her scoreen, Morrigan winced, remembering the caning Schoolmaster Winnett had recently administered to her knuckles. Of all the attendees, she was the worst offender, slipping into the forbidden Irish Gaelic as easily as a fish slips through wet hands. Even Betha had taken to notching Morrigan's scoreen when she spoke Irish at home, telling her, "There's no future for you without the English."

The Irish vernacular was a language of valley, lake, and glen, with place names venerating the natural world, not surnames of the powerful. Yet a language without the letters J, K, Q, V, X, Y, or Z, held no use to English-speaking rulers.

Having the English language forced upon her made Morrigan resist learning it. Her da told her she had stubborn Irish blood in her, too thick to adapt to the new ways. "Become a river when change is afoot. Like the Dunkellin as it flirts its way past boulders and ducklings," he'd said.

Morrigan found herself at odds with the interests and actions of most villagers, and thus, they distinguished her as "that strange Morrie." Perhaps something about her unusual birth in the caul—a rare circumstance in which a filmy veil covered a newborn's head—was the reason. An *en caul* birth bode good fortune, but because she had been born feet first, villagers weren't quite sure whether her *en caul* birth was lucky, especially because the trauma had left a long, thin scar from Morrigan's jaw to her neck.

Pausing by a stand of gorse bushes, Morrigan admired their full gold blooms. "Schoolmaster Winnett called me a poor learner, unfit for master's school," she said to a bee whose hind legs were fat with pollen. The bee hovered, almost as if it were listening. Do all beings listen—the trees and stones and sky, too? thought Morrigan. Something deep inside her answered, and surprise brightened her face.

"Schoolmaster Winnett would be outraged at the very idea of you listening, little bee." So would the village girls who labored to stitch perfect crewel. Morrigan held no interest in these activities. Instead, she felt at ease with the fishermen.

"Farewell, little bee," said Morrigan, turning back to the path. Suddenly a high whine grew loud in her ears. She staggered to the side, throwing her arms out to stop the dizziness. A flash of an image appeared before her eyes: Black and gold creatures curled in on themselves, unmoving. Dead bees, piles of them.

Finding focus on a large rock, she caught her breath, and balance returned. The image disappeared. "Christ almighty!" Never in her life had Morrigan witnessed such a scene. The little bee she'd spoken to was gone, but she saw no piles of dead bees on the trackway. Whose bees were they? And how had their deaths entered her senses?

Without answers, Morrigan finally convinced herself she was steady enough to descend the craggy slope down to the quay. She remembered her uncle's anger at her for taking his boat and Schoolmaster Winnett's promise of punishment. Will Uncle forgive me? I'd better get to whitewashing his walls. What punishment will Father Murray hand down? "Nothing happened to his bloody boat after all," she swore.

Morrigan's job, to transport the fish her da caught in the fierce North Atlantic to the market, was a way to escape the confines of her limited life. Though it was often the oldest girl in a family who was given this chore, Morrigan had been both pleased and proud when five years ago her da asked her to do it. Riona preferred the cleaner and livelier market where she could gossip with friends or perchance meet some of the gentry.

On many occasions, Morrigan had observed the fishermen at work, noting how they spoke and held themselves differently at the quay than at McDonaugh's Pub. Here, they referred to the sea as a woman and spoke about her in hushed tones, fearing the anger she could swiftly unleash. Knowing the fate of her own grandfather, Morrigan felt it was a right and true way to behave.

The docks pulsated with life—screeching curlews and gulls, brisk winds, unrelenting waves, and a tingly bite to the salt air. Here she felt fierce and more alive than anywhere else.

The men on the docks broke out in a song of the sea, as men who relied upon her for their livelihood had done for centuries:

She's the Mamoh who croons a lullaby
A baby who giggles in sleep

She's the temptress beyond where the seagulls fly
And the monster demanding to eat

She barks her furious orders
And moans her wanton release
To her we owe our greatest debt
So we sing the song of the sea

Oh! If the fisherman's life
Were gone, and were no more
We'd wander alone like true mad men
Alongside her white-breaking shore...

Morrigan reflected on the men's song. Music, along with the sea, was a necessity to the fishermen. Their Irish Gaelic word for music—*ceol*—meant lifeblood, and it was as if the blood in these men moved like the tides, their loyalty to the sea evidenced in every aching back and creaking knee. She revered their devotion and walked onto the quay greeting them as kin. They had abruptly stopped singing upon her arrival.

"Good morning, Mr. O'Malley." Morrigan made a show of tipping an invisible cap in the way Mr. O'Malley customarily greeted her.

"Morrigan," he said and turned from her. No tip of his cap. Eyes narrowing, she scrutinized the men.

She tried again. "The new babe, Mr. McMahon? Does he fare well?"

"Won't fare well if the season's cursed," he said.

"Is Mrs. McMahon all right?"

"She's a hearty woman, she is. Knows her place, too."

Morrigan froze as Uncle Colm came toward her.

"This will be your last day at the quay, Morrigan," he said.

Her mouth formed an O shape. She looked toward her da, but he and her brothers, Liam and Ruarc, were bent low inspecting the boat's keel. When she looked back at her uncle, his dark eyes bore into hers, and then softened for the briefest of moments.

"You're a good girl at heart, Morrie, but you can't be here," he said, turning from her and walking toward Tommy.

She caught a few words he rasped to her father under his breath—"…stealing the púcán was the last straw, Tommy… and her hair's turned ginger … can't have that here." Shoulders sagging, he walked like a sore man toward his púcán bumping against the dock.

A surge of shame and shock turned Morrigan's face scarlet. The ground of her life had shifted with Uncle Colm's utterance. As she filled the fish basket, Morrigan protested inwardly: I am *not* a ginger! My hair is gold with only a hint of red. Mean, selfish men you are!

For as long as she could remember, Morrigan had greeted the fishermen as they returned from their harvesting. No other had spent so much time at the docks, and she'd felt exempted somehow from their superstitions about redheads being unlucky. Now, marching the length of the dock, she felt the fishermen's eyes following her, and she shivered in the cutting wind.

Morrigan waded through sandy sludge toward the higher ground where her mum and Riona stood. Cries of "Fish!" filled the air and competed with gulls' fierce squabbles as an occasional scrap or a morsel dropped to the ground. She passed her friend Finnbharr McDonaugh, the pub owner's son, who shouted, "Duck's eggs! Sheep's cheese!" his voice cracking in puberty from a high tenor to a lower baritone as he advertised what he had for sale.

Finn saw Morrigan and asked, "Morrie, why so sad? Small catch today?"

Morrigan hesitated lest she burst into tears. When she remained silent, he teased, "Can't The Crooked Woman give you some cowslip to help you sleep? Christ Almighty, the circles under your eyes are as dark as night."

Morrigan kept her face guarded. Her lips trembled.

Finn's smile wavered. "Ah, Morrie, I was just funning with ya. You all right?"

Morrigan nodded and continued to her mother and sister.

"Morrigan's coming, ready the fish salvers," said Betha.

"Yes, Mum." Riona's knack for arranging fish trays at an angle *just so* on top of their wooden crates increased their appeal.

Betha greeted Morrigan. "'Tis a long face you wear, child. What troubles you?"

Morrigan hoisted the basket onto crates next to the display. "Uncle Colm said I wasn't to work at the quay anymore, Mum. Am I going somewhere?"

Betha pursed her lips. "Well surely you aren't going anywhere I know about."

Riona gave her sister an exasperated look and said, "Uncle Colm's been right cranky ever since Aunt Margaret passed on and the boys got work in Donegal, but you've given him cause by stealing his boat, Morrie." She turned to Betha, "Mum, will I have to carry the fish now?"

Shrugging, Betha shooed her eldest daughter away. "Off you go, Riona. Strike a good barter." Riona set out to neighboring stalls to trade fish for milk, eggs, oats, and butter.

Morrigan sorted the fish, a lump in her throat. The docks are all I know, she thought.

That night, after supper chores had finished and Tommy's lyrical harp had gone silent, after they'd said the rosary and the last candle had been snuffed, and with a soft glow of hearth embers shining in the darkness, Morrigan heard her da whisper to her mum. Private conversations were almost impossible in their cottage, sharing as they did the one large space. Despite the hush of his words, they fell like pelting rain upon the girl. "I don't know what's to become of her. The men don't want her around the boats. They think she's cursed the season, but mostly it's because her hair has turned ginger. Calling her a redhead. You know how they feel about seeing a redhead at the docks. It's what jinxed your da, most think…" His words trailed off. No one liked to speak about the demise of Betha's father at sea.

"Redheads do not cause the seas to storm, Tommy," hissed Betha. "Though perhaps she can help Connie McDonaugh in the kitchen at the pub."

"She'd be working such late hours, and she's a wild child. Gets restless indoors. Having to cook or do the washing will sap her spirits."

"Work in the pub will help with the rents. And she must learn to become a good wife and mother. She dallies in her chores and is useless at crewel." Betha sighed. "I should think few will want her for a wife."

At her mother's words, Morrigan cringed and felt for her scar.

"Maybe she is best learning the herbs and medicines from Cathleen. She seems drawn to The Crooked Woman."

"Cathleen is not a good influence. She's too steeped in the old ways, and they're pagan," Betha countered, repeating Father Murray's mantra.

"It's our heritage, Betha! Who would we be without our cures and charms, and Morrie's drawn to them. Spends hours at the stone circle, and she loves our festivals." He paused, and his voice lowered. "She's got something of the sight, Betha. The caul was a sign. Your grandmother had it. It's in the blood. She may not have a life like yours and mine."

"Not an easy child. Does nothing she hasn't the heart for."

Tommy didn't respond, and soon Morrigan heard his deep, even breathing. She lay, hands clutched into fists, willing her breath steady, willing her tears dry.

6

BETHA

A Promise

In the wee hours of the night, while everyone slept, Betha lay awake. That girl, she thought. Her youngest daughter seemed to have inherited Isla's gifts. In most families, the "sight" skipped a generation. Why had it skipped two? She'd been bypassed. She was aggrieved by this and somewhat relieved. A gift, such as the kind Grandmother Isla possessed, demanded self-sacrifice and could lead to danger, especially in these times.

In her mind's eye, Betha recalled Isla's ancient parchment, the one she'd hidden long ago behind the cupboard. It possessed mysterious etchings. She imagined in Isla's hands it held powerful medicine. But not in hers.

From time to time, Betha became obsessed with the parchment, stealing a moment to uncover it from its secret spot, tracing her fingers over the etchings. She'd felt no powers emerging from the old skin.

Father Murray declared the old ways *devil's work*, and she agreed. Still, something in her lineage tugged at her, refusing to be vanquished. If she'd just be more like Riona—or me, Betha thought. Tommy murmured in his sleep. Betha molded herself to his back. Fingering the cross at her neck, she made a promise: I will keep the parchment hidden. Morrigan must not follow Isla's pagan path.

7

MORRIGAN

Grim Calling Card

Morrigan awoke to skies swollen with rain clouds. The heaviness matched her mood. As she readied for school, she muttered to herself, "I will not work with Cook Enya in McDonaugh's kitchen, all closed up and smelling of smoke and fish parts. I'd get some extras, but I don't care! Cathleen can teach me medicines." Learning natural remedies held appeal, and her great-grandmother had been a healer, Morrigan reminded herself.

Her left shoulder tingled. Someone's coming. Since childhood, Morrigan experienced an eerie sensation whenever someone approached their home, and lately, she'd known the identity of the visitor before the door opened. She remained silent though, since Betha had forbidden Morrigan to make such pronouncements.

It was Finn McDonaugh, she was certain of it. Lately, he'd walked her to advanced charity school. This new routine differed from the many years of joining the McDonaugh boys at the pub and walking to school alongside Riona and her brothers. Just last week, Finn had escorted Morrigan twice. The second time they'd arrived laughing and disheveled, and to show his displeasure, Schoolmaster Winnett had made them remain after sessions to sweep out the hearth.

They heard a shout, "God bless all in this house!"

Her green eyes glowing, Morrigan swung open the door. Finn stood, clothes damp, face pale, sides heaving. "Morrie, hello," he said. "We just heard word at the pub. Father Murray's dead!"

"Father Murray? We saw him at Mass on Sunday," said Betha. "What's happened?"

"Found him cold and dead in his chair this morning, a bowl of mutton stew beside him."

Mamoh stood, crossing herself. "They'll be wanting our help to lay out the body," she said. She and Betha gathered their shawls and made haste for the door. Morrigan and Riona exchanged shocked expressions.

"I'll go with you, Mum," said Riona.

"I'll go to the quay to tell Da and the others," said Morrigan. They can't keep me from going there when I want, she thought, though she knew they could, and they probably would.

"I'm off to collect Cathleen," said Finn, his face shining with sweat.

Morrigan frowned as she took in Finn's condition. When they'd departed, the Lane women speaking in worried whispers about how Father Murray, who had not been old, might have died, Morrigan slowed. With a quick glance to assure herself of her mum's preoccupation, she ran to Finn, dodging puddles in the trackway. "Finn, are you having that reaction again?"

"Aye," he admitted, grinding his teeth, his eyes greyer today than blue, and troubled. "I get angry with myself, Morrie. There's no reason for it." But there was a reason, and they both knew it. Finn's mum, Kate, had died giving him birth. The heartbeat that had nourished his cells, the lilting voice that sang to him while he grew inside of her, had been lost just as he'd emerged into the light of life. Underneath his mischievous smile, he carried a sense of guilt for her death, though he had spoken of it only to Morrigan. Now the sudden death of anyone triggered the trauma of his loss like a grim calling card.

"Ah, Finn. 'Tis sorry I am to see you like this," said Morrigan, and caught herself from reaching out to smooth the creases in his forehead. She had a flash of an image, Finn resting his head on her lap, her hands stroking his flaxen hair. She gasped at its intimacy. Since childhood, she and Finn had been friendly competitors, racing along the cliffs, or stealing onto Sir Martin's land to catch trout, or playing chicken-behind-the-barrel, but his anguish touched her heart. "Mamoh says death is nothing more than parting company for a time," she whispered.

"I'll be all right, Morrie." Turning from her, he loped toward the village. Morrigan raised her shawl to cover her head as drizzle turned to spitting rain.

Scurrying to the quay, Morrigan mused about Father Murray's death. Though the priest's words had at times been harsh, she'd seen in him a real fondness for the villagers and would miss him. She shivered in the damp air as her thoughts returned to Isla's story. What had Manannán mac Lir possessed that her great-grandmother needed if she'd traveled to see him in the mysterious Land-Beneath-The-Waves? Then a chilling thought: If Manannán mac Lir ferried souls to The Otherworld, on the night she'd seen him, had he come for her and become angry when she'd turned her uncle's boat away from the churning waters? Had the sea god taken Father Murray as revenge?

Morrigan peered through her shawl to scan the rain-pummeled waters of the bay, half hoping the sea god would appear and answer her question.

Whatever had happened, one thing seemed certain: Mystery and otherworldly realms, past and present, had become like a prying wedge set under a stone, its shaft of light spilling into Morrigan's dark world.

8

BETHA

Gifted or Cursed?

The Parochial House, a spacious, three-room cottage, had become a wake house. In the parlor, women worked to bathe, shave, and dress Father Murray. In the old Irish custom, Mamoh placed candles at the priest's head and feet to remain lit until it was deemed the deceased's spirit had left the body. Another woman opened a window to allow the spirit to leave the house, keeping a careful eye no one crossed in front of it lest the spirit be blocked from leaving.

Adhering to the Catholic tradition, Betha wove Father Murray's most precious possession, hand-forged silver and amber rosary beads, around his hands so that the silver crucifix rested atop his thumbs. What a waste of a rosary, to be buried with him, she thought, and then, with a shudder, squelched her inner, devilish mind. "Set the clock to six, Riona. We cannot know the exact time of his death, but with the mutton stew, it's my best guess at the time he died."

"Aye, Mum."

As they worked, Widow O'Rooney whispered among the women, "'Tis queer the way Father Murray just stopped living."

"The heavens will be his bed this night," said another woman, as she lifted an ivory fabric, one of the priest's vestments, over a mirror in the entranceway. "You're right," she whispered. "And isn't it also strange, just after Morrigan saw the sea god?"

33

"The girl's gifted like Isla was. I'm certain of it, especially since she's seen Manannán mac Lir," whispered Widow O'Rooney.

"Or perhaps she's cursed," said another, "with her unholy birth. And though Isla healed many, she had her share of torments and tormenters."

Betha remained silent, hoping her lack of response would still their gossip. Inside, she fumed at the inference that Father Murray's death had anything to do with Morrigan.

Widow O'Rooney pursed her lips. "True it is, to bring healing to others demands courage to seek aid from those who live *between* things. Some have scorned the nature of it."

"The girl ought not set herself on the same course as Isla, though the temptation will be great. There's power in it, but her future would be grim," advised another.

"Indeed," said Widow O'Rooney. She moved closer to Betha. "Isn't it true, Betha, Morrigan is gifted in the way of Isla?"

"Hush and respect the dead," hissed Betha. She turned, and nearly bumped into Riona, who had leaned in to hear more. "Riona, fetch Schoolmaster Winnett. I'm surprised he is not here. Has he not heard the news?"

"Aye, Mum," said Riona. With a last prayer over Father Murray's corpse, Riona left.

Widow O'Rooney watched her go. "Now *that* girl of yours, Betha, is a beauty."

9

SCHOOLMASTER WINNETT

Self-Preservation

Despite his short stature, Schoolmaster Winnett was a handsome man, with eyes of palest blue, a straight nose, and a strong, capable jaw. But his own self-image, one as a serious scholar, kept him from using his most beguiling asset—a wide-mouthed grin that transformed his stern countenance to devastating appeal. He stood in front of the men and women gathered to say prayers over Father Murray's body. A droplet of sweat made its way along his temple. He wiped it away. With the priest's death, Winnett was expected to bear all Church responsibilities until a new priest arrived. A scarcity of priests meant it could take months. Bible clutched to his chest, he began, "The dead will not rest peaceably unless they're buried with their forefathers. Tomorrow I shall take our dear deceased pastor and brother overland to Tuam so he can rest with his kin." A murmur of consent passed among the villagers. Ancestral land was sacred, and a spirit knew its home. Anyone who left Ireland and died in a foreign land like America was considered an orphan spirit and grieved most wretchedly.

With his unexpected responsibility, Winnett saw an opportunity to shepherd the villagers in a more disciplined way. He had always believed Father Murray too lenient with his flock when it came to practicing the old Irish ceremonies and rituals. Now he could further restrict those abhorrent traditions.

Winnett bowed his head. He struggled for composure. Guilt flooded through him. My fault, he thought.

The scene from the previous evening played its drama in his mind. The servant girl had gone, leaving Father Murray some mutton stew. The priest had asked Winnett to join him, and thus, Winnett was in the priest's kitchen filling his bowl when he heard a throaty sound from Father Murray's study, followed by silence. Winnett hadn't heeded the sound because he was in full lecture mode, demanding Father Murray cease his undignified jokes at Mass, and insisting the priest would benefit from a more disciplined approach to his sermons. Not to mention the Lane girl and a suitable punishment for her.

By the time he'd noted the unearthly silence from the parlor, he'd come upon Father Murray ghostly white, hands at his throat, lips blue, eyes panicked, pleading. And then, a split second of giving over to something. Then nothing. It had happened so fast, and Winnett had stood frozen, unsure whether to run for help or hit Father Murray on the back.

As he relived the moment, Winnett struggled to breathe. He tried to pull himself back into the present—this moment with the priest, dead before them.

"Our Father, who art in heaven, hallowed be thy name…" began the villagers who viewed Schoolmaster Winnett's posture, bent over and clutching the Bible to his stomach, as one of deep prayer. Winnett reined in his emotions. He told himself it hadn't been his fault. Father Murray would have choked and died even if he hadn't been there. But a small voice inside himself asked, "If you were not at fault, then why did you clean your bowl and all indications of your presence, leaving Father Murray alone and dead?" Winnett had panicked, already guilt-ridden for not coming to the priest's aid. He'd thought of nothing except those times as a boy when his father had caught him in a misdeed and beaten him as though he were a dumb animal.

"Glory be to the Father, and to the Son, and to the Holy Ghost…" said the villagers, concluding their prayers.

Winnett gritted his teeth. It had been self-preservation to clean his bowl. Father Murray was dead, and that was that. Winnett would keep his presence at the scene a secret, and that was that.

Maybe it was meant to be. Now he could enforce a stricter piety among them, keep the villagers from drifting back to their pagan ways.

As they gathered around Father Murray's body, Schoolmaster Winnett braced himself to fulfill the role of nearest relative. He would touch the hand of the dead. According to tradition, if at its touch, a corpse uttered a cry, he was not quite dead. But Father Murray remained silent, as Winnett knew he would.

With a glass of whiskey inside her, Widow O'Rooney began the *ag caoineadh,* a high-pitched keening, her lament expressing a whole village's grief.

10

MORRIGAN

The Crooked Woman's View

The next morning, Morrigan went in search of The Crooked Woman, hoping Cathleen might help her decipher what to do with so much of her life in upheaval. Cathleen lived just beyond her village of Baile Ghort na Darach near an old stone circle. Morrigan decided to take the forbidden shortcut across the estate belonging to Sir Martin, the English landowner who authorized and apportioned the villagers' land leases and thus governed their lives.

She found a spot along the estate's stone wall, placed her bare foot into a ledge between stones and stepped up, grasping the top for support. She swung one leg over the wall, found a toehold, and soon, stood alongside gorse bushes on the other side. She braced herself for another bout of the eerie noise and image of dead bees she'd experienced a few days ago, but she remained clear and steady. She checked for signs of Mr. Eagan, the estate's overseer. Though she saw no one, a chill settled on her shoulders. She felt the sensation of being watched. Perhaps the overseer was hiding. Morrigan felt for the safety of the wall behind her, but only bird calls and the sound of wind moving through grasses met her ears. "Manannán mac Lir has spooked me," she chided herself. She made a sound of dismissal before walking through cow-pied grasses in the direction of Cathleen's cottage.

Halfway across Sir Martin's estate, Morrigan spotted Cathleen kneeling alongside a stream in pale blue skirts and wrap. She was foraging fen violets, laying them in her shallow, woven trug basket.

"God be with you, Cathleen," she said.

"Sodden skies are upon you, Morrigan," said The Crooked Woman.

"Sodden skies?" asked Morrigan.

Cathleen chuckled and explained, "'Tis my way of a greeting. I'm too bent over to see faces, so I try to feel into moods. I use sky descriptions, and your mood seems a bit—soggy. Are you in search of me?"

Morrigan hesitated, remembering her mum's cautions about the sea god. The urging to know more got the better of her. "At the well, you said if I had seen Manannán mac Lir, it would have been a distinction. And with Father Murray's death, I don't know if it is or it isn't."

"A distinction it certainly is. I learned from my grandmother only a very few possess the ability to see him. I m'self have had no encounter with the sea god."

Morrigan knelt alongside Cathleen and told her the story of Isla's voyages to the Land-Beneath-the-Waves, hoping for more information about its unknown realms.

Cathleen seemed unperturbed in hearing it. "Once there were many who had a special connection to Manannán mac Lir, who is a bridger to The Otherworld. These people were called Druids, a highly respected and oft-feared class in the advanced Celtic society. Oh, but 'twas a long time ago, some centuries past."

A memory flashed in Morrigan's mind of a younger Mamoh holding her small girl's hand inside an ancient stone circle, whispering, "The Druids gathered here, a leanbh, to listen to the wind and to talk to the stones, for the creator's wild nature held a powerful sway in their daily lives."

"Druids were greatly respected in Celtic society, training for decades in their craft. Some were storytelling bards, some were healers and seers, and some were priests. They wielded formidable power, but when the Catholic Church came to Ireland, the Druids were purged from the land."

"So how could my great-grandmother travel to the Land-Beneath-the-Waves?"

"The Druids are our ancestors. We all have a touch of Druid in us. It appears Isla was gifted at making connections to The Otherworld."

"But why did *I* see Manannán mac Lir, Cathleen?" asked Morrigan.

"Your name is quite like The Mórrígan, a powerful Irish goddess and shape-shifter who possessed magic and the gift of prophesy, as well as ferocity in battle. Perhaps there is a stronger touch of the Druid in you, too, though sadly, no one remains to teach you the old ways."

"Uncle Colm says I can't work at the quay anymore. They're calling me a redhead. I'll never see Manannán mac Lir again, and I'll never be a ship's captain."

"Sometimes it's a person like your uncle who gives you a gift wrapped in layers of disappointment," said Cathleen. "Perhaps he will propel you toward somewhere else you belong. It isn't the fish calling you, is it?"

"No," she gave a wry grin, "but I'm supposed to use my wits to learn English or Greek, stitch crewel, and get a husband instead. I would be so bored, Cathleen, stitching and sweeping." She ran her fingers over the velvety violet petals. "Ree fancies a countryman for a husband. She fits this life." An image of Riona from Sunday last flashed through her. Wavy black hair under her bonnet—hair like Da's, lustrous and thick; blue eyes with dark forests of lashes—eyes like Mum's. Only eleven months older, Riona had been surrounded by the village youth as she shared ideas about an upcoming Easter pageant.

"'Tis true you are different than most young women your age. Being different requires a willingness to seek your own answers. My mum told me something when I was about your age and stricken with this," said Cathleen, gesturing toward her crooked spine. "She said there is wisdom all around us. You only have to listen to receive it."

Morrigan plucked a violet. "What wisdom, Cathleen?"

"Powerful wisdom," she said, as if that alone was explanation. "And take care with those violet stems. Don't rip them, only pinch and tug. Ripping rends the spirit of the plant. And remember, too, when you forage, you must kneel and ask the king and queen of The Good People for permission before gathering plants. Then only take a few from each patch, never more than half, leaving some for others. The ancestors notice."

"Do you really think the ancestors notice, Cathleen?"

"I'm quite sure. The ancestors—sometimes we call them the Tuatha dé Danann—are in The Otherworld, the place where all the invisibles dwell, a beautiful realm merely a thin plane away. As close to us as the trees and the stones, the birds and the hills. And sometimes the trees and the stones, the birds and hills speak for the ancestors, so it's important to listen for their messages. Remember, when you are listening, everything is a part of the conversation."

Morrigan tried to imagine a divine realm all around her, as close to her as the violets she plucked, yet invisible. Her mum only talked about a Father in heaven who seemed somehow unreachable.

Cathleen continued her instruction. "To listen, you create an empty place deep inside." She pointed to the spot just above her stomach. "Then wait for messages to come to you. Trying equals *this much power*," she said, putting her thumb and forefinger together in a narrow gap. "Becoming an empty vessel leads to infinite power!" Morrigan watched as Cathleen attempted to throw her arms toward the sky for emphasis. "Everything," she said, as she caught her breath, "is here to teach us, even the biggest, ugliest thing. When you listen, you will find your place in the world. Or perhaps 'tis best said your place in the world will find you."

For the first time since she'd known her, Morrigan had glimpsed Cathleen's pale, youthful skin and deep blue eyes as she'd arched skyward. Cathleen was beautiful! And a much better teacher than Schoolmaster Winnett. Hers was an invitation to find wisdom in all things. Suddenly curious, Morrigan asked, "Have you always wanted to be a midwife and herbalist?"

Cathleen reached for her hazelwood walking stick and held it against her breast. "Once I stood tall, just like yourself. I fancied owning herds of sheep on a grand farm sweeping down to the bay, and a big, broad himself, who sang lullabies to the sheep and love songs to me. And armies of rosy-cheeked children, all laughing and teasing …" She paused. "Sometimes the spirits wish for us a different life, one we might not seek ourselves. So here I am, a midwife and herbalist." Cathleen lurched to her feet. "Perhaps we have tarried here too long. I sense the weather lowering. Rain's almost upon us." A bank of dark clouds hovered offshore. "I'll return for the last of the spring bloom, hopefully in time for Easter."

"Cathleen," said Morrigan springing to her feet, "will you teach me the forest medicines?"

"Is that not what I've been doing?"

"Thanks, Cathleen." Morrigan did not have the words to describe how safe she felt with Cathleen, how grateful she was for her kindness. This woman, so hunched over as to be called crooked, seemed not only a new mentor, but a new friend.

11

MORRIGAN

A Female's Place

Schoolmaster Winnett stood in the hovel turned Charity School. A slate tablet leaned against crates. At the top of the tablet, he had drawn the Greek alphabet and, below, what appeared to be a sentence in Greek. With no desire to teach poor females, Winnett had arranged what few there were in the back. All except for Riona, who occupied a front row seat, called the *master's seat* because he had selected her to assist him with lessons. When Winnett had asked the Lanes for permission to instruct Riona in schoolmastery, a rare opportunity for a female, they had agreed on one condition—that Morrigan obtain advanced schooling as well.

Winnett strode toward the back of the room and began his lecture. "This morning, I feel it important to discuss the philosophies of Aristotle, because Aristotle reminds us of a female's *place* in a family. Aristotle wisely wrote…" Winnett punctuated each word. "The relation. Of male to female. Is by nature. A relation of superior. To inferior. And ruler to ruled."

The room broke out in titters. Winnett's voice rose above them. "It is men who rule the waves, not women. Thus, when one of our females upsets the balance of place by stealing a púcán, a whole village upheaves. Isn't that so, Morrigan Lane? Isn't it true you've forgotten your place?"

A few of the boys sniggered and turned to look at Morrigan. A flush spread through her body and she felt the heat of it on her cheeks. *I want to disappear.* She bit the inside of her cheek and looked down. Then her face blazed. *No!* She dug her fingernails into her palm.

When Winnett leaned over to help William Cullen with his Greek, Morrigan slipped out the school door and ran toward a limestone ridge overlooking the bay. She erupted in a roar of outrage. She imagined the glare her teacher would direct at Riona in her absence, and how her sister would report Morrigan's breach of etiquette as soon as she returned home. To her sister, being proper mattered. In her brother Ruarc, she'd have found an ally. His mischief held no bounds. But he wasn't in advanced school. Uncle Colm now relied on him as first mate.

Already Morrigan regretted her misdeed. She'd be in trouble again. Schoolmaster Winnett's snobbery tore at her insides. Plus, he taught useless things. He'd known nothing of the edible leaves of purslane until Morrigan had shown him, and his insistence on clean hands seemed overly fussy. Unsuited to teach the children of fishermen, thought Morrigan. Nature as teacher, Cathleen's kind of learning, is best.

Climbing to the cliff's edge, Morrigan squinted into the bay's bright blue, scanning its vastness for signs of her father, brother, and the other fishermen even though they were beyond her vantage point. She unraveled her wrap to allow a briny breeze to caress the nape of her neck. As she plunked down on the spring grasses, Morrigan felt the renewed intensity of the sun. Winter had lost its power, and rebirth was upon the land. Finally relaxed, Morrigan put her face to the sun and whooped.

12

MISTRESS MARY

They Share a Secret

Mistress Mary, sixteen-year-old daughter of Sir Martin, breathed heavily from her mare's jump over a stone wall that bordered her father's estate. "Wouldn't Mother have been proud, Devona?" She spoke to her horse. Frowning, she slowed to a canter. "We'll keep this jumping a secret from Father, won't we?" She tossed the blonde ringlets that framed her porcelain face, and her hazel eyes flashed.

At the sound of a shout, Mary reined in her mare. She spied a peasant woman on the cliff's edge. The shout sounded full of—yes, joy. Mary wondered when she had last been joyful. It seemed a pinnacle emotion, coming over a person when some ineffable desire was fulfilled. Mary recalled a happier time, when at age twelve she and her parents had picnicked along the Kilcolgan on a linen blanket under an old willow tree. She and Father had burst into laughter as Mother told a story imitating Aunt Phoebe's nasal-sounding English. They had eaten a sumptuous supper of roast duck, drizzled figs, and pound cake. It had been a carefree day and Mary had been certain such times would last forever. But that was before her mother had been banished from their lives for something about which her friends whispered the Latin word *infidelitas*. Now Mary's tutor scolded her. "Joy, indeed exuberance of any kind, is unseemly for a lady."

Mary's bouts of restlessness coincided with her father's frequent trips to Parliament for work. While he was gone, she had no way to call upon her girlfriends in Clare and was often alone in the big manor house except for the servants and her tutor's visits, and her tutor was not her friend, as the formidable woman had once made plain.

Mary looked again at the young woman on the cliff. Was her shout because she'd been asked to Bealtaine, or better still, because she'd been kissed or even fondled by a beau? Remembering her own stolen kiss from a boy during a trip to London, Mary relived the thrill of it. Then she sagged in her saddle. It was proper behavior for a landowner's daughter to return to the estate and not engage in conversation with someone of a lower class. "Epidemics are rampant among the lower classes," she'd heard her father say. Straightening the deep green riding dress that accentuated her tiny waist, Mary shrugged, clicked her tongue to teeth, and moved the reins to signal her mare toward the young woman.

At Devona's snort, a young woman scrambled to her feet and turned, brushing bits of grass from her dusty red skirt. She curtsied. "Good day, Mistress Mary." Heat rose to her cheeks.

"Hello there," said Mary, struck by the woman's startling green eyes against her freckled skin and her unusual facial scar. She noted the woman's rapt attention on her finely chiseled gray mare just an arm's length away. "Go ahead and pet Devona. She'd like it," said Mary, sitting taller in her sidesaddle.

"Devona. A perfect name for this queen." Morrigan reached out to touch the horse's mane.

"She likes you. Look at her nuzzle your hand, and you've nothing to give her." The woman remained silent. "Tell me. You seemed so carefree just now. Why? Have you been asked to Bealtaine?"

"No, Mistress. 'Tis just … the sun is shining, and the breeze carries a bit of warmth this day. And it's lovely to see the bay blue like the sky. Oh, and the bees have begun their foraging for nectar, and…" she stopped.

Mary gazed out to sea. "No beau then?"

Once more, heat rose to the woman's cheeks. "There's a farm boy, Finn, but he's just a—a friend." She began making folds in her skirt. "I think Finn's sweet on me, a little." She shoved her renegade curls back into her bun.

"I'll bet he is sweet on you, with your eyes green like the hills, and if you wear your wrap around your chin like so," Mary motioned with her hands, "no one will even notice your, uh, disfigurement."

At this, the woman dipped her chin and moved her head to the side. Removing her hand from the horse's neck, she began to back away.

"Don't go. I like it. It's interesting! It's like a stem with a flower bud. It makes you special. Besides," Mary's voice softened, "everyone has something they want to hide."

A question in her eyes, the young woman stared at the Mistress.

Mary hesitated, then replied, "Even me. Look here." She removed her left glove and a gray, pebble-sized protrusion grew on the top of Mary's otherwise flawless middle finger. "I've got a wretched wart on my hand! It's despicable. I don't know what to do about it, and this year is my coming-out season."

"Cathleen can heal this," said the woman.

"The Crooked Woman? I've heard she invokes curses!"

"She's an herbalist and a midwife. Sure as the sun rises, she can heal your wart."

"She gives me the shivers, all hunched over like she is."

"She's the wisest person I know."

This girl is quite bold, thought Mary. "I'll consider it, … what is your name, then?"

"Morrigan. It's Morrigan Lane."

Mary chuckled. "So it's to *you* our piglet Shauna escapes. Puts Overseer Eagan in a proper huff."

Morrigan smiled at the mention of the young pig who seemed to prefer her company to the posh livery on the estate.

Abruptly, Mary looked back toward the manor. "I must go, Morrigan Lane. I oughtn't be riding outside the estate. Shhh!" She put a finger to her lips, and it now seemed they shared a secret. Turning, Mistress Mary urged Devona into a canter.

Morrigan stared after horse and rider as they grew smaller in the distance, and then cleared a wall, gone from sight.

13

MORRIGAN

Sir Martin's Increase

Walking the old cliff way home, Morrigan mulled over her conversation with Mistress Mary. For someone of the gentry class to speak directly with her kind was a rarity. Mistress Mary had spoken to her almost as if they were equals. She'd called Morrigan's scar *interesting*. Escaping school has brought its rewards, she thought. She couldn't wait to tell Finn what had happened. Now though, she would head home and face her mum's punishment.

Nearing the village, Morrigan heard angry shouts from a crowd in front of McDonaugh's Pub. Two of Sir Martin's agents were nailing a placard to a weathered column. Among the villagers, Tommy stood, his fist in the air. He shouted, "Two and a half pounds? Why another increase in rents?"

The agents faced the villagers and one declared, "It is by Sir Martin's own generosity you are leased the land on which you dwell. His reasons are not your business. The rents are due May third!" The agent hit the placard for emphasis. A protesting crowd followed the agents as they strode away from the village center.

Morrigan ran to her father. "Da! Are you all right?"

Tommy glared after the agents, lifting his flat cap to sweep the thick black hair from his weathered face. "Aye, Morrie." But they both knew better. For generations, the families of Baile Ghort na Darach had been subjected to oppressive acts and injustices as lands once stolen from them had been leased and subleased to tiny proportions. Rents were nearly impossible for the poor to pay. Most tenant farmers and rural workers lived in squalor and were spoken about as savages, blamed for their own impoverishment.

With the Legislature's Act of Union in 1801 that joined Ireland to the newly named United Kingdom of Great Britain and Ireland, the unrest had only intensified. The Irish people's plight under English rule had infiltrated song and story and cultivated rebellion. As hardship increased, so had the violence against the English, who were seen as foreign oppressors, and their proxy, Protestant landholders like Sir Martin.

East of Galway, as well as in more distant counties, a secret society of poor Catholics, The Ribbonmen, had clashed in violent skirmishes with police and military while fighting to prevent landlords from evicting their tenants. Though the fishing village of Baile Ghort na Darach had remained peaceable, like many places, it was a tinderbox.

Two years ago, Morrigan had witnessed a cruel eviction, seeing Mrs. Faherty on her knees, her five children wailing beside her as she pleaded with Sir Martin's head bailiff while the "crowbar brigade" tore the roof thatch from the Faherty cottage. Mamoh had turned Morrigan away from the scene before they set the thatch afire, but Mrs. Faherty's keening rose like the flames and attached itself to the winds, so, in truth, it was as though Morrigan had witnessed it all.

"Da, will we be all right?"

"God willing. What need have we of the comfort of sugar for our tea? We'll do without for a month or so…and fewer pints at the pub." Tommy gazed at the gunmetal bay in the distance. "Your brothers and I will have to sing sweet songs to the fish so they come right into our nets."

Morrigan nearly smiled at the image of her da crooning to the fish, but she stopped herself, seeing the deepened lines on his face, his shoulders slumped.

Thus, the men of Baile Ghort na Darach walked to their cottages where they'd bring news of the rent increase to their wives and wee wains. Morrigan latched onto Tommy's arm, brooding. *If I'd been a boy, I'd have joined the fishing fleet, increasing their catch.* She sighed in frustration, feeling her father's worry in his steps. "Da, remember what Mamoh says, 'Face the sun and turn your back to the storm.'"

"True, it is." Looking skyward, Tommy shook his head. The air smelled of rain.

14

MORRIGAN

God Bless These Fish

Tommy lifted the heavy lid of a clay-lined storage basin, his ropey muscles strong for his slight build. Buried into the ground on the shady side of the cottage, it was the coolest holding place for his catch. He placed whitefish into a carrying basket. On top, he added mussels, cockles, a rare baby octopus, and an early harvest of John Dorys.

Morrigan approached her da. John Dorys! Though uninviting in appearance with their spikes and spines, John Dorys were considered the most delicious fish at a feasting table. Likely, Cook Enya at the pub would make her acclaimed poached fish in wild garlic cream sauce for Easter. Morrigan's mouth watered; she couldn't hope to eat in such luxury.

Her father made the sign of the cross over the fish. "God bless these fish, God bless the sea, and may she forever bountiful be." Then he frowned as he gazed out over the waters.

"Why the sad face, Da?"

Tommy turned, wincing at his crabby knee. "'Tis the rent increase, Morrie. But," he put on a smile for his youngest daughter, "whether the sun rises late or early, the day is as God pleases."

Morrigan summoned her courage and asked, "Da, if I could fish, even from the shore, it would help us pay the rent." She clasped her hands together in a plea for understanding.

"Ah, you'd have the men in an outrage, a leanbh. In their lifetime, they've not known a woman like Gráinne Ní Mháille." Morrigan's face collapsed with disappointment. "Let's not think on it, Morrie. 'Tis Holy Thursday."

"All right." She threw out her hands to dispel her irritation.

"Might need two fish deliveries to McDonaugh's. Can you manage it?"

"Of course." With the sturdy leather straps of the fish basket over her shoulders and across her girth, and a smaller, creel basket looped over her arm, Morrigan would have little trouble carrying the fish to the pub. She appreciated that he had asked her anyway.

Tommy was quiet. Then he shook his head as if to banish his brooding, and conceded, "I know you love the waters like I do, Morrie. You've always been so cheerful about carrying the fish. We'll see what comes. I hope only for your happiness."

"Thanks, Da." Morrigan hugged her father.

Tommy looked skyward. "Let's hope the fog bank stays out to sea or it'll be a dank afternoon. Oh, and a hallo to the McDonaugh boys, especially that Finnbharr," he added with a wink.

Morrigan rolled her eyes at his ribbing, but she was eager to see Finn, for she hadn't yet had a chance to tell him about meeting Mistress Mary.

CONNIE

A Conversation with Kate

In McDonaugh's Pub, Connie McDonaugh, the proprietor, stood tall and stocky in his simple but spacious kitchen. "Spring onions, parsley, butter, cream. Got the lumpers already," he mumbled. The pub would offer a champ and a hearty fish stew during the no-meat fast of Holy Week. With the busy weekend before him, it wasn't too early to take a nip, and so he did. As if of their own accord, his hands washed, rinsed, and stacked the dishes from the previous night, pausing to rub his graying red beard and to take another pull of whiskey.

"It's these late nights, Kate," he whispered to his dead wife. It was his habit, a way of staving off loneliness. In his head, he heard Kate reply, "Connie McDonaugh, you're your own best customer. 'Tis the poteen whiskey you're drinking. The stuff'll make you blind! Or more daft than you already are." As often as not when she had been alive, Kate would have poked him in the ribs after a remark like that and given his meaty arm a squeeze. He sniffed the air and caught a whiff of her perfume made from wild orchids that grew on the limestone scree near the Burren.

"I try not to drink it, Kate. I know it makes me foggy and thick-tongued in the morning. And I'm curt with the boys."

"Those boys are growing wilder than a rockrose, Cornelius!" he heard her say.

"I know, Kate. Cormac's got a rag on every bush with the girls, and with his hot bent for justice, I fear he'll off and join the secret society that's rebelling against these new tithing laws. And why should we Catholics pay for the King's church? But he's a godsend with the customers, and his rendition of 'The Wind That Shakes the Barley,' well, there's none more beguiling." He squinted into the far kitchen corner and saw a mirage of his wife, her long red braid tinged with gray, her head nodding.

"James takes after me in size, doesn't he, Kate? Has to duck coming in and out of the farmhouse. He's willing to do the work here and on the farm. Just needs a bit of direction. And our Finn, Kate. He's got talent, and he's good to the bone, his features just like your own. I miss you, Kate." Connie swallowed a lump in his throat. After so many years, grief still overwhelmed him, especially when fatigued. He wiped his trembling hands on a rag near the sink and walked out into the damp morning air.

Morrigan came around the side of the pub with her fish basket. "Morning, Mr. McDonaugh. Da told me you might be needing more," she said as she handed him the basket.

Mr. McDonaugh hid his red-rimmed eyes. "He's probably right, Morrie. 'Tis Easter weekend. Many are out visiting as long as the weather holds." As the social center of the village, McDonaugh's Pub often overflowed with men who conversed about farming, fishing, and politics. "I'll send one of the boys to church this afternoon, let you know if we'll be needing more fish for tonight. He unloaded the fish into a basin and returned her basket. "Be a good girl and go tell the boys I need butter and cream, will ya?"

"Of course, Mr. McDonaugh."

"Tell them I shouldn't have to ask for it!"

Nodding, Morrigan hustled out the door.

16

MORRIGAN

Carving of Old Mother Oak

Temperate air hung dank and heavy as Morrigan walked through a meadow of wildflowers toward the McDonaugh farmhouse. A pale sun cast its limp shadow on the empty seedpods from last season's quaking grass. Morrigan thought: 'Tis one of those days. Can't decide whether to coo like a dove, or to screech like an owl. Mamoh would call them mackerel skies. "Mackerel skies, mackerel skies, never long wet, never long dry." She chanted the old fisherman's tune.

She felt a sudden unease, as though she were being watched. Yet a careful scan of her surroundings revealed no one. "I'm going daft," said Morrigan to a bumble bee that had landed on a clump of coltsfoot alongside the path. But the bee was immersed in a cauldron of nectar, not interested in answering. "Well then." Morrigan trudged to the McDonaugh farmhouse.

The wolf lay hidden behind a thick stand of milk thistle. For days he had observed the girl's actions and had judged her to be without guile, just as The Invisibles had predicted. It was nearing time for his message. He would wait until he caught her alone outside the village.

The farmhouse appeared like a disheveled uncle in worn clothes. It had once been distinctive, with its roomy three-bay, two-story structure, no doubt created for the large family Mrs. McDonaugh had intended before her untimely death during Finn's birth.

In the courtyard hemmed in by outbuildings, sheep milled about in one mucky corner, and ducks squawked from their clusters nearby. "God bless all in this house!" Morrigan called out as she approached the arched doorway, which stood ajar. She pushed it open, her nose wrinkling in distaste. Something poorly cooked congealed in a cauldron over embers inside the hearth. A half feral kitten nosed her way toward it.

"You do not belong inside, sweet kitten," said Morrigan. With a quick motion, she scooped it up and ushered it outside. She caught sight of a butter crock on the cupboard by the door and reached for it, then gasped as a voice penetrated the stillness.

"Look who's stealing your butter, little brother," said Cormac appearing in the doorway. Finn stood behind him.

Morrigan threw a wave of dismissal in his direction. "I am doing no such thing, Cormac. Your da sent me to tell you he needs butter and cream, and he shouldn't have to ask for it!" She looked at Finn, and a smile returned. "Hallo, Finn."

"Good to see you, Morrigan."

Cormac made a sound in his throat. "I'll get the cream," he said, and headed for the earth cellar. Turning back to Morrigan, he teased, "You're growing up nicely, UgMor." It was the name he'd used for her as a child, short for Ugly Morrie.

"Hush your irksome mouth, Cormac!" said Morrigan. She shook her head. She'd known him since he wore short pants and skinned his knees on the stones at the quay.

"Don't pay him any mind, Morrie," said Finn. "Here, let me take the crock. Butter's already churned." He reached for it, and his hands brushed hers for a moment. Morrigan felt a thrill surge in her veins. She looked into his eyes and eons of time seemed to pass before she blinked. His eyes asked her a question, "Do you see me differently as I see you differently?" She did.

A flush spread through her. "Thanks, Finn." She lifted her basket, lingering, not wanting to leave.

Finn seemed reluctant to see her go. He walked to the mantel and reached for a carving. "For you, Morrie. You're so taken by that oak these days." He held out a small carved replica of Old Mother Oak.

Morrigan's heart leapt as she turned the carving around and around. He had captured the way the oak's three broad limbs grew down as if to kiss the ground before reaching skyward. "Oh, Finn. 'Tis beautiful!"

Over the years, Finn had given her carvings—of salmon, currachs, and curlews—but none were as special as this one. "You must have spent hours and hours." Morrigan longed to touch Finn's hands to discover the magic inside them.

Finn shrugged. "You know I like to keep my hands busy. It's made from hazelwood, a branch felled in February's storm. I didn't want to cut a live limb from the oak to make it."

"Hazelwood. The wood of wisdom. The wood of divination." Morrigan chanted the words Cathleen had shared when she'd asked her about her walking stick. "How can I thank you, Finn?" Their eyes met, and Morrigan felt her breath catch at the intensity she saw in Finn's.

Cormac whistled as he made his way up from the cellar. The spell was broken.

"It's to remind you of home when you set out to captain your own vessel and conquer the world, Morrie," said Finn, now jovial.

"I'll keep it close." Morrigan brought the carving to her heart and gave him a warm smile.

As she started back across the field, Morrigan caressed the tree carving. What had she seen in Finn's gaze as their hands touched against the butter crock? Was it brotherly affection? Or attraction? She'd known him since they were babes. They'd played spinning tops and handball, competed in loy-digging for potatoes and in maths contests. Finn was eighteen, and to Morrigan's mind, the McDonaugh boy with the most promise. Have I *imagined* something different between us? she wondered. No, she decided. She hadn't imagined it at all. Humming "The Salamanca Reel," she skipped home.

17

MORRIGAN

The Once-and-Only Language

That afternoon the dank stone cottier's cottage bearing the grand title of Saint Joseph's Church was crowded with barefoot villagers in their homespuns who, in the absence of a priest, had come to hear Schoolmaster Winnett's scholarly version of Holy Thursday. Afterward, many remained in penitent prayer. Before a searing look from Betha could stop them, Morrigan and Tommy scrambled outside breathing away the musty air.

Morrigan latched onto Tommy's arm. A damp mist carried the scent of the bay over gold and spiky gorse-filled ditches to where they stood on the dirt trackway. Morrigan looked skyward. "Weather's lowering. Rain's on its way."

"True, it is," said Tommy sniffing the air with a chuckle. "You can read the skies as well as any fisherman, Morrie." With a nudge and a wink for his youngest, he said, "Oh, and your mum decided we'll have mutton stew for Easter." Betha had promised the rare indulgence if Morrigan took her advanced schooling more seriously.

"Praise be," said Morrigan, already salivating at the notion of aromatic mutton neckbones and shanks drenched in a stew of onions, garlic, and potatoes.

"Did you know, Morrie, your beloved Irish mariner Gráinne Ní Mháille spoke Latin when she met with Queen Elizabeth?"

"She did?" Morrigan stopped walking.

"Aye, and 'twas said she spoke Greek as well. She was a sea captain, smart and brave, but educated, too." Tommy leaned in and whispered, "If she could do it, so can you."

An image formed in Morrigan's mind of Gráinne sprawled on fur-lined pillows, surrounded not by attentive servants but by ancient Latin manuscripts and Greek writings, devouring them with gusto next to a roaring fire in a stone fortress she herself had captured. More than warrior-pirate, Gráinne had loved learning.

Da's right, Morrigan decided. I can love learning, too.

James intercepted them, chest heaving, "We're wild with people at the pub! We'll need more fish for the suppers," he said.

"I'll bring some directly," said Morrigan, turning toward the Lane cottage.

"I fancy m'self a nip at the pub before the fog settles in," said Tommy, a twinkle in his eye. "You'll tell your mum, won't you?"

"Me? Thanks, Da." They both knew Betha would raise her eyes skyward and make the sign of the cross, as though intoning, "Father, forgive his wayward deeds." Morrigan believed her mum blamed her as much as her da for his trips to the pub. As often as not, she'd sneak over after the men got to singing. Tommy's lush baritone was hardly rivaled, and it seemed the walls pulsated with the rhythm of the fishermen's bawdy seafaring songs. When Tommy ended an evening playing "The Erin Shore" on his lilting harp, father and daughter would walk home in the comforting envelope of darkness.

Eager to collect the fish and return to the pub, Morrigan ran home. From the cool storage place, she withdrew what remained of the week's catch and loaded her woven carrying basket, saying a prayer of thanks that Mr. McDonaugh bought his fish from her da. Often it meant the addition of a few niceties to their diet.

As she trudged back to town, she recited the last stanzas from her da's favorite poem, "The Rime of the Ancient Mariner," from Coleridge:

> *Oh! Dream of joy! Is this indeed*
> *The lighthouse top I see?*
> *Is this the hill? Is this the kirk?*
> *Is this mine own countree?*

The part she liked best near the ending suggested a close-up God, a creator who found equal value in the tiniest leaf and the biggest ocean.

> *He prayeth best, who loveth best*
> *All things both great and small*
> *For the dear God who loveth us,*
> *He made and loveth all.*

A blast of ill-disposed wind stirred bits of dried seaweed along the path. Chilled, Morrigan looked out across the bay. Fog had moved like a ghost over the water and now draped the fishermen's cottages in shadowy vapor. With everyone at church or the pub, Morrigan might have relished the quiet. Instead, she shuddered, and paused to shift the basket from where the weight of it rested on her shoulders. She looked up and witnessed, as through an ethereal veil, piercing yellow eyes. She froze and blinked twice to banish what her sight revealed—the formidable head and unyielding mass of a wolf. Its gray head was cocked, and its ears, silver at the base and turning ivory toward the tips, moved forward as though listening.

Fear gripped Morrigan's heart, froze her limbs, and coursed through her veins like silent screams. She fixed on a desperate action: Back! Up!

With slow, protracted movement, she lifted one unsteady foot and placed it behind her. She did the same with the other, her eyes riveted on the danger in front of her.

What happened next was most peculiar. With equally slow movements, the wolf settled back onto its haunches, gaze steady, body still—waiting.

Instinct propelled Morrigan to look for a weapon. Then, words entered her mind that were not her own. "It is for you I have come. It is to you I must speak." The words collapsed in on themselves.

Morrigan stared. Come for me? she thought. Because she had only *thought* this question, she was astonished to see the wolf's silver head dip as though in response.

"I carry a vital message to you from The Otherworld."

"The Oth-Otherworld?" Morrigan squeaked out words matching her thoughts but having a different sound than the language she usually spoke. She continued to take steps backward, so that the wolf moved forward a pace or two, and then sat to stay near to hear. Her mind scrambled to make sense of the wolf's presence. Had Manannán mac Lir shape-shifted into a wolf?

"No harm shall come to you from me, Morrigan Lane. I am here to give you a message. I have been chosen to deliver it. And you have been chosen to receive it."

At the mention of her name, Morrigan let slip the fish basket from her shoulders.

Scanning his surroundings the wolf said, "You notice we understand each other."

Morrigan nodded.

"We speak in The Once-and-Only Language. It existed long ago, a way of communicating being to being."

"The Once-and-Only Language?" Morrigan tried to remember if Mamoh had ever mentioned another language.

"The Once-and-Only Language happens inside the heart, not the mind. It is a felt sense, an exchange of meaning. It is nearly forgotten by humans. But I will speak more of it on the morrow. Shall we convene at the great oak in the forenoon?" The wolf stood, its head low, thick body in a crouch, paws spread to gain purchase on the stony path.

So close to his powerful animal presence, Morrigan felt fear overtake the strange trance that had beset her. But his riveting yellow eyes held no menace. With more certainty than she felt, she said, "Aye. If I can, I will."

Like fog's spectral twin, the wolf vanished into the night.

Shock numbed Morrigan's brain. She exhaled long to calm her breathing, willing her mind to become blank, but the predator appeared in it as if he had been called.

Morrigan found herself in front of Connie McDonaugh at the pub's kitchen door with no memory of having walked there. With shaking hands, she delivered the fish basket into his arms. He noticed nothing unusual amid the clamor of Holy Thursday supper.

That night, Morrigan lay on the pallet under the eaves she shared with Riona. The wolf's message about The Once-and-Only Language cracked open a long-exiled dimension of her being. She listened for some nostalgic old tune to reveal itself. Nothing came to comfort her.

She began to doubt what she had seen, the oft repeated Bible verse drowning her better knowing. "Trust in the Lord with all your heart and lean not on your own understanding; in all your ways submit to him, and he will make your paths straight."

As the night dragged on, Morrigan tossed and the bed moved and squeaked beneath her. Near dawn, Riona kicked her from where she lay next to her sister. "For Chrissake, Morrie, will ya be still?"

Finally, daylight showed through the cracks in the thatch. Deep down, Morrigan knew the wolf was real, just as she knew seeing the sea god was real. She'd meet the wolf, God help her.

18

BETHA

Morrigan's Wild Birth

Betha noted the way Morrigan played with her stirabout. "Not hungry? You look tired, Morrigan."

Morrigan clutched her stomach and complained, "My tummy doesn't feel well, Mum."

"Cathleen might have something for you," said Mamoh.

Betha nodded in agreement, but a frown settled between her eyebrows. Many contagions revealed themselves first as a stomach ache. "Twould be a shame if you were ill for Easter. You'd miss Riona's solo at Mass. Indeed, a trip to Cathleen is a good idea." She hesitated before adding, "And while there, please ask her for my remedy."

Though guilt-ridden, Betha ingested wild carrot seeds during her fertile time. As a young bride, she'd been told motherhood was a gift from the goddess and a sign a woman had been touched by the Divine. Tommy loved his two boys and two girls, and he'd have room in his big heart for more children, but Betha had harbored anxiety about childbirth since Morrigan's harrowing delivery.

Her mind spiraled back in time to the night of Morrigan's birth, one of the blackest anyone could recall. No stars had shone from the inky vault of the January sky and winds had come from the southeast. Africus winds, warm and stale like lion's breath, winds the old ones believed to be auspicious.

Awkward with pregnancy, frightened and in pain, Betha had realized her baby was birthing so fast there was no time to get Cathleen from her cottage outside the village. She implored Tommy to take Liam and the sleepy twins over to McDonaugh's Pub where they might find help from Cook Enya. Tommy had been reluctant to go, but when he saw the wild look in her eyes, he hustled his young family there.

Birthing her youngest, Betha had felt only waves of pain. She'd known something was wrong. Mamoh prayed first to the Virgin Mother, and then, as a violent pain took hold of her daughter, Mamoh turned to someone stronger, the ancient goddess *Bhride*, midwife for Mary. Morrigan's tiny foot had emerged from beneath Betha's skirt, not her head. It had been too late to do anything so Mamoh tugged her hard. When finally, the babe's shoulders were out, something strange had happened. Morrigan's head came through in the caul, covered with the "lucky" veil. But then her head had gone back in, as though something inside played tug-of-war.

Cathleen later explained that Morrigan was in the seam of not-yet and just-about, in both worlds at the same time, something the midwife had only heard about but never witnessed. Finally, Mamoh yanked Morrigan out as Betha's screams echoed across the fishing village and over the waters. A distressed Mamoh had ripped the veil from the babe's head and in doing so, tore and forever scarred Morrigan's skin from cheek to jawline.

Folding her arms across her midsection, Betha shook off the memory. Four children were plenty. The number four represented the four elementals—fire, water, earth, and air; the four great festivals—Imbolc, Bealtaine, Lugnasadh, and Samhain. And she'd read in Revelations about the four angels who stood at the four corners of the earth holding up the four winds. Four was enough.

Reaching for the tiny blue tin behind the mantel clock, Betha removed a few coins. "Give these to Cathleen for her trouble,

Morrigan, and be back for church at two. No lingering in the wildwood."

"Aye, Mum." Morrigan hurried out the door.

19

MORRIGAN

An Fhoínse

Under a gray sky mottled like whorls of sheep's wool, Morrigan headed toward Old Mother Oak. Her feigned stomach distress became real. Sounds of village life faded away. Morrigan's legs felt wobbly, and she almost turned back. But it was the peculiar language of mutual understanding that brought a measure of calm to the young woman.

She stood by the oak, one hand on its trunk for support. The glade rustled and revealed the wolf, more powerful in full light. He moved to close the distance between them, resting on his haunches where the woods met the small clearing around the oak.

Wolf legends were an inseparable part of ancient lore, a sacred symbol considered more companion and guide than cunning tracker and killer. Hunted to extinction in Ireland, none had been seen in generations. Perhaps Morrigan felt some deep ancestral memory of connection; inexplicably, she lost all sense of alarm and plunked down in the crook formed from two thick roots of the oak.

"I came as you asked, wolf," she said. She spoke in her mind the language she hadn't known she'd known until the previous night.

She heard his response in her head. "On behalf of The Otherworld, I herald you," he said, "for you have been recognized to fulfill a destiny on behalf of all creation."

"A destiny?"

"A destiny is the road of a soul. A life where the marvelous and the ordinary are one and the same if you allow them to be. A life of infinite, invisible connections as close to you as your own breath," said the wolf.

"You may think of me as a wisdom messenger. I, a being not seen for many decades, have come at the behest of The Invisibles, the guardians of The Otherworld. You cannot yet perceive them, although you have seen their bridger, Manannán mac Lir. Before I reveal the message about your destiny, how do you see your life as it is today?"

Morrigan hesitated. She had spent years keeping quiet. Experience had taught her attention was unwanted and often unpleasant. She collected her thoughts and began, "When I was little, people looked at me differently than they did Riona. They thought me unusual, and I don't know if it was because of my birth scar or because I was unusual on the inside, too." Morrigan twirled a strand of red-gold hair around her finger, gazing off in the distance before continuing. "Or if I became different because they looked at me as different. Da says I have a way about me. He calls it a singular truthfulness. Mum says it's an unbridled streak. Most times, it hasn't been helpful. And it's true, I see things differently. I've tried to hide it." Morrigan wrapped her shawl tighter around herself as a morning breeze rustled the hazel scrub nearby. "Mamoh tells me, 'I've gone inside myself but away from myself.' I feel like a salmon swimming upstream all the time. Lately, I want to break things, shout back, run away." She searched the wolf's yellow eyes for understanding. He nodded in confirmation.

"You have a vibrant life force, Morrigan," said the wolf. "Even if you stay silent, your true self will leak out of you. You are *An Fhoínse*. We would not understand each other if you were not. You would only hear growls from me, but instead, you can speak in The Once-and-Only Language. You have not lost your wildness the way others of your kind have. Your rare birth confirms it. We of the wildwood celebrate your gift, for you are needed now more than ever."

"*An Fhoínse?*"

"It means a spring from which the life force flows," said the wolf.

An Fhoínse sounded special in an important way, unlike being different and tormented by phrases like "Ugly Morrie, never a glory." Although Mamoh had hinted at something beyond the physical about her birth, the wolf's explanation sounded thrilling. "You, a wolf, describe me as *An Fhoínse*, a name I have not heard. And Mamoh tells me to keep quiet about my birth."

"Your Mamoh is a wise woman. There are those in power who long for more and are fearful of the potent power of your gift."

"Why do you seek me now?"

"The Wheel of the Year turned many times while The Otherworld awaited your birth, Morrigan. At last, you rode the wave through the cave of the ancestors, moving past row after row of inscriptions as old as the memories of the long-ago dead. At that time, The Invisibles proclaimed, 'This is a moment foretold in whispers around the council of stones. Let us hope there is still time, for the Great Mother, Máthair Mhór, is in grave danger. Thus, we waited to greet you until your gift began to emerge.'"

Morrigan opened her mouth to speak but no words came out. A buzzing sound filled her ears. The earth is in grave danger? She looked around the wildwood at the vibrancy of newly leafed ash and birch, moss-covered rocks, gold wood avens and dainty lemon primroses. It made no sense. Yet the memory of her dizzy spell and the flash of dead bees flitted through her consciousness.

Beings in The Otherworld had awaited her birth? Had the strange circumstances—how she'd come out and then gone back in—meant she'd been unwilling to emerge into the world? Whatever the wolf's message, had baby Morrigan wanted escape from it? Morrigan stood, fighting an instinctive urge to flee. "I hardly understand your words, wolf."

The wolf rose and stretched. "There is more to explain. Let us meet here again, Morrigan Lane," he said, little question in his tone. "The time has come for you to hear the full message I carry from The Otherworld."

Morrigan nodded despite herself. "I'll return directly after school on Easter Monday."

The wolf nodded, and then, as though by some sleight of hand, the forest swallowed him up.

Later, Morrigan arrived at Cathleen's small cottage and burst through the door. "Cathleen, I met a wolf who spoke of the old ways in an old language. He said he has a message for me from The Otherworld. They'd been waiting for my birth. Máthair Mhór is in danger!"

Cathleen had been sifting dried herbs. She motioned Morrigan to her side and hugged her to spread some calm. Then she reached for a glass jar from one of her shelves, opened the door, and scattered some of its contents across her threshold.

"What's that, Cathleen?"

"Saint John's Wort. It acts as the wildwood's representative for Archangel Michael's protective healing." She moved back inside. "Our Mother is in danger, is that what the wolf said?"

"Aye, and I am supposed to do something about that," said Morrigan. "I'm called, *An Fhoínse.*" Morrigan proceeded to tell Cathleen about her encounter with the wolf.

When Morrigan had finished, Cathleen placed her hands on the young woman's shoulders and gave them a squeeze. "Morrigan, seek out the wolf and learn that which is yours to learn. I know a small bit and will guide you as best I can, but I do not know The Once-and-Only Language. I am not *An Fhoínse*. Know you are in a wholly different sphere."

How is it Cathleen knows no more about these things than I do? "You'll help me though?"

"Aye, child, I'll teach you what I know of the ways of listening and acting in accordance with the ancients. But I urge you to listen for your own inner guidance."

After collecting the special remedy for her mum, Morrigan headed home. Every wind gust held a whisper, every bird call a response, "*An Fhoínse. An Fhoínse.*"

20

MORRIGAN

Holy Saturday Confrontation

On Holy Saturday morning, Mamoh knelt in the garden, her fine white hair stuck to her brow like a silken seed plume. She'd unearthed two precious heads of cabbage from where they'd been buried last fall. Patting the soil as she would a well-behaved child, the old woman sat back on her heels; a groan slipped from her mouth as her tired muscles protested.

Morrigan appeared before her. "I've brought potatoes and onions in from the earth cellar, Mamoh, and the last of the turnips and carrots."

"We'll have a fine stew for Easter then."

Morrigan bent down to help her grandmother to her feet. "Change is afoot, Mamoh."

Nodding in agreement, Mamoh answered, "The wheel of the year has its own rhythm, and with each season, come risks and rewards. We're now in the time of the winds, and soon, the time of brightness." For Mamoh and many others, the year had a distinct framework anchored by the four great festivals and its two solstices and two equinoxes. The wheel of the year also contained smaller divisions for planting, harvesting, and resting, as well.

"But some changes come outside the cycle, and without warning." Morrigan stopped herself from saying more. She'd been warned. "I'm off to collect wild garlic for the stew."

"Don't confuse the wild garlic leaves with those poisonous lords and ladies. Remember the difference?"

"In their smell most of all."

"Off you go then."

Morrigan left for Old Mother Oak, hoping to find the wolf. She waited for a time, her eyes scanning the undergrowth, but he did not appear, so she sneaked onto Sir Martin's estate. There carpets of wild garlic grew in the glen near where she and Cathleen had collected fen violets. With nimble fingers, she pinched off fragrant garlic leaves as an herb for the stew. She spied Cathleen just across the glen and approached her teacher. "God be with you, Cathleen. Where will you be celebrating Easter? Will you join us? Mum won't mind another at the table."

"'Tis kind of you, Morrigan. I've celebrated in my own way." Cathleen explained how Easter merged with many ancient traditions, including rituals to honor Ostara, the goddess of spring, and her companion, a rabbit. An impregnated egg symbolized the renewal of nature, where buds long dormant blossomed in the longer days and warmer weather, and sheep and cows became fertile.

"During the First Council of Nicaea, 325 years after Jesus of Nazareth was killed, the Catholic Church decided Easter would fall on the first Sunday after the full moon following our March equinox," said Cathleen. "At council, Jesus was declared divine—equal to the Father. That's when they began suppressing our native rituals and ceremonies." Cathleen made a derisive sound.

Remembering her mentor's instructions to seek out the wolf, Morrigan said, "I see no sign of the wolf today, Cathleen, but I promised him I'd return to the oak on Easter Monday."

"Be there as early as you can, child, for you cannot risk losing out on the message."

Morrigan nodded. A thick cord of tension tightened her stomach as she anticipated what the wolf's message might contain. Maybe she'd avoid school altogether and arrive at their meeting place in the morning. Could she risk it?

They heard snorting sounds. Soon the distinctive face and dull pink body of a piglet darted across the glen to where Morrigan stood.

"Hallo, Shauna!" said Morrigan, fondling the pig's soft ears.

She heard Cathleen's low warning, "Thunder clouds! Mr. Eagan's coming!"

The stocky overseer strode toward Morrigan, his head down like a bull ready to charge, his cheeks blowing from exertion.

"That pig," he huffed, "does not belong to you!" He glared at Morrigan, his posture rigid. "You will stop casting a counter-charm on her, or whatever it is you are doing to lure her from her pen!"

"But…" sputtered Morrigan.

"And you," he said, turning to Cathleen, "have been warned against foraging on these lands. They belong to Sir Martin now."

Cathleen grasped her hazelwood stick and struggled to her feet. "Mr. Egan, I know you have it in you to be a fair and reasonable man. Can I not select a few of the flowers and wild garlic for my purposes? These boundaries are only man's distinctions. The violets like to grow here and not on the drier soil nearest me. Shall we not encourage them to grow where they grow best, just as I encourage the gorse to grow on my land for use by all as horse feed?"

The overseer drew himself to his full five-feet-nine inches in height and thrust out his broad chest. "Rubbish! As Sir Martin's overseer, it is my duty to assert his preeminence over these lands. I do not care what grows where. I care about boundaries! *His* boundaries. I ask you to please remove yourself."

They heard a horse's gallop. Mouths agape, they watched a smartly dressed Mistress Mary soar over the glen and pull her mare to a halt only yards away. Looking down at Morrigan and Cathleen, Mary asked, "What is happening here, Mr. Eagan?"

"Nothing I cannot handle, Mistress," said Eagan.

"Perhaps," said Mary. She turned to face Cathleen, her voice cool. "Why are you on my father's property?"

Before Cathleen could respond, Morrigan felt a fierce surge. "Mistress Mary, once these lands belonged to Cathleen's kin before they were granted to yours. From time to time, she seeks the old herbs and medicines found here. Can you not allow her that small generosity?"

Mistress Mary glared down her nose at Morrigan, and then, as if having decided something, she replied, "You have a sharp tongue on you today, Morrigan Lane. What else would you like to say?"

Morrigan, whose knees had started to quake underneath her skirts, added the first thing that came to her mind. "The rent increase is far too steep at this time. It's not possible to pay it before the mid-May Fair where we can sell seaweed to earn the extra pence."

Cathleen cleared her throat. A warning. Morrigan looked down, and added, "Cathleen does no harm here." Then she turned to Mr. Eagan and said, "I can't explain why Shauna follows me, but I always see her home."

"Well, Morrigan Lane, you make an interesting point. Perhaps if you are brave enough to explain your reasoning to my father, I will ask him to give you a few moments by the pigs' pen. And while you're at the estate, you can help me with something," Mary said, removing her glove and pointing to her wart.

Morrigan's throat tightened. A meeting with Sir Martin? And how would she cure a wart? She feigned confidence. "When shall I call, Mistress?"

"Father's been away to London at the Parliament. He returns two weeks from yesterday. How about the next day, Saturday, in the forenoon?" She did not wait for a response. "Oh, and Easter greetings to you."

"And to you, Mistress Mary," said Morrigan, curtsying.

"Mr. Eagan, it seems we're done here. You can lead me and Devona home. The pig will follow along if the girl sends her." Without another word, Mary headed toward the manor atop a hill. The overseer gave Cathleen and Morrigan withering looks and then hastened to catch the horse's lead. Morrigan shooed the piglet in their direction.

"Landsakes! What have I done?" A skylark sang. Morrigan sighted the hovering speck whose long, liquid warble sounded like sunshine turned into song.

"Skylark seems to sing your praises. You've spoken up for me, for your family, and for the whole village by the looks of it," said Cathleen. "I'm proud of you, Morrigan. Your request to Sir Martin is reasonable, and it is perhaps a way you can help the village."

"I couldn't stay quiet," said Morrigan. "I was bursting inside. I'll be in trouble for it, sure as sunrise."

Cathleen retrieved her basket. "I wonder if the shape of your birth scar reveals your calling? The ancients said caul-bearers were born to rule or lead. Your scar shows the lines of a leader or a visionary, like the way you acted just now."

Morrigan traced her scar with two fingers. She shook her head and remained quiet. Manannán mac Lir. The wolf. Her life had been upended in only a few days. A memory arose from a simpler time when at six years old, perched on her da's lap with her ragdoll Lolly in her arms, they'd rocked to the soulful crooning of a songman in the pub. Morrigan remembered what her da had whispered into her ear, "We are the Irish, a leanbh. We are the music makers, the dreamers of dreams." In the sanctuary of her father's arms, she'd felt a profound sense of belonging. Now with her identity redefined by messengers from The Otherworld, she had no understanding of her gifts or how to use them. She feared whatever came next would require more courage than she possessed.

21

MORRIGAN

Easter

Morrigan loved the Lane family's weekly bath ritual. Sure, it was the warmth and the washing, but it was something else. Each time her hands sculled and made rivers in the shallow water of the wooden tub, she felt it singing a song. It was a caress, this song. Even more, it felt like an invitation to step out of the tub a different person. She had a sense of an open gate, unknown but welcoming at the same time. She felt it most when she was the first one in. Later in the rotation, it became a whisper, or went missing altogether.

It was Easter morning. As she heard the water's song, Morrigan felt a tingling sensation low in her belly. She smiled and began to hum a melody that matched that of the water.

"You're taking longer than a loaf to rise, Morrigan!" said Betha. "Wash and rinse and out. You know that."

"Yes, Mum." But Morrigan lingered a bit longer, wondering when to tell her da about her confrontation with Mistress Mary, and her supposed audience with Sir Martin. After Easter, she decided, not at all certain he would be as supportive as Cathleen had been. As she stepped out of the tub, Morrigan gave a satisfied sigh. Thank the good Lord I have Cathleen to talk to, she thought. And she'll teach me the forest medicines. This was news she would not delay. Around Cathleen, Morrigan had begun to feel important.

"Tommy, in you go now, and take your time. I'll lower another kettle to boil. It's you who should go first anyway," said Betha. Morrigan did not have to see her mum to know she was shaking her head in disapproval, lips drawn together in a thin line.

"I'll just turn the water into fish oil," he said. "I like my girls to go in first. Riona doesn't take long. She's worried about wrinkling her skin." He chuckled. "In you go, Ree-Bird, and watch you don't turn into a prune or you'll sing like an old crow," he teased.

"Oh, Da!" Riona darted behind a makeshift screen. Soon, wild splashing sounds came from behind it.

"Mind you don't give the floor a bath," said Betha.

"Yes, Muuuuum!" Riona trilled as she held the note. It was not out of the ordinary for Riona to sing her way through conversations, earning her the nickname Ree-Bird.

Morrigan stepped into her scarlet petticoats, and then slid her finest skirt of deep forest green over her head, pulling it down below her waist so it wouldn't look too short. She donned a coarse cotton top, admiring the embroidered collar Riona had sewn into it. With care, she slipped into new white stockings, her best frieze jacket, also in green, and, finally, put on her lace cap. Sliding into her one pair of shoes, Morrigan felt almost pretty. She was ready for Easter Sunday.

A soft mist permeated the air as the Lane family set out for Saint Joseph's. "'Tis a bonny foursome we have, Betha," said Tommy, gazing at his progeny. He was dressed in his best: a black waistcoat, breeches, white stockings and shoes.

"It is," said Betha, whose arm was linked with Mamoh's. Betha wore a finespun scarf of pale rose over deep crimson skirts.

"And you, my fair wife, look so fetching, I'm besotted all over again."

"Thomas, you've got more blarney in you than a tanked bard," said Mamoh. Riona and Morrigan giggled. Betha smiled, her shoulders relaxed.

"Mum," said Morrigan, who had noticed her mum's softened demeanor, "Would you have minded if Cathleen had come for Easter supper? I told her you wouldn't have, but anyway, she's already celebrated in some old way. I wish I knew those rituals." Morrigan spoke the last words more to herself than anyone.

A brief frown darkened Betha's face before she showed a smile. "A good Irish woman always welcomes another at her table."

"I thought so!" Morrigan took a little skip. "And Mum, she was kind enough to agree to teach me the forest medicines." Morrigan stopped talking when her mum stopped walking, her frown lines visibly deepened. "In case I truly cannot work at the quay."

"That's still to be spoken about." The Lane family had arrived outside the church along with hordes of enthusiastic villagers. "No more on this, Morrigan. I must ready Riona for her solo."

Morrigan bit the inside of her cheek, stuffing down disappointment. She had a sense she'd need her mentor's help to uncover the mystery of her calling. If Betha forbade it, Morrigan would have to find another way.

Betha guided Riona to the front of the damp and crowded church in preparation for her solo. The eldest Lane daughter looked beautiful in cobalt-blue skirts and matching frieze that brought out the blue in her eyes. She seemed lit from within. Betha arranged choral youth around Riona and stood ready to direct them in song.

Master Winnett, temporary service leader since Father Murray's death, led them in prayer and read from the Bible, and soon, it was Riona's turn to sing. Her voice, powerful but sweet, carried like blossoms on the wind.

A brighter dawn is breaking; Lo' the morning's nigh;
Long glories are awaking; comes forth our joyful cry......
Alleluia! King of Glory! Everlasting life in Thee.
Soar we now, with our Exalted! Sing ye heavens and hills and sea!

Churchgoers filed out after Mass into a steady rain, eager for a warm turf fire and their special Easter suppers. But not before greeting Schoolmaster Winnett and offering hearty *bravas* to a glowing Riona.

Betha pulled Winnett away, speaking to him in low tones, their eyes on Morrigan. Winnett's head shake turned into a reluctant nod. Then he stood before her. "Morrigan, your mum has asked me to keep you after school to learn the long-ago times of the Church. Your punishment for stealing the boat. I myself will enjoy the rigor," he lowered his voice, "so long as you comply."

Morrigan's mouth opened and closed. *Not* those *long ago times!* She looked at Tommy, who looked at Betha, who nodded at Schoolmaster Winnett, who said, "We'll start tomorrow. From Saint Patrick to the Council of Trent, we have an exciting history. Once priests celebrated Mass in secret, defying the penal laws. Heroes they were," said Winnett, "just like scholars."

"Yes, Schoolmaster Winnett," said Morrigan through clenched teeth. Wheeling around, she strode out into the rain. She'd promised to return to the wolf after school.

22

MORRIGAN

The Wolf's Journey

Late into the night on Easter Monday, Morrigan lay awake, listening for her family's soft sounds of slumber. She descended the ladder and crept out the door toward Old Mother Oak. As she hurried in the darkness, the familiar path simmered with primeval mystery. A wolf's long, discordant howl penetrated the night's stillness, and deep reservoirs of longing reverberated with the sound. Morrigan's heart thudded as she picked her way along the terrain. She came upon the great tree whose limbs loomed like black octopus arms.

"Wolf? Wolf?"

"I am here, Morrigan," the wolf said, appearing at the edge of the woods.

"Wolf, I am sorry I couldn't get away this afternoon. Mum convinced Schoolmaster Winnett to teach me the history of the Church in the afternoons. She says it's 'to counter Cathleen's undue influence' now that I'm learning the forest medicines. She's leery of the old ways."

"Let us move into the wildwood," said the wolf, leading the way. In the diminished light, Morrigan spotted a torn animal carcass and shuddered, looking away. *Am I safe here?* she wondered. Nonetheless, she followed him, pulled along as if by forces outside her control.

Soon Morrigan sat cocooned in a dense thicket. The wolf began, "The old ways your mother fears are needed now. You must learn to listen for the tune the land sings. When you can blend that note within you, then you have a way of knowing what is right in a situation. If a decision does not echo the note that the land sings, then it is the wrong decision.

"Long ago, in the days of balance, all was in harmony, and all beings lived side by side. No being had eminence. Each served the whole, yielding to a deeper connectedness within The World Tree, the sum of all creation. Indeed, each being was an ally of creation."

The wolf stood, ears alert, nose to the wind. He shifted his intense yellow eyes to focus on hers, searching for a sign of understanding.

Morrigan had been holding her breath. She exhaled and uttered, "…ally of creation," as though by saying the words she could conjure their meaning.

"Once, a reciprocal exchange brought balance to the world. In those days, a human, before setting bow to quiver, might have asked the spirit of a bear to give her life so that he might have food and fur. Equally possible, the bear might have asked the spirit of the human to give his life instead, for the sake of her cubs. In this way, the deepest possible collaboration existed between all beings. There was no trickery or mistrust because spirits were in cooperation. This way existed with all beings, not just animals. Old Mother Oak, for example. Notice how her trunk once grew toward the walled estate and has since grown back toward the wildwood?"

Morrigan squinted in the darkness, truly seeing for the first time the oak's distinctive curve.

"Once, another *An Fhoínse* created fellowship with this oak's spirit. She spoke to the tree in The Once-and-Only Language—of her worries about the tree's roots becoming rain starved or suffocated and her own wish for shade. She invited the oak, scarcely ten years old, to shift the direction of its growth. With the oak's agreement, together their spirits were in communion."

During Morrigan's recent conversations with the oak, she'd felt as though the tree had heard her expressed hopes and dreams. The oak's height and expanse gave her the courage to imagine something larger for herself. Morrigan believed herself alone in this thinking, though perhaps Cathleen would have understood. Now as the wolf described a long ago world of interwoven relationships, everything Morrigan had been taught was being shattered like a barrel of broken stones. She wrestled with the implications.

The wolf continued, "In time, humans began to believe their unique capabilities—to create tools, to form beliefs, to reason—gave them a superior status in creation. To the humans, it made The Once-and-Only Language seem primitive and unnecessary. So they separated themselves from the rest of the natural world." The wolf's words were strangled and low.

Morrigan thought about Schoolmaster Winnett's fear of dirt, or Riona's reluctance to play outside for fear of freckles appearing on her ivory cheeks. Spots of malice, she called them. Or of Mass being held in a stuffy dwelling with worn marram thatch that leaked. But her da spoke sweetly to the fish and said prayers of gratitude, and Cathleen always asked The Good People for permission before foraging. We haven't all separated ourselves from the rest of the world, she thought.

The wolf paused a moment before continuing. "Using their inventive methods, and the teachings of a powerful few to justify their actions, humans forgot even the tiniest creatures belong to a balanced whole, though they may never design, invent, or create anything except their own kind. Humans forgot that everything in creation has a spirit. Because humans have forgotten their place in The World Tree," the wolf growled low in his throat, "they have frayed the cords of connection."

"Cords of connection?" A vision emerged of her da's hooker sailboat with its braided ropes used for his rigging and netting, and the care he took to prevent their unraveling. Were there ropes like rigging in The World Tree? Though questions crowded her brain, one question rose above the others. "Why are you telling me?"

"If humans continue to ignore their imbalance with The World Tree, a counter-shift will occur, and humans will be at great risk. If this happens," the wolf slowed his speech, emphasizing his last words, "it cannot be reversed."

At their close range, Morrigan smelled the sharp, musky wildness of the wolf and had an urge to run away from him and his message. Still, she was fascinated by his depiction of humans and their relationship to the rest of the natural world. Again, she asked, "Why are you telling *me*?"

"At the center of humans lies emptiness," said the wolf, "and it must be healed, because humans, like all of creation, are sacred." The wolf put his nose to the wind and, turning to her, said, "Morrigan Lane, your birth has been prophesied in The Otherworld. Your destiny is to heal your village. Make your village whole and in harmony, for it is the way of things that the fate of the world rests upon the fate of your own, small village. It is the way of things." Having delivered his message, the wolf slipped away into the night.

Morrigan sat stunned before jerking to her feet. "Wait!" She crashed through brambles and fallen branches in pursuit of the wolf. He'd vanished. Rubbing the scratches on her legs, she considered the wolf's words. How was she supposed to heal her village when she'd witnessed no illness there? And what did healing her village have to do with healing the emptiness in humans and bringing harmony to The World Tree?

Following the familiar trackway home, again and again the message replayed in her mind. "Frayed the cords of connection... prophesied in The Otherworld...your destiny is to heal your village."

As night turned toward the pale peach of daybreak, Morrigan slipped home and climbed onto her pallet where she remained sleepless, seeing disquieting images of frayed cords, humans who looked hollow inside, the wolf's intense yellow eyes, and the black uncertain void of her life.

23

MORRIGAN

Fate of the Village

The next morning, Morrigan forced thoughts of the wolf from her mind. The meeting with Sir Martin was only days away. She found a quiet moment behind the cottage with her da as they barked the foresail for his boat, *Inis Ealga*. Morrigan loved the smell of the tree bark solution they used to dye a sail. She and her da customarily stood in companionable silence while a rust color emerged, at first in tendrils and then more boldly onto the dull sail cloth. Barking was a necessary thing. It kept the sails stiff and waterproof.

Morrigan cleared her throat. "Da, there's something I must tell you." Her eyes darted to where her brothers stood not far away, placing lengths of kelp onto wooden drying racks.

"Morrie, you look ready for confession at Saint Joseph's," said Tommy, steering her away from her brothers toward sedge bushes nearby.

Morrigan took a breath and said, "Da, before Easter I spoke out of turn to Mistress Mary. Miserable Overseer Eagan was being hard on Cathleen for foraging on their estate, and I couldn't help speaking out. Then the Mistress asked me what else I had to say, and I complained about the new rent increase." Hearing her own words, Morrigan put a hand to her mouth.

"You did what?" Tommy squinted into her eyes, a perplexed look on his face.

"Mistress Mary told me she would ask Sir Martin to give me an audience when he returns from London next week. Da, I'm to convince him to give us all a stay on our rents until after the mid-May fair."

"You're seeing who?"

Morrigan grimaced. "Well, the meeting is to be out by the pigs' pen." Somehow, a meeting near where Shauna and the pigs were paddocked seemed reassuring to her.

"Sir Martin's going to see *you* about a postponement of our rent increase?" Tommy's voice carried far and away beyond the privacy of the sedge. Liam and Ruarc had sidled nearby at his first bellow. "That's preposterous! Me own daughter's got an audience with Sir Martin? I've never even met the man, sending his agents to do the collecting like he does." Tommy roared with laughter. "By God, you've got pluck!" Tommy gave his daughter a spirited hug and yelled, "Betha! Come and hear what Morrie's done now!"

Morrigan turned away from her brothers' pestering questions. Meeting with a landowner conflicted with all protocols of society. Layers of intermediaries ensured an appropriate distance between the gentry and the poor. Mistress Mary must have known this. Why then had the Mistress suggested a meeting? Dismissing the idea of some mysterious connection between them, Morrigan decided the only reason Mistress Mary invited her to the estate was to cure her wart. If I'd only kept my mouth shut, Morrigan thought with a sigh. I'm in for it now.

Some days later, Morrigan leaned out over the cottage's russet-stained half door. Small patches of clouds rolled across a white sky.

"Come and sit, a leanbh," said Mamoh gesturing from a spot on the wooden bench. Potatoes boiled in a black kettle that hung over a turf fire. "You look tired. Is it the meeting with Sir Martin?"

Morrigan nodded though she also worried about what the wolf had described of The Otherworld and her destiny. She longed to learn more about what a destiny meant. But tomorrow's audience with Sir Martin came first. She leaned into her grandmother's reassuring bulk. "I don't know what to say, Mamoh."

"Remember what your da told you about the power of your stories," said Mamoh, stroking Morrigan's hair. "Storytelling has its own magic. Weave a story for Sir Martin like the seanchaithe do in their beguiling way. Make it about something meaningful to him, something that can only happen after he has done a good deed for the villagers, something to appeal to his conscience, Lord willing he has one. Then, be at peace with the result, knowing you've done your best."

So many instructions! Her head hurt from trying to come up with a plan. Plead with the landowner? Beg Mistress Mary for help?

For the villagers of Baile Ghort na Darach, eviction threatened like a goshawk over a field—one poor fishing season, one increase in rents, one accident upon the waters away. Morrigan's opportunity to speak with Sir Martin had planted seeds of hope in all their hearts. She couldn't walk through the village without a word of encouragement or a murmur of support. Even Uncle Colm had given her a brief pat on the shoulder yesterday. Finn had told her the men had placed wagers at the pub, though most were against her chances of success since Sir Martin was an exacting, even stingy, man.

Morrigan's left shoulder tingled just as a voice floated in from outside the door. "Blessings upon this house." She walked to the door to find Cathleen, speaking in low tones to Betha, who sat on her favorite stool spinning wool.

"Morrigan, Cathleen is here to prepare you for tomorrow's meeting with Sir Martin," said Betha, her mouth a tight line. "Cathleen will teach you about healing warts and speaking to a gentleman."

Morrigan smiled, relieved to see her mentor. "Thank you, Cathleen. I'd like that."

"There is much at stake, Morrigan, and I want to help in any way I can for I, too, am faced with a rent increase. You'll stay with me overnight to prepare," said Cathleen.

"I'll gather some things," said Morrigan. With a lighter step, she moved to collect them.

"Looks like I'll get the bed all to myself," said Riona, moving from where she stood in the doorway. "Certain persons have kept me awake for days." She looked at Morrigan, but her gaze held no sting. "We won't see you until after your audience?" Without forethought, Riona moved to the mantle where she kept a box of special things. "Take this, Morrie," she said, withdrawing a lace cap embroidered with an intricate flower pattern. "'Tis a gift for Mistress Mary. I hope she'll like it. I'll make her another if she wants."

Longing for a different social setting, Riona had made the cap in the hopes of wearing it herself one day.

Morrigan gazed at the exquisite handiwork. "Oh Ree, I cannot take it."

"Take it, you will and luck be upon you," said Riona, her eyes bright. She turned to make herself busy at the cupboard.

Betha led the womenfolk outside, while Morrigan remained inside to collect the things she needed. Soon Morrigan came out into the overcast morning, her belongings in hand.

"Remember to curtsy, and to do your family proud," said Betha. "Keep your wits and your manners about you. A prayer or two can be consoling. Ask the good Lord to hold you up when you can't do it yourself." The words caught in her throat. She moved to stand behind her daughter.

Mamoh shuffled toward the granddaughter of her heart. "Take this, Morrie," she said, handing her something in a cream-colored cloth. "It belonged to Isla. It's her *scian* dagger. She carried it in a pocket deep inside the folds of her skirt and used it for everything—eating, birthing, slaughtering, healing, and protection."

Morrigan unwrapped the dagger whose handle was fashioned from stag's horn. She unsheathed it from its doe-skin holder to find a blade the length of her middle finger, with a clipped point and scalloped file-work at the back. Carved into the handle was a symbol. It looked like a vertical ellipse made of smaller circles. Morrigan moved her thumb over the symbol, entranced.

Eyes wide, Betha backed away from the dagger with the strange symbol.

"Tommy sharpened it," said Mamoh, her voice thick with emotion. "Isla received it from her own mum, and I've held it safe for the one who could best use it—you."

Eyes misty, Morrigan reached for Mamoh, arms clumsy with belongings. "It's beautiful, Mamoh. Thank you." Their foreheads touched. It was enough.

"Cathleen! Teach Morrie whatever potions she needs to charm Sir Martin," boomed Tommy. Riona had gone to the quay to inform him and the boys of Morrigan's departure. Tommy placed his hands on Morrigan's shoulders, his dark eyes searching hers, and whispered, "Have heart, child. Only good comes from the heart."

"Aye, Da," said Morrigan, remembering all the stories he'd told her about Gráinne Ní Mháille. Now was a time for courage.

"I've wagered two good pence on you staying the rents!" hollered Ruarc, rhyming as was his custom. "Good luck, Morrie!" he said, patting her on the back so hard Morrigan stumbled.

Always serious, Liam placed a small mound of seaweed into Morrigan's hand and said, "This is what it's about, Morrie. This

seaweed will make the difference for us. Let Sir Martin know this."
He kissed her on the cheek, and then backed away.

Word had spread quickly of Morrigan's departure with Cathleen.
As she began her journey, she passed by a throng of villagers who
waved and wished her well. Dragging her feet, Morrigan wanted
to escape to the cliffs or Old Mother Oak. She did not want the
burden of all their hopes.

"You've earned the villagers' respect, Morrigan. Few receive
an audience with Sir Martin," said Cathleen. They approached
McDonaugh's Pub, where Connie McDonaugh stood in the
doorway to his kitchen waving a dish towel. "Come here straight
away after your meeting, Morrie! We'll be waiting for ya," he said.
With a nod to Cathleen, he turned back to his kitchen.

"Thank you, Mr. McDonaugh," said Morrigan. She remembered
their conversation some months ago when he'd revealed his secret
communications with his dead wife, Kate. He'd laid bare his sadness,
and in so doing, Morrigan had found herself longing to know
Finn's mum. A relationship with a dead wife seemed natural now
that she had conversed with a wolf.

Morrigan searched for a sign of Finn, failing at nonchalance.

"Finn's off brining mutton for the celebration when you return,
Morrie," said Cormac, leaning against the pub's solid door frame.
"Show Sir Martin what you're made of, UgMor. I wouldn't mind
losing my pence," he said with a wink.

Before arriving at her modest dwelling close by, Cathleen stopped
outside a stone circle, its seven large stones arranged by a very old
clan of people in a hollow formed between wildflower grassland,
a limestone-pocked ridge, and cobalt blue seas. Though Morrigan

couldn't see her face, she suspected Cathleen said a few words of salutation to the ancient stones and whatever energy resided there. The way Cathleen saw the world, everything, including stones, had a life force, though different from that of humans. Morrigan hadn't realized this truth until she'd spoken to the wolf. His words at their first encounter echoed in her mind—about how The Once-and-Only Language happened inside the heart, not the mind.

Cathleen walked around the circle from east to west, in the direction of the sun's journey. To walk in this rotation was considered the course of good fortune. Morrigan followed her, stopping where Cathleen stopped beside the largest stone, facing west, a stone that bisected the setting sun on Samhain, October's festival of the dead.

"'Tis here we begin," said Cathleen, caressing the stone and leaning on her walking stick. "Are you ready, Morrigan?"

"No," said Morrigan. "I don't know what to say to Sir Martin. I don't think I can go."

"If you go, you are one person. If you do not go, you are another," said Cathleen in a mysterious tone.

"It's a waste of time, and a distraction just as I've come upon the wolf."

"What did the wolf tell you about the fate of the village?" asked Cathleen. Morrigan had shared as much of the message as she could recall during their walk to the stone circle.

"He said, 'It is the way of things that the fate of the world rests upon the fate of your own, small village.' But I want to meet with him again, so I can learn what it is I'm to do."

"And doesn't this audience with Sir Martin also have to do with the fate of your own small village? 'Tis no distraction, Morrigan."

Morrigan's face flashed with understanding. "This audience with Sir Martin is connected with the wolf's words?"

"I don't know that the ancients would arrange happenings one after another like soldiers in a line. Yet if we recognize the world is many-layered and full of mysterious connections, then it might be you are being called to bring an attunement to moments such as these. Your audience with Sir Martin seems no accident."

"I don't know what you mean, Cathleen." Bright red patches had bloomed on her cheeks.

"A way of listening and acting in accordance with the ancients. Consider that harmony within the village supports harmony throughout the earth. Perhaps 'tis necessary to begin with the village.

"Here, sit among these old stones for half the day. Let the whispers of the ancients come to you. You might hear them on the wind or in the call of a skylark. You will know the messages of the ancients in your heart. I'll return for you just as the sun casts its long shadow on this stone circle, and tonight I'll show you how to heal a wart." Cathleen walked toward her home, then turned. "Morrigan? Remember to ask for permission."

Morrigan settled against a standing stone in the shape of a thick-waisted man, her mind a tumult of thoughts. Restless, she stood and retrieved the seaweed Liam had given her. She smelled the briny clump. *Maybe words will float up out of the this,* she thought.

Within the hour, Morrigan had shredded all the seaweed, letting tiny pieces slip from her fingers as she paced inside the circle. No words had come from the plant, and yet the letting go of it had quieted her mind. Finally, she became present to the stones. A robin hopped amid flowering grasses, and a cool wind came in intermittent gusts. "What will I say to Sir Martin?" She directed her question to the stones.

She heard a response: "When you sit in council, you will find a way, for indeed, we are a council of stones. Listen and see us as your elders."

"Fair skies are upon you, Morrigan," said Cathleen, returning to the stone circle. Her intuition told her something had shifted within her young protégé during her hours there.

"They call themselves a council of stones, Cathleen," said Morrigan from a cross-legged position inside the stone circle. Her eyes were closed, and she rocked forward and backward, entranced by the circle. "This one held ceremonies." She opened her eyes, and pools of leaf green reflected her inner stillness. "The stones prefer a loose, cordial arrangement approximating a circle, one that is natural. A stone or two can be outside the inner circle and still be a part of it. Sometimes, it's right to sit beyond the inner circle and listen in. And a tree can be a part of a council of stones, providing vision as well as canopy for protection. Even the smallest stone is part of a council and has a voice," said Morrigan.

Cathleen nodded. "Do you feel ready to meet Sir Martin now, Morrigan?"

"The stones tell me there is an old knowing I must know in a new way. I feel I need to tell a story rooted in the old ways and trust the right words will come."

"Going back *is* going forward, Morrigan. Think of it. Nature acts in a circular rhythm. Nothing is linear, including time. In nature's cycles, what was once an acorn is soon a fallen tree, decaying back to the earth, and then food for caterpillars who will soon become butterflies. In nature, what is a bank of fog off the seashore soon falls as rain on an inland meadow. What is past is also prophecy."

"A sending forth and a returning, a sowing and a reaping. Schoolmaster Winnett taught us the Latin word for it—*Reciprocus*," said Morrigan, nodding. She stood, and her trance-like state dissipated. "I'm not sure I'll know him when I see him, Cathleen. I know where the pigs' pen is, but—" she trailed off.

"You'll know him by the way he carries himself, Morrigan, for he is an important man. And how will you carry yourself in the presence of Sir Martin? Let's imagine this large stone is him, and you are walking toward him."

Morrigan closed her eyes and mentally placed herself at the estate approaching Sir Martin. She began to walk.

"Will-o'-wisp clouds! You are hesitant and scared," said Cathleen. "Try again." Morrigan stopped and reflected. Then she started again. "Gray overcast! Now you're a stiff, suffering servant. 'Tis no better," said Cathleen. "I wonder, do you think Sir Martin is more important than you?"

Morrigan shrugged. "Well, few receive an audience with him, and he is our landowner. I'm a mere fisher's daughter."

"There is nothing *mere* about you. Tell me, did Saint Francis have more influence when he was a nobleman or a penniless instrument of peace, a compassionate ally of heron, doe, hawk, and rabbit? Mighty power comes not from wealth but from the sacred alliances you make with yourself and your creator." Cathleen pounded her hazel staff onto the ground. "You have been recognized in the spirit world, Morrigan Lane. Stand up! Take notice. Honor them in the way you walk and present yourself."

A smile played on Morrigan's face. She couldn't believe the scar she'd always despised had somehow led her to this moment, this impending meeting with a member of the gentry. Too, her destiny had been declared by a wolf messenger from The Otherworld. She stood straight, thrust out her chest, pulled back her shoulders, and began to walk. She did not swagger; she did not march. She placed each foot with measured intention, feeling its impact upon the earth. And in recognition of her actions, deep within the wildwood, The Invisibles danced.

24

MISTRESS MARY

Mistress Mary's Wound

Sir Martin rode in his coach toward Rosderry Manor, his thoughts absorbed in the proceedings at Parliament. He'd finally made progress in passing a bill prohibiting the cruel treatment of animals, something he'd worked toward for years. The Cruel Treatment of Cattle Act was not entirely suitable because bulls weren't added to the list of animals that included ox, cow, heifer, steer, and sheep. Nonetheless, it was a start.

When the carriage stopped, it seemed Rosderry Manor emanated welcome. Or perhaps a memory of Elizabeth's once customary greeting had overtaken him—the door thrown open, her arms outstretched, and her hands already seeking the knot at the base of his neck, while her lips kissed the spot just above his clavicle. But her affair with the man from Paris had ended his relationship with Elizabeth. It had given him comfort to have sued Elizabeth's lover for criminal conversation. He still recalled the thrill of hurling every banknote of the £10,000 he had been awarded out the window of his coach on the long journey back from London. He hoped the poor sods who found it had bought good whiskey and gotten blathered. Shaking his head, he banished the memory, just as he'd banished Elizabeth from Rosderry Manor. With a weary groan, he emerged from the carriage.

"Welcome home, Father!" said Mary. His untucked white shirt and skewed bow tie revealed his exhaustion. Not long ago, upon his arrival, Mary would have launched into his arms and entertained him with stories of the mischief she'd gotten into while he'd been gone. But that was before her mother had left their lives. Now she felt estranged from him in some inalterable way.

"Good evening, Mary," said Sir Martin, looking past her to assess the state of his manor.

"Shall I hold supper, Sir Martin?" asked a housekeeper who peered from behind the dining room door.

"No, I'll be in directly. Mary, pour me a whiskey?"

"Yes, Father." As she poured, Mary's nose wrinkled at the fermented fruit aroma that emerged from the crystal decanter. She thought about the meeting with the peasant woman, Morrigan Lane. Had she been foolhardy in scheduling it for the day after her father's return from London? She'd tell him at dinner, once he'd relaxed. Hoping the whiskey would make him amenable to her suggestion to meet with Morrigan Lane, Mary poured another measure into his glass.

Halfway through their supper of roasted quail with sauteed turnips, dried cherries, and spring greens, Mary began, "Father, I wanted to tell you: I've asked one of the fishermen's daughters, a Morrigan

Lane, to the estate tomorrow. She has a request of you regarding this year's rents."

Sir Martin struck the dining table, causing Mary to flinch and teacups to rattle in their saucers. "Mary, you need *not* take on the affairs of my estate. What manner of lunacy led you to do such a thing?"

Mary couldn't remember such harshness from her father. She hesitated. "This Morrigan appeared quite bold in her reasoning, Father, and it made sense to me. Besides, it's out by the pigs' pen. You won't have to spend but a few minutes. Oh, and to warn you, she has a scar on her face, quite unusual."

"What's gotten into you, Mary?" Sir Martin ran a hand through his hair. "My own daughter meddling in my affairs."

Mary shrugged and bit her lip. What *had* gotten into her, to have had exchanges not once but twice with a woman so below her class? She had noticed something about Morrigan Lane, a shimmering vitality, and against her better judgment was drawn to the young woman.

"Next time you'll go with me to London. Cousin Gertrude will have you. She hasn't seen you yet this year."

Mary's eyes lit up. "Oh, I'd like that, Father!" She felt a rebel's satisfaction at having made her father think of her for once. Maybe the meeting with that Morrigan woman hadn't been such a bad idea after all. Now she'd get to go with her father to London.

Richard Martin gave his daughter a long, searching look. Then he turned his attention back to his plate.

Mary stuffed three cherries into her mouth and brooded. She admitted to herself that her father had become harsh, eroding memories of the carefree man she'd once called Da-Da. A stalwart and upstanding Member of Parliament, he had forbidden any contact between mother and daughter. Had her father become hardened because of her mother's indiscretion, or had he already become hardened due to his demanding work in Parliament? Mary's appetite had disappeared. She pushed her plate away, wondering if she'd ever see her mother again. Her longing, like an old wound, festered deep inside.

The sun's rays burst without apology into a long-windowed dining room at Rosderry Manor, announcing the day as bright and promising. Mistress Mary loved this room, where morning light played jester to the somber cerulean walls, and evening candlelight encouraged intimacy and romance. This morning, however, she pushed the black pudding and smoked salmon around her plate with disinterest and barely ate the apple-buttered biscuit. Her father had eaten hastily before retreating behind his heavy oak library doors. She'd made a face at his back, recalling the sting of his words the previous evening. She wondered if Morrigan would appear and whether her father would see her. She hoped the peasant woman would bring a remedy for her wart, because that was the most important reason for her visit. If Mary's mother had been in her life, she'd have brought in doctors who knew how to remove warts. As it was, Mary had to find her own solutions.

25

MORRIGAN

Meeting Sir Martin

Morrigan sat ramrod straight on a wooden bench alongside the pigs' pen. She'd arrived early enough to greet Shauna, who'd squealed happily at seeing her. Soon thereafter, Morrigan sent the pig away to finish eating before the other pigs ate all the feed.

Heart pounding in her ears, Morrigan's cheeks burned from the bright red spots that clung there. Her scalp tingled from the tight bun Cathleen had fashioned of her hair. As though holding a talisman, she gripped her great-grandmother's dagger inside her creel basket.

"I'm at the estate 'belonging' to Sir Martin," she whispered. As she said the word "belonging," she blinked her eyes and jerked her head the way all the villagers did when they said it. It was a secret, subversive act because not a one of them believed the land hadn't been stolen outright from the family of Cathleen Ó Nialláin during the strengthening of the Penal Laws in the late seventeenth century. English rulers had contrived to keep native Irish people impoverished and degraded. Among the deprivations: No Irish Catholic could practice his religion, receive an education, enter into a profession, hold public office, engage in trade or commerce, own a horse of greater value than five pounds, vote, or keep any arms for his protection. More than any of the deprivations, the confiscation of Irish land for the pleasure of the English gentry had torn at the hearts of the Irish. Since then, some of the laws had been relaxed, but the land was gone, and gone forever.

On this land that had once belonged to Cathleen's kin, Morrigan became aware of a thrumming coming up through the soles in her shoes. The ancestors were with her. She relaxed, no longer afraid.

"Always a smile on your face, then?" asked Mistress Mary, emerging from a stone pathway near the livery. She wore day-skirts of ochre and ivory and had what seemed a genuine smile of welcome on her face.

Morrigan curtsied, and said, "I've brought you a gift, Mistress Mary. 'Twas embroidered by my sister, Riona. She hopes you will wear it well." Morrigan held out the coarse linen fabric encasing the cap.

"Thank you." As manners dictated, Mary unwrapped the fabric and rotated the nightcap, her fingers caressing its embossed flowers. "It's exquisite! Mother's caps looked like this," she said, delight in her tone. For a moment, Mary had a faraway look in her eyes. "I wouldn't find one this lovely in Dublin, nor I daresay, in London," she added, giving Morrigan a long, assessing look. "Thank you. And please thank your sister. She is quite skilled."

"'Tis our pleasure, Mistress Mary. Thank you for this meeting with your father."

Mary frowned. "Yes! He wishes to meet you in his library. He is busy this morning, and cannot in his words, 'go traipsing down to the pigs' pen,' though if one of his precious brood mares were ill…" Mary didn't finish the sentence. "We've got some time, and I hope you've brought something else for me."

"Yes, I have. You should be seated."

Mary looked around. "There's a bench by the pond. We'll go there."

Morrigan followed Mistress Mary around the outside of a vast, three-storied, gray manor house as deep as it was wide. Thick expanses of ivy extended along the front, softening its imposing presence. Numerous chimneys protruded from the roof like hands raised at the hedge school. Long windows were supported by stone sills, promising a bright interior. Morrigan gasped at the sight of a pond filled with swans, its waters reflecting the manor house and its vast, landscaped gardens.

"We'll sit on this bench," said Mary.

Morrigan willed her wandering eyes to narrow their focus. Do your part, she told herself. She breathed in and out to steady her nerves and crouched on the ground in front of Mistress Mary.

Mary winced at the careful way Morrigan prepared herself and asked, "This won't hurt, will it?"

"No." Morrigan withdrew a small glass vial containing tiny dull green spheres and said in a firm voice, "Mistress Mary, I will explain as best as I can what I am doing. You do not have to believe in the details. Just imagine your wart disappearing from your hand. See your hand healed and beautiful. Nothing will work unless you believe!" Mistress Mary wavered. Morrigan imagined what it would take to mentally see something disappear right before her eyes.

"Close your eyes, Mistress Mary, and imagine your flawless left hand as it reaches out to touch the silkiest fabric you've ever seen," Morrigan instructed.

"Now you are wearing a new dress from that fabric, and your perfect left hand rests on the shoulder of a handsome gentleman. Believe!"

Mary closed her eyes. Soon her body swayed.

"Hold that image, Mistress Mary. It's working." Morrigan had, by instinct, touched on Mary's world—the fine beauty of being seen as beautiful in beautiful company, dancing and weaving from partner to partner, flawless and flowing as if on a cloud. She, too, visualized Mistress Mary dancing in the arms of a tall, broad-shouldered man. "Now I am placing five dried peas in your left hand." Morrigan reached for Mary's hand and deposited them. "Put them in your mouth and let them moisten there. Do not chew or swallow them."

Mary opened her eyes, one brow raised.

"Go ahead," said Morrigan. "They're just dried peas from a garden."

"Well, all right."

"Keep dancing, Mistress Mary."

Morrigan imagined the peas in Mary's mouth were five emeralds surrounding a diamond set in a ring on Mary's finger. A supreme lightness overtook her. Some moments later, she opened her eyes to see Mistress Mary immersed in her daydreaming. Morrigan instructed. "Now, with your right hand, remove the peas and rotate them sun-wise around your wart. As you do so, I invite the healing spirit within these peas to intermingle with your saliva to heal your wart."

"Like this?" Mary asked, hesitating.

Morrigan nodded and said, "Believe!"

On their walk to the manor house, Morrigan gave Mistress Mary the glass vial and explained the need to follow the same method with the dried peas for five days in a row.

"If the believing part works, Mistress Mary, you should begin to see your wart disappear in a fortnight, or at most, two."

"What have I to lose?" said Mary, accepting the task. She glanced toward the manor house and gasped. "It's Father. We're late, hurry!" Mary hastened toward him.

At the end of a curving carriageway, Morrigan spied a dark-haired, regal-looking man of medium build wearing a gray waistcoat and trousers with top hat and cane. Her heart pounded in her chest, and her legs felt heavy. But the healer's essence had lingered, and she recalled her rehearsed walk. Straightening her shoulders, Morrigan summoned her courage and walked toward a scowling

Sir Martin, who tapped his cane on the stones in short bursts of three. *Tap-tap-tap. Tap-tap-tap.*

Morrigan approached and dropped into a deep, slow curtsy. She whispered a prayer, "May Isla, the ancestors, and all kind spirits be with me." As she returned to standing, she reeled back, as though an invisible wave had washed over her. Something seared and bloomed in her heart.

"Father, here is Morrigan Lane," said Mary.

"Yes. What is it?" Sir Martin's growl seemed to bounce off Morrigan and return to him. He jerked back from his own belligerence, hesitated, and then gestured saying, "Please join me in the library." He walked into the front hall. Mary and Morrigan followed him.

"Good luck, Morrigan," said Mary. She motioned toward the library and then ascended the staircase.

A butler stood stiffly in the corner of the hall, waves of condescension emanating from him. Morrigan scarcely noticed him; her body tingled as blood rushed through her veins. She walked the short distance to the library, her steps speaking, *Old story. New story.* She sensed a great turning point in her life, a moment that could determine the validity of her destiny.

Sir Martin closed the heavy door behind her with a resounding thud, returned to his desk, and said, "Well?"

Morrigan took a deep breath in, prayed once more for help, and then began to speak.

Her words soared like seagulls banking on the wind. She'd entered a trancelike state beyond the business at hand. When she'd finished, silence lingered, and the lack of sound entered a timeless dimension that, later, neither were certain wasn't an eternity. Finally, the clip-clop of a horse's hooves drew Morrigan to present awareness.

Sir Martin blinked twice and shuddered. "Yes, you may have a stay," he said, but his words came out soft. To his ears they sounded weak, so he spoke them again with authority, "I, Sir Richard Martin, will grant the people of your village a sixteen-day stay on rent increases." Removing a sheet of stationery, he scrawled the words, lit a vermillion wax candle, and dripped it onto the folded seam of the stationary. Then he pressed his RBM seal into the wax.

He handed Morrigan the sealed letter and said, "I'll expect all the money and no defaults this year. If there is one, it will mean instant eviction, and the village will pay the rent all the earlier next year."

"Thank you, Sir Martin, and may the health of a salmon be upon you for your generosity," said Morrigan as she curtsied. To wish someone the health of a salmon bestowed long life, strength, and good fortune. Sir Martin did not respond, having already turned his back on the girl.

26

SIR MARTIN

Hoodwinked

Sir Martin ground his teeth and stroked his thick sideburns. What the devil had happened? He questioned his actions, for he had long held the opinion the fishermen were lazy, casting not a single net on Sundays or their Catholic holy days.

Had he been hoodwinked? Had he been influenced by what the girl said or in how she'd said it? His own estate taxes were due in one week's time, for God's sake! Yet there had been something about that young woman's words that had penetrated his long-guarded heart.

The agents would be angry at having to wait for their cut of the rents, and they were a rough lot, especially Muldoon. Sir Martin brooded over his life—the Parliament and its proceedings, his motherless child, Mary, and now this bizarre exchange with a fisherman's daughter. Finally, with a brisk push, Sir Martin left his desk to change into riding attire. A good, hard ride would clear his head. As he approached the livery, he realized how different times were from the heyday of economic boom while the Napoleonic Wars raged. Most of the villagers were still recovering from a poor potato crop two autumns ago.

He recalled his youthful courting days when he and Elizabeth had cantered across rolling green hills and through streams, her cheeks pink with exertion, her laugh easy, her bosom ample. He felt a tightening in his groin and made a dismissive sound, promising himself he'd stop thinking of her. He had no need for a wife now. Instead, Sir Martin forced himself to think about his never-ending work in Parliament on behalf of animals. He understood beasts far better than humans. Hearing the eager neigh of his stallion, he shrugged and mounted up.

27

MORRIGAN

Offering to The Otherworld

A s she returned to Cathleen's, a rushing sound filled Morrigan's
ears like the inexplicable sea-sound one hears in holding up
a conch shell. She felt light-headed; maybe it was from hunger.
How had she convinced Sir Martin? Her mind was blank. She
remembered curtsying, praying for help from The Otherworld, and
then little else. Whatever had happened, Morrigan had Sir Martin's
letter declaring a stay in their rents, and that outcome seemed to
confirm her destiny as one who can heal the village.

When Morrigan appeared at her door nodding, Cathleen guided
her into the cottage for tea and performed a ceremony of gratitude.
As she made ready to leave, Cathleen placed a small bunch of
herbs in her hands. "This is an offering for the inhabitants of The
Otherworld. Perform a ceremony of gratitude, dear one. When
you make an offering, you acknowledge the holy and unseen. Find
a suitable place to make the offering on your return to the village."
Morrigan nodded. "God be with you," said Cathleen, as Morrigan
walked toward the dirt trackway and the pub.

Morrigan's feet took her to Old Mother Oak. Into the tree's crevices she inserted small bunches of herbs and murmured words of gratitude.

"Everyone in the pub will wonder why I'm gone so long, Old Mother," she said in her solitary place against the oak. "I should feel fair lucky to bring this news. What has me so sad? Unsettled? Oh, I don't know!"

To Old Mother Oak, who stood quiet in her soil, it seemed the young woman had crossed an invisible threshold and was in a strange territory, like a ship without a clear heading and no land in sight.

28

BETHA

Hope Is a Tricky Thing

Betha sighed as she lifted two heavy buckets of water. As often as Tommy sang seafaring tales, Betha sighed. It was the language of her life. Careful to preserve the buckets' contents, she squared her shoulders and walked home.

Earlier, Riona and Ruarc had asked their mum if they could go to McDonaugh's Pub where the villagers would await the outcome of Morrigan's audience with Sir Martin. They had pleaded to be off, promising to work all the harder the next day. Betha had shrugged and waved them away to join the others, wishing they did not carry so much hope for Morrigan's chances.

Hope was a tricky thing. As a child, Betha had relied on hope like a babe does her mother's breast. She had observed her grandmother's healing ways, certain she would possess them some day. Her hope soured when she discovered she was not extraordinary, and again when as a young bride, she realized she was destined for a life of bone-wearying poverty. Then her da had gone missing at sea, and in desperation, Betha grasped at hope once again. But heartbreak claimed her when the remnants of his boat washed ashore with no body found.

"Hope is too close to expectation, and that in itself is a devilish thing," she said to Sean McMahon's two mangy sheep as she walked by his pen. "Better to give it to the Good Lord, is what I think."

Morrigan would be meeting Sir Martin about now. "Dear Mother Mary," said Betha, her voice low and urgent. "Please intercede on my daughter's behalf. Help her weave a story to convince the man. Give her courage to speak for our hardworking villagers. I humbly seek your help."

So absorbed was Betha in her thoughts that she tripped on a stony spot in the trackway. Cold water spilled from the buckets onto her feet. She set them down and made the customary cross-sign by thrusting her thumb between her fore and middle fingers, murmuring, "God between you and all harm," a prayer known to keep safe those who trod the paths of The Good People. A bemused smile spread across her face. Hands on her hips, she looked skyward. "I've already had my feet washed—on Holy Thursday!"

29

MORRIGAN

A Charm, Perhaps?

At the pub, Ruarc, Liam, and Finn broke into a run when they spied Morrigan in the distance. Tommy hobbled after them as quickly as he could, trying to glimpse Morrigan's face.

At seeing the boys, Morrigan stopped. They stopped, too. Her regal bearing belied her grave expression, eyes moving from one to the other, her lips curved into a smile as if sealing a memory. Tommy hurried by the group.

"Stay here," said Liam, his arm out to stop the boys. They watched as Tommy approached Morrigan. They watched as she reached into her creel basket and, in slow ceremony, removed a cream-colored paper. They watched Tommy's big thumbs struggle to open the wax seal.

Though he couldn't read, Tommy wanted to see the words anyway.

"It says, 'I, Sir Richard Martin, do hereby grant the village a stay on the rents until the day following the mid-May fair,'" said Morrigan.

Tommy whooped, and the boys began to run when they saw his fist pump toward the sky.

Finn and Ruarc carried Morrigan on their shoulders to the pub where Connie McDonaugh announced a rare free round for one and all.

Those in the crowd pestered her with questions. Connie McDonaugh's voice boomed above the others, "Tell us! How did you do it, Morrie?"

Morrigan squinted upward in thought. How could she tell them she'd appealed to the ancestors and then experienced a trancelike state, forgetting everything afterward? Instinct told her to keep quiet; the villagers wouldn't understand. *I need to reflect upon this strange day.* To them she said, "I don't know. I can hardly remember what I said, and that's the truth."

"You bewitched him, did ya?" yelled Cormac from behind the bar. He raised a glass of whiskey and said, "Here's to ya, Morrie, and to the scoundrel Sir Martin. And here's to the three that never bred—the priest, the pope, and the mule!"

"To Morrie!" yelled Finn, raising his glass amid the cacophony of rejoinders.

"Sláinte! To a reprieve!"

Someone began singing "Bold Soldier Boy," and soon a rambunctious chorus of voices burst into song.

Schoolmaster Winnett approached Morrigan, his cheeks flushed, and his pale blue eyes narrowed. "How did you do it, Morrigan?"

"Surely, I don't know, Schoolmaster Winnett," she sputtered. "It was a flow of words… I can't recall."

"A charm, perhaps? You used the devil's pagan arts, didn't you?"

Morrigan shook her head. A wild pulse beat through her veins.

The last strains of the song ended with shouts of triumph. Schoolmaster Winnett spoke so only Morrigan could hear. "If I were a priest, I'd hear your confession, Morrigan." He turned from her and brushed past Tommy, who had come to put his arms around his daughter. Tommy shouted, "We can't thank you enough, Morrigan!" The crowd cheered. Then he turned to them and said, "There mustn't be a one of us who misses payment. Isn't it right, Morrie?"

"Aye," said Morrigan, her eyes glued to Schoolmaster Winnett's retreating back. "Sir Martin told me if one of us is late, payment will be expected even earlier next year." Her voice had lost its authority. She felt depleted.

"Morrie, you've missed supper and must be hungry," said Connie. "With Finn's help, I've cooked a warming mutton stew."

"I'd love some."

More villagers stopped in at hearing the news. Morrigan was peppered with questions. It was all overmuch and after finishing her stew, she nodded off just as she overheard one of the men, "… lost another lamb, lads. That's three between us."

Morrigan snapped to attention. She strained to see who spoke in the crowded room. Mr. O'Hare from a ways inland.

"Ignoble pine martens! Must be one around," said Mr. O'Malley. Morrigan strained to hear their conversation over the din.

"… a strange thing. I could swear on Saint Patrick's grave I heard the howl of a wolf last week," said Mr. O'Hare.

Laughter erupted among the men. "'Twas the scream of the Banshee you heard. You'd best keep careful lest you take ill with such an omen," someone said.

"Still, we'll keep an eye out for a pine marten. Beastly things. Might have to take turns hiding away at night to catch it."

The wolf! thought Morrigan, remembering the carcass she'd seen when meeting him by the oak. She must warn him of the farmer's plans. She stood to leave, and as she moved toward the door, three men from nearby Village Cashelros came rushing in.

"We heard you've been granted a reprieve on your rents," shouted one of the men, unsteady from drink.

"'Twas my daughter here who did it. She took on Sir Martin and is the victor!" said Tommy, his face flushed with pride.

"So it's true!" The men looked at each other, astonished. "We've had no stay in ours," said another. "What did you say, girl? Or should I say, *do*?"

Furious, Tommy moved toward the men while Liam tried to hold him back.

"Enough! Leave my pub!" bellowed Connie McDonaugh. Chairs scraped the floor as villagers stood to confront the men.

One of the men looked around with a dismissive shrug and, steely-eyed, said, "If you were proper fishermen, you'd be able to pay your rents on time."

"I'll give you a sound drubbing for that!" shouted Tommy.

The men turned to leave though not before some grabbed at their coats while others charged them.

"Follow me, Morrie," said Finn, pulling her out the kitchen's side door to the back of the pub where they leaned against the limestone wall to catch their breath.

Morrigan fought back tears. The burden she'd carried on behalf of the villagers was gone but replaced with worry about the wolf.

"Morrie? Are you all right?" asked Finn. Morrigan wept at the tenderness in Finn's voice. He had always been her co-conspirator. Now he showed a gentleness she'd never experienced.

"…want to go home," she straightened and swayed as she stepped from the wall.

"Come, I'll take ya home." Finn held out his hand and she took it.

In silence, they crossed a field and soon were in near darkness, with only a crescent moon and stars to guide them. They emerged onto the road with its ruts and stones they knew by heart. They heard a gentle *seep, seep, seep* call overhead. A cloud of glow-flanked thrush passed them by.

"Frost birds. Headed back to the Faroes," said Morrigan. A sure sign of spring.

Finn turned her toward him. "'Tis a good thing what you've done, Morrie. I never doubted you'd do it." He grinned. "Soon I hope you'll tell me the whole story."

"Ah, Finn. There's much to ponder about it all." She wanted to hold close her experience, turn it over and over in her mind until she had a notion about how it had happened. She hugged him hard and asked, "Will I see you at Bealtaine?"

"Aye. You will. You're a wonderment, Morrigan Lane. Might be I'm under your spell."

Morrigan blushed. The cool sea breeze had revived her, and now warmth surged through her body. She swayed closer to Finn. At the same height, their mouths were a moment away. Words, like her bearings, slipped from her.

"I'd better get you home," said Finn, his voice hoarse. Morrigan nodded, not trusting her own.

30

CONNIE

A Gale's Upon Us

In the hour after midnight, Connie McDonaugh snuffed out the last lamp at the pub and with weary steps made his way across the field to his home. Looking skyward in the stiffening winds, he said, "Wind's from the east. It's good for neither man nor beast, Kate. I can almost feel that low black sky."

In his mind, he heard her response. "The geese are squawking already, Connie. And there's a shuffle of disquiet among the sheep."

"You aren't suggesting I herd them inside at this hour?"

"We've done it before, dearie."

Connie groaned.

"You don't want the sheep's milk to be turning sour, do ya? Or to lose eggs for a fortnight?" Kate was right, and Connie knew it. Still, he protested.

"Maybe it'll blow over," he said, though the strengthening gusts told him it was a fool's hope.

"No. Not this one," Kate said softly. "It's the *time of winds*."

Connie had little choice but to take on the burdensome task of herding the sheep and ducks inside. He paused at a crumbling stone wall to catch his breath. "'Twas grand, Kate, what Morrie did! I don't know how she did it, but we've got a reprieve on our rents!" At the memory, he felt buoyed again.

"She carries a belief in the marvelous, Connie, and that alone is enough."

Connie frowned. "The blaggards from Cashelros arrived, and there was a rushing about, but no real harm done. Though by Saint Patrick's staff, it won't be the last time they make trouble." As he neared the courtyard, he looked inside the gate, and blinked. No sheep. No geese. Then he heard faint sounds above the winds. He ushered himself on through.

"We've just finished," yawned Finn, as he stepped from the storage dwelling, his long johns shoved haphazardly into boots. He was followed by his brothers in similar undress.

"Gale's upon us," shouted Cormac.

"Aye," answered Connie, suddenly so relieved that the dreaded chore was completed, he sounded almost merry. "Thank you, lads! It's grateful I am."

They hurried toward the house just as great-sized drops of rain began to pummel them.

31

MORRIGAN

The Raven's Message

A beast of a gale struck the village in the early morning hours. No telltale signs had been evident, though in the way villagers had celebrated, it was possible no one had been looking. Eerie winds moaned and then wailed through the cracks in the Lanes' mud-and-stone cottage sounding like they were propelled beyond their control by a fiercer force.

Tommy emerged into fog-headed awareness, swinging his legs over the bed and onto the floor. "Liam! Ruarc! Get dressed! The boats!"

In the bay, waves heaved blankets of dung-colored foam onto the rocky strand where they clung until gusts lifted them away. At the quay, dories slammed against each other, and sailboats heaved up and down with each violent roller. Fishermen made their way to the sea, bent low against the termagant storm, lanterns made from rushes flickering in the blow.

Like all boat owners, Tommy and his boys had to row out to *Inis Ealga* to put another anchor crosswise over the bow or risk the boat becoming untethered. Relieved at seeing the oars were still in the dory, Tommy ushered in Liam and Ruarc and joined them just before a cresting wave crashed onto them, soaking them through.

In what seemed like slow motion, the oars moved, sometimes pulling water, sometimes pulling air, as the dory tossed over and through the waves. Finally, they reached the sailboat. Liam hoisted himself up and onto it while Tommy and Ruarc held fast the dory alongside the hooker's rails. Soon, Liam had thrown a cross-anchor off the bow, and they began their perilous row back to safety.

The Lane boys headed for the shore, hoisting and dragging their dory onto higher ground. Catching their breath, they turned to see who else needed help, for they were a fleet, and none would return home until all sailboats were double-anchored and all dories pulled to safety.

For two interminable days, rains pelted the earth and winds shrieked as if they knew no other way to carry themselves across the land. Tommy and his fellow fishermen took turns checking on the sailboats. In the days ahead, there would be many repairs, but there was nothing to do for it now.

In the Lane cottage, Betha calmed her nerves by carding some of Connie McDonaugh's sheared fleece that she and the girls had sorted, washed, teased, and oiled. Mamoh rocked in her chair endlessly singing an old Irish Gaelic song:

> *Come, Connal, acushla, turn the clay,*
> *And show the lumpers the light, go soon*
> *For we must toil this autumn day,*
> *With heaven's help till rise of the moon.*
> *Our corn is stacked, our hay secure,*
> *Thank God! and nothing, my boy remains,*
> *But to pile the potatoes safe on the flure,*
> *Before the coming November rains.*

Tommy and the boys slumped on the hearth bench, staring at rivulets of water that leaked through the thatch and fell to the earthen floor.

Tommy sought to cheer them all as he said, "We'll go to the strand as soon as the winds subside. Lord willing, we'll find an abundant harvest of seaweed to make the finest fertilizer this side of Oughterard." Often a violent storm spit red seaweed onto the strand, which, when dried and sold as fertilizer, supplemented the fishermen's meager income.

Morrigan paced. Questions churned in her gut. Keener than the accolades she had received after her audience with Sir Martin, there lingered a worry: Had the wolf or spirits from The Otherworld influenced her audience with the landowner? If so, were they pagan forces as Schoolmaster Winnett had suggested? And how could they have affected the exchange? Finding the wolf held utmost importance, both to warn him about the villagers' ire, and to get answers to her questions.

Just before dawn the next morning, the family began preparing to forage seaweed. Longing to escape to the wolf, Morrigan approached her da and said, "Da, won't we need more turf for the fire? I can gather some and bring it in to dry, and then join you at the strand."

Tommy stood by the door pulling on his boots. He thought for a moment and then said, "Morrie, see to the turf for the fire and whatever else Mamoh might need to make us a steaming potato and seaweed soup. You've earned it." She saw gratitude in his eyes.

"There's our lass," Morrigan heard as she hurried through the village amid salutes and shouts. She gave a half smile, and hastened onward, thankful the steady drizzle prevented the men from tarrying. Earlier, while hauling peat, she'd been set upon by women wanting to hear the story firsthand of how she'd persuaded Sir Martin to give them a reprieve on the rents. She'd faltered in trying to answer them. Eager faces had changed to polite frowns and disappointed looks when Morrigan had little to say.

As she picked up her pace to Old Mother Oak in search of the wolf, her mind reeled. I'm a curiosity. Even more different now. The wolf had told her she was *An Fhoínse*. That belief had given her strength during her audience with Sir Martin, and her power had grown with her decisive use of it. She assured herself the wolf would explain everything.

Soon she reached Old Mother Oak, and called, "Wolf?" Hearing only silence, she shouted above the drizzle, "Wolf?"

"Wolf is not here," said a voice in The Once-and-Only Language.

Startled, Morrigan looked beyond the tree's trunk, but she saw nothing. Hairs rose at the back of her neck. In a shaky voice, she asked, "May I know where he can be found?"

She heard a whooshing sound overhead, and a raven descended and perched on one of the oak's thick lower limbs, its knobby, charcoal-colored feet digging into the bark. She had never been this close to the bird considered a messenger of wisdom and prophecy and a protector of Celtic warriors. She'd heard Mamoh describe Isla as having raven's knowledge, the powers of a seer.

The bird's fierce dark eyes looked at her; its glossy, jet-black feathers were greenish at its head and blue-violet underneath.

Shivering, Morrigan remained still as a stone. Sparks, like fireflies, moved back and forth between them. Then she heard the raven say, "Wolf has departed. The messenger has delivered his message. It is time to rely on your own agency."

"But I don't know what it means to heal the village. No one is sick," Morrigan whispered.

The raven cawed three times, then replied, "Guidance will come from all sources, inner and outer, waking and dreaming, past and future, if you know how to ask." Then, the bird took flight into the wind. Morrigan stood in the chilly rain awed by her meeting with the raven, but, nonetheless, alone.

Part Two

DARK SIDE MOON

32

MORRIGAN

The Triad

That night Morrigan dreamed she saw the broad wingspan of a predatory bird descending toward her, its talons ready to sink into her flesh. Fearful, she launched toward the bird, intent on destroying it. She was shocked to discover she clutched only bones, with the tattered remains of feathers and flesh clinging to them.

Morrigan awoke, her heart hammering. She sat up, expecting to see an eagle skeleton at the foot of her pallet. Nothing. Riona shifted in sleep. The dream had seemed so real, and her hands felt sore, like they'd been gripping jagged bones. Why had she wanted to destroy the bird? Maybe it would have perched nearby and spoken to her. She chided herself for being so fearful, remembering Cathleen's words about dreams selecting a person for a reason. What had the dream meant? She recalled the wolf's words: "You have been recognized to fulfill a destiny on behalf of all creation, for it is the way of things that the fate of the world rests upon the fate of your own, small village."

Suppressing a cry of anguish, Morrigan climbed down the ladder, grabbed a wrap, and escaped out the door. Cool night air hit her with force as she walked to the sea. Staring out across indigo waters, Morrigan shouted in frustration, "What destiny?" She scooped a handful of stones, and hurled one into the water, shouting, "You left before telling me how to fulfill it!" *Plunk!* She heard the stone enter tranquil seas. She hurled another, and yelled,

"What am I supposed to do?" *Plunk!* No answers came from the lapping waves. Bereft, she sang to them.

Into the void, a labyrinth wide, nothing but darkness, nowhere to hide.
My burden is heavy, no dagger in hand, protect me now in this untrodden land.
Spare my heart, make safe the way, shrouded in gloom, 'tis a cruel fate.

To her surprise, a shimmering mirage of the sea god arose from the deep, his chariot floating beneath him in the calm bay.

Morrigan dropped her stones, and yelled, "Manannán mac Lir! I'm from the line of Isla!"

The sea god nodded and replied, "When you are ready, I will welcome you to the Land-Beneath-the-Waves." Then he sang in return.

Let the bones be laid bare, breathe into them life.
The task is for you, no matter the strife.
No, not powerless on this fated track.
Throw open your arms, for there's no going back.

He sank beneath the waters, his words echoing on the waves. "No, not powerless on this fated track. Throw open your arms, for there's no going back."

"No going back? Back from what?" Morrigan asked herself. Frantic, she scanned the waters, but the sea god was gone. She remembered the raven's words, "Guidance will come to you if you know how to ask." She would have to figure out how to ask. But who would know anything about her destiny?

When a high-pitched tinkling sound rose over the waves, Morrigan strained her eyes to find its source. A waning moon revealed nothing, yet the sound continued. Feeling drawn to it, and desperate for answers, Morrigan hurried toward the sound in the hope of finding help.

Breathing heavily on her climb from the strand, Morrigan confirmed the tinkling sound moved. It wasn't the bell of a sheep or a goat. They'd have stopped to browse along the heath. It couldn't be a tinker at this hour. Who or what could it be? Mamoh would have cautioned her about the lure of strange music, for music and dancing were the lifeblood of The Good People. "Many a fair maiden has been whisked away to nanny Fin Varra's children in the fairy halls of the hill of Knockmaah, Morrigan." Their popular superstition held that The Good People abducted young women to nurse their own young inside lavish underground dwellings.

"What have I to lose?" Morrigan said aloud, for her hopeful heart longed for another messenger to tell her how to follow her destiny. In her mind, she chanted, "Please," over and over in rhythm to her stride. Morrigan broke into a run to catch up to the sound. Too late, she noticed the stream in front of her. She jumped to clear it and twisted her ankle on the uneven ground.

"Saints alive!" she swore, as tears filled her eyes. She hung her head and took in gasps of air. Just then the tinkling stopped. Shivers ran along Morrigan's spine. There is a presence here, she thought. She knew better than to look around in case it *were* The Good People. She kept her head down, remaining motionless, and waited.

Later, Morrigan would not know if it were ten minutes or one hundred, she heard a musical voice whisper, "A triad to be perceived, and the one will be received." Then a gust of wind passed her, and the presence disappeared.

"Puh!" She pushed breath out from her lungs pondering what she had heard. It made no sense. Perhaps an instruction of sorts, though she had no idea who had sent it.

Morrigan assessed her surroundings. Pre-dawn light cast a murky glow on the trunks of gray yew trees encircling her like gnarled old women. She recalled a rhyme she had heard, "Of all the trees in the greenwood—oak, elder, elm, and thorn—the yew alone burns lamps of peace for them that lie forlorn." Yew trees were found in churchyards, their canopies dwarfing the slates atop the remains of beloved ancestors. Morrigan had never been in this yew grove north of the village. She knew few such old groves remained in the landscape. Here the trees radiated a powerful thrumming that tuned the chambers in Morrigan's heart.

After a time, Morrigan put weight on her injured ankle and groaned. She needed a crutch. Looking around, she spied a yew branch leaning against one of the oldest trees. She hopped to it and found it to be strong. In her heightened state of awareness, she chose to believe someone or something had conjured the branch just for her. She held it to her breast. Then she gripped the branch with both hands and put her weight on it, easing her way to the stream where she cooled her swelling ankle. "Morrie! No jigs for you," she scolded herself, thinking of Bealtaine only a few days away. "Finn! Can you hear me in your dreams? I need help. I don't know if I can make it home." Morrigan leaned on her yew crutch and gave in to tears.

33

MORRIGAN

Nature's Pace

In the early dawn, Morrigan paused to rest. She'd made it to a rough track used by itinerant folk—tinkers, travelers, and seanchaithe. She knew now she wouldn't make it home without help.

In the distance, Morrigan heard the sharp call of a chaffinch, a bird known to herald spring's chime, and then another in response. Close by, a rook cawed. She spotted it balanced atop a still-unleafed ash tree. Rooks were cousins to raven. Could he speak in The Once-and-Only Language? She tried using it, in her mind shouting, "Hello? Hello? May it please you to share in a conversation?" She was unsure of how to ask for the guidance the raven had said was available. Surely respect was necessary, as well as humility. She tried again, "I humbly ask the feathered ones for help. If any of you know of a stone circle just south and west of here, or if any of you could go to the cottage just beyond the circle, I wish to send a message."

Birdcalls stopped, and a rook alighted on a bush a scant distance from Morrigan. She tried again, "May I seek your help? I am far from home and have an injury to my ankle. 'Twould be like a hurt that made it hard for you to perch on a branch." The bird stood immobile, head cocked, one black eye looking at her. "If you venture along the coast in the direction of the midday sun, you will come upon a large council of stones, and just over the rise dwells a small cottage. There lives a gentle woman. She does not speak The Once-and-Only Language, but she is very wise and will know you are a messenger. Can you go to her?" The wolf had told her to try to connect with the spirit of a creature. Morrigan breathed in hope and breathed out gratitude.

With an explosion of movement and a loud caw, the bird swept across the short distance between them, and then turned toward the south.

Morrigan let out a sound. "Please let the bird get to Cathleen's, and please let her notice," she prayed. Her insides felt withered and shrunken, emptier than they had ever been. She scanned her surroundings for anything edible or drinkable.

In the slanted rays of the newborn day, saucy yellow buttercups flaunted their lustrous petals to the reawakened bees that boomed over glade and valley. Buttercups were poisonous. She spied sulphur-colored primroses peeping from among the rib-grass and violets, but she'd heard they were only good for the frenzies and could put her in a stupor. Near a rock-outcropping stood shepherd's purse, they were edible Cathleen had told her, especially the leaves. Morrigan grasped the yew branch and made her way to it.

"Thank you," she said aloud to the plant. She sat with her right leg stretched out on a granite rock chewing a fistful of shepherd's purse. Awareness dawned. It had taken a sprained ankle to slow her down to nature's pace and to realize she could reach out for help from non-human beings. She'd discovered the miraculous capacity for mutual exchange within The World Tree. The wolf had told her humans had frayed The World Tree's cords of connection. Morrigan wondered if healing the village required slowing to nature's pace. Perhaps only then would insights emerge about how to strengthen those frayed cords.

Imagining the world as a tree whose branches were inseparable cords brought a smile to Morrigan's face. A world like Old Mother Oak. As an image of the oak appeared in her mind, she caught a whiff of acrid air. Suddenly dizzy, Morrigan reached to brace herself on the rock. Her eyes closed to an image that entered her consciousness—a raging fire in the woodland, with flames cresting trees faster than Sir Martin's stallion could gallop. A fire that burned for weeks. A fire so hot it burned two meters down into the once-damp Irish soil incinerating everything in its path.

Morrigan groaned and fought for air. Pinching herself, she struggled to get back to *this rock, this dampness, this sprained ankle.* What was happening to her? I'm daft, she thought. She held her head, afraid to move, afraid to open her eyes lest she see the wolf's warnings had come to life.

34

SIR MARTIN

That Pig

In the dim morning light, Sir Martin emerged from Rosderry House. It had been another restless night. A list of manor house repairs spiraled into and out of his awareness and competed with legal arguments in the forthcoming trial against Billy Burns, the scoundrel who had been caught beating his donkey. As the first prosecution under the new Cattle Act, it consumed him.

He glimpsed his overseer, Edward Eagan, emerging from his cottage. Eagan yawned and scratched and began to stretch his arms overhead. "Oh!" Eagan grabbed his lower back. "Bloody storm," he swore. "I'm an overseer, not a laborer. Father would not have had to do work such as this."

"The carriageway repairs are sufficient, Mr. Eagan," said Sir Martin.

Startled, Eagan righted himself, eyes alert. "My apologies, Sir Martin. I did not see you there."

"You were saying something about your father?" Martin raised an eyebrow.

"'Tis nothing, Sir, only that as Lord Trimblestown's overseer, he would have a staff of his own to...'Tis nothing, Sir," Eagan sputtered as Sir Martin's jaw hardened.

"Lord Trimblestown's staff are not your concern, are they, Mr. Eagan?" Damn the man for mentioning that name, Martin thought.

"Have I not made it clear that my wife's family shan't be mentioned in my presence?"

"Aye, Sir Martin. It won't happen again."

Martin let out a long, slow breath. "It was a bloody storm," he conceded. "Let's walk to the livery. Repairs are needed there, as well."

"Aye, Sir Martin."

"We both share affection for the animals, don't we, Eagan?" Martin relaxed as they walked. "Well, perhaps not this one." Shauna raced around her pen like a whirling dervish. Up and back, round and round, she ran, her short legs pounding the ground as she dodged her littermates. Her behavior differed from the scampering, leaping, snorting antics she usually employed. Her full-throated squeals sounded serious to Sir Martin's ears. They approached the pen.

"What evil lies upon you, Shauna?" said Eagan. The piglet's movements appeared neither pained nor limited. She took a leap at the gateway to the pen. "So it's out you want? And where will you go, then? Off to that girl? Not this day, pig," said Eagan.

"She's determined, Eagan. Only a matter of time before she escapes."

"I've got too much to do to worry about you," said Eagan, ushering the pig into a stall in the livery and chaining her there. He patted the pig's head and whispered, "Don't fret. I'll bring ye a whole cabbage and some lumpers."

Sir Martin shook his head at the pig's behavior. As they walked away, he stroked his sideburns. "Strange pig."

But Shauna was not strange. A tiny, undomesticated part of her, the part that had not lost her wild, sensed the girl she felt safe with needed help.

35

CATHLEEN

The Rook's Signal

Cathleen watched the new mother hold a sixth baby to her breast and was in awe of all birthing women everywhere. Always after a birth, Cathleen felt a bloom of love followed by deep anguish at her own empty womb. She said prayers of welcome to the baby and placed three drops of water from a holy well on the girl's forehead. She dedicated the child in the name of the Trinity. Then she raised a woven Saint Brigid's Cross and carried it and a candle around the bed sunwise three times, chanting, "May the heavenly saints and angels provide a sunbeam to warm you, a moonbeam to charm you, a sheltering angel so nothing will harm you." The women bowed their heads to sanctify the sacred blessing. Cathleen nodded to the other women present and left for the home she'd departed twelve hours earlier.

The rook had spent most of its day around the cottage waiting and pecking at a window. A social bird, it had been a solitary time. But it had never before experienced a call for help from a human, mostly shouts and stones thrown by farmers with fists in the air. It had stayed to fulfill the woman's request, not because humans were special; rather, because this woman seemed to know she could not thrive without the help of feathered kin. And she had spoken in the ancient language. So, the rook waited and fed upon nearby worms and larvae. Finally, it saw a figure emerge across a daisy-spangled meadow.

Fatigue had dimmed Cathleen's attunement, so she was almost at the threshold to her cottage before she noticed the rook's unusual darting moves.

"What's all this about?" She hadn't a sighting of the bird so much as the sound of its flapping and cawing. The rook landed at her feet and began to caw a persistent caw—three, four, five, six, seven times—its head turned toward the village and the north.

"Are you trying to send me a message?" she asked the bird. Then: Morrigan! She must have found a way to speak to the bird. The girl is remarkable, thought Cathleen, and probably in trouble.

Cane in hand, The Crooked Woman walked across the estate's meadow. She spotted Mistress Mary on her mare and struggled to throw her arms in the air to catch the young woman's attention. The mistress was too far away to be heard, but Cathleen watched her recoil. I suppose I look like a flailing buzzard, thought Cathleen.

"What in all manner?" said Mistress Mary, with barely concealed disdain.

"Mistress Mary," said Cathleen, shoulders heaving, "I hesitate to concern you, but I am certain Morrigan is in trouble. With due haste, I must go to the family and tell them."

Mary asked, "Where is she? What harm has befallen her?"

"I do not know. I know only a messenger has signaled trouble. Perhaps you can go to the fishing village and alert Morrigan's family, or search your grounds? Any help would be a blessing," said Cathleen.

"I've ridden all over the estate this afternoon, and Morrigan is not on it," said Mary. "No, the villagers will no doubt wait to hear from you anyway, only trusting their own," she said under her breath. Removing her left glove, she caressed the middle finger where a wart once grew. "I've changed my mind. I'll go speak to her family and join the search." Mistress Mary motioned her mare toward the village. "I'll be known far and wide as Mary the Rescuer," shouted Mary to her horse as they galloped away.

Cathleen smiled. It seemed the girl longed for an adventure. We all want to feel needed, she thought.

36

BETHA

Spirited Away?

The sight of Mistress Mary resplendent in a dove-colored riding dress atop her regal mare caused a stir among the fishermen's wives. Something was wrong. Their new heroine Morrigan had gone missing.

Betha had already sensed trouble because Morrigan never missed a meal. She'd sent Ruarc and Riona off to look for her. Cathleen arrived a short time later confirming her inkling that Morrigan was stricken by something, somewhere. Betha had dispatched Tommy and Liam to help in the search as village women whispered in ominous tones about what could have happened to Morrigan. Mamoh was thick among them.

"Could it be Manannán mac Lir? Is she with him now in The Otherworld?" said Widow O'Rooney.

"True for you, though they are going fast, The Good People— the Lord be with them—are very active at this time of the year. Morrigan could have been spirited away!" suggested another.

"Many an illness comes upon a person sleeping out near the time of Bealtaine," said Mamoh with a shiver.

"Aye, the *time of no time*. Ill fortune could be upon her. Could be *Them* returning from their winter respite, full of mischief and carefree delight," still another whispered, quick to cross herself.

The village women dared not use other words to describe the pantheon of sylvan beings in their lore—the Daoine Sidhe, the fairies, the wee chap with his Frenchman's cap and yellow breeches, the pooca, the Irish ghost, the thievish, to name a few—for fear of insulting their sensibilities.

Talk like that unnerved Betha. As a child, she'd heard too many compelling stories to dismiss The Good People as mere fancy. Father Murray considered them fallen angels. She and most villagers believed them to be the prime agents of all accidents, diseases, and deaths, and equally responsible for the health of cattle, crops, and babes. Claiming a nervous headache, Betha retreated to her cottage.

As she added a meager turf to the fire, Betha shivered, remembering the story old Darby Doolin, a shanachie, from Connaught told years ago as he sat smoking his *Dúidín* in their chimney corner.

"Now, if you'll hold your tongue for a short space, I shall tell you all about Connor Maguire, the hearty, red-haired tailor who lived in Kilrandy, just as you pass the door of Dermott Reilly and get upon the common. I shall tell you all about him being the likeliest boy in the parish. Sure, 'twas no later than the day before yesterday week I saw him with my two living eyes riding home on the quietest mare ever ridden, and how that same mare bolted at a wisp of straws whirling at the crossroads, and off she set, galloping, ever, ever, till he fell on his head just outside his own door, and when they lifted him up, he was speechless and never tasted a bit of the world's bread from that day to this. Well, everyone knows The Good People had a hand in it."

Now a devout Catholic, Betha would not let herself believe The Good People had spirited Morrigan away. Still, knowing Morrigan had the gift of connecting to spirits she herself had once desired, she paced inside the cottage, anxious for any word that Morrigan was safe.

37

BETHA

The Parchment

Betha leaned out the half door of her cottage and spied Mamoh and the other women walking toward the sea. Everyone else had been dispatched to search for Morrigan. She made a quick decision and groped behind the cupboard, contorting her thin body to reach a parcel that had long been hidden there. A coil of nervous tension wound its way along her spine. With fingers trembling, she untied a ribbon and pulled open an ancient goat-skin scroll. She longed to feel tingling or to see a bright light in its presence. As always, she felt nothing.

She'd found the parchment three decades ago, or perhaps more aptly, she had stolen it. Grandmother Isla had gone missing in a storm and been presumed dead. While her mum was comforted by her women friends, Betha had sneaked into her grandmother's forbidden chest, the one she had used to heal countless people who had walked or ferried long distances to see her, so renowned was she as a gifted seer, foreteller, and healer.

With curiosity, Betha had opened the parchment to see a loose arrangement of unfamiliar markings, three wide and three deep, inscribed on the goatskin. Betha had stared in wonderment at the center symbol, which seemed strangely illuminated as if from behind. Eleven round shapes formed an elliptical glyph, with loops joining one clover shape to another.

Even as a child, Betha had sensed the parchment had great import. Back then, she believed she, the granddaughter of the great Isla, The Healer, came from an extraordinary healing line and would, in time, be known as gifted, too. Unwilling to wait for her mum to bequeath the parchment to her, Betha had taken and hidden it, and not even Mamoh knew of its existence.

In the weeks and then years since its discovery, Betha had hoped and expected to intuit something from the parchment, believing if she wanted to be a healer strongly enough, or prayed fervently enough, she would understand the parchment's mysterious symbols, and a healer's knowledge would be transmitted to her. However, eventually she realized she was not a gifted healer and seer as her grandmother had been, and she would have none of the villagers' admiration either.

Although the Church denounced divination and the gift of sight, many villagers secretly relied on them, in the same way they still performed the old rituals, such as passing burning sod three times under a pregnant cow's belly or three times over the nest in which eggs lay.

Betha was only a poor fisherman's wife. Disappointment lodged in her heart, accompanied by an odd relief, and that made her feel like a coward. Sometimes, she wondered if stealing the parchment had changed the course of her own destiny. After all these years though, she didn't dare tell Mamoh about it. And of the hundreds of moments Betha had knelt for church confessional, this deed alone remained unforgiven because she had never confessed it.

In time, other teachings had become her belief system. She'd concluded the parchment, with its etchings, had no value, at least for her. Father Murray had taken great pains to instill in her the Church's condemnation of the old ways as incompatible with the Catholic faith. Still, whenever Betha had been tempted to burn the parchment, a voice inside her begged her to keep it. And so, she'd hidden it behind the cupboard in the cottage.

On the eve of Morrigan's trip to the estate belonging to Sir Martin, when Betha had seen her grandmother's dagger, she'd been shocked to see on it the same glyph symbol as on the parchment. She remembered a story Mamoh had once told the family: "A woman came to the island all the way from Inis Diamain. She had with her a son who had ceased to speak owing to having witnessed the drowning of his friend. Isla used her dagger to make a strong tea from the root of horseradish and gave him three cups. She applied a tincture of usnea lichen and honey to his throat, wrapping it in coarse linen. She then instructed the mother to leave him in the presence of the sky for three nights, to lay him in a soft spot beneath the limestone karst.

"While he lay there, Isla and the woman performed sacred ceremonies to the spirits who lived in The Otherworld. When the sun hit its zenith on the fourth day, Isla told the woman to return for her son. She said the curlews had sung his voice back to him, and they had."

Mamoh spoke of Isla in reverent terms, and despite an instinctive affinity for healing, Mamoh, like Betha and Riona, did not have the gift. Only Morrigan had shown signs of Isla's knowings. In spite of this, as Betha held the parchment, she longed for a flash of intuition about her missing Morrigan. Feeling, hearing, and sensing nothing, she wondered if it wouldn't be best to rid herself of the parchment forever.

38

MORRIGAN

The Transit

From her spot on a rock by the traveler's way, Morrigan watched the sun transit across a bold blue sky. At first, her senses were attuned to the sight or sound of a traveler. Then she tired of such alertness and reflected on what had happened to her in the past few weeks: Dreams had invaded her nights and dizzying images of earthen disasters her days. A mysterious sea god wanted to ferry her somewhere. Uncle Colm now forbade her a future at the quay. Schoolmaster Winnett declared her a devil's apprentice just as a wolf called her special, *An Fhoínse.*

Now another message: "A triad to be perceived and the one will be received." It had to do with her calling, she was clear about that, though she hadn't any idea who could have been speaking, as there were many Invisibles, at least according to Mamoh, who spoke of them in hushed tones even as Betha called them fallen angels. Mamoh had told her the queen of The Good People traveled with bells on the harness of a great white steed. Could the bells have been the tinkling sound she heard?

"I'm a lamebrain. I'll never captain a boat. Mere folly," she muttered. "I'll marry some dullard and have twelve wee wains." The pain in her ankle had become a persistent ache, and her hot hunger had vanished, replaced by a throbbing at her temples. Encased within the wrap, Morrigan breathed in the salty, odorous smell of her unwashed body and lashed out through clenched teeth, "Not a single traveler? Where is everyone?" She yanked the wrap off and yelled, "Cussed sound! Why didn't you just kidnap me like the old ones say you do? Where's my family? Have they not missed me all drasted day?" She gulped in breaths of air.

"Da, where are ya? Mum? Finn?" her words choked out. At last, she fell silent, numb and spent.

Sometime later just before the gloaming—twilight's descension into night—an improbable sight appeared in the distance. Shauna ran toward Morrigan, grunting and squealing, mirroring Morrigan's own joyful cries. Mistress Mary followed behind, her mare in a canter. In the distance, men rushed forward.

"Shauna! You've found me!" Morrigan shouted. She launched from the rock, forgetting about her ankle as she reached for the pig. She landed in a heap as pain shot up her leg. Lightheaded, her body sticky and cold, Morrigan fainted to the faraway sound of Mistress Mary's scream.

39

MORRIGAN

If I Can, I Will

From a deep, sonorous place, Morrigan heard a summons. She opened her eyes and blinked once, twice. Faces of the women she loved—Mamoh, her mum, Riona, and Cathleen—blurred before her eyes. She closed them. She'd been in a dream where a wild-haired crone stood, her gaze fierce. She'd held a vessel in one hand and a rolled parchment in another. In a limbic state, she had heard the crone rasp, "Your destiny is in your hands." Then the crone had turned into a long, trailing green vine. The vine had begun to wrap itself around her, not to suffocate, but as a garland. Then the vine had turned into a bird, perhaps a merlin or peregrine falcon, one not too small and with a flash of white the color of hawthorn flowers in bloom. In her dazed state, Morrigan could not be sure which world was real.

"Morrie! Can you hear me?" asked Riona, her voice shaky.

"My destiny?" whispered Morrigan, as the room came into focus. She lay in Mamoh's bed closest to the hearth. Da, Liam, Ruarc, and Finn stood behind the women, speaking in whispers, respectful of female authority in matters such as these.

"She'll need some St. John's Wort tea," said Cathleen, now in command.

Riona retrieved the cure-all Tommy and Liam used for aches and pains rendered by the sea. Betha lowered the kettle to the hearth.

Morrigan tried to sit and discovered her right ankle propped, a cool cloth around it. Her arms were aflame from sunburn. Spying the yew branch alongside her, she reached for it.

"You wouldn't part with that branch, Morrie," said Finn. "Clutched it all the way home, ye did."

"'Twas the pig that saved you, Morrie," said Tommy, scratching his head as he heard his own words. "Mistress Mary, too, and Cathleen, who enlisted her aid."

Morrigan remembered with astonishment Mistress Mary coming for her. The rook had found Cathleen!

"How the dickens did you happen on the old traveler's road?" asked Tommy. "What were you doing out there?"

"I couldn't sleep so I went for a walk on the strand." Morrigan hesitated to tell the truth. She knew her mum and Mamoh would be angry to know she had followed a tinkling sound. She reached for the teacup Cathleen handed to her. It smelled of autumn leaves warmed by the sun. A story was expected, and the truth could not be revealed. Morrigan continued, "With May Day just two days hence, and the seven herbs the very thing everyone needs for their pails before milking, I wondered if I could find a new foraging place. The moon guided my way. I found yarrow, and speedwell, and an old yew grove. Then I got careless when jumping across a stream and sprained my ankle."

All heads turned toward Morrigan's ankle wrapped in a cloth saturated with the oil of St. John's Wort. Mamoh reached forward and lifted the compress. "Hmmm," she murmured. A blue bruise was forming.

"'Twas in the yew grove where I found this branch to use as a crutch. I limped as far as the old road, knowing I couldn't get all the way home, so I waited and hoped someone would find me. It's sorry I am to have caused you worry," said Morrigan.

"How kind of you to think about collecting the seven herbs," said Cathleen. "You'll need some fresh chickweed to cool your sunburned skin. I'll gather some, and Riona can help you apply it afterwards. I must get home before darkness sets in."

Riona made a sound of disgust. She had never liked the feel of chickweed. When it came to her skin, she preferred to stay out of the sun altogether to avoid the remedy. Often the first to rise on Bealtaine, Riona would bathe her face and neck with dewdrops glittering like gossamer in the flowery meadows, a remedy thought to prevent freckles. For Morrigan, keeping freckles away was a lost cause.

"You can't dance around the May bush, Morrie," said Finn.

Mamoh made a sound of encouragement. "She'll be there anyway, won't you, Morrie?"

Yawning, Morrigan answered, "Aye. If I can, I will." The same words Morrigan had used in response to the wolf's request for a second encounter. Whatever war waged in her heart, her willingness to trust in mystery had become like a rudder on a vessel, carving a remarkable course into the flow of her life.

40

CATHLEEN

The Sea Green Dress

The Seven Sisters star cluster rose just before sunrise on the morning of Bealtaine. Fitful April, at once warm and witching, then harsh and gloomy, had come to an end, and the sweet, blue-eyed harbinger of summer settled upon them. May Day! The oldest celebration of sun's full light. The time when human spirits attune with the seasons and burst, alongside all of creation—forest monarchs and marsh marigolds, feathered fowls and multi-legged creatures, on hill and hollow, land and sea—all hailing the dawn of summer, the Sabbath of the year.

Villagers had thrown off the cares of life and in the past few days had gone *Collecting for the May*. Revelers paraded from door to door for scraps of gaudy silk, ribbons, or handkerchiefs for the May bush, and turf coals or old bones for the propitiatory fires. Garlands of yellow primroses, cowslips, posies, and buttercups were prepared for the dance, while green rowan boughs with white hawthorn sprigs and marigolds decorated windows and doors and even cows' tails to fend off The Good People who reveled in mischief at this time.

In her cottage, Cathleen heard a noise outside. Door knockers were for the gentry and priests, those who could afford such a thing. Often visitors began to speak outside a door and then pushed it open to make their entrance. "Wide is the door of the little cottage," said villagers with pride.

In bounded Ruarc, followed by Riona, her friend Colleen, and Finn. "Cathleen, you seem to live farther and farther away each year," said Ruarc.

"Sometimes the most precious of things requires a bit of a journey, isn't it so, Ruarc?" said Cathleen, her voice merry.

"Your wreaths are as beautiful as ever, Cathleen," said Riona, as she lifted a wreath of noreens from the worn pine table to examine its skillful weaving. Riona, too, had fashioned a dozen wreaths for Bealtaine.

"It's as if the daisies wove themselves. It happens when you are mindful of the direction they are already bending," said Cathleen.

"Morrie wants us to carry the wreaths on this yew, Cathleen," said Finn, stooping to show her the yew branch Morrigan had found just two days prior.

"I recall that branch. Morrigan's got a fine sense of the potency of a yew, and that, I did not teach her," said Cathleen. The yew tree was considered a connector with ancestors, a bringer of dreams, and a symbol of magic.

While Riona strung the wreaths onto the branch, Cathleen moved toward her faded wardrobe. In a far corner hung the remains of one of her great-grandmother's finest gowns. For the last dozen years, Cathleen had provided strips of this golden gown for the May bush, observing the fabric's deterioration over time as a marker of the loss of riches that were once her lineage. Fingering the softness of the silk, stories of long ago came back to her, times when her family had owned acres and acres of rich land filled with streams and ponds, natural meadows and deep woodlands—nothing like the poor limestone soil upon which her diminutive cottage now stood.

Cathleen glanced at a dress in the farthest corner of her wardrobe. Its sea green colors made her heart leap. She remembered wearing the dress when she was sixteen and upright, with long chestnut hair twisted in a fetching style and a daisy wreath crowning her head. In her mind's eye, she saw Henry Rooney, tall and strong, holding a garland in front of her and looking again and again into her eyes as they serpentined around the May bush. She had been mesmerized by the promise she saw in them. But disease had crippled her spine shortly after that long-ago Bealtaine. Now, savoring the memory, Cathleen grabbed the folds of her sturdy cotton skirt as if to curtsy and then dropped her hands. The memory slipped away. She removed both the golden gown and the sea green dress from her wardrobe. One would be used for another Bealtaine ribbon, and the other, she'd give to Morrigan, who had embraced her uncertain call with increasing assuredness, becoming a treasured student.

41

MORRIGAN

Bealtaine

Blue bonnet skies provided a backdrop for the festive Bealtaine gathering near the market. Tommy Lane, along with Connie, James, and Cormac McDonaugh, carried the May bush, a white hawthorn. They were followed by musicians with harp and fiddle, one in a home-patched Green Man costume—a symbol of the ancient spirit of nature—another playing The Fool—a symbol of the fairies whose touch, *poc sídhe,* or "fairy stroke," could cause seizure or even death. Behind them, adorned with garlands and boughs, danced Liam, Ruarc, Riona, Finn, and others. Spectators following the procession sang:

> *This morning as the sun did rise*
> *We dressed the bush you to surprise*
> *With our fiddle and our pipes so gay,*
> *To bring you good cheer on the first of May.*
> *Summer! Summer! Milk o' the heifers*
> *Summer! Summer! Nature from her slumber wakes!*
> *Summer! Summer! Milk o' the heifers*
> *Summer! Summer! Worship the sun and sweeten the cakes.*

Nearby, Mamoh and others less mobile were seated on wooden crates. Morrigan stood next to them, wearing Cathleen's sea green dress and waving a garland in time to the music. Earlier Riona had presented Cathleen's dress to Morrigan, along with her message, "I wore this dress at a long-ago Bealtaine. Now it is yours to wear. Remember, your new life comes as you live it." Morrigan had been thrilled with the dress that reflected the colors of Ireland—a leaf green, silk-poplin bodice and flouncy skirt with a sky-blue organza overlayer. She felt transformed from awkward to graceful. As the troupe approached, she whooped with glee.

"Though your feet can't dance, your eyes can," said Mamoh.

"The May bush is a sight to behold," said Morrigan. Festooned with wildflowers, strips of colored silk, and ribbons, it was a fitting herald to summer. Trees were a symbol of knowledge, and for centuries, Irish people danced around the May bush to reflect their veneration for nature.

The men faltered as they moved to set down the bush. "Ooooooh," shouted the crowd.

"The scoundrels must have brimmed their morning milk with whiskey," said Mamoh, smiling. Finally, the bush rested on the ground, and musicians and dancers circumambulated it three times in a ceremonial way they would repeat later as the two Bealtaine bonfires were lit for a safe and prosperous season for bulls, heifers, and calves.

Morrigan spied Finn among the dancers and grinned. Instead of his usual open-collared, stained shirt and muddy trousers, he wore a fresh white, buttoned shirt, finespun brown trousers, vest, and tweed jacket. He saw her in her new dress, and his eyes widened in surprise. She blushed at the appreciation she saw in them, even from a distance. "Finn's wearing a smile like a buttercup, Mamoh," she said.

"He's got spunk. Clever, too. I heard he's fashioned a conveyance for the whiskey barrels into and out of the pub. Makes it easier for Mr. McDonaugh. One likes a man who eases the work of others. He'll make a fine husband, no doubt." She turned away from the festivities and winked at Morrigan, her gray eyes crinkled with mirth beneath dabs of white eyebrows.

"You're daft!" said Morrigan, but her mind wandered. All her life she'd looked at Finn as one would a brother, but lately, she'd seen in him something different, something potent. Her heart fluttered at the memory of him carrying her home from where she'd been stranded on the travelers' road—rolled up shirtsleeves, flexed forearms, and strong hands gripping the cot as though he would never let her go. She imagined his hands, sensual and slow on her awakening body, and for the first time in her life she felt a hunger different from her usual one for food, a feeling both scary and wondrous.

That evening the Bealtaine tradition from as far back as the Celtic great ancestors began. Before they journeyed to summer's fruitful pastures farther from the village, cattle were herded across a gap between two sacred, purifying bonfires thought to prevent the spread of contagious bovine diseases. Then, with turf, old bones, and coals, the fires were built higher. Flames shot into the air warming the already sunburnt faces of those gathered. Musicians paused from their jigs and their reels to watch, too, mesmerized by the blazes.

Villagers believed that leaping forwards and backwards three times through the gap between the fires would grant success, even invulnerability, in their endeavors. Since most waited for the fires to become "friendly," their colors changing from white hot and sparking to yellow-orange and mellow, Morrigan cried out when Finn leapt through the fiery gap with flames at their highest. He shouted, "Tralee!"

"Saints alive, Finn! What're you thinking?" Morrigan shouted into the roar. Connie, James, and Cormac, who were seated nearby, cheered.

What did Finn mean about Tralee, worlds away south of our village? she thought. Have I missed news of another uprising? No one's talking about it.

"Your turn, Morrie!" Finn swaggered over to where she sat alongside Riona and Colleen. He smelled like burnt hair. Morrigan looked at her still-bruised ankle and then up at him, her mouth opened to upbraid his foolishness. He deflected her words with his own urgent ones. "It's smoky by the fire, Morrie. Let's find fresher air." He reached out to help her.

"I cannot go far, Finn."

"Lean on me, Morrie."

And so, the pub owner's son and the fisherman's daughter wound their way around groups of men smoking pipes and sharing stories, the smell of sweet tobacco lingering in the air as women packed what remained of the feast to deliver to village widows.

Though Finn matched Morrigan's slow pace, she felt his impatience like a horse barn-weaving in its stall after a long winter.

"What, Finn?"

"Just a bit further, Morrie, so you've got some place to sit."

"We're in fresh air, Finnbharr McDonaugh. Say whatever it is you have to say."

"Ah, Morrie. You've never been one for shallow concerns." He stopped alongside her, removed his flat cap, straightened his posture, and said, "You know I'm the third son in the line of McDonaughs."

Morrigan nodded and braced for something important.

"Da's land can fit just one house for Cormac as the eldest. He'll take on the pub as Da ages. Then there's James, who'll live with Da and Cormac forever." His words held a tinge of sadness. James's simple mind required family care throughout his life. "Then there's me, Morrie. I can't make anything of myself here," he said, spreading his arms and looking around.

Morrigan's heart began to thrum. She leaned back as though to evade a punch. Finn moving away? She panicked and put weight on her weak ankle, gasping in pain.

Finn moved closer to support her and surged on. "To Tralee I go, and soon. I hope to become a carpenter's mate. I've heard there are jobs for those like me who are good with their hands."

"Tralee?" To Morrigan's ears, it sounded as far away as Africa.

"Aye! There I can earn the money to go to America. She's bursting with shipbuilding and commerce," said Finn, looking out to sea.

Morrigan's breaths were sharp. Finn off to Tralee? Finn going to America? She swallowed a lump in her throat.

"'Tis either this or join His Majesty's Service. Or become a priest," he said. "Morrie, I don't want to become a priest." His gray eyes searched hers as he reached for her hands. "I want you to come with me."

It took a moment for Morrigan to comprehend his words. Go with him to Tralee? Or America? "You do?"

"'Tis you I want for my bride, Morrigan Lane, and no other," said Finn. "Between the jigs and the reels, I'll get the fare for the both of us to go to America."

A stirring sea breeze caressed her gossamer gown. Morrigan leaned into Finn, turning her face upward, her eyes on his lips. This boy-man who her mind had known as capable and safe, bright and promising, had become someone her heart now felt was strong and alluring. Her body and mind were locked in battle. How could she go to America if she was called to heal her village? Closing her eyes, she swayed just as Finn's lips found hers and they kissed.

The sounds of a piper's plaintive love song came drifting toward them:

I knew a valley fair,
Eileen Aroon.
I knew a cottage there,
Eileen Aroon.

Far in that valley's shade
I knew a gentle maid,
Flower of the hazel glade,
Eileen Aroon.

"Is that you, Morrigan?" Betha's harsh voice broke them apart.

"Coming," shouted Morrigan, as Finn slipped away into the darkness.

Betha's posture was rigid; Morrigan suspected she'd get a lecture in the morning. She felt guilt but a fiery resistance as well. Finn loved her, and she was a bird ready to fly away, perhaps over the seas themselves to the shores of America.

Morrigan joined the Lane women and without a word, began to limp home, her thoughts on Finn and his wondrous, worrisome news. In the distance, the fires smoldered, and a few pregnant women stepped across the gap to garner luck, while couples snuggled against each other. Mothers, reluctant to return home, held sleeping children in their arms while men finally got to talking low and quiet. Morrigan heard Finn's shout out of the darkness, "Tralee!"

42

MORRIGAN

To Be Going Somewhere

Morrigan awoke too early to rise for the day. She shifted on the pallet, and Riona stirred, turning to face her.

"What was it like? The kiss?" asked Riona, excitement in her whisper.

Morrigan could feel herself blush in the darkness. They had never spoken of such things. "His lips. Time stopped." She pursed her lips, remembering. "Gentle but persistent all the same."

"'Twas a good thing you went straight to bed. Mum was in quite a lather though she said nothing. Won't do you any good in the morning."

"Maybe I'll be gone to Tralee in the morning," said Morrigan. Her heart leapt at hearing the words. She imagined what it would be like to simply escape with Finn.

"Tralee?"

"It's where Finn's headed to become a carpenter's mate. He says he wants to make me his bride and take me to America!"

"Ah-Merica!" Riona whispered the sacred words. She perched on her elbows to look into Morrigan's eyes. "Are you going?"

"It's too soon to know if he'll even get an apprenticeship or be able to save enough for passage. He says there is no life for him here, Ree, and I think he's right."

"Is there a life for any of us?" asked Riona.

Morrigan didn't rush to answer. In truth, she didn't know why they were so poor that Finn and many Irishmen had to set out for foreign shores in search of a better life. Here there was kinship—a fishery and farming village who watched over each other. What she really wanted was a small holding, a wee cottage by the sea away from prying eyes so she could fish and live on forest medicines. A life with Finn. Right here. Perhaps she would find a conjuring spell to get what she wanted. For now, Finn was going away. Despite the lingering memory of their kiss, a weight settled onto Morrigan. Finding Riona's hand, she squeezed hard and held fast.

A few days later, on a morning of clearing skies, Morrigan limped across the threshold in a hurry to see Finn off to Tralee. Her ankle had improved, its bruise now yellow, the swelling gone.

Betha lifted a basket off the pine cupboard. Underneath a festive red scrap of cloth lay a loaf of newly baked oatbread, with a mixture of boiled milk, honey, and seaweed slathered on top for sweetness. Betha's mouth watered. The rents were due soon, and there was scant left to barter with and little food for the family's supper. But she had made the bread for Finn, knowing he had no mum to send him on his journey.

"Give Morrie a moment with Finn, Betha. You've had her repairing nets and drying seaweed for days since Bealtaine," said Mamoh.

"How can you be so easy on her, Mum? She almost caused a scandal at Bealtaine. After all the homilies we've heard about the sin of moral weakness. A kiss is like mead—sweet to drink but bitter to pay for," said Betha.

"Finn's a good boy, not a rogue like Cormac. Anyway, give him my love," said Mamoh, as Betha hurried out the door.

"What do we know about Tralee?" asked Riona.

Keeping her eyes on the quay, Morrigan said, "Da says it's a three-day sail from here, and they've started building big merchant sailing vessels there."

"Well, it's awfully exciting to be going somewhere," said Riona, holding her arms out dramatically. Then she lifted her skirts, made a quick pirouette, and began a song of her own spontaneous creation:

> *To be going somewhere, on a journey*
> *To be going somewhere—out there*
> *To be going somewhere, stepping boldly*
> *Just trusting the winds are fair.*

Riona's arms raised, body twirling, raven curls escaping her loose bun, and blue eyes flashing unloosed something in Morrigan. Was Riona singing her impromptu song for Finn, or for her? Perhaps she sang for herself. The song was infectious, and soon Morrigan sang for all the times she had longed for freedom:

> *To be going somewhere, can you feel it?*
> *To the wild seas, heart carefree*
> *Casting aside all that is certain*
> *Glowing with possibility.*

> *Fare thee well, the time draws near*
> *Fare thee well, it's now, it's here*
> *Fare thee well, go without sorrow*
> *Fare thee well, on your passage to tomorrow!*

The Lane girls burst into laughter at their antics. Even Betha chuckled.

Was Baile Ghort na Darach a small and smothering place? A land, a sea, and a people who were "a bit wild and a bit mad," as her da had always said. "A stop on the road from nowhere to nowhere in between the desolate scree of the Burren and the heather-rich Galway bogs."

It was home, and yet, to go through the "Golden Door" to a land of fairness and abundance filled many Irish with longing. What would it feel like to set sail with Finn for America? Could she survive without her family, Cathleen, or Old Mother Oak? What about the wolf and his message, her calling? While Finn was away, she felt a clarion call to discover more, for she had nothing but questions.

"Looks to be a beam-reach to Tralee if the winds hold," said Tommy to the packet boat captain in the ageless language of sailing. He caught the dory's line and pulled it alongside the quay.

"Aye," said the captain.

"'Tis a fine day for it." Tommy cast an appreciative glance at the calm waters. "You'll have a boy on board, a Finn McDonaugh." Tommy pointed to where Finn stood near the rest of the McDonaugh men, canvas haversack over his shoulder. "He'll come to good use while you're under sail. He's got a natural hand with wood and all things mechanical, that one."

"Is that so?" said the captain looking dubious.

"'Twould seem he's too lanky for any hard work, and his easy grin hides his smarts, but we Irish have strength and tenacity beyond what the eyes can see," said Tommy.

"True it is," said the captain.

On the strand, Morrigan limped ahead of Betha and Riona, nearing Finn with a wide smile.

"There's my daughter," said Tommy. "She loves the sea as much as I do, and she can read the skies as well as any fisherman. She wants to join our fleet, but it's just not done. She'd never drown, though, being born with the caul."

The captain paused from unloading cargo bound for the village. "So she carries luck in spite of her red hair," he mused. Superstitions surrounded a baby born with a caul. Many believed the child would be protected from drowning as long as the tissue was preserved. Others thought caul-bearers had supernatural powers over water.

Tommy remained silent. Then he chuckled as he watched Morrigan. "She's hoping to catch a rare moment with her sweetheart."

"You can't blame her if he'll be gone long. I remember those days of longing for my own dearie."

"A man is incomplete until he marries," said Tommy. "After that, he's finished!" They laughed.

"Finn, you never told me how long you'll be gone," said Morrigan, leaning in so his brothers couldn't hear.

"If luck is with me, Morrie, I'll be back before you hear the bleating of the lambs next spring," said Finn.

Morrigan's face fell. All those months seemed like forever. Finn had always been a short walk away, their moments together filled with fun. "If you can, send us a post to let us know you're all right. But don't be wasting your pence on letters, Finn, if it helps you to come home all the earlier."

"Aye, Morrie, and I'll work m'self to the bone for it." Finn's gray eyes searched hers. Then he looked up and tipped his flat cap. "Good day to ya, Mrs. Lane, Riona."

"The sun shines her good fortune upon you today, Finnbharr," said Betha. "I've brought you some sweet oatbread for your journey."

"Thank you kindly, Mrs. Lane."

"Are you excited?" asked Riona.

"Aye, and sad to be leaving all at the same time. It's a bewilderment, Ree."

An urgent sound came from the two-masted brig, a long, low-pitched whistle, followed by a short, high one—a boatswain's call. Time for Finn to board. He shook hands with Tommy and gave his father and his brothers quick hugs. Then he turned to Morrigan. "You'll be needing more cowslip for under your eyes, Morrie," he joked softly. "Take good care."

"Aye, I will. And you keep out of trouble, Finn." She threw her arms around his neck, not caring one whit what her mum thought just then. She bade him Godspeed, feeling his deepened squeeze and then sudden release.

"Thanks. I've got my mother's brooch with me for luck," he said, his voice husky.

Blinking back tears, she watched him walk to the dory. It would be almost a year before she'd see him again. "Please watch over him," she prayed.

Tommy, Liam, and Ruarc went back to work while the women stayed to watch the crew row the dory through the breakers and out to the brig. Soon they viewed Finn's wiry frame as he climbed the ladder to the brig's deck.

"The boat. What's her name?" Morrigan asked Connie McDonaugh.

"She's called *Hope*."

As Finn sailed off, the McDonaugh men and the Lane women walked back to the village and their lives.

43

MORRIGAN

The Mysterious Vessel

Under brooding skies, Morrigan sat outside the Lane cottage, carding fleece and conjugating Greek verbs. She had been allowed to stay home from charity school while her ankle healed, and she loved studying in the fresh sea breeze while seagulls squawked and wheeled overhead. Her attention was caught by three decorated caravans in the distance. "The travelers, Mamoh!"

Mamoh rose from her spinning wheel. "Go tell your mum." She made haste for the caravans. The travelers were a sight to behold—festive wagons overflowing with children, beautiful women, and hardworking men and their sturdy beasts. They came to barter work or household items for food, camping in a field for a week or a fortnight and then moving on to whatever destination suited their fancy.

"Mum, the travelers are coming," said Morrigan through the open half-door.

Betha boiled potatoes at the cauldron. "Good. We'll need help with your da's fishing gear." She lifted the pot from the fire and placed it on cool stones.

As Morrigan followed her mum, she reflected on the travelers' free and simple ways. They were closer to nature's cycles than to the rest of the world. With no rent and dependent on the kindness of strangers, they seemed to understand what it meant to move at nature's pace.

Morrigan spotted Mamoh and other women cooing over wee wains and conversing with the travelers at the far caravan. Betha stood in conversation with a man and a woman at the nearest one. Reaching for what looked like a vessel of sorts, Betha suddenly shoved it back at the man. "No, not this," said Betha. Morrigan's body tingled as she glimpsed the ancient-looking vessel with umber patina and carvings.

"What's that, Mum?" she asked, approaching Betha.

"Nothing." Betha's words were rushed as she turned to walk to another caravan.

Eyes on the vessel, Morrigan stalled, watching the traveler place it on a hook alongside other objects for barter at the rear of the caravan. "Can I see it?"

"We needn't take their time. The travelers must camp before the rains come." Disappointed, Morrigan followed her.

Back at the cottage, Morrigan couldn't stop thinking about the vessel. She had a strong urge to hold it. Then, an idea. "I'll get water for supper."

Betha nodded, and Morrigan took off in earnest, buckets jangling on her arm just as rain started falling. The pathway to the open space where the caravans camped was soon saturated. Careful of her ankle, she walked around puddles of water. Something pulled her to the vessel, the same sensation she'd felt in seeing Manannán mac Lir.

The traveler peered from behind an unfurled cloth at his rear door. He gave the half-soaked young woman a measured look.

"I've come to see the old vessel my mum held," said Morrigan, prepared to square off with the man. Her stance told a story—she was more than a mere female. Of course, no one who observed her extraordinary facial scar disagreed, for it told the same story.

The man pulled at one end of his mustache, considering her request. "I'll let you hold it, and then we shall see what the powers say." He opened the curtain to let her inside.

Morrigan had no idea who or what the powers were. Nonetheless, she dropped her water buckets and pulled herself into the caravan.

She found herself in a small-scale world of habitation where practical living merged with an air of conviviality. Cooking pots, tools, stringed instruments, and woven wraps hung from nails or hooks. Two long wooden benches stretched along both sides of the space, with brightly patterned blankets, cushions, and bolsters for the little ones. A jug of wild purple orchids rested atop a diminutive chest, their sweet fragrance filling the space.

The man ushered his woman and children deeper into the caravan and pulled a saffron-colored cloth across its width. Confined in the dark, narrow space remaining, Morrigan felt afraid. "I haven't much time." She bit her lip, and edged backward to the entry curtain. Her eyes, like those of one hunted, locked onto the man's movements.

He frowned at her seeming discomfort. "Among our ways, there is no tolerance for transgression or harm." His voice, like his face, seemed weary. "'Tis a pity, the misjudgment, even from the young," he said under his breath.

"Oh." Morrigan let go of the curtain she'd been holding. She felt chastened by the man's words. From the moment she had arrived, she'd been coarse, and his eyes, like his actions, had only been kind. "I meant no harm," she said.

"I met a stranger yesterday," said the man, in a voice born for storytelling. He reached into a small wooden cabinet as he spoke. "I put food in the eating place. I put drink in the drinking place. I put music in the listening place. And the stranger blessed me and my family and my horse. And the lark sang in her song: 'Often, often, often goes the Christ in a stranger's guise.'" He unwrapped the vessel from within its makeshift holder and handed it to Morrigan.

"Thank you." This man with his simple message—any encounter was an encounter with kin—had taught her a lesson. Heart pounding, she studied the vessel, forged from bronze and several inches deep. It had a curled edge at the top and an eroded old carving: Paired spirals with snake's heads bordered either side of curved markings—a waterfall with three salmon swimming upstream—among the most powerful symbols in Irish folklore. A moon was on the wax, and a dark bird was on the wing. Though hard to see in the low light, feel it she did. As Morrigan rotated the vessel, she gasped. The glyph! The same symbol that is on her great-grandmother's dagger.

"There is another carving, of a tree, with a bear, a fox, and a boar resting under its canopy. Do you see it?"

Morrigan rotated the vessel and traced the marks with her fingers. "Aye."

"These are symbolic carvings," he whispered. "I think it's a ceremonial vessel from long ago. When you hold it, what do you feel?"

She closed her eyes. "Power, surely. But something else. Love? Joy? Oh, a rainbow of feelings—openness, and ease, and, and hope." Because the glyph matched that of her dagger, Morrigan wanted the vessel. They belonged together. "Sir, I would like to have this vessel though I don't have much to barter with. Maybe I can ask my da for some fish. And I'll help you find edible herbs and flowers. I can bring you water each day, and my sister, Riona, has a skilled hand at crewel…"

The man placed one roughened hand under hers as they held the vessel. Morrigan stopped talking. "Take it. Since my boy found it at an old yew grove northaways of here, it has brought only disquiet to my eyes, and to the eyes of everyone else who has held it, except for you."

"An old yew grove?" Was it the ancient forest where she'd learned about the triad? Now she knew the vessel was meant for her. "You mean I can have it?"

"Aye. It would please me if you found with it what you seek."

Morrigan held the vessel to her heart and said, "Oh, thank you. I won't forget you or your kindness."

She left the caravan on the showery late afternoon, raindrops on her face like a jubilant baptism. In coming to the traveler, she had followed her inner urgings. She had little doubt the vessel was tied to her destiny. She picked up the water buckets and headed to the well. The traveler's voice lingered in her mind: "Often, often, often goes the Christ in a stranger's guise."

44

SIR MARTIN

A Wicked Eagerness

Sir Martin heard a knock at his library door, and in filed his footman, followed by three agents, serious and sullen.

"Your agents, Sir Martin," said the footman. They tipped their bowlers and shifted from foot to foot awaiting his instructions.

"Lads, you've had to wait a bit, I know," said Martin. "Today we collect the rents. I must be informed if there are any among the villagers who cannot pay. We will evict them immediately."

"Aye," said the largest man, Itchy-Fingers Muldoon, a brute who had survived two shipwrecks and won countless duels. "Sir, we should remind the villagers the reprieve this year is not to be expected next year."

Sir Martin frowned at Muldoon's audacity in telling him what to do. Hadn't he provided these agents with jobs for years? The man was signaling that he would not tolerate such a delay again since their pay was tied to the rents. It had been bad enough he had had to wait for the rents himself, but so had they. Martin stroked his chin. In truth, he needed them. "All right," he said. "Remind the villagers it is by my generosity they are tenants." Glancing at the stately portrait of his father on the wall across the room, he reminded himself he was, after all, the son of Thomas Martin, a wealthy and distinguished landowner. He stood just as regally as his father appeared in the painting, and said, "As a Member of Parliament, I will not sanction outright violence."

"Aye, Sir!" the three replied in unison and retreated. Their expressions bore a wicked eagerness for which he had no appetite.

45

MORRIGAN

The Agents' Revenge

Despite darkening skies, Morrigan's steps were unhurried as she walked toward McDonaugh's Pub. Her ankle was well enough to deliver fish again, and she was content with the task. It kept her from worrying about the mysterious vessel now in her possession and about Finn, who had been gone only a few days. Out in the bay, the sea's waters were choppy. She imagined Finn aboard *Hope*. She smiled at the ship's name, hoping *Hope* handled well in rough seas.

The Lanes had sold all their dried seaweed at yesterday's fair. Morrigan recalled an image of her mum afterward. Betha had smoked her dúidín, a dreamy smile on her face, as happy as Morrigan had ever seen her.

Morrigan's reverie was interrupted by a shout. "There's the one who done it!" Three men surged toward her, carrying satchels. They had crazed smiles on their faces. Agents!

She recognized the biggest one, Muldoon, often hired by landowners to carry out evictions. All evictions were cruel, but his bordered on viciousness.

Her heart pounding, Morrigan glanced around. She was alone. Her instincts told her there would be trouble. "Run!" her body screamed. But her ankle lacked strength, and she was impeded by the fish basket across her shoulders. She bit her lip, willing herself to stay calm. She cursed under her breath. She'd left her dagger at home in the bottom of the creel basket. Suddenly, they were upon her. She stepped aside. They weren't passing.

"So, this is the little witch who delayed us our money," said a slight man with eyes like a mouse.

"Aye, her ugly scar gives her away," said Muldoon. Snarling, he reached toward Morrigan, who raised her arms to deflect his hand, her shout cut short by his strong grip on her jaw. He squeezed hard.

Eyes panicked, Morrigan clutched his wrist. He leaned in, his pockmarked face a hair's breadth away. "The village heroine," he leered. He smelled like whiskey and rotted gums.

Swallowing an impulse to vomit, Morrigan made a fierce sound from the back of her throat and turned into a wild thing, kicking the agent in the shin and raking her fingernails across his arm. The other agents jeered.

"You little devil!" Muldoon glared. He threw her to the ground. She landed on her fish basket. *Can't breathe.* She fought to pull air into her lungs. Muldoon came closer, his eyes glittering. "You need a lesson in keeping to your peasant station." He pulled her up by her red curls.

Hands on her head, Morrigan uttered a cry of pain, "Please. Let me go." Muldoon grabbed her arms and pinned them behind her back. "I've got her now." Turning to an agent, he cried, "Tommy, bring me yer knife so I can scar the other side of 'er face."

The man laughed but hesitated. "Sir Martin said…"

"Bugger Sir Martin. Stop fighting, girl, or I'll break your arms, too."

"Cabhrú! Cabhrú!" shouted Morrigan, the Irish cry for help. A hand came over her mouth and clamped down with brutal force. In the seconds that followed, Morrigan observed herself as though from a distance—her eyes wide and panicked; her feeble kicks at Muldoon who stood behind her; her arms pinned and unmoving, muscles straining from their unnatural position; the metal taste of blood filling her mouth. She saw white caps on the water against a leaden sky. A fleeting thought: *Hope* is sailing to Tralee. Finn is gone.

"Leave her alone, Muldoon!" roared Cormac McDonaugh. He stood behind the men with a large limestone rock raised in the air.

Muldoon swiveled and yelled, "Get 'im, lads!" In a brief moment, his grip lessened. Morrigan exploded sideways and scrambled away.

Cormac cracked the rock on the head of the small man, who collapsed amid the debris. Muldoon and the other rushed him.

"Cabhrú! Cabhrú!" Morrigan returned to her cry for help. She needed a weapon, and clawed the trackway for a stone. It wasn't working. The sound of fists landing on bones and skin filled her ears. Desperate, Morrigan scooped up road dust and took in the sight.

The smallest agent was coming back to consciousness, while a second was on one knee clutching his belly from a blow. Cormac bled from his nose as he and Muldoon squared off like fighters in a ring.

Muldoon cocked his arm to land another blow. With a fierce cry, Morrigan ran at him and threw a cloud of dust into his face.

Muldoon coughed and spat, rubbing his eyes.

Just then Connie McDonaugh, James, and two others from the village raced toward them and grabbed the men. "It's bad enough you axed one of my whiskey barrels, Muldoon," said Connie. "Don't kill our son as well." He used the word *our*, for Kate was so much a part of him as to be right there with him at the crunch in the situation.

Muldoon spit out a tooth as he shook off the men who held him. Cradling his sore fist, he growled, "You'll have no more reprieves."

Then he helped his fellow agents to their feet. James ushered a staggering, bloody-nosed Cormac toward home.

Connie put his arms on Morrigan's shoulders to steady her. One villager picked up her broken fish basket, while another retrieved fish strewn in clumps where Morrigan had fallen. Connie spotted her shawl on the ground, and following a motion of his head, a man went to retrieve it. "Are you all right, Morrie?"

She nodded, but her eyes seemed vacant; she'd gone somewhere.

Connie and the others salvaged as many fish as they could and deposited them into the broken basket. He lifted it, carrying it as he would a young lamb. "Tell your da I'll use whatever fish parts I can for a stew, and not to worry. I'll send James back with the basket in the morning. It was a stroke of luck that Cormac was out breaking stones and heard you." Worry deepened the lines in his face. "Can you make it home, Morrie?"

"Aye." She began a slow walk toward home, and then turned back to Connie and the village men. "'Tis thanks I owe you," she said, her voice like dried leaves skittering across a frozen moor.

46

SCHOOLMASTER WINNETT

A Dark Fascination

Schoolmaster Winnett rode his sturdy donkey away from the school. The Archbishop of Tuam had given him permission to use the donkey until a new priest replaced Father Murray. He winced at the priest's name in his head, but he no longer heard the voice of conscience that had once protested his cowardice in watching Father Murray die. Still, he feared his inaction would one day be exposed.

To curry favor among the villagers, he had taken to riding around as temporary shepherd of Saint Joseph's, offering counsel to whoever might need it. He'd reveled in his expanded duties and the greater esteem shown him by his flock, as he now thought of them.

Winnett's attention was drawn by an odd sight outside the pub. A barrel of whiskey lay on its side with a deep gash spewing amber contents onto the trackway. Cook Enya worked with a kitchen maid, shoving towels into the break in a vain attempt to stop the flow. How odd, he thought. Then: what would it be like to suck on one of those towels? An image surfaced of his father, leering with rage after a night of drinking. As a boy, he had hidden underneath his bed when his father had become mean. Not for me, he reminded himself. When he drank whiskey, he became his father, and though there was something in it that felt like home, Winnett had disciplined himself to break the cycle of abuse and avoid whiskey. Most times it worked.

Someone had mutilated that barrel. He made a *click-click* sound, and the donkey picked up its pace. "Cook Enya? What's happened?" yelled Winnett.

"Good day, Schoolmaster Winnett. The agents slashed it," said Enya. Her apron was stained, and a sweet smoky aroma surrounded her.

"Why?"

"None too pleased about the delay in rents. As Muldoon axed the barrel, he shouted, 'Never again!'" She made a sound like disgust in her throat and lowered herself to her task.

Winnett looked out along the trackway and spotted James, assisting an injured Cormac. Then he spied Morrigan, surrounded by Connie McDonaugh and some others, and further on, the agents, walking toward the fishermen's cottages. The agents had clashed with Cormac, and perhaps the Lane's youngest daughter, too.

Fear clutched Winnett's heart. How to respond? Should he try to stop the agents? It was his flock they had attacked. He tried to summon up outrage. But it was also not his business, he reminded himself. He was a temporary stand-in for a priest. The agents, after all, had been sent by Sir Martin, and he could not risk opposing the landowner. "They're exacting revenge for Morrigan's unholy charm against Sir Martin," he muttered to himself, feeling a grim satisfaction at the idea of Morrigan learning her lesson. Perhaps now she'd cease her devil's arts.

A dark fascination overtook him. At a distance, he followed the agents, watching them harass the villagers, collect the rents, and then ransack their possessions. When the agents left the hamlet bound for inland farms, Winnett approached them. An idea had formed in his mind. Weren't their actions a form of justice? Through them, he'd seek some justice of his own. His heart pounded as he approached the bruiser, Muldoon.

"God be with you on this dreary day, gentlemen. I see you are about Sir Martin's work," his voice squeaked.

"Aye, and you'd better stay out of it, Winnett," growled Muldoon, omitting the schoolmaster's title. The three agents surrounded Winnett on his donkey.

Winnett swallowed his panic and tugged on the reins to make the donkey back up, but it stood still. It had never taken to backing up, a blind move for an animal. "Oh, no, of course not. I just wanted to remind you about The Crooked Woman's abode just beyond the village. She…" he stumbled on a reason for his suggestion. "She taught Morrigan Lane to put a charm on Sir Martin," he said in a rush.

Muldoon looked into Winnett's eyes, as if assessing him. "We forget no one this day, teacher," he said in a contemptuous tone. "And you'd better take this beast home before I decide to ride it. Good and hard." He gave the donkey a vicious slap on its hindquarters, and it took off, with Winnett bouncing on it like a flea on a dog.

As drops of rain began to spatter his clothes, a shaken Winnett rode home, murmuring words from *Romans*, which seemed deeply comforting, "For the one in authority is God's servant for your good. But if you do wrong, be afraid, for rulers do not bear the sword for no reason. They are God's servants, agents of wrath to bring punishment on the wrongdoer."

47

MORRIGAN

Danger of the Calling

That night a persistent rain fell. Tommy had placed a sod of turf over the door to signal *good liquor within*, as was customary in troubling times. The Lanes' cottage bustled with visits from hard-bitten fishermen, each one describing the small, mean deeds done to him or his possessions by Muldoon and his fellow agents. They'd heard about shattered windows, smashed wagons, and tenants upended in their own dung heaps. Cormac had suffered a broken nose in the altercation.

Perched on a rung halfway up the ladder to her bed, Morrigan had a bruise forming on both sides of her jaw, torn fingernails, aching arms, and a sore hip from her fall. She wanted to be invisible.

"Tommy, God love ya, it's the whiskey I want," said Uncle Colm, as he entered.

"Aye, Colm. We're needing the steadier this night," said Tommy, sliding the bottle toward him.

Betha leaned in from her bench by the hearth, gave Tommy a pointed look, and said, "You've had enough steadying, Tommy." He had already shared the whiskey with four others.

"Betha, don't get huffed. Colm needs company, isn't it so, Colm?" said Tommy.

"Aw, now don't go getting me involved in it, Tommy. A man knows not to counter another man's wife," said Colm. Nevertheless, he reached over and poured Tommy a nip. They drank silently. "One of O'Malley's young'uns might lose an eye, have ya heard?"

"Aye, a shard of broken glass. Lord willing it'll heal." Tommy ran his hand through his hair. "By God, they think they can do this to us at every clang o' the town clock!" His voice told the story of the powerless and poor Irish. These injustices, or worse ones, were commonplace, and there was not a whit to be done about it. They were the guilty ones. Guilty of being born poor. Tommy's glass made a loud *whumph* as he banged it on the pine cupboard.

Colm nodded. Close to the turf coals, the kettle sang. To Morrigan's ears, it was a lament. As each visitor had shared his ill-fated news, Morrigan had withdrawn further and further into herself, sickened with shame.

Violence had descended upon the village. Violence Morrigan believed she had caused. Had she done the right thing in convincing Sir Martin to postpone the due date of the rents? Though it had kept some from certain eviction, a chorus of accusations ran through her. Soon, Uncle Colm said what had been on the minds of many.

"I wonder, Morrigan, whether it was proper for you to speak on behalf of the village. Look what's come upon us now? Our reprieve has made things worse," he said, shaking his head.

"That's enough, Colm. Time to go," said Tommy, and with some forcefulness, shoved his younger brother out the door.

With an aggrieved heart, Morrigan climbed to bed. She heard the door slam behind Uncle Colm. She heard her mum serving a round of tea. The yeasty aroma of warming stirabout made her stomach growl, but she did not move from the pallet.

How could she face the families of the village in the coming days? She'd been tasked with healing the cords of connection, and instead, the village suffered discord and destruction. She'd tried her best to speak out on their behalf, but like a counter-charm, it had come back on her. Perhaps her calling came with danger. Perhaps not all people wanted her in the role of healer.

"Morrie, come for some tea and stirabout," said Betha.

"No thanks, Mum." Betha tsked as Tommy climbed the ladder. Leaning into the shallow space under the eaves, he held out a small glass. "Take this, Morrie. 'Twill help you sleep."

She smelled whiskey vapors on her da's breath. "Are ya daft?"

"Go on. Drink it in one quick swallow. It'll warm you. 'Tis a night for it." He pushed the glass toward his youngest, his lined face a carving of worry.

She reached for the glass and drank it. Distilled whiskey burned her throat, and soon, she felt its warmth flooding her chest. It was not an unpleasant feeling.

"There's my girl," said Tommy, his voice husky and his weather-raw hand gentle. He patted her head as though she were a skittish colt. Morrigan's mind began to peel away from his soft words. "We Irish live like the tree in Job 14:7, 'For there is hope for a tree, if it is cut down, that it will sprout again, and its tender branch will not cease.' It's not your fault, Morrie. Now don't you be thinking it is."

"Yes, Da," she answered from a faraway place. Muscles in her body that had held tension for hours finally relaxed. She was being carried like a leaf on a river, swirling in an eddy, and then, she was only the water, fluid and unconstrained.

She was not awake to hear Tommy descend the creaky ladder or the family's low tones as they finished the stirabout. She was not awake to hear Riona beg Mamoh, "Toss the cups for us, Mamoh!" She was not awake to see Mamoh nod and enact the old way of divining the future—the way her mother had done for her islanders, and her mother before her.

Mamoh gave a teacup a particular twist anti-clockwise in the left hand three times, and placed it mouth down on the saucer to remove the dregs. Then with ceremony, she lifted it up to examine the tea leaves as they were strewn hieroglyphically along the inside. All heads save Betha's strained to peer into the cup. Mamoh's voice, trancelike, said, "There's a ship going across the sea, and I see a girl carrying a letter in her hand. There's something—following the ship."

"What something?" asked Riona.

"Sea Sirens, up from the deep!" said Ruarc.

"Hush, Ru!" said Riona. Mamoh seemed not to know or was unwilling to share.

"That's enough nonsense," said Betha. She took the cup from her mother, taking a quick peek inside. Then she shook her head, and dropped it into the rinse water, breaking Mamoh's trance.

"You'll have some repairs to do on Morrie's fish basket, Ruarc," said Tommy.

"Aye, Da."

"Surely others will be needing our help." Somber heads nodded, as they moved toward their beds.

With the help of the whiskey, Morrigan was sound asleep.

48

MORRIGAN

The Sea Turtle's Revelation

Morrigan dreamed she swam with the current, searching for something. The moonlight first revealed and then concealed an object that lay beneath the fathomless waters. She took a deep breath and dove down toward the ocean's lightless bottom. A hulking sea turtle glided by. Its hundred-year-old eyes blinked and said, "You know more than you think you know." Morrigan dove deeper, fighting buoyancy, trying to remain calm under increasing pressure from the sea, from her lungs. Just there! She scarcely made out the object half buried in the silt. As she reached for it, her lungs screamed for air. She grasped it just as her lungs burst. Her eyes shattered like porcelain, and there was a sound. One true note so full there was nothing else but the sound.

Morrigan awoke from the dream, and like many, this one lingered. She made a fist with her hand, wondering what she'd reached for and what the turtle's message meant. Trying to understand the message was like looking into a mirror and glimpsing something just beyond her reflection, beyond her normal way of seeing. Did the message imply she possessed some inner wisdom about her calling to heal the village? The raven had told her she had to learn how to ask for guidance. She had received clues from conversations with Cathleen, instructions from the wolf, encouragement from Manannán mac Lir, and a mysterious voice commanding her to find a triad. Now this message from an ancient turtle in a dream. The clues seemed to point to a vast interconnectedness and a need for deeper listening to some inner knowing in order to help and heal others. Though they filled her with awe, the clues also weighed her down like stones in a pocket.

Moving, she winced, sore all over from her encounter with the agents. A thought: Cathleen! Morrigan hadn't heard about Cathleen's fate at the hands of the agents. She'd been so distraught to hear about Lettie O'Malley and Cormac, she'd forgotten about Cathleen. "Ree!" Morrigan shook her sister awake. "I'm going to check on Cathleen, make sure she's all right."

"I'll tell Mum," said Riona in a sleepy voice. Ever since Morrigan's disappearance and sprained ankle, Betha had required her wayward daughter to report to a family member wherever she was headed. Morrigan slipped from the house.

Early dawn air smelled damp with the vestiges of yesterday's rains. The fishermen's hamlet suddenly felt unsafe. It was Sunday; none of the fishermen were out. She did not want to face the villagers so soon after the agents' vindictive deeds. But there would be Mass at eleven, and she'd have to face them. Would Schoolmaster Winnett mention the agents' evil deeds at church? A man who craved power would no doubt say little against Sir Martin.

She looked toward the white-washed cottages in the distance, each clinging to its own green hillside. Away from here, she thought, and it struck her why Cathleen had set her cottage outside of town. Hurrying, her mind returned to the disaster she called *yesterday*. How would she thank Cormac for his help? She supposed she'd beetle his bloody clothes, a scrubbing chore her sore body would find painful. I'll bake Lettie O'Malley's family an oatbread, she thought, groaning as her imagination conjured a grotesque image of Lettie without an eye.

As she neared the stone circle, a narrow plume of smoke rose against a salmon sky. Was Cathleen's cottage in ruins? Cathleen herself burned in the fire?

At the top of the rise, Morrigan spotted Cathleen wrapped in her usual sky-blue scarf and skirts. The cottage sat as it always had, a beacon for lost souls. "Thank the good Lord!" said Morrigan, rushing to the tidy, whitewashed abode where a small pyre burned atop a naturally hollowed stone near the cottage.

"Cathleen, it's me."

"Storm clouds, like sinister flocks of raptors, have come and gone," said Cathleen. She placed bundles of herbs atop the fire.

"Are you all right?"

"Aye."

"Have you heard about the village?" Morrigan squatted down so Cathleen could see her. "That agent Muldoon attacked me and said he would make a cut in the other side of my face. If it weren't for Cormac, I—I might have been truly harmed."

Cathleen put a hand on the girl's shoulder. "Though I can see you were not truly harmed."

Morrigan shook her head, no.

"If you focus on what could have happened instead of what is real and true in front of you, you'll forever be enslaved by your fears."

Morrigan considered these words, but her wounds were raw, too fresh for her mentor's philosophies. "You weren't there, Cathleen."

"I see." Cathleen's soothing voice was the one she used for newborns, shocked into the world.

As she added more herbs to the flame, Morrigan asked, "Why are you burning your herbs?"

"There's no delicate way to tell ya. Those men directed streams of their yellow poison piss onto my racks."

"Your medicines, Cathleen!" The Crooked Woman's healing remedies were her livelihood, used to barter for barley, goat's milk, duck's eggs, the occasional mutton, as well as much-needed shillings.

"Not all of them, just those drying outside. No matter, I'll replenish. I've decided to burn them to purify the air and calm my disquiet."

Morrigan moved to the far rack to transport herb bundles, their fragrances following along like reluctant children.

"Thank you, child. Now I must make haste, for Sean O'Hare came to tell me about Lettie O'Malley."

"Her eye," said Morrigan, looking down. She remembered her father's words about the gross injustice villagers endured as a matter of course. She longed for a judgment day for the agents. A time Father Murray had often spoken about.

"I'm told Doc O'Brien removed the shard. I'll try a combination of fresh red seaweed and sea buckthorn to help keep her sight from being lost."

"I'll go with you, Cathleen. I've caused this lot of bad fortune."

"Morrigan, it's true storm clouds come, but they also go. Don't let this situation deter you from what you've been called to do. I daresay it makes your destiny more urgent."

Morrigan hadn't thought of it the way Cathleen had. If the rents hadn't been delayed, there might have been evictions, and The Ribbonmen might have caused violence in the process. As it was, the agents had caused the violence. Either way, the village was not in harmony and needed healing.

"You're right, Cathleen. Anyway, I don't have a choice, do I?"

"There is choice in any life, no matter how confined one might feel." Cathleen placed the last bundle on the fire. In silence, they watched it burn. A sweet, woodsy smell surrounded them. "Come along, Morrigan. We'll collect some sea medicines."

As they made their way to the cliff road in the direction of the strand, Cathleen explained, "Sea buckthorn is found at the verge of cliff and strand. Look for bright orange berries and clumps of silver-leafed bushes. We need a half basketful of each. A climb might be in order."

"Aye." said Morrigan, already searching where the sand rose away to become cliff. "I think I see some!"

"Ouch! They've got thorns!" shouted Morrigan, after having scaled the side of the cliff.

"Ah, yes, mind the thorns."

"Thanks."

Cathleen walked toward something farther along the strand while Morrigan returned to her task and soon had what she needed.

Approaching her mentor, Morrigan froze. An object stuck out of the sand. She let the basket slip from her hands.

"Whatever it is, it is powerful, Morrigan. Can you feel it?" said Cathleen. With her hazelwood stick she'd carved a circle around the object in the sand.

"I had a dream in which a turtle told me I know more than I think I know, and I reached for something that looked like this at the sea bottom." Morrigan knelt and removed sand to reveal what appeared to be a bone. Her hands pulsed as she reached for the object.

Cathleen chanted something in a low voice.

Morrigan held a narrow, oyster-colored shaft. It had a small ball head at one end with a rectangular hole at the other. Five tiny, circular holes ran along the shaft to a sawed-off, hollowed end.

"Is it some kind of wind instrument?" asked Morrigan.

"'Tis a bone, made into a flute, too small to be a deer bone, too big to be a hare bone, perhaps a fox femur. Looks to be quite old," said Cathleen.

Morrigan turned the object over in her hands. "The symbol. It's the same as on Isla's dagger and the vessel I got from the traveler!" She looked again at the looped, circular pattern carved into the flute on the side opposite the holes. "How can this be, Cathleen? Who put it here?" Morrigan assessed their surroundings. A cool ocean breeze quickened, scattering low clouds into floating puffs of islands. Piper shore birds pitter-pattered their way along the strand in search of edible creatures. Otherwise, they were alone.

"I don't know, though I sense it was meant for you. It's wet but nevertheless, blow into it. See what happens."

Morrigan held the bone flute to her mouth, recalling how Mr. O'Hare held his flute on Sunday evenings at McDonaugh's Pub—off to the side, right hand at the far end, left closer in, fingers covering the holes, mouth puckered over the end hole. She directed a stream of air downward over the hole. *Pfff. Pfff. Pfff.* "Nothing. Nothing that sounds like a note, anyway."

Positioning her fingers along the bone, Morrigan tried again. A water-logged note sounded. She felt chills. Notes seemed trapped within the flute, wanting to escape, waiting for their waves of sound to find the tiny hairs of an ear drum willing to hear another melody, the one just below the surface of everyday conversation.

Morrigan had experienced moments of keen awareness like this ever since she'd spoken to the wolf in The Once-and-Only Language. Tremors of truth, they'd held certainty, though she had no control over when they occurred. But she'd begun to trust them, just as she'd *known* she had to see the vessel in the traveler's possession.

Just as she'd realized if the Druid-seers of the past were highly educated, then she, too, must learn everything possible. Tommy's story about Gráinne's education had changed Morrigan's attitude toward charity school despite the fact Schoolmaster Winnett treated her new interest with mistrust.

"Take the flute home, Morrigan. Immerse it in water from the holy well at Craobhach Dearg to remove the sand and restore its purity, then let it dry in the sun. Be gentle with it. Not a toy to be passed around."

Morrigan nodded. She couldn't shake the image of the flute as a drawn bow ready to release its notes. She caressed the carved symbol. Her mouth flew open as an idea dawned. "Cathleen, this flute must be the third piece in the triad. The voice in the yew grove told me, 'a triad to be perceived.' I have my great-grandmother's dagger, the vessel from the traveler, and now this flute. I wonder if they all once belonged to Isla, and if so, how they got separated? And what do I do with them?"

"A dagger, a ceremonial vessel, and a flute together hold the possibility for healing, isn't it so? And it seems you haven't had to search for them as much as avail yourself to them," said Cathleen. "Perhaps as your understanding of your destiny grows, you will soon know what to do with your triad."

"Oh! I remember a second part of the message: '...and the one will be received,'" said Morrigan. "How can I find *the one?*"

"Send your thoughts out in all directions as an invitation. 'I am ready,' you say. Then, be alert like a deer. Trust there will be an opening. Power is unleashed into the realm of infinite possibility when you do so," said Cathleen.

Morrigan turned in a slow circle, sending a silent invitation outward. She imagined it traveled to the sun, moon, and stars. Trust *the one*, she told herself.

Together, student and mentor, healers both, made their way toward the village.

49

MORRIGAN

I'm Curious

Schoolmaster Winnett rapped the slate tablet where he had written a Greek phrase. "Who can pronounce this phrase?" From her seat in the back of the crowded room, Morrigan raised her hand. Winnett made a sound through his lips and ignored her. "Who *else*?" he muttered. "Ah, Riona! Give it a try then."

Morrigan lowered her hand, as her sister stumbled through the foreign phrase. Once Morrigan had committed to learning Greek, the letter combinations and their sounds came easily to her.

"Now who can tell me what the phrase means?" asked Winnett.

Morrigan shouted, "In the beginning was the Word. John, Chapter One, Verse One."

"Morrigan Lane, I will not tolerate unruly outbursts here," said Winnett.

"Yes, Schoolmaster Winnett." Then Morrigan raised her hand. "I'm curious, Schoolmaster. You told us the Bible was first translated from Hebrew into Greek. The Greek word for word—λόγος—is masculine. Is that why we think of God as a he? I know Jesus was a man, but do we really know if God is a man?"

Winnett's face reddened. "Go!" he said, pointing toward the door.

"I just wondered." Amid the titters of her fellow advanced students and an exasperated headshake from Riona, Morrigan lifted her head, smiled broadly, and left.

It was a logical question. Morrigan kicked a stone. She'd become fascinated with Greek mythology, which had as many goddesses as gods, as had old Ireland. If there was now only *one* god, why did everyone presume he was masculine?

Recent experiences had changed her views about who held the knowledge and where wisdom had come from. It was reassuring to consider there were spirit allies—both male and female—all around her, as the messages she had received had indicated. She vowed to continue learning Latin and Greek from Schoolmaster Winnett, though she felt a strong dislike for the man and his suffocating views.

Cormac appeared before her. "Morrie! We've had a letter from Finn. Da hasn't opened it. He wanted you there."

They hurried the short distance to the pub, matching stride for stride. "Seems your limp is gone, Ug-M...Morrigan," said Cormac, his voice softened at the use of her real name.

Morrigan raised an eyebrow at his new refinement. "And your nose is healed well all right," she said.

"The slight bump only adds to me charms," said Cormac with a wink, tipping his flat cap at wildflowers growing along the track as though they were clusters of young women.

Morrigan rolled her eyes though it was true. Cormac's stature had grown from dubious rogue to esteemed hero as word had spread about his fight with the agents.

50

CONNIE

The Letter

Connie McDonaugh stood outside the pub shielding his eyes from the brightness. He scanned the trackway. Morrigan and Cormac headed his way. "Good!"

Back in the kitchen, he hoisted the cast iron kettle filled with colcannon away from the flames and grabbed the letter from Finn off the cupboard.

Surrounded by Cormac, James, Morrie, and other villagers, Connie slid a thin sheaf of paper from a homemade envelope and, for once grateful he had learned to read English, began: "Dear Da, and all, I've had to go even farther away, to Cork, beyond Tralee. But I got a job as a laborer at the quay, and soon, I hope, as a carpenter's mate. I passed the apprentice test. It was all those maths contests that did it, Morrie!

"The lads at Mrs. O'Mahoney's Boarding Home are from all over. Some with such funny accents I can scarcely understand them. We start work at the docks at half four, get a break at eleven, finish at half five, and then go to O'Mahoney's pub next door for supper."

Connie paused as Tommy rushed into the pub.

"…a letter from Finn," Cormac whispered. Tommy walked toward Morrigan—a waft of briny fish slightly on the turn clung to him. Placing his arms around his daughter's shoulders, he leaned in. "The packet man told me there was a letter," he whispered. Morrigan smiled a greeting even as she wrinkled her nose at his pungency. She'd grown used to the smell.

Connie continued reading. "Mrs. O'Mahoney says I've got the carver's sight. She's hired me to carve a new sign for the pub. She watches me work, and it puts a twinkle in her eyes. She says the carving will keep me out of trouble.

"I hope you are all keeping well. And ever to you, Miss Morrie. I think of you all in my lonesome hours. Your affectionate son, brother, and friend. Finn."

As the group conversed about the news, Connie leaned back against the bar, taking a deep breath, a lump in his throat. He longed for his beloved Kate. "Finn's making his way, not lured by the devil's hand to gaming or whoring. You'd be proud of him, Kate, as I am." Sadness laced Connie's words. "He'll be off to America before this time next year."

"Well, dearie, it's the best thing for him after all," said Kate, strong and certain in Connie's mind. He shook his head, stood, and poured himself a pint with shaking hands and a heavy heart. "I know it's what I'm to hope for, but 'twould break my heart to lose our Finn, he of your own sparkling spirit, Kate."

"Now, Connie, don't you be getting all sentimental." Connie glimpsed a mirage of his dead wife at the other end of the bar, waving a tea towel with merry eyes. Then he blinked, and she was gone.

"Good news, isn't it, Mr. McDonaugh?" said Morrigan.

"Aye, but he's a long way away in Cork."

"True, it is. I miss him, but it's good Finn found work."

"A great turn of fortune."

"Thank you for waiting to read the letter, Mr. McDonaugh."

"Ah, you know how he feels about you."

Morrigan gave him a hug and left the pub.

"She's a good girl, that one, Kate." In his mind he heard, "She's grand."

51

MORRIGAN

Mistress Mary's Summons

Although Riona had tattled about Morrigan's banishment from Winnett's schoolroom, Betha used her influence after church on Sunday, and soon, a reluctant Schoolmaster Winnett had allowed Morrigan to return to master's school. She sat on a hard bench in the far back corner of the room, where Winnett had taken to ignoring her, though on occasion he'd surprise her with a question. She knew the answers, but staying focused was agonizing. Was it possible she had a better grasp of Greek now than he did? She was every bit as advanced in maths, though she struggled with reciting Shakespearean sonnets by rote. That's where Riona, full of dramatic flair, shined, and Winnett had taken to more memorization lessons as a result.

As Riona stood, reciting a passage from scripture, Morrigan willed her restless legs still. This afternoon, she planned to try out the bone flute.

Under a sapphire sky dabbed here and there with fists of clouds, Morrigan picked her way along the outskirts of the village, past hedge bedstraw with its rambling blankets of ivory flowers, beyond banks of fox-and-cubs, with their clusters of orange flower heads, and into the darkened woodland.

Arriving at Old Mother Oak, her canopy thick with summer's growth felt like visiting a dear friend. Morrigan gave the tree a silent salutation, touching its rough trunk. She directed her attention to the palm of her hand, listening for something like a heartbeat. Words came to her, "Give us this day our daily bread." The tree gave her peace of mind, like a kind of daily bread. In gratitude, she gently kissed its trunk and wriggled to her usual spot against it. She withdrew the flute, caressing the looped glyph, as if to discern its meaning.

Putting the flute to her lips, Morrigan readied herself for an exploration. Though she didn't know how to play a flute, she hoped if she expressed reverence and sent out a silent invitation to receive guidance, her hands would move of their own accord. Blowing through the flute, she moved her fingers in various positions along the length of it. She'd know the right sound when she heard it. Finally, placing her ring finger on the third hole from the top, she blew. A low bass note emerged with a mysterious vitality. She repeated the note. "Yes!" There was something about it. She tried other hand positions, each note sounding dull and somehow *off* in comparison.

She sat still, remembering she was in the very place the wolf had spoken to her using The Once-and-Only Language, the place where her life had shifted in an instant toward some undetermined destiny. She listened. A world of sounds came at her. Breezes gusted through the boughs of the oak, a flying insect buzzed into and out of her awareness, a field mouse, perhaps, rustled through the undergrowth, and farther in the distance, a thrush sang melodious notes. Focusing on the thrush's melody, one high note seemed to ring truer than all the others. She remembered Cathleen's words: "Everything is here to teach us." Morrigan asked her hands to find the place on the flute where the thrush's note could be found. Instinctively, they moved to a new position, and she blew.

"Hooooough," the note rang out, sounding like the thrush.

Astonished, she opened her eyes and memorized her hand position. "I've got two notes, Old Mother Oak!" she said, patting the oak's roots. She then played the notes in succession over and over until her hands moved automatically: "Mmmmmm, Hooooough."

Yet something told her the sequence was not complete. She tried the higher note first. "Hooooough, Mmmmmm," but it didn't sound right. She returned to the original pattern and continued to listen and experiment.

Fighting disappointment, she lowered the flute onto her lap. "Helpers visible and invisible," she whispered. The word *God* seemed somehow not large enough. Then she squared her shoulders, lifted her head to the skies and said, "God, ancestors, Isla, spirits of The Otherworld, I ask you to please consider my request. Please show me what to do with the triad. I'll be here at nature's pace, listening and waiting." With a renewed sense all would be revealed in its time, Morrigan rested her head against the oak and closed her eyes.

An explosion of sound interrupted her reverie. Something plunged through the forest. Morrigan stood just as Shauna appeared, a lead rope around her neck. Mr. Eagan held it, his pudgy face flushed.

"There you are," said Mr. Eagan. "Was sure the pig would find you."

"A good day to you, Mr. Eagan." Morrigan slipped the flute into the pocket of her skirt, gave Shauna a pat to calm her squeals, and raised her eyebrows in inquiry.

The overseer seemed ill at ease. Their encounters until now had been altercations. "It's the Mistress. Illness is upon her." He turned in the direction of the estate. "Doctor's been to her." His eyes locked onto hers, as misgivings turned his expression stern. "Seems she's asking for you."

52

MORRIGAN

The Trouble with Mary

"**M**istress Mary's asking for me?" Morrigan considered for a moment. "I'll go to her straight away." Moving toward the estate, she stopped. "Does Sir Martin know about this?" She was not eager to see him after his agents' abuse.

"He's aware she's been asking for ya, but not that I've come." Mr. Eagan looked skyward, his face a struggle of emotions.

"What are you expecting me to do? Go to the door, fancy as you please, and say, 'I'm here to see about Mistress Mary?'" Morrigan couldn't help keeping the irritation from her voice.

"I thought to take you up the servants' staircase. Just to see her," he said, shuffling his feet.

"Oh. All right. I'll go."

At the back entrance to Rosderry Manor, Mr. Eagan held out his arm to stop her. Heart thudding, Morrigan stopped. The overseer ducked inside. With a glance behind her—no one was working in the gardens—Morrigan considered sneaking away. She heard a few low words from Eagan, followed by the hiss of a woman's response.

With a quick motion, Eagan ushered Morrigan inside the kitchen, a massive space filled with hanging copper pots, a wall of cupboards, and a marble carving block the size of her pallet. A cook stood with her back to them wearing a crisp white, full-bib apron. She stirred something in a kettle, its savory aroma filling the room. Morrigan clutched her belly as her stomach groaned in hunger.

The overseer gestured toward a swing-door close by, and Morrigan tore herself away from the tantalizing smell and slipped through it. A narrow hallway led them past several wide, decorated doors. She followed Mr. Eagan, maintaining a hair's breadth distance away until they came to a wooden staircase. As she ascended, Morrigan relaxed. By the spareness of the walls, she knew they were on the servants' stairs. Soon they emerged onto a landing where ornately framed portraits lined the walls—of men astride great steeds surrounded by wolf hounds, and women nestled on wool blankets underneath shady groves. Morrigan felt overwhelmed by the opulence.

Mr. Eagan stopped in front of a door with carved flower panels, knocked lightly, and said, "Mistress Mary? It's Overseer Eagan. May I come in?"

They heard a muffled response that sounded affirmative. He opened the door, and Morrigan walked into a world of roses and ruffles. Vast and bright, the room had a large white armoire and matching chest of drawers, a carved mirror, and paintings of serene landscapes. The heat from a robust fire in the grate, though, felt oppressive, and on an ocean of a bed unlike any Morrigan had seen lay Mistress Mary.

Swallowing a gasp, Morrigan stared. Gone was the confident and saucy young woman she'd encountered atop Devona. Instead, Mary appeared diminished and sickly. Moving closer to the bed, Morrigan brushed her own errant curls from her face, embarrassed at her appearance in contrast to the fineness of her surroundings. She was aware of a sour smell, a stagnant essence that seemed to pool around Mistress Mary. With the same knowing she'd had about the vessel, Morrigan was certain the mistress was gravely ill. Fear gripped her. She thought: Mum won't approve of me being here. Foul and quick-spreading afflictions are a constant worry for her and the villagers.

Mary attempted a smile through cracked lips as she gazed at Morrigan shifting from foot to foot near her bed. Instinct overcame Morrigan's fears. She crouched low at the bedside, eye level with the mistress, noting her breath was labored. "What sickness is upon you, Mistress Mary?"

"We none of us know," said Mary. As though riding a wave of nausea or pain, Mary winced and swallowed. "It hurts here," she motioned to her abdomen, "like a jagged piece of glass." She raised a trembling hand to her temple and added, "And I'm getting these furious headaches that build and build. Then I bring up what's in me, a greenish mess."

"Oh, Mistress Mary," said Morrigan. The Mistress seemed alone in a hazy, pain-filled landscape, in which no language was sufficient, no words suitable as solace. In only a few encounters, Morrigan had felt something special between them. Mary had helped Morrigan get a reprieve on the rents. Morrigan had cured Mary's wart. And with the help of Shauna, Mary had rescued Morrigan. Now Mary suffered greatly and Morrigan longed to help her.

"Doctor O'Brien's been here twice," said Mr. Eagan, his voice harsh. "Says it's some kind of miasma. He's done nothing for her that I can see. It's no contagion," he added under his breath, as though he'd noted Morrigan's earlier hesitancy.

"The laudanum helps," said Mary, her voice weak, "but I— lose myself."

There came a light tap on the door. "Mistress Mary?"

"Come in," said Mary.

A girl appeared holding a chamber pot against her gray-and-white pinafore apron. Morrigan recognized her as one of the

O'Hares from the village. The girl nodded at Mr. Eagan, and her eyes widened at Morrigan's presence alongside Mistress Mary's bed. "I've returned your, uh, this, Mistress Mary," said the girl, her voice faltering. Mary nodded as the girl stepped around to the opposite side of the bed. "Mistress Mary, Sir Martin is home, and is coming up straightaway." She curtsied, glanced in Morrigan's direction, and left the room.

Morrigan backed away from the bed, her eyes darting to Mr. Eagan and the door.

"Stay. Morrigan. Please," said Mary, her arm outstretched, a look of fear on her face.

Morrigan wanted nothing to do with Sir Martin, and she was not prepared to deal with Mary's illness. Mamoh's story about Isla having no dead hand in her possession flashed through her mind. As Morrigan moved toward the door, Mr. Eagan shrugged and said, "You'd better stay."

Within seconds, they heard heavy steps approaching the door. Morrigan stood straight-backed, nervous, and sweating by the fireplace. Mr. Eagan opened the door and said, "Welcome home, Sir Martin."

"How is she?" Sir Martin asked as the door swung open to reveal the room. He stopped when he saw Morrigan. "What are you doing here?"

"Father," said Mary, holding her hands to her temples, her dull eyes beseeching his. "I asked Mr. Eagan to fetch her. He has only obeyed my order."

"What can she do? She could have lice or some other infestation!"

"I do not!" said Morrigan, squirming, for she was dirty.

"She knows the forest medicines, Father," Mary whispered. At her words, Morrigan felt desperate for it to be true.

Sir Martin sighed. "You have your mother's contrary quality, Mary," he said, his voice gentle. "Are you feeling better?" Hope dwelled inside the question.

From Mary, there came no response. She had leaned over the bed, and soon, the sounds and smells of vomiting filled the room.

Part Three

FULL MOON

53

MORRIGAN

'Tis in Her Blood

"No fever, no cough. Just headaches, vomiting, and pain in the gut," Morrigan chanted Mistress Mary's symptoms to herself in the twilight, matching her strides to its rhythm. As unprepared as she felt to help Mistress Mary, the wolf's message came to mind. Mistress Mary lived in the village, and thus her illness related to Morrigan's calling.

Shivering in the chill, Morrigan thought about all the medicines Cathleen had taught her. Which are good for the Mistress's symptoms? she thought. The root of wood avens? Tiny white fairy flax? Her mind swam with the names of herbs and wildflowers, but the knowledge was not in her bones. Not in the way wildflower wisdom lived within her mentor. For Cathleen, the land's medicines were as close to her heart as were her ancestors. She knew them as separate beings, with unique personalities.

Morrigan decided she'd go in the morning to seek Cathleen's help. She'd have to ask Riona to deliver the fish from the market, which would not please her sister, though she supposed Riona would have to get used to it. Overwhelmed at the task in front of her, Morrigan raced home in the near darkness, reassured by the glow of a candle from inside her cottage.

In a rushed voice, Morrigan shared the news about Mistress Mary.

"You are *not* going back to that estate!" thundered Tommy. "After his agents drove the nail-rods through us? 'Tis his problem, not ours, and may he be afflicted with an itch and have no nails to scratch with."

Morrigan pleaded, "Da, Mistress Mary called for me and she could die. Sir Martin likes the idea no better than you do."

"What can *you* do, Morrie? Whatever it is will be like spitting at a burning house to put the fire out."

Mamoh interrupted her son-in-law before he could add anything further. "Tommy, you know if there's any saving to be done, Morrie will find a way to do it. 'Tis in her blood, after all."

Perched on the rungs of the ladder, Morrigan smiled at her grandmother's support.

Betha had been quiet while Morrigan spoke about Mistress Mary's sickness. Now Mamoh gave her daughter a stern look.

"Do you want to do this?" Betha asked.

"She's asked for my help. What else can I do?" Not that I know for sure what to do, Morrigan thought.

With a nod, Betha turned to her eldest daughter, who sat with her back to the wall on the hard earthen floor alongside Liam and Ruarc. "Riona, please deliver the fish tomorrow."

Riona glared at Morrigan. "Aye, Mum."

"Visit Cathleen to see what can be done about Mistress Mary, Morrigan, and if she is the better person to go, see to it, won't you?"

"Thanks, Mum."

Outvoted, Tommy moaned and walked to the cupboard. He rummaged until he found the whiskey Betha kept trying to hide. "I'm becoming mildewed with the blight of conscience," he said. Nonetheless, he gave Morrigan a wink.

As, one by one, the family departed to bed, Morrigan descended from her perch on the ladder and sat next to Tommy by the hearth. She felt a strong pull to share her strange visions with someone, and Tommy was the likeliest.

"Da, can you leave a little poteen on a dish?" she whispered. "I'll keep out a portion from the milk pail." It was well known that The Good People, should they hold a council after humans had gone to bed, liked something to drink by the hearth.

"Your mother seldom makes those allowances anymore. What has you so nervous, a leanbh?"

Morrigan leaned into her father, speaking as lowly as she could. "I've seen scary images, Da. Dead bees, raging fires, and a goshawk turned to bones. Death is everywhere. Where are they coming from? I fall into a dizzy stupor most times." Tommy stroked his daughter's curls. "Da, I fear I'm going mad. And now with Mistress Mary's illness. I don't know what to do except ask The Good People for help."

Tommy wrapped his arms around his youngest. "I think I know what it's about."

"You do?"

"It's Schoolmaster Winnett. Hasn't he blathered on about the vengeance of God, making the wicked a fiery oven whose fire shall devour them? Sure picks the most frightful Bible verses."

"Yes, but…"

"Don't fret, Morrie. You don't have *fairy stroke*, and you are blessed with a caring heart as big as our sky. Schoolmaster Winnett isn't here to see us place these offerings for The Good People. And thank heavens Mamoh doesn't rake out all the hearth at night. The Good People would think it mean. Rest now my daughter. Have sweet dreams."

And with that, Tommy ushered Morrigan up the ladder to her pallet, shushing and calming her as she went.

54

MORRIGAN

A Snarly Operation

J ust past the stone circle, Morrigan crested the rise, surprised to see Cathleen moving in her awkward gait away from her cottage. "Cathleen!" The words were lost on the wind. Morrigan set off at a run, the sheathed dagger and bone flute slapping against her thighs in her skirt pockets. A gathering basket bounced in the crook of her arm. "Cathleen!"

Finally, Cathleen stopped and turned around.

"Where are you off to?"

"'Tis the birthing time for Mrs. Walsh. You're a thundercloud, Morrigan. Speak."

"Mistress Mary's got a sickness—headaches, vomiting, and pain in her gut. Da says I can go, but Mum says if you are the better choice you should go, and…"

"Slow down, Morrigan. When you slow down, you gain a different view of things, not confused by your own clamor. Now tell me again what ails Mistress Mary."

Morrigan recounted what she had seen the previous afternoon.

After hearing her story, Cathleen said, "Vomiting is the body's way of getting rid of something not wanted in the digestive organs. You say the headaches go away afterward?"

"At least for a time."

"If we focus on the digestive area, we may heal the headaches, as well. Tell me, what have you learned about stomach remedies?"

"Aren't the roots of wood avens, when boiled, good for stomach problems? And fairy flax, if boiled? They're in bloom now," said Morrigan.

"Ah, my sweet fairy flax. But the flowers need to be dried not boiled, and there's no time. Plus, it's a purgative and can be poisonous in large doses. Have you thought about milk thistle?"

"The big green plant with spiky leaves?"

"Aye."

"'Twould be a snarly operation collecting them," said Morrigan.

"Sometimes the snarliest plants carry the most powerful medicine, isn't it so? You can boil the roots and leaves straight away. Soak the stems to reduce their bitterness and then use them as a following remedy. And you were right about the root of wood avens. They would be helpful, too," said Cathleen.

"You can't come with me?"

"No, and it's off I go now to Mrs. Walsh, for soon she'll be welcoming an infant into the world. But think on these things, Morrigan: What does it mean to heal? And what are you being called to heal?"

"I don't understand."

"Consider this question: Is there more to a person than a body? Sometimes I get a strong intuition that a sickness goes deeper than the physical, into the spirit, too."

"Surely she'll die if we cannot cure her stomach pain."

"True, it is, and it is also true when applying medicines, I set an intention for everything to be healed, even what I cannot know or see."

"I think I understand." For weeks Morrigan had ruminated about the wolf's message. It hadn't made sense the wolf had used the word *heal* when no one in the village was sick. Cathleen had presented a broader way of thinking about healing.

The Crooked Woman reached out to give Morrigan a reassuring squeeze. Then she began her slow, lumbering walk toward the

Walsh woman's home. She stopped after a moment, turned back, and said, "There's a stand of milk thistle at the cliff's edge, back of McDonaugh's Pub. Mistress Mary will need a few armfuls of it. You'll want something larger than your gathering basket, or you'll be all scratched up before you get home. And remember to ask for permission before you collect."

As Morrigan set out to gather milk thistle, she spied Cormac walking from his farmhouse to the pub. "Cormac! Glad I am to see you. I need your farm cart for half a day."

"James has it. He's breaking stones," said Cormac. "What're you needing it for, Morrie?"

"To gather milk thistle from the cliff's edge. Mistress Mary's ill. 'Tis a matter of urgency."

"You aren't telling me you are coming to the aid of the land-owner's daughter?" Cormac's scowl was fierce.

Morrigan would not be deterred. She squared her shoulders. "Cormac, you're right to think I'm daft, but I helped cure a wart on her hand, and she thinks I can help her again. She's desperate, Cormac, and she's called to me, so I aim to do whatever I can."

"All right. I'll dump the stones and bring the cart to ya."

Morrigan gave him a spontaneous hug. "I'll be at the cliff's edge. Oh, and Cormac? Thanks."

Cormac opened his mouth to say something. Morrigan braced for one of his brash remarks, but this time he shrugged and turned away.

He has seen something different in me, she mused. Maybe it's because I'm taking charge.

Morrigan stood in front of a huge growth of milk thistle as tall as a fish-curing barrel and half again as wide. Dozens of purple flowers bloomed atop thick stalks. She reached out to stroke one of the large, bright green leaves with its telltale milk-colored veins. She gave the plant a silent salutation and listened for something in return. Tracing a finger around a hole carved out by some chomping insect, she marveled at how canny it must be to sup without getting pierced by the leaf's sharp spines. "Maybe you'll keep those spines away from my foraging fingers?" she asked the plant.

Dropping her basket, Morrigan reached in the folds of her skirt for her dagger. "I'd be grateful for some of your healing medicine," she said to the plant, recalling Cathleen's words, "Spirit is everywhere and in every living thing."

"From the tips of your flowers all the way to your roots is what I need." She talked as she walked around the plant. "Is there a part of you wanting to become this medicine?" Her eyes were drawn to a bee that flew onto a purple-flowered section growing away from the rest. She could dig there without being ravaged by spiky leaves. "This part?" she asked and listened for a yes or no feeling. "Well then, I give you my thanks, and I'll try not to hurt the other roots."

It felt natural to talk to a plant. She'd heard Cathleen speak about them as though they were kin. The plant's utter aliveness sent a wave of shivers down Morrigan's spine. She smiled. Perhaps she'd just been kissed.

Morrigan pushed the squealing old farm cart along the rough trackway toward home. She'd received no scratches from the milk thistle, and for that, she murmured words of thanks. Had it truly been in the way she'd asked the thistle? The raven had said much the same, "If you know how to ask." Not everything had a logical explanation. She hadn't an explanation for how peas and saliva had cured Mary's wart, but they had. Isla had never told Mamoh how the curlews had sung the boy's voice back to him, but they had. Maybe it was unknowable. Maybe the truest things were. In just a few months, the landscape of Morrigan's life had widened, and anything, anything at all, seemed possible.

55

MORRIGAN

The Healer's Calling

Morrigan sat beside Mamoh close to the turf coals. A cauldron of milk thistle bubbled. Mamoh hummed while Morrigan stirred; tendrils of steam emerged from the concoction. Soon it would reduce to a thick, greenish astringent.

Morrigan had followed Cathleen's instructions, placing the milk thistle stems into a separate tub to soak. A somber mood overcame her. A terrible burden, this healing. It seemed to have layers to it, more than what was visible. She'd have to learn how to interact with the spirits of the land.

The triad had potency. After all, Isla must have used the triad for healing. Morrigan reminded herself she didn't need to know *how* the triad worked, only to believe it would. Confident now, she withdrew the dagger, the flute, and the vessel from their hiding place and showed them to Betha and Riona when they returned from the market.

Betha's eyes widened at seeing the vessel. "What did you give the traveler in exchange for this?" she asked.

"Nothing. He said it belonged to the one whose face lit up in the holding of it," said Morrigan.

Riona scowled and examined the glyph. "The symbol on it looks like a tangle of knots to me. Morrie, I don't understand. What does this old thing mean to you?"

"I've received a message about three connected objects. This vessel is one, as is our great-grandmother's dagger. Then I found this bone flute. See, Ree? It has the same symbol. It must mean something." She hoped she'd ignite her older sister's love for the dramatic.

Without warning, perhaps from having to carry the fish that morning, Riona erupted, "It means I'm tired of your strangeness." She spat the words out. "We've given you quarter all our lives, Morrie. 'Leave her be, she's simply different,'" mimicked Riona. "Mum's told me many a time. Lately you've gotten worse. How am I ever going to attract a countryman if I have a sister who's as daft as you are?" Riona stormed out of the cottage.

Mamoh, Betha, and Morrigan stared after her, not knowing what to say. Riona was the golden child, perfect in everyone's eyes.

Morrigan collapsed on the bench, a maelstrom of emotion. What had she done to upset Riona? Mamoh patted Morrigan's shoulder and said, "Have no worry about Riona. She'll be fine. And your thistle mixture looks well and done. Perhaps your vessel ought to carry the remedy, isn't it so?"

"Yes," said Morrigan, bringing the vessel forward to receive the liquid. "Thanks, Mamoh. I'll go now." Morrigan left the Lane cottage bound for Mistress Mary. She tightened her wrap against stiffening east winds. The skies had become as dark as black currants. A storm threatened.

56

SCHOOLMASTER WINNETT

Fair Riona

Schoolmaster Winnett fingered the letter he'd received from the Bishop, one hand absently patting the donkey he had grown fond of. The letter spoke about the Church's goal to recruit and train hundreds of priests for Ireland as her people's faith solidified. He smacked his lips. "Good."

His star pupil, Riona, came rushing toward him along the trackway. Was she in tears? Frowning, he nudged the donkey forward.

"Schoolmaster Winnett, good day to you," said Riona, wiping her eyes.

"Glory be to God for this fine day, Riona. What has you in tears?" asked Winnett.

Riona swallowed, "'Tis nothing. Just Morrigan. You know how she is."

Winnett scowled. "I'll speak to your mum about her. Morrigan should model herself after you, a monument of fine breeding."

Riona gave him a searching look. "I am all right now, thank you kindly. I'm off to Colleen's at present." Riona turned to go, a brief smile brightening her face.

What a beauty, he thought. Had her smile held fondness? Her eyes had sparkled, but was it only the tears? For months, the vibrancy of Riona's poetic recitations had invaded his dreams. While many lads were interested in her, Riona had accepted no suitors. It seemed her sights were set on someone finer. Perhaps she was waiting for him. As he trotted away, a shiver of excitement moved through him. He was Sir Galahad, the Arthurian knight, his donkey a white stallion. He, a rescuer of the fair maiden Riona. She will make a fine wife.

Morrigan appeared, hurrying through the village. Schoolmaster Winnett seized the opportunity for a lecture. "Good day, Morrigan."

"Good day, Schoolmaster Winnett," said Morrigan, balancing something on her hip, her fingers drumming its perimeter.

"Riona came by just now. Seems you've upset your fine sister. Why would you do such a thing?" Despite his being on the donkey, Morrigan stood almost at eye level.

"I didn't mean to." Morrigan shifted from foot to foot. "I must go. Mistress Mary has asked for my help. An illness has befallen her, and I've made her a porridge of milk thistle. I must bring it to her at once."

"She has asked for *your* help? How strange." Winnett narrowed his eyes. "I'd like to see this concoction you've prepared."

Hesitant, Morrigan lifted a cloth to show him.

He leaned in and sniffed it, noting its earthy smell. Then he recoiled as he spotted the symbol on the vessel. "An unusual carrying bowl, isn't it?"

"'Twas a gift from the travelers," said Morrigan, biting the inside of her cheek.

He felt a chill in her demeanor. "I'll say a prayer for Mistress Mary. And pay heed to your actions, Morrigan," he said. "In all things, there are consequences. Good day." He nudged his donkey, and they trotted down the track.

57

MORRIGAN

The Power of Believing

Winnett's words didn't worry Morrigan. She felt the same. In all things, there *were* consequences. It was the root of the wolf's message: "Because humans have forgotten their place in The World Tree, they have frayed the cords of connection." Still, unnerved by the schoolmaster's rudeness and judgment, she fantasized about never returning to charity school. "And your sermons are giving me bad dreams!" she said into the air. She could not abide the man, although he held influence and would be risky to cross.

Finn would not have judged her the way Winnett had. He'd have encouraged her to be herself however unusual that might appear. She missed Finn, who had no idea about the triad or any of the changes in her life since his departure several weeks ago. She wished she could talk to him. In her mind, she saw him outside his boarding home, with the late afternoon sun casting a warm glow on his jaunty flat cap, sandy hair, and soft gray eyes. Finn, reading a letter from her, his carver's hands caressing its rough rag paper. She imagined she had written:

Dear Finn:

Surely the objects I've found will bring healing for Mistress Mary. If you had seen her, you'd be scared as

*I am. I think she's dying, Finn, and I don't know how
I'm to use the three objects I've found to help her. But
I never told you about a voice at the yew grove where
I fell, or about a message I received there. Mamoh
would say the message was from the Queen of The
Good People, but I never told her either.*

Morrigan arrived at the estate's stone wall. She scaled it and
trudged through the pasture to the back of the manor, saving
the time it would take to walk around on the new road. She
continued the letter in her mind:

*Finn, I never told you something else. In the spring,
I encountered a wolf with a message, and we could
understand each other because we spoke what he
called The Once-and-Only Language. I know you'll
think me daft, but it's true! He said the beings in The
Otherworld have been waiting for me, that I'm to,
well, heal the village. I don't know what it means,
but Mistress Mary wants me to help her, so I think
it's part of that calling the wolf described.*

How strange it all sounded, and yet how right it felt, too. None
of Morrigan's experiences seemed accidental. *Finn, my love, I'll
tell ya all about it when you return.* But his return was a long way
away, and she had mighty healing work to do.

As Morrigan neared the estate, she spied Mr. Eagan walking a
horse. "A good day to you, Mr. Eagan!" she shouted. "I've brought

some medicine for Mistress Mary." The overseer looked across the pasture, and blanched. Morrigan appeared like some mystical, wild-haired goddess from tales of yore.

"Whoa, Gleanna!" Eagan tightened the reins on the startled bay mare he'd been exercising. "Rival! Venus! Stay!" he commanded two growling gray wolfhounds at his side.

"I took a shortcut across the fields," said Morrigan, eyeing the dogs.

Eagan scowled as he looked at the young woman's dirty feet. "Did you avoid the cow dung?"

"I think so. How is Mistress Mary?"

Eagan turned to look at an upper room in the manor house. "Sir Martin sat by her bedside all night. He tells me she's no better. Been five days now." Eagan's eyes were bloodshot, his mouth tight. "Doctor's come and gone, clucking like an old hen. Sir Martin wants to take her by carriage to Galway, but she's saying no. I think Mistress Mary is out of her head."

"May I go to her? I've brought medicine."

"Aye," he said. "Go to her."

Escorted by the servant whom she now knew as Maeve O'Hare, Morrigan gasped at the wave of stagnation that assaulted her when she opened the door to Mistress Mary's room. The mistress looked far worse.

"Mistress Mary, Morrigan Lane is here," whispered Maeve.

Though Mary's eyes were closed, her hands moved as if in recognition. Her pallid face, gaunt body, and the circles of violet around her eyes were enough to tell Morrigan she had to act quickly. She set the vessel on a table nearby, crouched down, and whispered, "'Tis your lucky day, Mistress Mary. I've found just the right medicine. How about I give you some?"

Mary opened her eyes and reached for strands of Morrigan's red hair that had escaped her bun, spilling onto the bed. A wisp of a smile graced her face. "No tape, then? Your curls."

"No," said Morrigan, who'd never have the means to tape her hair. She gestured for Maeve to move to the other side of the bed. "We'll have to prop you against the pillows, Mistress Mary."

"Thank you, I don't think I can take what you've brought," said Mary.

"Do you want to get better or don't ya? 'Tis a fight you're in, make no mistake, Mistress Mary," said Morrigan, fear for Mary's life making her bold.

"Call me Marée. That's what Mother called me," said Mistress Mary.

Something had shattered inside the Mistress. Morrigan was in over her head. She wished Cathleen were with her. Remembering her mentor's guidance, Morrigan said a silent prayer to heal whatever ailed Mistress Mary, physical or otherwise. "Have you heard of milk thistle, Mistress—Marée? 'Tis a large plant with showy purple flowers and hidden inside all its spiny beauty is medicine for just the ailment you have. Surely you can take a sip of its healing magic," said Morrigan.

Seeing no reaction, she continued, "Remember when I came to cure your wart? I told you to believe. The same is true now, Marée. You must believe, for this plant wants to give you its healing medicine and the process requires belief to work." Morrigan hoped her words made sense to Mistress Mary. She herself wanted to believe in the medicines and in the triad.

"All right," came a faint response.

Morrigan and Maeve boosted Mary. Then Morrigan sat on a wooden stool near Mary's bed. A vigil chair. The stool had not been in the room yesterday. Lacking a spoon for the remedy, Morrigan asked Maeve to get one from the kitchen. In the meantime, she'd use the dagger. She placed a dab of the still warm mixture along the dagger's blunt edge. "Marée, think about welcoming this magic potion into your body, believing it will heal you."

Mary opened her eyes to see the greenish mixture on the silver knife-tray, Morrigan nodding her reassurance. Mary choked down a small amount and then another. Morrigan let out a breath. It's like priming the water pump in the village, she thought.

For twenty minutes, Morrigan fed Mary small amounts of the mixture, replacing her dagger with the spoon Maeve had retrieved from the kitchen. While she did so, Morrigan conjured images of Mistress Mary living a rich and happy life. "I see you, healed and galloping across the estate on Devona, Marée, soaring over stone walls, your laugh of delight ringing across the green fields and silver streams.

"Now, Marée, I see you on a grand staircase in a soft peach gown that sweeps the stairs as you descend. Everyone turns to see who you are, especially a handsome, dark-haired gentleman who leans against a carved column, his deep brown eyes staring at you, Marée. You glance his way and smile. There are others, too, and soon you're surrounded by them all."

Morrigan sensed Mary listened, though she had trouble describing the scene in detail having never lived that kind of life. She had no idea what to expect from the remedy; in her heart, she hoped for a fast miracle.

When Mary held her hand to signal a stop, half the mixture remained.

"'Tis a good start. We'll rest a while," said Morrigan. Mary closed her eyes as Morrigan reached for the flute inside her skirt pocket. "I'll play something for you, Mistress," she said. "It could be part of the healing." She brought the flute to her lips, positioned her fingers, and blew, hearing, "Mmmmmm, Hooooough." She held the higher, second note longer than the first, and then played them again and again. To her hopeful ears, it sounded like a simple, two-note lullaby. If Isla's curlews could sing back a young man's voice, then her flute could carry waves of invisible medicine into Mary's body. She blew the notes three times, and then went silent. They were all quiet. Morrigan matched her breathing to the shallow rise and fall of Mary's.

"Tell me what it's like," whispered Mary.

"What it's like?"

"To have siblings. And a mother at home with you." Morrigan was struck by how lonely Mary must be and hesitated to respond. "Tell me a story," said Mary.

"All right," said Morrigan. "Fadó fado." She spoke the Irish words that began every old tale, then continued. "Long ago, there lived a fisherman's family, just beyond the wood. If you traveled that-a-ways toward the sea, you might notice a kindly old white-haired woman tending the potato and turnip plants, shooshing away the bugs and the pigs roaming too close. That's Mamoh, and although she can't see as well as she used to, no one can sow seeds quicker. She's putting seeds in now for spring cabbage. Waits until the moon is full, she does. Says the full moon invites the seedling to emerge into the cycle of life."

Mary's eyes were closed though her lips had curved upward. Morrigan's stomach began to rumble. She hadn't eaten all day, so hunger entered her story.

"This family is in the hungry months since their crops aren't ready for harvesting and the harvest herring are yet to appear. So, you might notice a fair-haired and blue-eyed woman walking the roadway to and from Saint Joseph's Church where she exchanges some cleaning for a bit of butter and milk. That's Mum. She's a worrier, though she doesn't speak about it. It's in her eyes, and in the way her mouth turns severe when she thinks no one's looking. She gives it over to the Lord often enough. But from time to time, her blue eyes dance in merriment. Do you want to know why?"

"Tell me," said Mistress Mary.

"Because of the strong and wiry fisherman, Da. You'd laugh just to hear him storytelling at his supper table or singing at the pub. "The Boys of the Irish Brigade" rings out on his harmonica, and in his own rich singing voice. His wild black hair and wrinkles around his dark eyes would tell you how fiercely he loves life. And this man is well loved in return. He often says, "There is no need like the lack of a friend.""

At these words, Mary winced. "I have no real friends," she said, a small tear forming in the corner of her eye.

"I can be your friend sometimes," said Morrigan. Her mind understood the unlikelihood of this statement, but her heart did not. Maeve sniffled and turned away to tend the fire.

In times of illness, nothing mattered except essential things, such as breathing, knowing someone loves you, and remembering happy times.

"In my top bureau drawer. The lace cap your sister made. I want to wear it. What am I waiting for anyway?" Mary's voice trailed off.

Though Maeve and Morrigan exchanged worried looks, they put the pearl white cap on Mary's head. She held a ghostly loveliness in wearing it.

"You look beautiful," said Morrigan.

Maeve overcame her bashfulness. "Aye, Mistress, you do."

Mary focused first on Maeve and then on Morrigan. "Thank you. Please, stay with me, here," Mary said, gesturing at the end of her spacious bed. Then she closed her eyes to the world of the living.

58

SIR MARTIN

No Carriage, Father

"**G**euh!" Sir Martin awoke from a dream in which his wolf-hounds were writhing in agony from slashes to their abdomens. Disoriented in the dim light, he rubbed his eyes. Only a dream. Something else though; he tried to remember what was amiss. Mary's illness! He flung the coverlet onto the Chesterfield sofa where he'd slept. Stepping across the stack of Parliament proceedings he'd intended to review, he hurried from the library.

Mind racing, Sir Martin ascended the grand staircase to his daughter's bedroom, arguing with himself. Why had Mary refused to go to Galway? Why hadn't I simply put her into my carriage and taken her to a skilled doctor there despite her wishes? Out of her head refusing me like that. Yes, the ride was long and arduous. Seven difficult hours. How had this happened? And so quickly?

A man who liked control, it shook Martin to the core, his inability to control this thing that had happened to his only child. Opening the door to Mary's room, Sir Martin scanned her face, relieved to see her asleep. Then he noticed Maeve and Morrigan lying on opposite sides at the bottom of Mary's bed, curled like seashells, as if to safeguard her.

"Ahem!"

Morrigan and Maeve jerked awake and sprang from the bed.

"Mistress Mary asked us to stay with her," Maeve said, curtsying and backing away from the bed.

"Never mind." Martin walked to his daughter and whispered, "Mary, can you hear me? I'll order a carriage now. We must go to Galway."

"No. No carriage, Father."

Though Mary could have endured the ride two days ago, she was too weak now to make it. Sir Martin raised a hand to his head and made an anguished sound.

Holding the vessel, Morrigan approached him and, after a quick curtsy, said, "Sir Martin, Mary has had a good amount of this healing milk thistle and will need more. It has stayed down."

Sir Martin gave her a searing look and said, "What? Mary looks no better."

"Sir, it might just work. She feels very alone just now, and healing intentions, such as I carry, can help. I've got the root of wood avens to try also…" Morrigan gasped as Sir Martin grabbed her arm and pulled her from the room.

A vein pulsed in Martin's forehead. "It's utter nonsense. Why are you here anyway? What good are you? She's dying, and you've done nothing but waste my time!"

"No! I, I think …"

"Don't think, Morrigan Lane. Leave." With that, Sir Martin reentered the room and shut the door.

59

MORRIGAN

A Moon in All Things

Morrigan stumbled home. She sat on the hearth bench to warm herself as Mamoh lowered the pot of leftover stirabout into the coals to heat it. "I thought it would be enough," she said to Mamoh as the others listened in. "I suppose it's too early to know if the milk thistle will work. Sir Martin wouldn't let me wait and see."

Tommy scowled, patted her shoulder, and said, "Morrie, I don't care about Sir Martin's daughter so much. It's you I worry about. You've done your best, a leanbh. Prepare yourself, for a disease such as this does not tell a lie. It kills at last." None needed reminding of the many tiny slates in their cemetery—young ones lost to disease.

At the other end of the bench, Mamoh made a noise of disapproval and said, "Let us devote the rosary to Mistress Mary this night. We'll pray she does not meet her maker just yet." She turned to Morrigan. "From time to time, Great-Grandmother Isla would say, 'There is a moon in all things.' Think about it. A moon in all things."

"What does that mean, Mamoh?"

"Well, I don't know myself, exactly. Something about the mysterious ways of the world. Long ago, when I asked her to explain, she said only to understand a thing I had to see it with more than my eyes alone. 'Become the moon,' she said, 'and you will understand.'"

As Mamoh spoke, Morrigan saw a flash of an image behind her closed eyes. A red-haired woman with a scarlet wrap walked along a cliff drenched by the light of the moon. *Is that you, Isla? How do I become the moon?*

Morrigan, like all fishermen families, understood the moon's pull on the tides, but it didn't seem the same as becoming the moon. The forceful moon was made visible by something outside itself—the sun. Yet it was equally powerful when invisible, outside the view of those on earth.

How do I become the moon? she wondered again. And how does it help Mistress Mary? She remembered her favorite quote from Hamlet, where, after seeing a ghost, Horatio says, "O day and night, but this is wondrous strange!" And Hamlet responds, "And therefore as a stranger, give it welcome. There are more things in heaven and earth, Horatio, than are dreamt of in your philosophy."

Brooding, Morrigan made her way to the door and slipped outside in search of the moon's mysteries. Clouds drifted and the moon, nearly full, hung in the sky, sometimes in and sometimes out of view. Walking to the sea, she considered the ever-changing phases of the moon.

"Sometimes visible, sometimes not," she said, "just like Mary's disease." Maybe everything had both visible and invisible parts, the way plants had their physical appearance and their hidden healing powers. The structure and shape of her triad objects are quite apparent, but their spiritual potency is not.

"All things visible and invisible, all things new and full," she sang to a melody of her own conjuring. The world has physical and spiritual creatures—the material world, and The Invisibles beyond it. "Still, if there's a moon in all things, how does that heal Mistress Mary?"

60

BETHA

The Truth of Our Deepest Nature

Betha lay staring at the ceiling in the narrow bed she shared with Tommy. It was the wolf hour, the moment when an unearthly void of silence reigned and, like the infinitesimal pause at the end of an exhale, *night* finally surrendered her power while *day* had not yet made up his mind whether to break. It was the time when creatures who moved in the dark became still and before morning's songbirds heralded dawn. It was the time when babies were born and the old or the sick died, when deepest dreams claimed their dreamers and restless sleepers claimed despair. It was the time when no lie survived as a thought, even in a mind of greatest denial.

Betha had known the old parchment and the three objects Morrigan now possessed were connected. They shared a mysterious glyph. She had not wanted to face the implication that Morrigan was the rightful heir to her grandmother's gifts.

Once, Betha had longed to decode the parchment's meaning and claim its knowledge as her birthright, but she'd failed to understand it. Hidden away for decades, only in the last few months, as Morrigan's intuitive powers had emerged, had Betha felt compelled to rid herself of the parchment's hold on her and, thus, on Morrigan. Whatever its meaning and powers, its origin was ancient and therefore pagan.

Betha took comfort in the rituals and traditions of her youth, and Mamoh reminded her that ideas taken as science less than a century ago were considered heathen superstition today. But Betha was a woman who wanted certainty, and the old ways—of a belief in an Otherworld and its beings—held far too much influence outside her control. In the Catholic faith, if you followed the Ten Commandments, were pious, and devoted yourself to the Father's teachings, there was certainty; heaven was your destination. It brought her peace.

Surely the parchment, though it had belonged to Isla, and perhaps Isla's grandmother before her, held the devil's influence. She must not bequeath it to Morrigan. Betha flinched as she heard Grandmother Isla speaking in her mind as though she lay right beside her.

"Our ways have existed long before time could be measured," said Isla. "They ring with the truth of our deepest nature. Long before Father Murray's sacred texts, we had our own sacred texts. His Church turned our original stories into empty ones. The institution calling our powerful old ways, with our impeccable relationship to all of creation, 'the work of the devil' has lost its way."

Betha gasped at Isla's words and made the sign of the cross to safeguard herself from their potency. She had been young when her grandmother died. She'd never heard her speak words like these. As only a conversation in her mind, Betha pushed her grandmother's words down and away from her heart, for to look at them was far too difficult.

Sleepless, hours later, unable to rid her mind of Isla's admonishment, Betha made an anguished sound and relented. She'd give Morrigan the parchment. Her daughter and the old scroll were intertwined, and that seemed beyond her influence or control. She prayed Morrigan would not understand the parchment any more than she had. Relieved of the great burden squeezing her heart, Betha rolled over and, merciful Lord, found sleep.

61

MORRIGAN

Message from the Dead

Morrigan awoke after a few hours' sleep, her perspective restored. She thought it quite possible the milk thistle had worked. Still, as a following remedy, she'd harvest some wood avens. Easing herself off the pallet, she climbed down the ladder, gathered her yew stick, basket, and dagger, and edged out the door.

A full moon hung luminous in its sky, dwarfing points of light from millions of stars and offering Morrigan light shadows to see by. She walked to the woody scrub near Old Mother Oak, delighting in the night's envelope of mystery. As she had done before, she searched for a glimpse of the wolf's silver-white coat but saw nothing. Her mind returned to the brief flash she'd had of her great-grandmother walking across the island, foraging just as Morrigan did now. "Am I like you, Great-Grandmother?" she asked and, in response, felt a stirring of presence she was certain was Isla's.

The sky brightened in the east. Carrying the wood aven roots, Morrigan made her way to Rosderry Manor. The incessant churring sound of a nightjar arose, the bird who was noted for its astonishing twists and turns while pursuing its prey. The nightjar gave her a churr of encouragement. She felt certain of that. Soon Mary will have more healing medicine, even if I must sneak it in to Cook, she thought.

Later, against soot gray clouds, Morrigan walked home from the estate, refusing to cry. The cook had accepted the remedies with gratitude and promised her Maeve would take them to Mistress Mary, but the news she'd shared hadn't been good. Though Mary's vomiting had lessened, and the cook believed Morrigan's remedies had helped, Mary was weakened beyond measure. Sir Martin had called for ministration by an Anglican priest, something like a Catholic's last rites.

Morrigan had begged to see Mary, but Cook shook her head no. "'Tis himself up there now, sitting vigil," she'd said. "You've done all you can, and for that we are thankful."

Before Morrigan left, Cook had insisted on filling the young woman's vessel with some mutton stew. "No one will eat it here. Take it." When Morrigan protested, Cook shushed her. "Few would have done for the Mistress what you have, especially after the agents' misdeeds." Cook had placed a rough cloth filled with a loaf of brown bread over the top. "God be with you."

Morrigan felt a lump in her throat. Though Mistress Mary had everything she could want—a mare, fine clothes, trips to London, and food—anything her father could buy, none of that mattered.

Home! Exhausted, Morrigan staggered to the door of her cottage. "Mamoh!" she said, her voice trembling. The old woman rushed to open the door.

"Oh!" Mamoh cried. Morrigan placed the vessel and cloth on the cupboard and turned into her grandmother's outstretched arms. "A leanbh," Mamoh murmured the term of endearment against Morrigan's red curls as she hugged her. Tears made a damp spot on Mamoh's gray sweater, as if the old fabric itself were meant for it. The two rocked in an embrace, one giving comfort to the sorrowful, and one receiving it, in the way women had been fated to do for centuries.

"Uh, Morrie?" Connie McDonaugh loomed in the door frame, lungs heaving.

Mamoh and Morrigan stared. Something was amiss. Connie seldom left his kitchen at supper hour.

"Good day to you, Connie. Kettle's on the boil," said Mamoh, moving to add a turf to the embers for tea. Connie tipped his flat cap in response, ducked under the door frame, and stood shuffling in their small space.

"Sit here, Mr. McDonaugh," said Morrigan, pulling Tommy's chair from the corner toward the bench by the fire. "What brings you out this late afternoon? Have you news from Finn?"

"No, it's not about Finn," he said, his voice bouncing off the walls. He leaned toward Morrigan, who had positioned herself on the bench nearest him. "It's about Kate, Morrie. I've had a message from Kate." He looked at Mamoh for her reaction. She made a supportive sound, busying herself with tea.

"She revealed a curious thing. She said, 'The girl need not despair, for her mother has hidden that which holds the sovereign wisdom.'" Connie had repeated it to himself all the way from the pub.

"Sovereign wisdom?" asked Morrigan. "Are you sure she meant me?"

"Aye, we speak of you as often as we speak about the boys. You are the daughter she never had, we never had," he said. "I'd best go. Supper's late already."

Morrigan thanked Connie and then turned toward Mamoh and asked, "What does it mean?"

Mamoh made a sound low in her throat. "I think we'll know when your mum returns from Saint Joseph's."

Morrigan went to the open door, hoping to see Betha. Instead, she saw Tommy, Liam, Ruarc, and Riona coming from the quay, arms filled with net-making supplies. "The Lane netmakers will arrive soon," said Morrigan, leery of their impending clamor. The harvest fishery time was near, a season when large schools of herring moved along the Irish coast. In preparation each year, the Lanes established a work area outside the cottage to make or repair the special-sized nets required for fishing the herring.

"Clouds could open at any time," said Tommy, as he and the boys placed their fishing gear across two barrels acting as tables. "Ree, take the thin rope and the netting needles inside so you and Morrie can load them. Let's stack the floats there and roll the old nets to this side."

Morrigan stepped outside to rinse the teacups just as Riona made her way in.

"Morrie! How's the mistress?" Riona asked. She'd taken a keener interest in Mary's health after hearing she'd worn the crewel cap Riona made.

Morrigan shook her head and said, "She's not responding. I didn't get to see her again."

Over and over, Connie McDonaugh's words rang through Morrigan's mind. I need to talk to Mum, she thought. Ominous clouds were closing like a noose around a pale sky. After another failed search of the trackway for a sign of her mum, Morrigan decided to go find her.

62

BETHA

The Revelation

Betha closed the door to the Parochial House with a firm click, her blue eyes dull with pain, one hand pressed to her temple where a headache had been building all day.

Within a month, a new priest would arrive. Thus, Betha had been readying the residence. Today had been floor-scrubbing day, and each time Betha had bent down to scrub the floors, the blood pounded against her skull.

As she walked home, she noticed for the first time the bright morning had been ousted by chilly winds and sinister-looking clouds. She carried a basket containing a small loaf of brown bread and butter, making a *tsk* sound. "Breaking my back for a loaf no bigger than me own hand!" Still, she'd be absorbed in gear-making for the autumn fishery and would have to curtail her work at the Parochial House. That meant even fewer extras.

"Extras!" She spat the word out. To label it so suggested the existence of enough already. She didn't know how to take this poor life in stride the way Tommy did. Even after days away on rough seas, Tommy returned in good spirits. She thought about how many times she'd heard him say, "The Irishman's merriment begins at his christening and ends when he has been well waked."

Mamoh often said, "We're rich in love and the blessings of a beautiful land." To Betha their lives were a struggle, with the family half starved for months on end. She mumbled to herself,

"I've got no dowry for Riona. What's she to do? And we're at the mercy of the landowners and the fisheries." She kicked a stone on the trackway, and then winced at the throbbing at her temples.

Betha paused as Morrigan strode toward her, each step more vigorous than the next. Was it trouble or grief replacing her daughter's customary lightness?

In the distance, Betha heard a rare rumble of thunder. "Wind's from the east. 'Tis good for neither man nor beast," she muttered the old saying.

"Mum, are you all right? You were just standing there," said Morrigan as she reached her.

"I'm fine, Morrigan, just an ache in my head from too much scrubbing. We should get home with this storm coming."

Morrigan hesitated, giving her mother a penetrating look. Betha was none too comfortable under her daughter's scrutiny.

"Mum, Mr. McDonagh came to see me today," said Morrigan low and soft. "He said something strange. He received a message from Kate."

"A message from Kate?" Betha asked, shivering at the thought of any communication with the dead.

"He said you had something hidden away for me. Do you have something hidden? Meant for me?"

Betha swallowed hard. The parchment! She sucked in a breath, fear making an encampment inside her body. She set down the basket to rub both temples and said, "There is something that could be for you. I planned to give it to you when I got home."

Morrigan whispered, "What is it, Mum?"

"It's an old parchment with the same marking as your dagger and the other things you've come across," said Betha, looking away.

Morrigan winced as if touched by a hot fire-iron. "Where did you find it?"

"'Twas your great-grandmother's."

Morrigan took one, then two steps back. "Where is it?"

Betha stooped to retrieve her basket, aware once again of her pounding head and the freshening wind that chilled her thin body. "I'll retrieve it for you as soon as we get home."

Morrigan stood with a stubborn set to her jaw. "Where," she hissed through clenched teeth, "is it?"

Betha looked away. It wasn't supposed to have happened like this. "Behind the cupboard. Wrapped in a red ribbon. On a nail."

Morrigan took off at a run leaving Betha behind, staring, her eyes sunken and in pain. The daughter she resented, the daughter she loved, had run from Betha as though she were the devil himself. To the north, a flash of lightning pierced the sky.

63

MORRIGAN

The Before Time

What happened next blurred into what Morrigan came to call "the before time." She exploded into the cottage, startling both Mamoh and Riona. She took two steps to the cupboard, gave it a rigorous heave as it scraped across the dirt floor. After a long reach, air escaped Morrigan's lungs as her shaking hands grasped a rolled parchment of unknown age. Mamoh and Riona leaned closer as Morrigan slid the ribbon across its skin.

It possessed intensity, a treasure of sacred origins. As she unrolled the thin sheath, she sensed something escape in a luminous flash just outside her vision and then disappear. The word *messengers* came to her, though she had no notion of who or why.

Then, she felt wave after wave of shivers as she stood, entranced by strange but familiar etchings. With its own life force, the central glyph pulsed, the same carving as on her dagger, flute, and vessel. Surrounding it in fine symmetry, three on the top, three on the bottom, and two alongside the glyph, were distinct markings burned into the parchment by a hot scribing tool.

"It's *the one*," Morrigan whispered to herself, "and the one will be received." The message from the yew grove had been fulfilled! She felt a weight settle into her body, aware she now had what the voice in the yew grove had promised.

A flash of lightning pierced the cottage, followed by explosive thunder. The women jumped. Tommy, Liam, and Ruarc came bursting in, their shouts of alarm shattering Morrigan's trance. In haste, she collected vessel, dagger, and flute, and placed them inside her creel basket, resting the parchment on top. Lastly, she grabbed her yew stick.

"Hurry, Betha!" Tommy yelled as he spotted his wife walking toward their home. She did not hurry. "The skies are vexed," he said. A green tint merged with the clouds' bruised violet.

From behind him, Morrigan pushed aside her father, making a small noise of apology. She rushed outside, taking off at a run toward the quay, covering her head and the creel basket with her wrap.

"Morrie! Where're you off to?" Tommy's shout disappeared in a sudden gust of wind that seemed to come from all directions. He made a movement to run after her, but Mamoh's hand stopped him.

"Thomas, it's her destiny, and it rises with urgency. Let her go."

Tommy turned to his mother-in-law. "'Tis no trifle of a storm, Mamoh!" He broke away from her and went out into the whipping winds.

From the doorway, Mamoh, Riona, Liam, and Ruarc watched as Tommy started after Morrigan, and then turned and ran to Betha. They witnessed an exchange as each stood in the raw tempest—Tommy's wild gestures and Betha's small ones. They watched as Betha shook her head and Tommy stomped his foot.

"What's going on? Where's Morrie going?" asked Tommy.

"She's probably got the parchment," said Betha.

"What parchment? She could be hurt in this storm!"

"Grandmother Isla's. I'd hidden it. I didn't want her to have it."

"You did what?" shouted Tommy.

"It's the devil's handiwork!" Betha's hands went to her temples.

"By God, Betha! You think your grandmother's healing gift is the devil's handiwork? You've denied your own daughter her legacy." He turned from her just as a flash of lightning came so close the smell of sulphur filled the air. Betha cried out. Tommy grabbed her arm and hurried them home.

64

MORRIGAN

A Confluence of Initiation

Morrigan retraced the steps she had taken on that fated night in May when she had followed the tinkling sound to the yew grove. There she had felt the presence of a being from another realm and been given the command to find the triad.

The skies looked otherworldly, with churning masses of slate clouds, jagged bolts of lightning, and echoing thunderclaps. She had no room for thought except the mantra, "Get there! Get there!"

Light bled from the sky as Morrigan moved across the terrain. On a cliff north of the fishing village, she caught her breath. Across the bay, sheets of rain extended like thick tentacles into the sea. Closer in, waves pitched and plunged against the rocks. Just then, escorted by a chorus of wind, the rains met her where she stood.

Hard driving rain pelted the initiate, for surely Morrigan was inside a confluence of initiation. She placed her wrap over the creel basket. Lifting her face into the onslaught, she shouted, "I am coming!"

Amid the downpour, Morrigan bent to protect the parchment, chastising herself for risking it. Though the parchment was made from skin with etchings burned-in, not scribed, she couldn't be certain it was impervious to rain.

The curtain of rain had lessened, its roar replaced by distinctive drops that plopped onto leaf and stone. Morrigan listened intently, uncertain whether she'd heard a high-pitched tinkling above the rain. The track had become so narrow that despite her use of the yew stick as a clearing tool, her skirts caught on branches of prickly burdock and heath, slowing her down.

Finally, she glimpsed the stream where she had injured her ankle. Standing on her tiptoes, Morrigan spotted the spikey crowns of a yew grove. As she did so, her rational mind emptied and withdrew, and in one whoosh of an exhale, she felt a powerful pull. As if in a waking dream, she floated toward the yew grove, waded through the rain-swollen stream, and entered the grove.

Thick, gnarled limbs had kept out much of the rain. It felt warm and safe in the dark space. Morrigan knelt on dried needles covering the earthen floor. She had lost her hairpins, and her curls dripped on her face and back. Gathering her hair into a loose knot, she leaned forward on her haunches, and lowered her head in deference. "I have come," she said. "I have the triad and a parchment." She laid her crimson wrap on the needles and arranged dagger, vessel, and flute in a triangle in front of her. Then she unfurled the parchment and laid it on top. She waited for the presence to respond.

"You have entered a nemeton, a sacred grove." The voice, indistinguishable as male or female, spoke in The Once-and-Only Language. Morrigan closed her eyes; blood sang in her veins. She felt cold and hot at the same time—charged, like her insides were jumping against the constraints of her skin. In the distance, the *tweet-tweet-tweet* of a robin saluted the end of the day. Leaves spilled their raindrops onto the earth. She waited.

The voice continued, "Those who have come here have been in many shapes before assuming the form you will see. I have been a lanternlight. I have flown as an eagle and dreamt as a lizard on a rock. I have been a drop of dew and a currach on the sea, a sword in battle, and a string in a harp. I have absorbed fire and been a beast with a hundred heads. I have fought at the battle of Goddeu Brig and sang the swans down from the stars. I have been a blackthorn full of spines and a sweet-smelling apple blossom. There is nothing of which I have not been a part, for I am the singer of the underlying song of the universe."

Morrigan searched the blackness of the grove. She felt a presence just outside her perception. An instinct cautioned her to not try so hard. She relaxed and widened her gaze, taking in everything and nothing.

In her peripheral vision she discerned light from tiny particles seeming to dance in and out of feathery form. When she gazed in their direction, they disappeared. To see them, she must not focus on them directly. It took great effort. Facing the most powerful presence she had ever known, her eyes wanted to narrow in and focus.

The breathy voice continued: "A triad was perceived, and now the one has been received. You are an initiate. In ancient times, you would have spent two score years working through twelve levels of knowledge to achieve the Three Illuminations—Tenm Laida, Dichetal do Chennaibh, and Imbas Forosnai. There is no more time."

To Morrigan's ears, the strange words sounded like "illumination of song, divination, and the light of foresight." She strained to hear more.

"For over two millennia, humans have strayed from their deepest knowing. When Pádraig, Saint Patrick, outlawed the natural connections with the ancestors and the gods, humans lost their prophecies and insights. Now we must intercede. Take the parchment into your hands."

Morrigan lifted the parchment as if it were a holy scripture. Its center glyph was alit and pulsing. She touched the glyph and heard a song ringing through everything—the trees, the full moon just beginning to show from behind clouds, the beat of a hare's heart, and the quiet absorption of a drop of rainwater.

"Do you hear it?" asked the voice. "It is the hum of Earth."

"Aye," whispered Morrigan.

"Now what do you hear?"

As she continued to trace her finger over the glyph, one persistent melody, a progression of five notes, emerged from the symphony of the whole. The first two notes were ones she'd discovered playing the flute. The third note exploded with a rapturous sound.

"This is your healing song, Morrigan Lane. Your flute will call us from The Otherworld as helpers and guides," said the voice.

"What does this song mean?" asked Morrigan wanting to imagine something when she played it on the flute.

The melody built on itself, and then a chorus of vibrant voices erupted. Even though her eyes lost their trance-like gaze, she saw brilliant lights coming up from the earth like steam from a teapot.

Believe believe that anything's possible if you see it differently.
Magic's happening all around you, open your eyes, and see really see.
Imagine an impossible thing, and before you know it has come
to pass.
Place your trust in the power of dreaming
take off your blinders and shatter the glass.

Only, only only joy lives here! Only, only only joy lives here!
See it swirling around, sparkling golden light
feel it easing away all your pain inside
Only, only only joy lives here! Only, only only joy lives here!

Morrigan felt the power of the song in her being. It offered the same advice she'd given Mistress Mary—to believe. Had Great-Grandmother Isla her own healing song?

"Each being has one true song coursing through them like underground rivers," said the voice in response to her thought. "We in The Otherworld say when all souls sing their true songs, then all of creation will once again be perfect."

Morrigan considered this a daunting proposition. Even Schoolmaster Winnett and the agents had true songs? Did Mistress Mary's healing have to do with singing her true song?

"The parchment is from the time before the wheel of the year, before the silver branch and the animal helpers, before the battle of trees and the dark words. In the hands of *An Fhoínse*, it has witnessed raptures and sorrows nine-fold times nine-fold," the voice continued.

Morrigan shivered through her wet clothes. The parchment is that old? How had Isla received it? And what sorrows would she, *An Fhoínse*, witness?

This time the voice did not answer her. Instead, she heard, "You must remember three truths in the use of the parchment. First, its power can only be invoked if the holder is trustworthy," said the voice.

"Trustworthy?" Strange word, she thought. "Worthy of trust. Whose trust?" she asked.

"We in The Otherworld, The Invisibles, the ancestors, and the not-yet-born nine generations hence," answered the voice.

Morrigan nodded, thinking of Cathleen's advice about asking for permission before foraging.

"Second, its potency is only effective if there is a reciprocal desire for, and interchange within, the healing."

"Reciprocal." Again that word. "You mean both I and the person who is ill must want the healing to occur in order for it to work?"

"Yes. Healing cannot be compelled upon another. And to bring complete healing, you must consider the entire circle of a life. You shall learn about what is meant by healing in a moment. Or a lifetime," said the voice.

It seemed the wolf's message about healing the village was as multilayered as Morrigan had considered. "The third?" she asked, feeling overwhelmed, her body chilled.

"Third, it has great potentiality. Over its dozens of lifetimes, when discovered by those who have desired to wield power, it has been perceived as a grave threat. Its existence, therefore, must remain a secret from all except a very few in whom you would entrust its preservation over your own life," said the voice.

After a silence, the voice continued, "For now as an initiate, the parchment shall work in this way. There are eight carvings accompanying the glyph. Three are symbolic representations of the dagger, flute, and vessel—the top middle, and bottom left and right. The other five represent the five cords that contain the circle of a life.

"When a person is ill, something lies broken within them. One or more of their cords are fractured, becoming discords—separations from the song of creation. The five cords are of the body, spirit, terra, mind, and heart."

Morrigan remembered Cathleen's mysterious question, "What are you being called to heal?"

"The Crooked Woman understands to heal means to make whole," said the voice. "Consider Mistress Mary. Hold the parchment while envisioning her state. You shall move your left hand—the intuitive hand—over the five markings from bottom center, to center right and left, to top right and left."

What was broken in Mistress Mary? Morrigan wondered, moving her left hand over the etching at the bottom center of the parchment.

"This is the cord of the body," said the voice.

As she traced the etching, an image popped into Morrigan's mind of the vessel containing the remedies she had prepared and something else. She was moving her hands over Mistress Mary's stomach in a downward, spiraling motion, dislodging something necessary. Morrigan's heartbeat quickened. Mary's body was in discord.

She moved her hand to the middle row, right side.

"This is the cord of the spirit," said the voice.

Morrigan felt nothing. No image popped into her mind. She grunted.

"Understand in this moment, Mary has no discord of the spirit; her spirit cord is whole," said the voice.

"Oh, I see. Not all cords need healing." She moved her hand to the middle left of the parchment.

"Next is the cord of the terra," the voice said. "One's ability to belong to, or be allied with, nature and all of creation."

Morrigan felt nothing. Then she moved her hand to the etching on the top, right side of the parchment.

"This is the cord of the mind" said the voice.

Again, Morrigan felt nothing. Finally, she moved her hand to the etching on the left side.

"This is the cord of the heart," said the voice.

An image popped into Morrigan's mind of a much younger Mistress Mary running after a carriage, shouting, 'Mama! Mama!' A woman's face appeared out the side of the carriage, her look anguished, tears making tracks down her cheeks.

"Mistress Mary's mother was cast out of the manor," said Morrigan. "The Mistress's lone rides outside the estate; her questions about me and my family; her apparent lack of friends. She needs her mother! Is there still time to heal Mistress Mary?"

"Only by attempting the journey into healing will you know. Your three healing tools—the keen-edged dagger for action, the nurturing vessel for remedies, the flute to call upon us, and the parchment shall guide you in all ways. Remember to remain trustworthy, ensure there exists a reciprocal desire for healing, and keep the parchment a secret," said the voice.

Morrigan could no longer see the flit of lights from the periphery of her soft gaze. Their presences ebbed away. "Don't go!" she shouted in her mind. Among The Invisibles, she felt at home after a long journey away from herself.

"I offer you great thanks," she said into the blackness as she lowered her head once again. "I vow to heed my calling to heal the village and its concerns. I vow to make whole any cords that have been fractured, adhering to the three rules." After gathering her sacred items, Morrigan bowed, and backed out of the yew grove. She felt the power of the parchment and the triad. The responsibility, too. With her intuition, as revealed through the parchment, and her three healing objects, she would claim her destiny.

65

BETHA

A Mess of Things

From within the constrained silence of the cottage, Tommy urged Betha, "Go to her before you've lost her, and I hope something in you finds an explanation, for I myself cannot understand." Betha nodded and grabbed a shawl from a hook by the door.

The storm had passed out to sea after a fierce, long downpour. Brisk salt air cooled Betha's trembling heart and mingled with her salty tears. I've forever alienated me own daughter, she thought. Never meant this to happen. But an inner voice reprimanded her, saying, "You withheld the one thing Morrigan needed." Betha had only wanted to protect her youngest, so different from everyone else with her sharp mind and her wild ways.

Isla's life had not been easy, and Betha had wanted to spare Morrigan that kind of life. Then, a sinister thought occurred to her. She was jealous of her own daughter, the one who had what Betha longed for—her grandmother's gift. Betha groaned and the truth of it struck her hard. There was no hiding from it. She was a poor fisherman's wife, bitter and hard-hearted. "I've been so selfish!" Her words were lost inside a sudden release of waves on the strand. Her footsteps had taken her to the sea. Over and over, the ocean's restorative powers called to her, even though she had lost her own da to its waters.

"Da!" she cried. She heard only the waves.

Where had Morrigan gone? Betha had an inkling. The old oak on the far side of the village. She picked her way along the track as dusk slipped into night.

66

MORRIGAN

Magic Is Happening All Around

Morrigan's teeth chattered despite her long strides to the estate. Her wrap, though sodden, provided a shield against the wind's bite. The moon shone luminous in a clearing sky, lighting Morrigan's way. Divine timing had been at work with Connie receiving Kate's message on the eve of a full moon just as Mistress Mary neared death. Morrigan felt someone else captained her story, as if she'd stepped out of her ordinary life and now inhabited a character in a traveling seanchaí's fable.

What could she say to convince Sir Martin to send for Mary's mother, the woman he had once banished? She imagined him wild with fear and grief at the prospect of losing his daughter.

It had hurt Morrigan to learn Betha had withheld the parchment. She couldn't understand why. She hadn't asked for her unusual birth scar or her uncommon life. As though her thoughts had conjuring power, Betha rushed out of the darkness.

"Morrie! I've been looking everywhere for ya," cried Betha, her skirts wet from the sodden landscape. She looked at her daughter whose height exceeded hers.

Morrigan noted the new imbalance of power between them and felt the truth of it surge through her. In a flash of insight, she realized she'd never be a healer if she held on to her hurts, so she let them go. "Mum, I'm sorry I ran off."

Betha let out a breath and stepped forward to hold Morrigan's face in her hands. "I've made a mess of things, Morrie. I knew you were special. I knew it on the eve of your remarkable birth. I wanted to be special, too. But I'm not." Tears welled in Betha's eyes.

Morrigan had never seen her mother cry.

"Will you forgive me, Morrie?"

Morrigan felt a surge of compassion for her mother as in a flash, she saw images of Isla cradling Mamoh as a baby and then Mamoh cradling Betha, and finally, Betha cradling her. She said, "Aye, Mum, and I'll need your help." It would take Mary's mother to help heal the Mistress, and only another mother could persuade Sir Martin to send for her.

Betha and Morrigan walked the new road toward the estate. Morrigan spoke in low tones about what she hoped would happen there and how her mother could help. Soon they arrived at Rosderry Manor. It was long before sunrise. Believing no one would be awake, Morrigan turned the knob to the back door. It opened and she slipped in, motioning for Betha to follow. Slumped over the kitchen table, the cook snored softly.

"Cook," whispered Morrigan.

The cook jerked and lurched from the table.

"I've come back. There is something else I must do," said Morrigan.

"Oh, Morrigan, I think you're too late," said the cook, exhaustion showing in her eyes. She glanced at the clock perched on a shelf above the hearth.

"Is Sir Martin with her?"

"Aye. Last I knew, he was."

"May we see her? I'll say you had no hand in it."

The cook turned her back and moved toward the low embers of her fire. "I didn't see ya," she said, gesturing toward the servants' staircase.

"...not a good idea, Morrigan," whispered Betha.

"I'll go in, speak to him, and bring him out to you," said Morrigan. Though her heart pounded, she told herself to trust in the parchment and in The Invisibles.

Betha sighed, crossed herself, and began moving her lips in silent prayer.

Morrigan tapped on Mistress Mary's door and slipped inside. A strong smell of incense permeated Mary's bedroom and on the mantelpiece above a turf fire, a dozen candles burned low in their sconces. Morrigan was relieved to see a slight rise and fall in Mistress Mary's chest. Sir Martin had not awoken in response to her knock. He appeared innocent in sleep, sprawled back against the wall on his stool, a half-filled glass of whiskey on the nightstand.

Morrigan crept to the far side of the bed, hoping the distance provided some protection from his rage. She knew not what to do, except to play the flute possessed of the full five note song, her healing song. From her heart, she sent a message to The Invisibles, the ancestors, and the not-yet-born nine generations hence, "Guide me. I am willing to do whatever is necessary."

She withdrew the flute from her basket, closed her eyes, and breathed in and out, quieting her mind. Her fingers moved over the bone instrument, and then she began: "Mmmmmm, Hooooough, Huuuuuuh, Mmmmmm, Mmmmmm." In her mind, she sang the words, *On-ly joy lives here.* She repeated the sequence.

"What?" Sir Martin leaned toward Mary, searching for signs of life. Then he stood and walked stiffly toward Morrigan.

She curtsied, moving as close to him as she dared. She stood erect and proud, flute in her hands. "Sir Martin, something more can be done."

Under different circumstances, Sir Martin would have angrily ushered her out the door. This night, he was drowning in something outside his control, too filled with pain for fury.

"Sir, if I described one thing you could do to restore Mistress Mary to health, would you do it?" whispered Morrigan.

"Of course," he rasped.

"And if I said it would be the hardest thing for you to do, but that it would work beyond all doubt, would you do it?" asked Morrigan.

"Yes," he said, without hesitating.

"Come, please." Morrigan said, gesturing toward the door. She opened it to reveal Betha, who curtsied and then motioned for Sir Martin.

"Sir, there is something I must tell you. It will make all the difference," said Betha, her blue eyes seemingly lit from within. Her prayers had brought her serenity. They stood in the hallway as Morrigan gently closed the door.

Her full attention on Mary, the initiate healer leaned over and sang the words that had been seared into her heart at the yew grove, "Mistress Mary. Marée. Believe, believe that anything's possible if you see it differently. Magic is happening all around you. Open your eyes and see, really see." She felt chills move up and down her spine. Her hands were hot, pulsing. She began moving them in a counter spiral a hair's breadth from Mary's stomach. Mary opened her eyes from some far distant place.

"Mary, something must be dislodged from within, and I must move my hands this way," said Morrigan. Mary did not respond to the motioning of Morrigan's hands.

"Impossible!—not enough time—" Morrigan winced when she heard Sir Martin's voice rise from the hallway outside the room,

Then her mother's voice, pleading, "—just knowing she is coming—"

"—not coming!"

Morrigan felt the cold wave of Sir Martin's negativity penetrate the room. To counter it, she repeated her healing song.

Believe believe anything's possible if you see it differently. Magic is happening all around you, open your eyes, and see, really see.

She sang the song as much to herself as anyone.

Imagine an impossible thing, and before you know, it has come to pass.

Morrigan's hands circled Mary's stomach. "You want to live, don't you, Maree? Think of joy."

Only joy lives here. See it swirling around, sparkling golden light. Feel it easing away all your pain inside.

Never had Morrigan wanted a thing as much as she wanted Mary healed. She imagined herself at the yew grove surrounded by love from The Invisibles. She heard their voices join hers. "Only joy lives here!" Mary must have heard, too, for her mouth opened. Morrigan told herself Mary sang along.

67

SIR MARTIN

Healing the Discords

Sir Martin dispatched a horse and rider who rode out hard under an eastern horizon layered with hues of salmon and royal blue. He kicked at a stone in his carriage way as he watched the figures become smaller in the distance. It would be four days before Elizabeth arrived if his Cousin Gertrude could locate her, the journey a grueling one of rider to packet boat, to rider, to yet another rider, to packet boat, to rider.

"Elizabeth," he muttered. He hadn't spoken the name in seven years and had no interest in where she lived or with whom. He spat on the ground. He was not prepared for his former wife's return. Worse, Morrigan Lane had insisted Elizabeth must become a part of Mary's life once again. "One visit alone won't work," she'd said.

He shook his head in disbelief. How had he allowed the Lane women to persuade him to seek out Elizabeth? He recalled how Betha Lane had described the special kinship between mother and daughter. "You have nothing to lose and everything to lose," she'd said. Perhaps the Lane women were right, and it would give Mary something to live for.

"God," he pleaded to an unseen deity, "I don't care about anything else. Just cure my Mary." Wearily, he walked toward the house, the first rays of light bringing clarity. He'd tell Mary he sent for her mother. He'd have to convince his daughter that despite his wife's banishment seven years ago, her mother would now be welcomed at any time. The idea was galling, but he would do it because deep down he knew it had been cruel to sever ties between a mother and a child and because he had given his word to the Lane women. Ultimately, he was, and always had been, a man of his word.

68

MORRIGAN

Waiting

Three days had passed since Morrigan and her mum visited Mistress Mary, and they'd heard no word about her health. After delivering fish to McDonaugh's Pub, Morrigan made her way to the oak. "What's happened to Mary, Old Mother Oak? And what really happened at the yew grove?" She recalled the three truths about the parchment's use: the importance of trustworthiness, reciprocal healing, and the need to keep it hidden. The five cords—body, mind, heart, spirit, and terra—remained mysterious. Yet everything was interconnected, and it felt right that the five cords of connection created a whole. If one or more were frayed, healing was necessary.

With grunts and squeals, Shauna appeared, her tail wagging like a dog's.

"Shauna," said Morrigan, kneeling to scratch the pig behind her ears. Soon Mr. Eagan emerged from the wood.

"Mr. Eagan, what news?" asked Morrigan.

Catching his breath, he wheezed, "Mary's coming along. I wanted you to know. She had a bad night after you left, with pain unlike any of us had seen. It passed, and she's been without symptoms, sleeping, and recovering ever since."

"Thank the good Lord!" said Morrigan. "And the mother?"

"We expect Lady Vesey will arrive tomorrow."

Mr. Eagan had become a co-conspirator, even a friend. Morrigan threw her arms around the pudgy overseer. "Oh, Mr. Eagan, I could kiss ya! Thanks for letting me know."

Mr. Eagan's face turned red. "Best be going," he mumbled. "Now relinquish Shauna, if you please."

"Home you go, Shauna. Thanks again, Mr. Eagan!"

Morrigan did a dance around Old Mother Oak, singing, "Thank you, Invisibles. Thank you, ancestors, and, and all beings in The Otherworld." The parchment and the triad worked! Her mother had played a role, and by doing so, had made amends for hiding the parchment.

She wondered: Will others appear to help me in the future? The Invisibles referred to a person's "circle of a life." Cathleen had said what is past is also prophecy. Morrigan was a healer, just like Isla. In the way of all healers, she made an offering to show her gratitude.

69

SIR MARTIN

Elizabeth's Return

At the sound of an arriving carriage, Sir Martin walked to his daughter's window and parted the brocade curtains. A dark Bians coach-and-four slowed to the driver's low-throated "Whoa." Four matching bay-colored horses snorted and tossed their heads, their sides heaving. Elizabeth Vesey, daughter of Lord Trimblestown, appeared in the doorway of the coach.

Sir Martin felt his heart leap. He ground his teeth to stifle his body's betrayal of happiness. Martin swiveled around to see if Mary had heard him. She lay asleep, her breathing stronger than it had been for days. He watched as the coachman placed a box-step on the ground below the door. Elizabeth disembarked wearing a modest midnight blue traveling dress. Although he could not see her face beneath the bonnet, he noted the slenderness of her once buxom form. He glanced at his own girth spilling over his gray breeches. He felt clumsy and vulnerable in his country suit. Perhaps he'd change to something formal, all black, an attire that felt like a suit of armor. Not enough time.

What had Elizabeth's life been like these last seven years? His own had changed drastically. Just then, his former wife looked at Mary's bedroom window and their eyes met. He saw concern, almost panic in hers. He suspected she saw a haggard and hardened man. He closed his eyes and leaned into the window, his forehead resting against the cool glass. Image after image of him and Elizabeth flitted into his consciousness—eyes following each other as they moved around other courtly dancers, a young Mary cantering ahead of them through meadows to their favorite picnic spot, he and Elizabeth in sensual morning lovemaking. He gave himself over to one moment of sadness and longing and then forced the memories out of his mind. It was over.

As he descended the stairs, he saw Elizabeth, one arm on the curved railing at the bottom alongside his housekeeper, who wrung her hands, uncertain of protocol.

Elizabeth hesitated and soon rushed toward him, her attention on Mary's bedroom. She stopped and whispered, "Sir Martin. Richard, may I see our daughter? Is she…?"

During the many hours since hearing the news of Mary's illness, Elizabeth had wondered whether her daughter lived or died. Her Marée, of the saucy smile and boisterous ways, so like her own, was her daughter through and through, and Elizabeth wanted to see her child, whether the breath had left her body or not.

Sir Martin felt a stab of guilt for all the years he'd forbidden the two he loved to see each other. He nodded and motioned. Elizabeth raced up the stairs ahead of her escort, heedless of convention. She had always been her own woman.

Some days later Sir Martin looked out the French doors of his library at scurrying maids and servants on the grounds. The mild, fair morning matched his mood. Clumps of high clouds gathered like cream-colored skeins of yarn across an otherwise blue sky. A fresh breeze gladdened boughs and bent rushes lining the pond where white swans glided like felicitous hosts.

In a move that had surprised him, Sir Martin planned a picnic. He chuckled as he recalled how the accounts clerk's eyes had widened upon hearing the news. The clerk had cleared his throat once, twice, and then inquired, "For *all* your tenants, Sir Martin?"

"Of course," he'd said. "I'm of a mind to celebrate." Then he slapped his gloves against his open palm and added, "There'll be mead, boy!"

Grabbing his top hat and cane from a hook in the library, Martin strode across the foyer to the front doors, his step light. With Mary's illness came circumspection. In these past years, his life had become doleful, and he'd been too self-absorbed to notice it. Now that Mary grew stronger each day, he vowed he would change.

He had to admit Elizabeth's return had not been the acerbic affair he had envisioned it would be. Elizabeth had been adamant about not residing at the estate. Rather, she stayed with Lady Richardson in Clare. Her attitude had been one of humility and grace, and her propensity for simple, unadorned gowns only enhanced her beauty. Though it had disarmed him, he pushed away any fantasies of a different life.

Elizabeth made the trek to visit Mary every other day. They were inseparable. Yesterday he'd heard Mary's giggle and Elizabeth's boisterous laughter erupting from the drawing room.

Even the servants felt the change. His housekeeper had become less timid and, from time to time, ventured a jovial comment. He approached her now as she arranged stacks of bowls on serving tables placed in an L-shape on the grounds.

"A fine day, Mrs. Donovan."

"Aye 'tis so, Sir Martin. And the tenants who don't get bowls will have to share with others. We aren't furnished for the many who are coming," she said.

"Something tells me there won't be a complaint, Mrs. Donovan. Thank you for your help here." Sir Martin turned to walk back to the manor house to check on Mary.

Cook had boiled milk with fresh sea moss and allowed it to thicken. Afterward, she mixed it with honey to create a pudding. She had placed the dessert at one end of the table alongside seasonal fruits, jam, and bread. At the other end of the table were jugs of mead, made from pure fermented honey, fruits, and natural herbs.

Servants stood in front of a second table, ready to dole out portions of colcannon and lamb roast to the tenants from both villages where Sir Martin's holdings were located.

Women and their children sat on woolen blankets, spread in a colorful array on grasses overlooking the pond, each woman imagining Rosderry Manor was hers. Men stood in clusters talking about their farms or the fisheries, telling tales of heroism and cowardice.

Mistress Mary sat on a parlor chair in a sunny spot closest to the house, her thin body wrapped in purple and blue woolen blankets. She wore a tired smile. It was, however, the look of someone who had heard in the distance the rumbling wheels and pounding hooves of the Cóiste Bodhar, the death coach, seeking to claim a body for the empty black coffin mounted at the rear; the look of someone whom the death coach had passed by.

On one side of Mary stood Maeve O'Hare, who fussed over her—would Mary like her parasol opened or closed? Was she warm enough? Did she want more tea? On the other side of her stood Sir Martin, a glass of mead in his hand, surveying the scene with an air of contentment.

70

MORRIGAN

The Picnic

"Tell us again, Mum, he invited the whole village?" It was Ruarc, bounding alongside Tommy, who escorted Betha as they steered down the new road toward the estate. They were dressed in their very best.

Betha smiled and nodded. "As I understand it. 'Tis rather a break with tradition." She looked back at Morrigan. They shared a smile.

"A man with gratitude in his heart is apt to do unusual things, isn't it so?" It was Mamoh, shuffling alongside her as ably as her old body would go.

"Aye, Mamoh, 'twould seem so," said Morrigan. Her stomach gurgled, and her mouth began to water at the thought of whatever feast awaited them. She stifled a desire to wrest herself away from Mamoh's arm and run to the estate. She couldn't wait to see for herself that Mary was well.

"I haven't heard of another landowner who opened his grounds for such a party," said Tommy. "Aren't we lucky for it? But what do you suppose he wants?"

"Can't a man celebrate the life of his own daughter?" Mamoh asked.

"Besides, we're bringing our own contribution," Betha reminded her husband.

"Aye, Mum. A crewel cap for Mary's mother, a loaf of bread, and a big jar of bilberry-gooseberry jam for Mary. A crewel cap, a loaf o' bread, and bilberry-gooseberry jam; a crewel cap, a loaf o' bread, and bilberry-gooseberry jam," Riona launched into another one of her instant melodies, and skipped to its rhythm.

"Slow down, Ree," said Morrigan. Mamoh had stopped to take a rest. Just ahead stood a broad brick archway whose filigreed wrought-iron gates were swung open. A long, sweeping carriageway ran to the estate. Ruarc whistled under his breath.

Betha straightened her spine. "Remember to be on your best manners, Ruarc and Liam. Thank Sir Martin straight away and offer him your assistance."

"Aye, Mum," they answered.

"You too, Tommy."

"Acushla, when have I ever transgressed?"

Betha opened her mouth to retort, but Tommy cupped a hand over his mouth and made a mock-guilty expression. They laughed, and headed for what they hoped would be a grand day.

Approaching the tables, Tommy Lane boomed, "'Tis the Lane family at your service, Sir Martin." He bowed and tipped his bowler to Mistress Mary. "I'm Tommy Lane, Morrigan's da," he said, chest puffed with pride. "Greetings to you, Mistress Mary. We're all cheered to know better health is upon you, especially my daughter here."

"A couple of fine strong boys you have there, Mr. Lane," said Sir Martin. "I've, uh, met your wife and one of your daughters."

Morrigan crouched in front of Mistress Mary. "Good day, Mistress Marée—Mary," she corrected.

"Have you been well, Morrigan?" Mary's words were formal, though her eyes reflected warmth.

"Aye. And you, Mistress? I hope you'll be galloping across the meadows soon."

Mary nodded and smiled. Then she leaned toward Morrigan and whispered, "You might see my mother galloping with me sometimes. We'll come visit you on the cliffs."

Morrigan swallowed a lump in her throat. "I'd like that."

The intensity of their experience had, for a brief period, bridged the chasm of their classes.

As the Lane family moved toward a picnic spot near the pond, Sir Martin called out, "Morrigan, a word." He walked a distance away from where Mary sat. Morrigan followed. At least I'm presentable, she thought, proud of her deep green skirt and jacket, shoes, and hair in a tight, braided sweep.

Mead had softened Sir Martin's demeanor. "Morrigan Lane, I don't know how you did it. Mary's life was slipping away. I don't know how you knew what to do to help her and I'm grateful to you all the same. How can I repay you? Not that I can repay you for Mary's life. Perhaps something to bring ease to your family?"

"My brother Ruarc would request mutton stew once a week for the rest of our lives," she said, and a smile crinkled her green eyes. "'Tis kind of you, Sir Martin. Payment never occurred to me. May I share a story?"

He chuckled. "I'm not surprised. You seem to have an affinity for spinning and weaving words." Indeed, Morrigan had an unusual presence and a broader vision of things than most people Sir Martin had met, regardless of class. "Go on, then."

"Long ago, before the invention of clocks and calendars, people lived in rhythm with the cycles. Work started when the sun rose across the fields and finished when the sun sank into the sea. So, too, did life revolve in accordance with the cycles of the year and with what each season brought. Winter gifted people with another herring fishery. Spring brought forth lambs and new life in all things. With summer came the gifts of the gardens and the moors while autumn yielded the harvest, including the herring fishery. So it was, exchanges were made in alignment with the abundance of the land or the sea. Sir Martin, if you consider the earth's seasons when determining when rents are due, villagers would be better able to meet your demands, and be most grateful."

Sir Martin gazed skyward. "Rents are set by forces outside my control. I must pay my taxes when they are dictated, but I will see what I can do. In the meantime, do you want a pound or two to tide you over until the harvest fishery? Or the pig that follows you around?"

"No, I couldn't accept that," Morrigan said, and then hesitated. "Perhaps Shauna can visit me though, and when she has a litter, maybe we can have one of the males?"

"I'll see to it. And I'll give thought to your suggestion, though I make no promises." He gave Morrigan a searching look. "Thank you, Morrigan Lane."

"'Tis my honor, Sir Martin." Morrigan curtsied, glanced at Mary, and joined her fisher family in their picnic on the manor lawn.

71

BETHA

Pagan Forces

The Lanes picnicked on high ground overlooking the pond. Nothing in recent memory was as unexpected or as grand as this, with a feast better than they'd ever had at Christmas. In the rare afternoon of leisure, Betha admired the flowering bushes and trimmed shrubs that dotted the front grounds of the estate. It seemed they existed solely for viewing pleasure. She couldn't imagine the effort it took to maintain both the manor house and grounds.

Mamoh dozed on a blanket in the warm sun. "Time for supper, Mamoh. I'll bring you some." Betha ushered Tommy, Liam, and Ruarc into the line, followed by Riona and Morrigan.

"I can carry Mamoh's bowl, Mum, so you can fill your own," said Morrigan.

"Thanks, Morrigan." A new ease existed between them. One day they would speak about what had happened with Mistress Mary. For now, Betha felt satisfied that the mistress grew stronger, and Morrigan seemed the better for it.

Schoolmaster Winnett intercepted Betha after she'd filled her bowl. He guided her away from the table. "Glory be t' God for this fine day and this fine supper," said Winnett.

"Aye. A real gift from heaven."

He put a hand on her arm. She stopped. "Morrigan is responsible for Mary's upturn?" he asked, his tone sounding critical.

"Though we cannot know for sure, it would seem so. Cathleen taught her the herbs and remedies that seem to have healed Mistress Mary," said Betha.

"Though the Lord has given us the fields and the flowers to do with what we wish, we must repel the old pagan forces wanting to rise again and again like weeds in a garden."

"What are you saying, Schoolmaster Winnett?"

He leaned in. "Do you really know what went into the concoction she brought to the mistress? Let us speak plainly, Betha. Morrigan is caught up in your grandmother's ways, and they're not aligned with the Church's teachings. As Father Murray's surrogate, I must remind you against encouraging her."

Betha fought off a learned, guilty feeling. Then she felt the stirrings of a mother's protective posture. *I haven't done anything wrong, and neither has Morrigan.* She lifted her chin and made her voice chilly. "The Lord works in mysterious ways, Schoolmaster Winnett. And may we all give thanks to the Lord when our new priest arrives. Good afternoon."

She nodded to the schoolmaster, and joined her family, but the altercation left her in turmoil. What *had* happened between Morrigan and Mistress Mary at Rosderry Manor as she'd stood in the hallway with Sir Martin? She had no idea. She'd heard singing and flute playing. What was pagan about that? Hadn't her daughter saved a life? In this toilsome land, there were more deaths than miracles. She decided to think no more about it, nor about whether the parchment had influenced what had happened. The Lord worked miracles. She believed it.

72

MORRIGAN

Trawler Trouble

Morrigan slipped away from the villagers, feeling overwhelmed by the glad praise she'd received for her role in healing Mistress Mary. "Shauna, I've brought you a potato and some carrots," she said to the pig, who stood in the pen on the far side of the livery. With her telltale brown markings, Shauna squealed at seeing Morrigan and danced in circles. The other pigs crowded in for a moment, and then meandered away.

"Of course I would come to visit. You needn't have fretted," said Morrigan, as she reached through the wooden slats to offer food to the pig, feeling the roughness of Shauna's tongue. "Good, wasn't it?" Morrigan scratched behind the pig's pink ears. The pig pushed against her hand for more. Now that she'd seen Mary in better health, the heaviness slid from her shoulders and Morrigan fell quiet, anchored in the certainty she'd been an instrument through which healing had occurred, from her and *not* from her, all the same. Perhaps the feeling came from a place words couldn't reach. She rested in it, hoping she could help others in the future.

The sun began to descend from its zenith in the sky. Flies buzzed and landed on her and the pigs. Morrigan leaned against the pen and smiled. "What is my future, Shauna?" Altogether different from who she'd been six months ago, Morrigan sensed her calling to heal the village wasn't as literal as she had once believed. It involved a way of walking through the world, with a focus on making whole the broken cords of connection. Perhaps her village could expand beyond its actual boundaries and could include anyone, anywhere.

"Shauna, you've always had faith in me, and when you have a litter, Sir Martin said I could have one of your piglets—that is, if it's all right with you," said Morrigan. Shauna grunted and wagged her curly tail in seeming agreement.

Morrigan stood and shook her best skirt of debris. She made her way alongside the livery toward the festivities. She spotted Cathleen and Mister Eagan, and her face lit up with delight. Cathleen usually kept to herself. Morrigan hadn't expected her. Red-faced, Mister Eagan was scowling as Cathleen held his hands. Morrigan overheard her words, "I'll make you an ointment from hart's tongue straight away. There're plenty of fronds growing along the shady side of the stone wall."

"'Tisn't necessary. Just a wee burn.

"You're a dark overcast, Mister Eagan. It's already starting to blister."

"What's happened, Mister Eagan?" Morrigan peered at his hands.

"Scalded my hands on Cook's big kettle is all," he said.

"Oooh! That looks painful. Cathleen will care for you." Mister Eagan blushed and Morrigan raised an eyebrow at her mentor.

Cathleen said, "Enjoy the picnic today. I'll be off to collect hart's tongue."

Walking back to the festivities, Morrigan spotted Riona, skirts flying and arms waving as she ran toward her.

"Morrie! We've got to go before there's a scuffle."

"What's happened?"

"There's a new tenant from Village Cashelros, a Mr. Dillon who's a trawler owner. He's got all the fishermen riled. Uncle Colm's watching him like a terrier after a weasel. Mum says we have to get Da and the boys away now."

The sisters hurried toward the picnic. Alongside the mead table stood a small cluster of men from Morrigan's village. Her Uncle Colm's voice rose above the rest. "Devil to your trawler! Your day's haul is bigger than three of ours. Trawlers aren't allowed in our bay!" Colm's voice was tight with anger.

On the opposite side of the table stood Mr. Dillon, speaking in low tones to his men as they drank their glasses of mead and looked threateningly at the fishermen from Morrigan's village.

"This is devilish trouble, Riona," said Morrigan.

They tiptoed past the men, and soon intercepted Tommy, Ruarc, and Liam, who'd gotten wind of the newcomers' presence. At their heels were Betha and Mamoh, picnic items hastily gathered.

"Girls, your da and the boys need help remembering the way home. Please escort them," said Betha looking alarmed.

"The lads need us," said Tommy.

"Not here they don't, Tommy. You can do your fighting at the quay or at McDonaugh's Pub or over to Cashelros. Not as a guest at Sir Martin's feast," said Betha.

Morrigan grabbed Tommy's arm, steering him away from the looming conflict while Riona grabbed Liam and Ruarc by the arms.

"Three without rule—a mule, a pig, and a woman," said Tommy under his breath as he allowed himself to be led away.

"I'll give your thanks to Sir Martin," said Betha.

By the time the Lanes reached the carriageway, Tommy was fuming.

"What does it mean, Da?" Morrigan asked.

"A threat it is to our customs and way of life," Tommy said. "We fishermen have seen the newfangled Brixham trawlers in the deeper waters of the bay, waters our small hookers can't sail in. And if Dillon and his like are coming closer to shore, their trawlers will wreck the fish stocks and upset the natural cycles."

"Da, I don't understand," said Morrigan.

"Unlike the way we hooker fishermen set our nets and then wait, a trawler drags its nets along the sea bottom, and the constant movement disturbs fish, especially herring and their spawn. I fear the bay's plentiful stocks will be depleted by such a greedy method of fishing. Might come a time when no hooker boatman can make a living in this bay."

Morrigan chewed on a piece of grass, her thoughts in a jumble. Another example of what the wolf had meant by humans' fraying the cords of connection? As exciting as fishing in deeper waters sounded, she had a new worry. Dillon's trawler might disturb the natural cycles and it might also cause a war among the fishermen.

Part Four

FATEFUL MOON

73

MORRIGAN

The Shoals of Herring

In Galway Bay, change was afoot due to the new trawler, captained by Michael Dillon. In the days since Sir Martin's picnic, Dillon had visited McDonaugh's Pub, disputing what he claimed were self-imposed superstitions about when and where to fish. With only three weeks until the commencement of the harvest herring fishery, villagers sensed trouble.

One evening Morrigan pestered her father to help her better understand the stakes.

Tommy explained, "Harvest herring are considered a superior species to winter herring. They sell for higher prices on the market. The whole livelihood of a family or a village rests on the luck and fortune of the harvest herring fishery. For generations, we hooker boatmen have been knitted together in our loyalty—our give and take with the silver fish. We've regulated ourselves, allowing the herring to run for five full days before commencing the harvest."

Reciprocus. Her da had described the rhythm of nature, a time for waiting and a time for fishing. Tommy went on to explain the yearly Blessing of the Harvest ceremony. Just after the September fair, as many as five hundred hooker and púcán boats from all over Galway Bay commenced the harvest herring fishery at the precise signal of a Dominican friar, who stood in a command boat ready to give the blessing. Any who acted contrary to this custom suffered loss of nets or even boats and were given a good drubbing from the faithful.

"Dillon's trawler could be the start of many. If he comes to our bountiful bay, others will follow," said Tommy. "I cannot afford a trawler, nor would I want one. 'Tis *Inis Ealga* I'll sail until the life has left me body. If trawling wins out, our old customs will be lost, and anyway, what will happen to the fish?"

That night Morrigan could not sleep. As she turned on the pallet, she felt that same dizzying feeling she'd had from other images. She heard the wolf speak as though making a pronouncement to all beings in The World Tree. "The herring has taken its last breath. The silver-of-the-seas is no more." In a trance, Morrigan watched a herring sink to the bottom of the ocean, dead. She understood herrings had left earth's waters.

Morrigan pinched herself back to the present. Careful not to disturb Riona next to her on the pallet, Morrigan stared at the dark thatch above her head. She couldn't shake the image of one humble ten-inch fish, its iridescence gone, sinking to the ocean floor. The fish, whose frothy, migrating schools had inspired poetry, songs, and festivals, was gone.

The image had seemed so real. Was it foretelling the future? If herrings were to leave the waters of the bay, her family and most of her village would be destitute. Tommy's oft-spoken words rang in Morrigan's ears, "Is ann an ceann bliadhna a dh'innseas iasgair a thuiteamas." 'Tis at the year's end the fisher can tell his luck. That luck had everything to do with the shoals of herring.

Perhaps it wasn't Schoolmaster Winnett's sermons. Perhaps The Invisibles had sent messages to her dreams and waking life all along. One thing was clear: A fissure was growing among the fishermen, and the natural rhythm of the herring's reproductive cycles was threatened.

Morrigan rolled on to her side and closed her eyes, hoping for sleep, but the image of a sinking herring persisted. Then, the beginnings of a plan formed in her mind. She would go to Cashelros and speak to Mr. Dillon.

Determined to see for herself the gear Mr. Dillon used, Morrigan walked to Cashelros south of Baile Ghort na Darach. With all the fearful talk about the new fishing method, was it part of her calling to find an answer? She considered asking the fish directly whether the trawler's nets disrupted their egg laying. Could The Once-and-Only Language work with fish? First, she'd speak to Mr. Dillon.

As she walked onto the quay at Cashelros, Morrigan shielded her head and face from view with her shawl. Summoning courage, she spoke to a group of fishermen, "Good day, sirs. I wish to see Michael Dillon."

"Dillon here, miss," said a man, wiping his wet hands on his trousers.

"My name is Morrigan Lane. I've come to talk to you about your boat."

Dillon frowned and said, "Isn't it your uncle who has stirred the resentment toward us trawler men? Why are you to be trusted?"

Morrigan ignored the question. "I can see your trawler is bigger than our hookers. Can you show me how you fish? Your gear. How is it different? And why are my villagers so worried about it?"

Staring at Morrigan, Dillon retorted, "Maybe you're after making trouble? Or are you touched in the head?"

Morrigan answered truthfully, "I've always wanted a boat of my own and the life and freedom of being a ship's captain, like Gráinne Ní Mháille from long ago. I only want to know how your boat works. I know sailing. I've hoisted a foresail all on my own."

Dillon shook his head and said with a look of disdain, "I'll not show you anything, and you would do yourself good to ask your uncle or your father why there is more need for fish than can be supplied by their hookers." He assessed her tall, narrow frame. "I suspect you yourself are hungry."

Morrigan made a pained face. It was true. Every day hunger lurked like a predator. "I don't understand. Don't the fish limit our supply?" she asked.

"Utter suspicion and nonsense. I've seen the schools. The ocean is teeming with fish. Your father's boat is not designed to withstand the wild Irish seas. My boat, with its powerful build and many broad sails, allows me and my crew to venture into any waters, shallow or deep, to harvest fish. Like your father, we've no guaranteed wage, but we have a boat that can take advantage of the bounty of the sea. And *we* are not hungry."

"Closer in, where the herring spawn," said Morrigan, "isn't it wiser to avoid the breeding areas? It's like what Cathleen Ó Nialláin tells me to do when foraging for medicines—never take more than half."

"And I should listen to you, the daughter of a fisherman who can only fish in shallow waters?" Dillon said, waving his arm in dismissal.

Morrigan shouted out so Dillon's crew could hear, "You must find some accord with the hooker boatmen, Mr. Dillon. How do you know the fish will last forever? What about nine generations hence?"

"I think it's best you go home now," said Dillon. "Shame on whoever sent you, a female to talk me out of fishing where I want."

"No one sent me. They don't even know I'm here."

"Well, then, you're a brave young woman, but a strange one," said Dillon.

Morrigan nodded, looked him in the eye, and said, "Aye. I *am* different." I've been recognized in the spirit world. I am An Fhoínse, she thought. Then she continued aloud, "Think on what I said." Head high, she turned to leave.

"I don't think you know the truth of it," Dillon shouted to her retreating back. "And tell me, if you *were* Gráinne Ní Mháille, if you *were* a ship's captain, would you have your own people starve if they could be fed?"

Morrigan walked toward her village pondering Dillon's words. She had to admit he'd given her good justification for trawling in their bay. Why then had she received the dream and its warning image? Perhaps it was a caution—to pay attention and see what unfolded among the fishermen. Could she use the power of the parchment to reveal whether Dillon and his men had discords that needed healing? No, she decided. The Invisibles had said she could not impose healing on something or someone who did not wish for it, and Dillon and his men had no wish for her healing.

74

MORRIGAN

Her Golden Shores Await

As Morrigan neared home, her attention drifted. A robin's delicate lilt arose from the undergrowth of a nearby shrub. She smiled and slowed to nature's pace as she had become fond of doing, sending a silent greeting to the bird.

A two-masted ship approached the harbor, tacking back and forth with grace. Who could be on it? At the mid-day hour, none of the hookers were at the quay. Morrigan decided to greet the ship. Before doing so, she made her way to McDonaugh's Pub. Peering inside the open front doors, Morrigan called, "Mr. McDonaugh!"

"What has you hollering like you are?" said Cormac.

"A beauty of a ship is making its way to the quay. Could be some rooms needed. I'm going down to welcome them."

Cormac started toward the kitchen and said, "Let me tell Da, and I'll be right with ya." Together they hurried to the quay where seagulls screeched and picked from the remnants of small crabs or shelled creatures whose good fortune had come to an end in the shallow waters of the bay.

"'Tis a schooner," said Cormac, squinting out to sea. "A fine one."

The ship anchored a distance offshore. Her sails began to lower. "Maybe it's our new priest. I've heard Father Murray's replacement is as rigid as a stone," said Morrigan.

"God help us."

They sat on the remnants of a tree trunk that had washed ashore. Soon the prettiest pulling boat Morrigan had ever seen advanced toward shore.

"They're rowing in."

Morrigan didn't answer. A strange buzzing had overtaken her.

"It looks like Finn!"

"Don't be daft. It can't be Finn. He's gone until spring. Anyway, how can you tell?" Morgan shielded her eyes from the sun.

"I'd know me own brother. Isn't it Finn on the starboard side oar? Finn with three others?"

Morrigan hitched up her skirts and rushed onto the dock to secure the dory, her heart pounding. "I think it's him!"

At her heels, Cormac bellowed, "Finn? Is that you?"

"'Tis himself!" said Finn.

Mouths agape, Morrigan and Cormac shared grins and a celebratory jig. "Finn's home!"

"Morrie!" Finn shouted, leaping from the boat, and nearly spilling his shipmates into the sea. He hugged her and kissed her hard on the mouth.

"Finn!" Morrigan gushed, her laugh combined with tears. "How is it you are home? 'Tis grand!"

Finn turned to greet Cormac and then declared, "That is a tale best told at the pub. Come along, Morrie!" He held out his arm, and they paraded toward the pub.

At McDonaugh's, Finn sat on a stool surrounded by a dozen villagers as others burst through the door at the news. Connie McDonaugh, James, and Cormac stood behind the bar. From time to time, Connie reached out to touch Finn, as though to convince himself his son was home.

It wasn't proper for Morrigan to sit at the pub's bar, so she positioned herself against the wall where she could watch him. Finn had grown taller and had filled out some. In his new waistcoat and trousers, he carried himself with confidence. She had changed so much in these last few months without going anywhere. She couldn't imagine all Finn had experienced.

Questioners peppered Finn from all sides. "Can't a lad have a pint first?" he said and raised a glass. "Here's to eyes in your heads and none in your spuds!"

"Sláinte!" the men lifted their glasses in a toast to good health.

Finn winked at Morrigan across the pub and said, "Now I'll tell you my story, though the main character hasn't appeared yet. Sir Thibideau and the rest of the crew should be rowing in soon."

The hubble bubble inside the pub lessened as Finn began to speak, "I secured a job as a laborer in Cork and having passed the carpenter's apprentice test, I was to be trained as a carpenter's mate." Murmurs of assent moved through the gathering. "When Sir Thibideau arrived with a broken bowsprit on his schooner, L'Immortel, I joined the lads to fix it. Then he noticed me carving a new sign for O'Mahoney's pub." Finn looked toward the door, and his voice lowered. "Sir Thibideau's a fancy man from Paris, but his mum was from Oughterard. When the war broke out, he secretly sided with the Bugs against Napoleon. He put all his money into English investments, and when the English won, he vowed to sail to Ireland to visit the slate that marked his mother's memorial in Oughterard. For if it hadn't been for her, his money would have been on the losing side."

Mixed reaction followed this information since most Irishmen had rooted for Napoleon against their English oppressors. "He may be a fancy man, but he's right bobbish," said Connie.

"Aye, Da. And he's made a clever pick in his cabin carpenter, too," said Finn, pointing to his chest.

"You're his carpenter?" someone asked, skepticism in his voice. Apprenticeship lasted years.

"Not officially, but the captain needed a pair of trail boards repaired for his bow, so he offered me the work. Sir Thibideau plans to set sail for the tropics soon. The captain will hire a ship's carpenter then. So I've got the job for a little while—and the coins," Finn said with a gleam in his eye.

Cormac gave his brother a suspicious look. "You don't think he's got unnatural acts on his mind?"

Finn's eyes widened at the question. Then he lowered his voice to a whisper. "No. Word is he likes dark-skinned island men." He raised his eyebrows and chortled. Morrigan had never seen Finn command a room before.

Just then, in strode the French aristocrat, Sir Thibideau, his captain and crew, escorted by Tommy Lane and the other fishermen. The pub rumbled with introductions, greetings, and shouts for pints. It was noisy and crowded, too much for Morrigan.

She squeezed along the wall against the tide of villagers pushing to reach the bar just as she heard the ship captain say, "Oui, we have ze lad and hiz *mains experts*, uh, skeels with ze wood, until Liverpool, where he leaves for Americah—departs in ten days."

Morrigan stopped and turned. Had she heard the captain right? Though she stood on tiptoes, she couldn't see Finn over the crowd.

"Is that so, Finn? You're off to America?" shouted a voice.

"Aye, lads. Her golden shores await," said Finn.

Morrigan swallowed a sensation of panic, and pushed her way out of the pub. She stumbled a few steps and leaned against the pub's cool limestone wall, taking deep breaths of air.

Finally, she stood, trying to assemble meaning from what she had heard. Finn's arrival had come as a shock. She needed to speak to him alone. The world had opened and closed in on her and she wanted to run, but where? To the yew grove? To Old Mother Oak? To Cathleen? Anywhere, she told herself, but her steps led her through the village to Old Mother Oak.

Once there, Morrigan collapsed onto her favorite spot on the ground, leaned against the tree, and gave in to an inexplicable desire to cry. Afterward, she dried her face with her wrap and took deep breaths to regain her composure. Her hands traveled over the big roots as they wended their way from the trunk into the earth below. She looked around, reassured by the familiar landscape: same perky yellow wood avens tangled amidst dark-leafed ivy, same faraway call of a song thrush, same rambling purple vetch lining the edge of the woodland, same damp Irish breeze. It settled her.

"Old Mother Oak, Finn's back, and why do I cry when I should dance? 'Tis happy I am to see him, looking so handsome. And he's got promise as a carpenter and the confidence of a French gentleman and a ship's captain." She smiled as she recalled the countless times he'd whittled away on sticks when they were younger. "But if I heard right, he's going to America." Morrigan gulped back a sob. "Does he want me with him? Do I want to go?"

"Of course you do, don't be daft!" she heard Riona's voice in her head. "When you're in America, married with wee wains of your own, and living on a farm by the sea, you'll both laugh at your panic."

"Maybe Riona's right, Old Mother Oak. Maybe I'm just scared." The wink Finn had given her across the bar spoke volumes about his intentions, or so she hoped. But maybe he'd fallen in love with a girl from Cork and didn't want her to go with him. And maybe she didn't want to go with him. After all, she hadn't expected him for months, and she was no longer the same person she was when he'd left. "I've been given a calling," she said, speaking the words out loud. In truth, Morrigan knew little about Finn's plans, so she decided she'd go home, and, soon enough, she'd find out.

75

MORRIGAN

The Love of a Man Who Loves You

That evening, after a supper of boiled nettles with new potatoes, the Lane family talked about Finn's return.

"He's got himself a fine job," said Tommy. "I sailed past *L'Immortel* on my way to the quay. She's a bonnie boat."

"What have you heard, Morrie?" asked Riona.

All eyes turned to Morrigan. She swallowed. "The pub was too noisy and crowded to learn much," she said, shifting her position on the ladder.

"Time enough to hear Finn's news," said Mamoh, who stood at the door. "He's coming along the trackway now." Riona made a motion with her hands, as if to direct her sister to straighten her wayward tresses. Morrigan began to do so and then shrugged and let her hands fall. Riona made a hag's face. Morrigan smiled. Some things were more important to Riona than they were to her.

Before the family could draw him into conversation, Morrigan greeted Finn. "You've had a grand welcome, Finn," she said by way of hello.

"Morrie! Will you stroll with me?" Finn asked, looking beyond her for permission.

Tommy made an ushering motion. "Of course, Finn. Glad we are to see ya," he said.

"Not too far. It's almost twilight," said Betha.

They walked a distance toward the quay, their silence like a seam ready to burst. At the shore, waves pushed one against the other until they spilled themselves onto the strand in what seemed a clumsy display. Morrigan felt shy, uncertain of Finn. "Both the Frenchman and his captain have fancied your handiwork," she said. "'Tis great news, Finn. Your da must be proud of you."

"Are *you* proud of me, Morrie?" asked Finn, searching her eyes.

"Of course! Never prouder," she said. Then, lowering her eyes, she whispered, "You're so sure of yourself, Finn. You stand differently now."

Finn lifted her chin so he could see her eyes. "I've thought of no one but you since I left, Morrie. I've toiled long hours with you on my mind, imagining how the money I earned would buy us passage to America and what it would be like to work as a carpenter's mate on our way there. It's any man's dream," he said, throwing his hands to the heavens. "Sir Thibideau thinks it's possible with a ship called *Newburyport*. He knows the captain, so he sent a letter attesting to my skills as a carpenter's mate. In case I cannot get the job, he also included banknotes to secure two tickets in steerage. I've already begun repaying him from my woodworking on *L'Immortel*. Morrie, we're going to America!"

Morrigan's hands went to her mouth. "Finn! America! Can you believe it?"

"*Newburyport*'s going to a town by the same name, somewhere north o' Boston. They build ships there."

Morrigan's excitement faltered. "Did the captain say he leaves in ten days?"

"Aye. *L'Immortel* must depart in ten days in time to catch *Newburyport* before she leaves from Liverpool on the third of September."

Panic surged through her. "It's so soon, Finn. Ten days," she said, her body seized in protest.

Finn put his arm around her shoulder. "I can read your eyes, Morrie. Like a frightened hare you are. But few ships leave in the coming weeks. The captain told me the North Atlantic makes passage risky this late in the season. Any longer and we'd have to wait until spring. I wouldn't have the chance like I do with Sir Thibideau knowing the captain of *Newburyport*."

Morrigan bit her lip as she watched the sea. "How can I leave our home, Finn?" How could she abandon the wolf's message and her vow to The Invisibles?

He flung out his arms and said, "I have the same question, Morrie. This place is all I've known, everything I've loved. Sunrises o'er green hills, sunsets o'er blue waters, the farm, our pub with all its music and jesting…." He turned to her, gripping her hands in his, "I can make something of myself in America where food and jobs are aplenty! You know there's no life like that for me here. If I have you with me, I'll have my home with me, too. Anyway, if I become a ship's carpenter, maybe I can get work on a vessel that sails to and from Ireland and you can sail with me. You might even learn captaining. We'd come home often," he said, his voice husky.

Morrigan was swept up in the possibility of it all. Finn had a strong mind and worked hard, and if anyone could rise above his station, he could. Her mind argued for his cause. Perhaps the "village" the wolf had spoken about, charging her with its healing, extended to anyone she encountered, even in places like America.

Her eyes glistening, Morrigan took a deep breath and said, "Finnbharr McDonaugh, you won't be going to America without me." Then she laughed. "Can women be ship's captains in America?"

"Yes, Morrie, and hurrah!" said Finn, throwing his flat cap into the air and leading her in an impromptu jig on the stony terrain by the quay. "Morrie, it's all I've dreamed of! We've got to make plans. I want to marry you so we're man and wife proper like!" Then he turned serious. He touched a curly tendril escaping Morrigan's bun and said, "I'll make ya proud, Morrigan Lane." He pulled her close, his eyes on her lips. She parted her own, and like a soul desperate for fulfillment met his.

That night neither Morrigan nor Riona could sleep. They lay on their pallet under the thatch and pretended. Then Riona whispered in the darkness, "Morrie. Do you think Finn's going to ask Da for permission to marry you?"

Morrigan rolled over to face her sister. "Aye, but it's so sudden, Ree. I don't think I'm ready for it."

Riona chuckled. "It's not a bad thing, I imagine, having a husband to warm your bed."

"It's not *that!* America is just so far away."

"Indeed it is. One moment you'll be here, and the next you'll be married and gone. I wish I were gone from here," said Riona under her breath. "Well, I'll have to get busy stitching a crewel cap for you, won't I?"

"I wish we could wait until spring," said Morrigan.

"What for? Finn's got a chance at apprenticeship on the ship leaving in September. He's got to take it, Morrie," said Riona. "It seems any who can are going."

"Sometimes I don't think I should go."

"Ach, do you know how lucky you are? To have a chance to leave this hard life for a new one filled with promise. I'd give anything to go."

"Maybe I'm not brave enough," said Morrigan.

"Not brave enough? You have more courage than anyone I know. Think of how you handled Sir Martin about the rents and how you fought past him to heal his own daughter. It's not courage you're lacking."

"Ree, I've had dreams and visitations from The Otherworld."

Riona exhaled a long breath. "I know you love Cathleen, but she's filled your head with fables."

"I know my own experiences, and they aren't fables." She longed to defend the ancient healing ways her sister had brought into question, but she knew Riona wouldn't understand.

"Oh, you've gotten all rigid on the pallet, Morrie," said Riona, "Listen, Cathleen's a kindhearted woman, and she's taught you a lot. I do think you see where others can't. But don't throw your life away for the notion of it. You deserve the love of a man who loves you and a life filled with promise," whispered Riona. "We all do."

Long into the night Morrigan struggled with questions: Why was a life filled with promise not possible in Ireland? Were the triad and parchment only useful in the land of Isla, the land of her ancestors? Was her destiny bound to the lush green hills and brooding skies of Ireland and Ireland alone?

76

MORRIGAN

A Jolt, Like a Lightning Strike

Morrigan fought to wake herself from the dream. Drenched in sweat, her heart pounded. She'd dreamt the same scene—the wolf's voice, the tragic image of one last herring as it sank to the ocean floor and, then, silence. Empty seas. The dream burned into her brain though she breathed in and out to make it go away. Cathleen had taught her dreams came for a reason, and they came in their specific timing for a reason. The dream brought with it more than sadness; it brought grief.

Morrigan dressed, gathered the triad and parchment, and escaped to the stone circle for guidance.

At the stone circle's perimeter, Morrigan summoned her courage to face the presence within the old stones

She stepped into the circle, aware of her heightened alertness. "Here I am," she said to the silence, finding a spot to rest against a large stone in the dim light before dawn. "I am pulled in two directions," she said to the stones. "Finn wants me to go to America, and I love him. Yet The Invisibles want me to heal the village, saying there is much at stake. What should I do?"

Silence. Could the parchment work on her? With trembling hands, she removed it from her creel basket and opened the scroll. I don't know what question to ask, she thought. Why did I have the same dream? What is it trying to tell me? She placed her hand over the first cord, body, and closed her eyes. No image came to mind. She moved her hand to the second cord, spirit. Again no image appeared. Then she moved her hand to terra, mind, and finally, heart, yet not a single image popped into her mind.

I suppose the parchment is a tool for healing, not answering questions about what to do, she thought. She returned it to her basket, and then willed herself to create an empty space deep inside the way Cathleen had instructed.

Shifting onto her belly on the hard ground, Morrigan sighed. "Wolf, where are you? Who else can give me answers?" Many minutes went by. Her mind quieted as the stones anchored her thoughts. A progression of images floated before her closed eyes. In the first, a rook hopped close to Morrigan, cocked his head, and took off toward Cathleen's abode. The rook who carried my message to Cathleen, she thought, remembering the mysterious exchange when she'd sprained her ankle. In the second, Finn's smoky gray eyes looked lovingly into hers. A moment she did not recognize as having happened. In the third, she stood at the stone circle surrounded by hooker and trawler fishermen. Some were inside the circle and some were outside. A premonition of the future! She felt a jolt like a lightning strike.

Knowing flooded in. Finn loved her and she loved him. Yet something beyond her ken had chosen her as *An Fhoínse*, a spring from which the life force flows. She was healer and ally of creation, and her vow to The Invisibles outweighed everything else. Now she knew what she must do.

Morrigan walked the stone circle sunwise, in the direction of good fortune, and called out, "May The Invisibles, the ancestors, and the not-yet-born nine generations hence give me strength." She must accept the great responsibility she'd been given. To risk believing her village could be anywhere, even in America, was too great. As heir to Isla's healing lineage, the triad, the parchment, and her calling were about this Irish land.

Dawn's golden glow spilled onto the land just as Morrigan stepped out of the stone circle and headed toward the village.

As she approached McDonaugh's farm, Morrigan's stomach roiled. Her decision was heart-wrenching, but she assured herself once she'd explained everything to Finn, they'd find a way forward together. Spring isn't far away, she thought. Maybe we can stay, and I can fulfill my promise. I just need time to figure things out.

At McDonaugh's door, she shouted, "Finn! Are you awake?"

The door swung open, and Cormac stood squinting in the bright light. "Morrie, you're quite the trollop, howling for Finn."

"Cormac. I've no time for jest. I must see Finn."

Cormac smiled at her small fury. "He's having a lie-in this morning." He turned and hollered, "Finn, it's your darling sweetheart coming to roust ya from sleep."

"A minute, Morrie." Finn's voice sounded hoarse and sleepy. "I'll meet you in the courtyard."

Morrigan made ready to leave.

"Will ya have some tea?" asked Cormac.

"No thanks. I'll be outside," said Morrigan, apology in her voice. She backed out the door. What will Cormac think of me after I tell Finn? It bothered her to disappoint them both.

"Morrie! I'm sorry to keep you. We had a raucous night at the pub," said Finn, looking peaked.

She turned from him before he could read her face, taking long strides to combat her nerves. They walked along fields strewn with pink foxglove, pale white dropwort, and blue harebell, cool counterpoints to the warm morning light. How was she going to tell him about her experiences? Finn was her mate for life. Would he believe her? Morrigan recalled her da's advice once before: "Take heart, Morrie. Only good comes from the heart." She turned to Finn. "I've got something to tell you. I never had a chance to tell you before you left how some things have happened to me, and, and how they've changed me."

"What things?"

"I've had a messenger from The Otherworld. 'Twas a wolf! Do you remember the tales we've heard from Seanchaithe?"

"Those long-ago stories?"

"Yes. As it turns out, my *en caul* birth and the mark I have," she touched her jaw, "mean I can speak in a language older than our Irish, older than anything. When all beings spoke it, accord existed across the land. Now, everywhere you turn there's strife. Hookers and trawlers, Irish and English, the Church and our ancient ways, landowners and us poor, our livelihood—the herring at risk."

Finn put a hand out. "Slow down, Morrie, the blasted poteen's made me slow this morning." At the pub, Finn had been the recipient of endless rounds of toasts to him and Morrigan's future together.

Morrigan struggled to find words to help him see as she saw. She chose a different tack. "Finn, I love you! I've never loved another. You make my heart sing, and I love your new confidence. I love how we've competed in games and laughed at crazy nonsense. I want you alongside me until my dying day. I want to become a mother with ya," she choked, and pushed on, "but I've been given a message that the fate of the world rests on how our village fares, and I have an obligation to try to heal this village."

"Heal the village? Is there a sickness going around?"

"Not in the usual way. But I must stay here for a time."

"Are you saying you won't marry me and sail to America?" Finn's mouth hung open in disbelief.

"I'm not saying no forever. I just can't go yet. Perhaps in the spring…" Morrigan closed her eyes to the pain she saw in Finn's.

"Just yesterday you said you'd go."

"I had a dream. Twice it came. About the last herring. It's The Invisibles trying to share a prophecy."

"The Invisibles?" Finn nearly shouted. Morrigan started to turn away, but he grabbed her shoulders and swung her around. "*I'm not invisible, Morrie! I'm here. Right in front of you! It's you I love.* I've worked myself to the bone for this! And the captain has already secured two passages. It's the break I need. We won't have this same chance in the spring."

"I know, Finn. I know." Morrigan's whole body ached.

Finn put his hands to his temples and took a deep breath as if trying to comprehend what she'd said. "All right, you have these—special gifts, Morrie. And you've had some strange happenings. But what can you do about a whole village? What can you do about the Irish and the English? What can you do about us being so poor I can't make anything of myself here?"

Morrigan shook her head. She took a step back from him to evade his anguish.

"The chance is now, and I'm right here in front of you, asking, Will you come with me, or won't you?"

Morrigan looked upward as though to draw strength from the unseen Otherworld. "Finn, I just….don't think I can!" she cried out, spun around, and fled through the meadow.

77

MORRIGAN

The Fates

The days flew by. As silent as a snowflake drifts upon the moor, Morrigan went about her work. She hardly slept, often walking the cliffs and talking into the air. She searched for the wolf. She called for Manannán mac Lir. She looked for signs she'd made the right decision, despite her broken heart.

Tommy and the boys fished like they'd always done, and Mamoh, Betha, and Riona focused on making or repairing gear for the harvest fishery. But their hearts weren't in it. Their minds were elsewhere. No one knew what to say to Morrigan, for they themselves did not understand her choice.

One Sunday morning after church, Riona linked her arm in Morrigan's and said, "Morrie, let's play 'What If.'" It was a game of fancy they'd enjoyed as children.

Though Morrigan's interest in games had disappeared, she conceded, "All right, Ree. Me first. What if you ate just one thing for a month? What would it be?"

"Ah, you've asked this question every time we've played, Morrie. I'd eat warm, apple-buttered biscuits."

"Well, it's a new answer, anyway."

"Because I had them at Sir Martin's picnic. My turn. What if you had only one chance at happiness? Would you take it, Morrie?" At the implication of Riona's question, Morrigan tried to pull away, but Riona wouldn't let her go.

"You don't understand, Ree."

Riona squeezed her sister's arm. "Maybe I don't, but you're crazy, Morrie! You have a man who loves you and a promise of freedom in America. That's not enough?"

Morrigan tore from her sister's grasp. "I made a promise to the ancestors. They are not to be trifled with."

"The ancestors are not here, trying to eke out a life, you senseless girl."

With a sharp breath, Morrigan glanced around them. "You distain the ancestors?" She turned from Riona and began to run as though her sister's words were a bad omen. Riona's full-throated cry came to her ears like a spear. "America beckons! For God's sake. Go!"

On a morning just days away from Finn's departure, Morrigan went to the stone circle. This time she walked in the counter direction. It matched her dark mood. She spoke aloud to the stones, "Is staying the right thing? Why does my heart want to break?" She touched each stone as she walked. "There's no making it right with Finn. He owes the captain for two tickets. Please send me a sign I'm doing the right thing."

She paused for a sign and seeing nothing, she walked further inside the stone circle, anger now quickening her pace. "It doesn't make any sense. Finn's right. What can I do for this village, anyway? One unlucky redhead? One skinny, dirty fisherman's daughter?" She had a wild impulse to push over the great stones. Just then she felt a sharp sting on the pad of her foot. "Ouch!" she said and quickly sat. A bee, no longer moving, was squashed into her foot. "Oh, little one, I'm so sorry." Morrigan pulled off the bee's wasted body, laid it atop a stone, and with both hands, squeezed the venom out of where the bee had stung. Tears pricked her eyelids and the stones blurred.

Tiny points of light began to dance in and out of her view. Then she heard a stern voice say, "You may be one skinny, dirty fisherman's daughter, but you are *An Fhoínse*. If you go to America, you spurn the Moirai."

The Moirai! Morrigan shuddered. The fierce Greek goddesses often called *the fates*.

"If you go to America, you spurn your namesake."

The Morrígan, goddess of war and fate. Standing now, Morrigan shivered in a sudden cool blow. "I mean no harm," she whispered.

The wind calmed and the voice softened. "This is your homeland. The bones of your ancestors feed this soil. Their ceremonies, the ones you love, mingle with the wind. Their sacred stones hold the stories just as they hold the warmth of each day. The Irish language, our ancient customs, a wildwood alive with beings, who are you without these?"

"I am lost without these."

"Then let your troubled heart be still."

Morrigan rocked back and forth as the tiny points of light disappeared.

She headed toward the village. I am not strong enough to defy the fates, she thought. My calling must be honored. An image of Finn arose in her mind, and her heart shattered. How can I let him go alone? She must pay him for the second ticket somehow. An idea formed in Morrigan's mind. She turned and took the shortcut to Sir Martin's estate.

At Rosderry Manor, Morrigan waited by the livery. She had nothing to lose. Desperation prompted Morrigan to seek Sir Martin. Desperation spurred action; of that she was certain. She had observed it in Sir Martin when Mistress Mary lay dying. She had observed it among the fishermen in the presence of Dillon and his threatening trawler. She'd heard the stories about desperate lads as young as eleven during the Rebellion of 1798 who were given the half-hanging torture and then killed.

Though she hoped to encounter Mr. Eagan or Mistress Mary as intermediaries, fate brought Sir Martin into view. He rounded the corner of the livery in his riding ensemble.

"Sir Martin, it is improper of me, and I beg your pardon. Might I have a moment?"

A startled Sir Martin said, "What is it?"

She hadn't rehearsed what to say, so her words tumbled out. "Though I would love one of Shauna's piglets you said I could have as a thank you for helping heal Mistress Mary even though I didn't ask for anything but it would seem I have a greater need just now—" She stopped, imagining Sir Martin's mental assessment. "The girl is just another of the begging set after all—ignorant and idle."

In truth, though Sir Martin's lips were pursed, he was working through her rush of words.

"—for a passage to America, and I won't ask for anything ever again." She bit her lip, waiting, heart thudding, searching his face.

"You want to go to America?"

"Not for me, Sir Martin. For my older sister, Riona."

Martin scratched his long sideburns considering her words. "You're a strange sort, Morrigan Lane. For Mary, I'll honor your request. Wait here."

Morrigan waited at Shauna's pen, her hands traveling over the pig's sturdy back. "I cannot believe Sir Martin has said yes, Shauna. Will Riona go to America with Finn? Maybe he'll take James with him instead." To herself, she thought, why can't it be me? But she knew better than to curse the fates, so she clenched her jaw and was silent. Soon Sir Martin returned and handed her an envelope.

"This should cover the fare, Morrigan."

She stared at the envelope and the words from her healing song came to mind. "Imagine an impossible thing and before you know, it has come to pass." Can more miracles happen for me? she thought. "Thank you, Sir Martin, and may the health of a salmon be upon—"

"Yes, yes, I know the blessing. It's little enough."

Morrigan curtsied and made to leave.

Martin held up a hand and cleared his throat. "Tell me, Morrigan Lane. Your, uh, powers. Do they work with people?" He looked out at the mares in the paddock, his arms folded. "I mean, could it mend my hard heart where her ladyship is concerned?"

Morrigan looked down to conceal the flush that had spread across her cheeks. She sensed the enormity of effort it took for Sir Martin to ask her this question. "I've seen Lady Elizabeth riding with Mistress Mary. They're so happy together."

"Riding is not a gentle sport, and both are quite accomplished. We are, or were, a premier equestrian family."

"A ride together might prove, uh, fruitful," ventured Morrigan. Then she turned to face him. "Sir Martin, I don't think you need the help of a curative. Perhaps if you simply choose to forgive her."

"You don't know enough about life." His words were punctuated with the slap of gloves on his forearm. Again, he turned away. Morrigan felt the heaviness of his inner struggle and, with a gasp, realized it matched her own.

"Love is its own healing force," she whispered, "like a gallop over the green hills of home."

78

SCHOOLMASTER WINNETT

Counter Charms

Astride his donkey, Schoolmaster Winnett felt the bird's presence as an intake of air. Then he heard the whoosh of its wings. Startled, he turned toward the sound. A lone magpie came at him, suddenly rolling its body, flying upside down. Winnett put out his arms for protection, but a stick, held in the bird's beak, grazed his forehead. The bird flipped upright and soared out of sight.

Schoolmaster Winnett grunted, checked his bald scalp, and found a scratch and a little blood. A single magpie was a bad omen. The old curse burst from his lips, "May fire and water be in you, bird of evil, and may the judgment of God be on your head for ever and ever."

It had been like this all summer. He'd felt besieged by things his rational mind could not understand, but his fearful mind suspected Morrigan Lane.

Like an infection, she had erupted these past months, her silent presence giving way to something more churlish. A nuisance she was, making a mockery of his authority with her ever-emboldened actions. And then those happenings in which she was embroiled—the rents and Mistress Mary. She seemed to simply *know* things. It was this fear that fueled Winnett's paranoia. Could Morrigan read the guilt in his eyes? Would she one day know he had stood passively by while Father Murray had choked to death?

He'd had to endure a harsh rebuke from the girl's father, for Christ's sake! The man said Morrigan was having nightmares and spells because of his sermons. The fires of hell were far more extreme than what could be found on earth. Whatever she was seeing was of her own conjuring.

He had been relieved to hear Finn McDonaugh had proposed to the young woman, and he'd hoped she'd soon be off to America, with his secret safe from her penetrating eyes. He imagined the old ways would vanish with the sailing ship, and the village would appear chaste and pious for the arrival of the new priest, expected within a fortnight.

Although Winnett would be reluctant to relinquish many of the duties and the benefits he'd experienced as temporary stand-in, he would soon have another focus. Riona. He was determined to marry Riona and start a family. He smiled, thinking of her blue eyes, her porcelain skin, and rosy lips.

It had all been planned. Except Morrigan had suddenly rejected Finn's invitation, a strange turn of events. He wondered if The Crooked Woman had invoked a counter-charm on Morrigan to advance her own wayward influence. Cathleen was beyond saving, and anyway she scared him. There remained time to save Morrigan with her quick mind and appetite for learning despite her recent contrary and even dangerous behavior.

He came to a crossing where the old trackway met the new road and startled Morrigan herself. Her clouded face and dark circles revealed an inner turmoil. Perhaps Cathleen *had* invoked a counter charm. "Good day to you, Morrigan. What brings you out on the new road?"

"Good day, Schoolmaster Winnett." Morrigan reached out to pat the donkey's muzzle.

She's ignoring my question, thought Winnett. He'd be direct. "I wish to speak to you, Morrigan. About your future."

"Oh?"

"It would seem you have a singular opportunity to go to America. It is beyond reason why you would turn down young Finnbharr. What could be at work? Do you feel strange? Perhaps it is one of Cathleen's counter-charms."

Morrigan stepped back from the donkey and looked at the schoolmaster. "Cathleen does not manipulate fate with counter-charms," she said, her face fierce.

"Surely you cannot have us believe you, of all village girls, do not want the freedom America promises? And with a fine man like Finnbharr who'll take you despite your disfigurement?" said Winnett. Morrigan winced. Winnett felt a thrill of satisfaction after the ways she had humiliated him in the master's school. Something seemed to be tucked under her arm. "What's that you carry?"

Biting her lip, Morrigan looked in the direction of her home.

"Let's have it!" Winnett demanded, holding out his hand.

Morrigan hesitated, then handed him the cream-colored envelope. "It's for my father, from Sir Martin. It's private."

Winnett noted Sir Martin's vermillion waxed seal. He dared not open it. "And what would Sir Martin be after, giving your father something?"

Morrigan glared, her disregard for him evident. "Kindly return my envelope or I shall tell Sir Martin you are a thief!"

Winnett felt the cold clutch of fear in his gut and lashed out. "Something irregular is happening, Morrigan, and it would seem you are right in the middle of it." He shoved the envelope at her. "I won't abide it! And you will regret any choice you make save going to America. Be forewarned: There is one who will lament it more than you. Your friend, Cathleen." Winnett gave the donkey a firm kick and headed away, his threat hanging in the air like the stench of rotten fish.

79

CATHLEEN

Is There One True Destiny?

Cathleen grunted as she carried a basket laden with turf inside her cottage. Her trips to the dried bog stack promised a warm and cozy home, her one indulgence.

Ah, the smell of turf. Acrid, yes, but with pungency so familiar, it was as if she'd emerged from her mother's womb craving it. The solid black peat formed from oak or yew was considered best. It came from deep in the earth and had the longest burn time. In contrast, Cathleen loved the heather peat, formed from decayed flowering shrubs and grasses. Its burn was shorter, but to her, it smelled like earth's perfume.

She set the basket in the chimney corner, lowered the tea kettle, and readied some buttered brown bread to have with tea. She had everything she needed: a full churn, a hot fire, tea, and shelves of her friends, the herbs. She began to hum a tuneless melody.

"Cathleen? Are you home?" Morrigan said outside her door. The Crooked Woman smiled. She'd had an inkling to put out an extra cup and saucer.

"Aye, Morrigan. Come in." She hadn't seen Morrigan for days, though she'd heard the news of Morrigan's decision not to go to America with Finn.

Morrigan entered in a whoosh of cool air, and instantly, Cathleen sensed her unease. She poured tea for her young friend and sat in her chair by the fire, motioning for Morrigan to sit on the bench nearby.

"Schoolmaster Winnett does not favor you or your medicines, Cathleen. I worry he could turn the village against you. He has threatened to do so. I think he's afraid of you."

"Schoolmaster Winnett is a learned man. In time he will realize the creator's world is filled with sacred succors."

"Maybe he wants the village to need him more than you."

"It is true the old ways have power and some don't want that power in the hands of us poor Irish. Nonetheless, we will continue to rely on our ancestors' methods."

"He told me I must go to America. Riona says I'm crazy not to, and I can be free in America."

"Free? Free from what?"

Morrigan stayed quiet for a time, thinking, and then said, "Once I thought freedom was being a ship's captain. Now I think freedom is being all lined up on the inside, knowing what is right for you to do." As she sipped tea, she recalled the crone's words: "Your destiny is in your hands." Would her decision bring her peace in the end? "Cathleen, Schoolmaster Winnett thinks you've performed a counter-charm to keep me here."

Sensing Morrigan's unspoken question, Cathleen said, "No I did not. 'Tis not for me or anyone else to alter your course, Morrigan, though sometimes it's easier to believe a thing outside of ourselves is the cause of our circumstance. Morrigan, you must decide whether to go or stay yourself. Tell me, have you really had a change of heart? 'Tis difficult to turn away from the promise of love." She felt a pang remembering her own dream of a husband and family.

"I want to go with Finn, but I made a vow to The Invisibles to heal my village. And this is the homeland of our ancestors. These are my people. Seems the fates have plans for me. There is looming conflict with the new trawler fishing boats risking our herring fishery. I am needed, I suppose."

"I wonder. Is there one true destiny a person is fated to have? Or does a person create a destiny choice by choice?"

MORRIGAN

Lower the Kettle

On her walk along the cliff way, Morrigan slowed her pace. She reflected on Cathleen's question about whether destiny is fated or created choice by choice, uncertain of the answer. Maybe I can choose to go to America with Finn first. Use the banknotes for myself, she thought. Maybe I can choose to return in a few years, with Finn, coins in my skirt, and our own wee wains. We could have our own cottage holding, and Finn can work as a carver and I can fulfill my vow to The Invisibles...

It was her heart's dreaming, but it contrasted with the steely instruction she'd heard earlier in the stone circle. Manannán mac Lir's words settled into her: "No, not powerless on this fated track. Throw open your arms, for there's no going back."

Morrigan arrived at the quay just as the sun sank below the horizon. Fishermen rambled in twos and threes making their way home.

"Da, I've got something to ask ya," said Morrigan.

Tommy steered her away from the others and said in a gentle voice, "What is it, Morrie?"

She dragged her feet as she struggled to find the right words. "I know you were surprised I changed my mind about going to America. Something has me rooted here, at least for now. True it is, I may never leave."

Tommy put a hand on her shoulder. "For my selfish heart, I am glad. But don't be breaking your shin on a stool that's not in your way, a leanbh. You can't know what tomorrow will bring."

Morrigan steadied herself. These next words would change all their lives. With them, Riona's dream of America could be realized and her own calling honored. They were hard words to speak. "Riona has stars in her eyes and a hankering to go to America. She's told me so. And Finn's beholden to the Frenchman for two tickets. I wondered if she should go instead of me, so I asked Sir Martin to pay for the extra ticket. He'd planned to give me a piglet from Shauna's first litter, but I asked for the banknotes instead."

Tommy cocked his head. "He gave you money for a passage to America? Either I've misjudged the man, or he's gone daft."

"He did." Morrigan reached into her skirt and produced the cream-colored envelope. "He said it was because of Mistress Mary. Will you take it to Finn as payment for the ticket I won't use? And do you think Riona could go?" Morrigan gulped the words.

Tommy searched her eyes and asked, "You sure you want to do this, Morrie?"

Morrigan looked down and nodded.

"I'll deliver the banknotes. About Riona, I'll talk to your mum." He added, "I understand your tie to this land; 'tis in me, too." He gave her a hard squeeze. Arm in arm, they walked home.

Later in the evening Tommy encouraged Betha to go out walking with him. Hands dripping with dishwater, she protested, but Morrigan ushered her away. Soon Betha returned, her shoulders drooped like cabbage needled with hoarfrost.

"A walk's supposed to put a bloom in your cheeks, Mum. You look paler than when you left," said Riona.

Betha turned and held Morrigan's gaze. Their eyes shared sadness at what would be put into motion. "Your da went to the pub" was all she said.

Frowning, Mamoh said, "I'll lower the kettle."

81

MORRIGAN

The Decision

On a morning four days before Finn's departure, Cormac arrived at the Lane cottage, cap in hand and said, "I'm here on behalf of Finn."

"Cormac, come in," said Mamoh.

Riona and Morrigan sat loading rope onto netting needles. "What's this? Cormac here on behalf of Finn?" whispered Riona. Morrigan bit her cheek and said nothing.

"Will you have some tea?"

Cormac shook his head. "Thank you, kindly, Mamoh, but I've got more work than a thieving fox. Where's Himself?"

"Tommy's out loading nets." Betha gestured toward the quay. "Tell us why you've come."

"Finn wanted me to say…" Cormac paused, his usual mockery gone. He looked at Morrigan and shook his head. Something like pity showed in his eyes. To Betha he said, "He will escort Riona to America."

"What?" said Riona, stunned. She looked at Cormac, who shrugged his shoulders. Then she looked at Morrigan.

"'Tis you who dream of it, Ree."

"It can't be true. Me? Going to America?"

Betha placed a hand on Riona's shoulder. "You'll find a country-man there, sure as sunrise."

Riona clutched her mother's hand. "Mum, can you believe it? I'm going to America!"

Like a brigade on a mission, the Lane family rushed to ready Riona for her long voyage across the sea. Hoping to send her off with a few extra coins, Tommy and the boys risked fishing *Inis Ealga* at the edges of her capability in search of a bigger harvest. Mamoh mended anything of her granddaughter's looking threadbare, her fingers skilled despite her poor eyesight. Morrigan feigned a new interest in netmaking and repairing. Without Riona, the job would fall to her. Betha visited women in the village whose relatives had braved the voyage. She returned home, anxious and bursting with news.

"Landsakes! There's to be a medical inspector, Riona, and if you don't pass, you'll be left at the Waterloo loading dock in Liverpool!"

"I've never felt better, Mum," said Riona.

"Still, keep your wrap tight. And there's no bedding in steerage. Mary O'Hare said her brother bought some in Liverpool. Said there're loads of merchants by the boarding houses near Waterloo Dock and northwards of a Clarence Dock. You'll need a night or two at a boarding house. Mary says don't go to Marshall's at Clarence Dock if you can help it. It's filthy there and destitute of comfort. And avoid Union Hotel on Moorfield Street. They charge ten pence a day!" Betha stopped to catch her breath.

Riona laughed at her mother's concerns. "I'll be fine, Mum."

"Oh, and you can bring aboard some of your own provisions. I'm told passengers get the basics—oatmeal, biscuits, flour, sugar, molasses, and tea, sometimes rice."

"No potatoes?" Riona hadn't lived a day without potatoes.

"They don't stay fresh in the hold, I suppose. Not enough air." Morrigan shuddered at an image of a dark, airless ship.

"Oh, merciful Lord, we'll all have to help since there's loads to do!" said Betha.

"God is nearer to us even than the door, dear," said Mamoh. "We will all help. I'll go see Mary O'Hare about the honey, and Morrie, can you see if Cathleen has some helpful herbs?"

"Aye, Mamoh."

Betha added, "Now, Riona, go and collect Finn. We're to meet Schoolmaster Winnett here. He wants to explain about finding a Catholic parish just as soon as you land in America."

Morrigan winced as she imagined Finn and Riona together landing on America's shores. She felt a squeezing in her heart.

82

BETHA

Her Heart Is Pure

Betha heard a noise outside the cottage, followed by the customary words, "God bless all in this house!" She opened the door to Schoolmaster Winnett hobbling his donkey. "Schoolmaster Winnett! Come in and warm yourself. I've made tea," she said, moving aside to permit the man's entry, noting the way Winnett folded his arms as if for protection.

During his ride to the Lane cottage, Winnett had rehearsed what he intended to say as his whole future depended on this one conversation.

"Riona's collecting Finn, and they'll meet us here. Everyone else is out preparing for their departure. We are anxious to hear how the two can connect with a Catholic parish in America."

Winnett would not sit. Rather, he drew himself up as though giving an oration at Saint Joseph's and said, "Well, that's not why I am here, Mrs. Lane. I am here to tell you it is Morrigan who must be on that ship."

"Morrigan? She's decided to stay. She's knitted to this land as breath is to wind."

"She is a bedeviled child. Our new priest arrives soon. We must display only utmost piety in Baile Ghort na Darach. And you, a model Catholic woman in this village, should understand, despite your *particular* upbringing—we mustn't bring shame upon this parish. For the love of God, you must send Morrigan instead!"

Betha gripped the kettle hard to resist smashing it on his head. "You are out of line, Sir. Shame upon the parish?" She leaned in, her words clipped and cold. "My daughter has a gift for healing, and her heart is pure in its intent. There is no shame in that."

"She listens to The Crooked Woman, with her spells and charms."

"Cathleen has brought life to nearly every babe in this village. She has a gift for midwifery and forest medicines. I have no knowledge of any charms."

Schoolmaster Winnett shook his head, slumped a bit, and then admitted, "Mostly, Betha, I came to speak to you about Riona."

Just then Riona burst through the door, followed by Finn. "I'm sorry we're late, Mum. Good day, Schoolmaster Winnett. What about me?"

The man blushed and asked, "May I have a word with you, Riona?"

Betha started to protest, but Riona replied, "Of course, Schoolmaster Winnett."

Once outside, he ushered her a distance away from the cottage and said, "Riona, you are my best student. Your refined ways and the manner in which poems and songs burst from you are like a salve to my soul. I'd like to bring my own wee ones into the world with a mother as beautiful as you." He bowed as though embarking upon a courtship. "I'd like to have you for my wife."

A bubble of laughter erupted from Riona, but upon seeing Winnett's face, she stopped. "Schoolmaster Winnett, I don't know what to say."

"Consent to my courtship, Riona," he pleaded, grasping her hands in his.

Riona squirmed and said, "You are kind, Sir. And you've been a strong and intelligent teacher. For that I thank you. But I've already decided. I aim to find a man of fortune in America, and America is where I am going." Then she withdrew her hands from his and stepped quickly through the door.

Schoolmaster Winnett stood stunned; his face darkened. "Well, you shan't have any help from me!" he shouted and, with jerky movements, mounted his donkey and trotted away.

83

MORRIGAN

Final Acts

When she arrived at Cathleen's, Morrigan asked, "Do you have any curative herbs or teas Riona could take with her on the ship?" Morrigan couldn't keep the grief from her voice.

Cathleen turned her attention to the healing herbs. "Of course, especially meadowsweet oil and lemon balm oil," she said. From large vials she poured portions into smaller bottles. "Meadowsweet staunches bleeding and heals wounds. Smell," said Cathleen, removing the wooden stopper. Morrigan leaned in and sniffed saying, "Smells like wintergreen."

"Lemon balm oil repels bugs and rats. It can be rubbed on the skin to deter them and placing a dot under the nose will help if the ship's odor becomes unpleasant."

"Imagine Riona administering dots of lemon balm under everyone's noses," said Morrigan, a smile forming.

Cathleen couldn't imagine the refined Riona on a ship at all, but she said nothing. Next, she showed Morrigan a tin. "Dandelion and burdock tea, for sore throats, and swollen glands. If Riona is feeling poorly, she should take this. Then there is hawthorn tea for sleep. I imagine 'twill be noisy in steerage, and this nettle tea is warming on a dank day. That should do it, Morrigan."

As she made her way to the door with the medicines, Morrigan said, "I hope to know these medicines as well as you know them one day, Cathleen. Mistress Mary needed your knowledge of milk

thistle as much as the insight about her loneliness I received from…"
Morrigan stopped. The parchment's inner workings were a secret.
"First you, and then The Invisibles taught me the hand, without
the spirit, brings no healing."

"I am fortunate to pass on what I've learned to one of Isla's kin,
one as quick-witted and lionhearted as you, Morrigan. Consider
your birth scar a signal—you are a leader *and* a healer, both."

Morrigan nodded, considering her words. "I'll think on it,
Cathleen. And may all good spirits, the ancestors, and the not yet
born nine generations hence bless you. You've helped me realize I
won't be sad or angry forever. Da's right. The future's unknowable."

"Tell your mum there's no charge for the medicines. They're my
gift to Riona. May she go with God."

On her way home from Cathleen's, Morrigan's dark mood lifted
despite the brooding skies. She imagined what life could be like
as a village healer and leader, a voice for her people. Morrigan
believed she was smarter than Schoolmaster Winnett. Maybe I can
be like Gráinne Ní Mháille of the land, she thought. I will write
to Finn in America, and we'll come together soon. She would not
rest until she found Finn there, and, with this thought, Morrigan
felt comforted.

At the sound of a horse's whinny, she turned, and there
approached Mistress Mary atop Devona. Morning light illuminated Mary's pale face, and determined set to her lips, but her
eyes were bright.

Morrigan curtsied. "Good day, Mistress Mary."

"Hello, Morrigan. Your mum told me I might find you here."

"You're looking well, Mistress Mary."

Mary smiled. "I'm getting better each day. I carry a letter of recommendation for Riona. I heard from Maeve she leaves soon." Mary searched Morrigan's face. "The letter speaks of Riona's fine skills with embroidery, lace, and weaving. With it, she should be able to get a job in a gentry's home."

"Mistress Mary, you are kind. Thank you."

Mary hesitated. "Morrigan, I would have written a letter for you, too, though with different words." They shared mischievous expressions. "The letter would have said what a competent and fun schoolmistress you'd be, or a nanny."

Morrigan looked away. "I cannot go, Mistress Mary. 'Tis no good trying to explain why."

At the sound of voices coming down to the quay, the horse's ears flicked forward. "Whoa, Devona." Mary shifted in her saddle. "I'll be going to London for a time with Mother. And off to Paris to shop for the season's parties."

"That'll put the glow back in your cheeks."

"I've instructed Mr. Eagan, anytime you want, you can walk Devona for exercise. That is, if it's something you'd want to do."

"It would be my pleasure, Mistress Mary." Morrigan patted the horse's neck.

"And maybe when I return, we can sit by the pond. I'll describe every party to you, and all the gowns."

Mary searched Morrigan's eyes, "Mother told me sometimes a friendship can supersede the blood one is born with."

Morrigan laughed. "'Tis a strange world, Mistress. I'd like to sit by your pond."

An awkwardness settled on them. Mary squirmed in her side-saddle. Morrigan hesitated, squinted up at the mistress through clouds seared with sunlight. What else? she thought.

Mary burst out, "Father and Mother are to be remarried! There's to be a wedding soon! Oh, Morrigan, I hope you will come. I'll tell father the livestock will need soothing and you are the perfect one to do it, but you can enjoy the party, too."

"I would be proud to help on such a happy occasion," said Morrigan.

Mary smiled. "May your sister go with God, Morrigan, and to you I'm forever indebted." Her words came from her heart. Then she turned away and urged Devona into a canter.

Morrigan hurried home carrying a basket filled with Cathleen's medicines and Mistress Mary's letter.

"Mistress Mary brought a recommendation for you, Riona. She has written of your fine skills in the gentry's appreciation for crewel and weaving."

"Saints be praised!" said Betha. She added softly, "That Winnett refused to tell us how to connect with a parish in America."

"It's because I rebuffed him, Mum. He made me feel ill at ease," said Riona.

"Thank the good Lord for Mistress Mary's endorsement," said Mamoh. "And don't we owe thanks to Morrigan, as well? Without her healing help, Mistress Mary would never have written it."

MORRIGAN

True Lovers Don't Sever

In a wink, the evening before Riona's departure arrived. The Lane women prepared John Dorys in cream sauce with potatoes and early cabbage. Seldom did Tommy keep John Dorys for his own family, but this night was an exception.

An unaccustomed orator, Tommy declared he would like to say a special prayer of blessing before they ate. "Dear Lord. Our hearts are filled with hope and sadness all at the same time. We ask for your grace. We ask you for strength. We ask for all good things to happen in the end. And we ask you to bless this food, from thy bounty, through Christ our Lord, Amen."

Mamoh wiped away a tear. The boys bowed their heads. Riona sniffled. Betha and Morrigan said nothing and ate little.

Just after Tommy had played a lonesome tune on his harp, there came a shout at the door. "Morrigan?" It was Finn's voice.

"What does he want, Morrie?" asked Riona, her brow set in a frown.

Morrigan shrugged, but her heart pounded. *Why has Finn come tonight before he departs in the morning? Has something changed? Maybe he is staying after all!*

"She's coming," said Tommy, pushing Morrigan toward the door. "May God be with you on your journey, Finnbharr, and we'll see you off in the morning," said Tommy, though there was a slight question in his tone.

Morrigan left the cottage. "Hello, Finn," she said, blushing. She'd forgotten how chiseled his jaw, how muscular his arms, how lean his torso. And those eyes. Gray and blue and clouds and sea.

"This way, Morrie," Finn directed, walking inland, away from the quay, past other candlelit fishermen's cottages. A waxing moon cast its glow on the landscape known as home. As they walked, Finn said in the darkness, "Since we were babes, Morrie, we've been together. I can't leave without telling you something."

Her heart sank at his words, "can't leave." He was still going. In the low light, she could just make out Finn's features. She told herself to memorize them.

Finn drew her to him and said, "I know you're special, Morrie. You're special because you're the girl I never felt awkward around. You're the girl I fell in love with. And I've known you were special in a different way. You have something the rest of us don't—a way of seeing the world beyond ours."

Morrigan softened. "Aye, Finn."

"Now, I don't know how your gift has gotten in the way of us being together, and I think it's breaking both our hearts, but I want you to know I respect your devotion."

"Ah, Finn! It's true, my heart is breaking." Suddenly she recognized the scene from her dream in the stone circle. Finn's smoky gray eyes poured love into hers. She leaned into him. His eyes caressed hers and when his lips found hers, he kissed her like one whose hunger could never be satisfied. Finally, they separated.

"I want you to have this, Morrie." Finn placed a large pin in Morrigan's hands. "My mother's brooch. The stone is chalcedony. I've kept it for good luck, but I think it needs to stay here in Ireland with you."

Morrigan looked at a stunning stone of celestial blue in a plain gold setting. "It's beautiful, Finn! Kate's brooch. I'll wear it close to my heart." She lifted the gem to her breast. "But I will get to America, Finn. Soon. I will join you, soon."

"I'm counting on it, Morrie. I'll be waiting for you in America. Come when you can. Because true lovers don't sever." Then in a winsome voice, he sang:

> *Come in the evening, or come in the morning*
> *Come when you're look'd for, or come without warning:*
> *Kisses and welcome you'll find before you,*
> *The oftener you come, the more I'll adore you!*

> *Light is my heart since the day we were plighted*
> *Red is my cheek they told me was blighted*
> *The green of the trees looks greener than ever,*
> *And the linnets are singing, "True lovers don't sever!"*

Morrigan heard the screech of a barn owl. It sounded like the cry of her own heart's wound. She sang:

> *And with love like ours, as unchangeably beaming,*
> *We trust, when in secret, most tunefully streaming;*
> *Till the starlight of heaven above us shall quiver.*
> *And our souls flow as one down eternity's river.*

> *Imagine sweet flowers I'll pluck for a start;*
> *To honor my memories while we are apart;*
> *I'll send from the mountain its breeze to inspire you;*

I'll send from my fancy a tale that won't tire you.

Together they sang:

> *So, come in the evening, or come in the morning*
> *Come when you're look'd for, or come without warning:*
> *Kisses and welcome you'll find before you,*
> *The oftener you come, the more I'll adore you!*
>
> *Light is my heart since the day we were plighted*
> *Red is my cheek they told me was blighted*
> *The green of the trees looks greener than ever,*
> *And the linnets are singing, "True lovers don't sever!"*

Their voices faded. Neither wanted to break the silence. Finally, Finn embraced Morrigan and said, "I'll always love you, Morrigan Lane. I hope you finish what you're meant to do. I'll be waiting."

Overwhelmed by a mixture of love and sorrow, Morrigan answered, "Never have I felt this more strongly, Finn: If I can, I will." Holding hands, they walked one last time toward her home.

85

MORRIGAN

Like Ireland Herself

The next morning the sea glittered like diamonds on a silver ball gown. While Riona prepared for her departure, Morrigan walked to the quay and stared out at *L'Immortel* rolling in the swells. "Help me make it through the day," she whispered. Perhaps she'd pretend she was someone else, someone whose heart was not in tatters. Someone who was not holding the shears that had done it.

She recalled her dream of becoming a sea captain and Manannán mac Lir's alluring words, "Come to me, explore the sea. I shall ferry you to the free." The sea god had offered her a new opportunity to see into hidden realms.

She remembered singing with Riona, "to be going somewhere," as Finn journeyed to Cork. Now Riona was truly going somewhere, over the seas, while she remained in Ireland.

In a different way, she had been on a journey guided by the spirits and helpers of The Otherworld, and she was heir to Isla's gift. The thought brought her a breath of comfort. She chided herself for her poor attempt at consolation and returned home.

Clustered outside the door, ready to depart, stood her family. Riona and Finn, two soon-to-be Irish emigrants, walked to the quay along a path lined with villagers who bid them farewell and offered them words of encouragement and counsel. Shouts of good fortune filled the air culminating in a wild Irish cry.

Blank-faced and rigid, Morrigan willed herself to join them, walking alone. Need air, she thought, her gasps betraying the turmoil inside.

The villagers whispered about Morrigan, the one who would stay behind. Though they admired her loyalty to their native Eire, they wondered about the wisdom of her decision.

"The whole countryside's come out to see you off, Ree," said Tommy. As had many, he'd started the morning with a whiskey-milk punch at McDonaugh's. It was possible Betha held him steady as she latched onto his arm.

"It's like a party, Da," said Riona, pirouetting once in her new woolen shawl and skirt, stopping as she saw Morrigan's face. Guilt prompted her to whisper, "You can change your mind, Morrie. All my clothes will fit ya. Just pull down the skirts."

Morrigan shook her head and said, "I can't, and please," she bit her lip, "don't ask me again. I couldn't bear it."

"When you're ready, Morrie, just come. And when I get work, I'll send money. I'll miss you more than anyone. I can't think about how much, or I won't want to go either. And what are you going to do with all that room on the pallet?" She squeezed Morrigan's arm, and they shared sad smiles.

Soon the rest of the villagers fell back, and only the families of McDonaugh and Lane walked the last steps to the quay. An onshore breeze had stiffened, moving the petals of sea asters where they clung to the coastal cliffs. Commands from the captain and returning shouts from crew members silenced the group.

Connie McDonaugh, brimful of whiskey and grief, threw his arms around Finn and held him. Then he tore himself apart, cleared his throat, and said, "You've got to do your own growing son, no matter how tall your grandfather was."

Finn nodded.

Cormac sputtered, "Come back to us one day, will ya? Maybe as a captain of your own ship." He and James formed a circle of brothers around Finn patting him on the back, and then moving aside.

Tommy gave Finn a hearty hug. "May God be with ya, Finn. Keep a watch over Riona," he said.

"Aye, Mr. Lane. I'll tell the lads she's my sister, and I like to fight," he said.

Riona said a teary good-bye to Morrigan and Mamoh, and received a strong hug from Betha whose face was hardened with grief. Riona kissed her brothers on the cheek, and then Tommy escorted her to the dory.

Finn approached Morrigan, who looked out to sea as if trying to spot something on the horizon. "It's time, Morrigan. We've said all there is to say." He turned her toward him and lifted her chin.

"Kiss me farewell, Finn."

Finn's lips pressed into hers, and, with a sound like a distressed animal, he turned toward the sea.

As the pulling boats pushed off from the quay and began to row out to *L'Immortel*, Betha ran after them. "I love you, Riona! Go with God." Never had Betha declared her love so directly.

Morrigan stood a distance apart, her eyes huge wells of tears, holding her wrap tightly across her body as the dory carried Riona and Finn away. With a low sound in his throat, Tommy took a step toward Morrigan, but Mamoh held out an arm to stop him.

"She is not alone. She knows this. She is doing as she must. Let her come to you." Then Mamoh wrapped her arm around her son-in-law, leaning into him as though she could no longer hold herself up.

Once aboard the ship, Riona walked to a place near the stern and began jumping up and down, waving her arms. She held her hands to her mouth and shouted something that was lost in the wind. She would stand this way, waving and shouting while sails were hoisted, and the anchor was aweigh. She would stand this way during the schooner's tack out into the bay. She would stand this way until they could no longer see her on the boat.

Once on the ship, Finn turned, waved a final gesture of farewell, and then, with head down, went below decks. Brisk winds caught the schooner's sails just beyond the quay, and *L'Immortel* accelerated toward the horizon.

Hands to her cheeks, Morrigan collapsed into herself. "Come. Back." Turning, she fled the quay, running through the village and onto the old cliff way as if to escape some inner demon. At the cliff's edge, she watched the ship grow smaller and smaller in the distance. She clutched the chalcedony brooch Finn had given her, and in her grief, she did not see it glow nor did she see a similar glow from deep in the recesses of the forest.

When her inner storm had exhausted its fury, Morrigan gazed for a long time across the empty, glistening waters of the bay. Her spirit strengthened, rising like a tide that spills upon the shore.

Morrigan stood like Ireland herself, infused with vitality from invisible forces and fortified by her dreams.

Guide to Characters

Morrigan Lane
    Father: **Thomas (Tommy) Lane**
    Mother: **Betha Lane**
    Grandmother: **Mamoh** (MamOH)
    Siblings: **Liam** (LEEam) **Ruarc** (RUerk) and **Riona** (REEuhna)

Colm Lane (CULLuhm) Uncle, Tommy's younger brother—sails a smaller type of hooker sailboat, a púcán.

Cathleen Ó Nialláin, (CatLEEN oNYElin)—The Crooked Woman, —herbalist and midwife

Sir Richard Martin, gentry landowner
    Daughter: **Mistress Mary**
    Overseer: **Mr. Edward Eagan**
    Pig: **Shauna**

Connie McDonaugh, pub owner
    Sons: **Cormac, James,** and **Finbharr** (FINvar)

Schoolmaster Winnett, schoolteacher

Father Murray, priest of Saint Joseph's parish

Michael Dillon, trawler owner

The Otherworld—The mysterious, magical, holy space that lies in between things, or across the veil, or deep inside

Guide to Pronunciation

Ag caoineadh (aKEENnu)—a rhythmic praise of the dead, keening

A leanbh (ahLANuv)—my child

An Fhoínse (anEENcheh)—a fountainhead, used here metaphorically as "spring from which the life force flows

Baile Ghort na Darach (BALLeh Girt no DARach)—Village name meaning, "Village of the Field of the Oak"

Bealtaine (beeELtinuh)—a festival celebrating the beginning of summer on the ancient Celtic calendar. A cross quarter day, marking the midway point between Spring Equinox and Summer Solstice, today it is celebrated a few days earlier, on May first.

Cabhrú (COWru)— help!

Caul (CAll)—a rare birth phenomenon in which a piece of the amniotic sac is still attached to a baby's head or face

Cóiste Bodhar (coeshteh BOWer)—Death Coach

Daoine Sidhe (DEEne She)—The Good People, Fairies

Dúidín (DUdeen)—pipe

Gadaí (GODee)—thief

Gráinne Ní Mháille (Grawn-ya ee WALLia)—daughter of the Irish Ó Máille chieftain, a warrior-pirate and ship's captain during the reign of Queen Elizabeth

Imbolc (IMulc)— a festival celebrating the beginning of spring on the ancient Celtic calendar. A cross quarter day, marking the midway point between Winter Solstice and Spring Equinox, today it is celebrated a few days earlier, on February first.

Ionsaí (UHNsee)—attack

Lughnasadh (looNAsa)—a festival celebrating the beginning of harvest season on the ancient Celtic calendar. A cross quarter day, marking the midway point between Summer Solstice and Autumn Equinox, today it is celebrated a few days earlier, on August first.

Manannán mac Lir (MAnanan MAC lir)—Sea God

Máthair Mhór (mawher WOR)—Great Mother

Púcán (POOcahn)—a small hooker-type sailboat

Quay (KAY)—docks

Samhain (SOWan)— a festival celebrating the beginning of winter on the ancient Celtic calendar. A cross quarter day, marking the midway point between the Autumn Equinox and the Winter Solstice, today it is celebrated a few days earlier, beginning at sunset on October 31st.

Seanmháthair (shanaWAW her)—Old Mother

Scian (SCHEENn)—dagger

Sláinte, Sláinte mhaith (slANcha wah)—a toast, "to your health"

Seanchaí (SHAN a chee) "ch" as in loch; (Plural: Seanchaithe)—storyteller who roves from village to village, in the old tradition

Tuatha dé Danann (TOO-hot day-DA-naan)—the people of the Goddess Danu, thought to be an ancient race of Ireland who ruled from 1897 B.C. to 1700 B.C.; allegedly defeated by the Melesians and consigned to mythology and the underground

Original Song Links

"LET THE BONES BE LAID BARE"

Page 130

Lyrics: Jennifer Comeau
Music: Jennifer Comeau and Michael Farquharson
Vocals: Nell Ní Chróinín
Guitar: Jim Kelly
Uilleann Pipes, Flute: Ivan Goff
Violin: Oisín McAuley
Cello: Natalie Haas

"TO BE GOING SOMEWHERE"

Page 162

Lyrics: Jennifer Comeau
Music: Jennifer Comeau and Michael Farquharson
Lead Vocals: Maureen McMullan and Nell Ní Chróinín
Guitar: Jim Kelly
Flute: Ivan Goff
Violin: Oisín McAuley
Cello: Natalie Haas
Bass: Michael Farquharson
Percussion: Billy Sutton

"ONLY JOY LIVES HERE"

Page 247

Lyrics: Jennifer Comeau
Music: Jennifer Comeau and Michael Farquharson
Lead Vocals: Nell Ní Chróinín
Guitar: Jim Kelly
Flute: Ivan Goff
Violin: Oisín McAuley
Cello: Natalie Haas
Bass: Michael Farquharson
Percussion: Billy Sutton
Backing Vocals: Jennifer Comeau, Delilah Poupore, and
Andrea Wollstadt

Author's Notes

I wrote this novel to honor my Celtic ancestors, their ceremonies, and their exquisite relationship with the visible and invisible realms within their raw and beautiful landscape. The idea of *A Moon in All Things* came to me in a dream. I awoke with four nouns in my head: woman, wolf, the Burren (a landscape in Western Ireland), and ancestors. One image, which I intuitively knew would be both the start and end of a story that wanted to be written: A woman standing alone on the cliffs overlooking the Irish sea, "… like Ireland herself, infused with vitality from invisible forces and fortified by her dreams."

Growing up in my suburban Tonawanda, New York, home, the lot of us (eight kids and our parents) loved the Clancy Brothers and Tommy Makem. We sang Irish songs while my mother told stories of the ancestors or quoted poet scholars. The Irish Gaelic word for music—ceol—means lifeblood, and music is the lifeblood of the Irish. As a songwriter, I felt a story set in Ireland would only come to life if it included music.

Some readers have asked me what's real in the story. That's a question for you to decide. I can share that the pea-saliva curative that Morrigan applies to Mistress Mary is real. I once had a wart on my foot, and a friend of a friend told me to apply the pea-saliva method every day for two weeks. The wart went away.

Most of the dreams in this story are my dreams. For example, the dream where Morrigan's eyes are opened after a ceremonial leader offers the medicine of sheep's cheese and water—its own kind of *holy communion*— just before a wolf pack leader upends her, was my dream. The dream of a predator bird descending on

Morrigan as she sleeps, where she grips it to kill it and discovers only bones and feathers, was my dream. The dream Morrigan has two times about the last herring sinking to the bottom of the sea was mine, except in my dream, it was the last dolphin. And yes, sadly, I also had the dream *twice*. More of my dreams will feature in the sequel.

The five meta cords of connection—Body, Mind, Heart, Spirit, Terra—I believe are real. So many examples exist in healing modalities today under different names. Five element acupuncture, and Former Harvard and Columbia University professor, Tal Ben-Shahar's happiness studies and Wholebeing SPIRE model—Spiritual, Physical, Intellectual, Relational, Emotional—to name two. And couldn't it be possible the parchment is a physical representation of our intuitive capacities?

I have many stories about how experiences in the natural world informed the choices I made in my writing. I look forward to sharing them with you at a book club or talk. To those who may wish to know *what happens next* to Morrigan Lane and her clan, I am immersed in writing the sequel and look forward to sharing it with you one day soon.

Research into the Galway Bay area of Ireland in the 1820s was an important part of my journey. I took pains to ensure the veracity of the festival descriptions, fishermen's lives, herbal medicines, class and gender inequities, and the plethora of superstitions and rituals that represented everyday life. I have taken some artistic liberty. For example, I portrayed the Irish as less destitute than they were at that time and I sited a church in the small village of Baile Ghort na Darach—a town too small to have had a church or a priest, as priests were scarce in those days. Any research errors are my own.

Resources

1. Hely Dutton, *A Statistical and Agricultural Survey of the County of Galway* (Original edition: University Press, Dublin, 1824; annotated and indexed edition: Clachan, 2013)

2. Sir William Wilde, *Ireland: Her Peculiarities and Popular Superstitions* (Dublin University Magazine, c. 1850)

3. Garret FitzGerald, *Irish Primary Education in the Early Nineteenth Century: An Analysis of the First and Second Reports of the Commissioners of Irish Education Inquiry, 1825–6* (Royal Irish Academy, 2013)

4. Lady Wilde, *Ancient Legends, Mystic Charms, and Superstitions of Ireland* (Ticknor and Co. Publishers, 1887)

5. Terence A.M. Dooley, *Estate Ownership and Management in Nineteenth and Early Twentieth-Century Ireland* (Irish Academic Press, 2000)

6. *First Report of the Commissioners of Inquiry into the State of the Irish Fisherie*, (Alexander Thom, Dublin, 1836, House of Commons Parliamentary Papers Online, © 2006 ProQuest Information and Learning Company)

7. Sharon Paice MacLeod, *Celtic Myth and Religion*, (McFarland Publishers, 2012)

8. John Matthews with Caitlín Matthews, *Taliesin: The Last Celtic Shaman* (Inner Traditions, 1991)

9. John Matthews, *The Sídhe: Wisdom from the Celtic Otherworld* (The Lorian Press, 2004)

10. Alexander Irvine, *My Lady of the Chimney Corner* (original edition: Eveleigh Nash, London, 1913; annotated edition: Books Ulster, 2015)

11. Maria Edgeworth, *Castle Rackrent* (original edition: J. Johnson, 1800; World's Classics edition: Oxford University Press, 1995)

12. John J. Marshall, *Popular Rhymes and Sayings of Ireland* (original edition: 1924; third edition: Books Ulster, 2015)

13. Patrick John Kenedy, *The Universal Irish Songbook* (original edition: P. J. Kenedy, 1884; reprint edition: Forgotten Books, 2015)

14. Eddie Lenihan and Carolyn Eve Green, *Meeting the Other Crowd: The Fairy Stories of Hidden Ireland* (Jeremy P. Tarcher/Putnam, 2003)

15. Seumas MacManus, *The Story of the Irish Race: A Popular History of Ireland* (originally published 1921; revised edition: Devin-Adair Company, 1990)

16. Thomas C. Irwin, *Irish Poems and Legends* (original edition: Messrs. Cameron & Ferguson, date unknown; reprint edition: Forgotten Books, 2015)

17. Mara Freeman, *Kindling the Celtic Spirit: Ancient Traditions to Illumine Your Life Throughout the Seasons* (HarperCollins, 2001)

18. Kathryn Miles, *All Standing: The Remarkable Story of the Jeanie Johnston, the Legendary Irish Famine Ship* (Simon & Schuster, 2013)

19. Penelope Ody Mnimh, *The Herb Society's Complete Medicinal Herbal* (Dorling Kindersley, 1993)

20. Stephen Harrod Buhner, *The Lost Language of Plants* (Chelsea Green Publishing, 2002)

21. Stephen Harrod Buhner, *Plant Intelligence and the Imaginal Realm* (Bear and Company, 2014)

22. Website: Wildflowers of Ireland, https://www.wildflowersofireland.net/

23. Website: Irish Wildflowers by Jenny Seawright, https://www.irishwildflowers.ie/index.html

24. Website: The Irish Language Forum, https://www.irishlanguageforum.com/

25. Film: *Call of the Forest: The Forgotten Wisdom of Trees* with Diana Beresford-Kroeger.

Acknowledgments

Where to begin Thanksgiving for a ten-year project such as this one? The tapestry of readers, cheerleaders, inspirational catalysts, and project supporters is richly woven.

As Morrigan Lane said, "'Tis thanks I owe you."

To:

The ancestors (especially Kate and Connie O'Rourke, from whom the characters Kate and Connie McDonaugh were derived) and the invisibles in The Otherworld who invaded my dreams, inhabited my mother's stories about *the old sod*, and guided my writing.

12 Willows Press and Steven Long's troupe—Elizabeth, Jordan, and the cats—for believing that a story written in a time two hundred years ago is still a story for our times. For exquisite editing by Annaliese Jakimidcs, Deborah Burke, and Blessingway, from whom I learned how to be a better writer. For a masterful layout and map by Mariella Travis of Alleiram, and a beautiful sketch of the parchment by John Forssen.

NUI Galway History professor, Niall Ó Cíosáin (now retired) said yes to a phone call from a strange woman in Maine who dared to write a novel set long ago in the land of her ancestors. For the vast assemblage of books and research information he generously provided during my visit, and the follow-up emails as well.

My friends in Ireland who may not even know how influential they were in providing grounded magic for the story, and the Irish filmmaker Vivien de Courcy (*Dare to Be Wild*) who not only read an early manuscript but sought out my editor to "give her some Irish guidance."

The mythologist, author, and Arthurian expert, John Matthews, whose chronicle of his encounter with a member of The Good People in his book *The Sídhe*, inspired much about what I called, "The Once-and-Only Language" in my novel. And to Robin Wall Kimmerer, whom I hope will return to Maine. Whenever I was stuck in my writing, I opened *Braiding Sweetgrass* (Milkweed Editions, 2013) and remembered the wisdom that all original peoples had (and most still have), and was inspired once again to tap into the wisdom of my people.

The musicians who brought my original songs to life, especially Donegal's own Oisín McAuley and Michael Farquharson, my producer, and co-creator. (Our mantra: "Better than Disney!")

My dearest friends, and members of book clubs, writing groups, and Maine Writers and Publishers Association, who faithfully read sections, Chapters, and/or the manuscript with enthusiasm. And for those who taught me the importance of dreams, divination, and listening. You know who you are.

My mother, Mary Margaret Mattimore Elwell, for her singing and storytelling and for being the hearth of our home. My father, Gordon Elwell, who loved Irish music as much as Mom did. My seven brothers and sisters—and the in-laws—who weighed in at various times about the story trajectory and its themes, and who patiently read my texts, calmed my worries, and cheered me on. For my mother-in-law, Stella, who loved to hear me read aloud some Chapters in my clumsy Irish brogue.

For John Comeau, who is the man of my dreams, and for whom my gratitude is endless.

For the stunning landscapes and moody skies of western Ireland. I hope my writing has been a tribute to your beauty; and to the unconquerable Irish people, whose resiliency, humor, and poetry I deeply respect.

I conclude with this blessing. As the Irish have said during those times, *May you have the health of a salmon!*

Conversation Guide

1. TONE

The book begins with Morrigan summoned by the mythical sea god Manannán mac Lir. Against all dictates, she steals Uncle Colm's boat. With this start, what tone has the author set for the story?

2. POWER

Track Morrigan's feelings of power and freedom versus powerlessness and suppression/oppression in the story. When does she move with her own power; when does she suppress it?

3. FAITH

The idea of *faith* is prevalent throughout the book. Describe how the juxtaposition of *faith* versus "the (Catholic) faith" existed in parallel in those times in Ireland.

4. SETBACK

Morrigan faces an uncertain future after being banished from the place where she feels most alive—the quay. Her dream of becoming a ship's captain seems impossible. Cathleen tells her, "Sometimes it's a person like your uncle who gives you a gift wrapped in layers of disappointment." When in your life have you experienced a setback or hardship that, with hindsight, can be seen as a gift?

5. MENTOR CATHLEEN

Cathleen uses sky descriptions to describe moods because she is "too bent over to see faces" (e.g., "Sodden skies are upon you, Morrigan"). Why do you suppose the author chose to give Cathleen a physical spine disability? Have you had a mentor in your life whose words seemed drenched with import, wisdom, or significance?

6. "NEW EYES"

In a dream, a teacher gives Morrigan a small square of sheep's cheese and a tin of water, asking her to partake and "see with new eyes." During her journey, in what ways does Morrigan begin to see with new eyes?

7. ROMANCE

Finn is an affable friend whom Morrigan begins to see differently. Can you recall the sensory experience of an early spark of romance in your life, of innocent mutual attraction?

8. BIRTH/DEATH

Morrigan has a harrowing birth, and finally comes into life *en caul*. Finn's mother dies giving birth to him. Cathleen is a midwife. Kate McDonaugh speaks to Connie from the dead. In what way do birth and death, the seen and unseen, play a role in 1820s Irish culture?

9. LEARNING

Morrigan is drawn to nature, and prefers "nature as teacher, Cathleen's kind of learning" to the "useless things" Schoolmaster Winnett teaches, but then learns there are benefits to both. Besides the more institutional or traditional education, what learnings have you drawn from the broader landscape of your life?

10. THE ONCE-AND-ONLY LANGUAGE

In the story, Morrigan learns she has not forgotten the Once-and-Only Language, although most other humans have. Do you feel a personal kinship with any part of the natural world? Have you ever had an experience that you would describe as a "conversation" with some part of nature, such as a river, a tree, a sunset, or a field of flowers?

11. WOLF'S MESSAGE

The wolf tells Morrigan, "It is the way of things that the fate of the world rests upon the fate of your own, small village." In what ways can this be viewed as an axiom for life?

12. SHAWNA THE PIG

Shawna the pig has an unusual attraction to Morrigan. What does their relationship signify? In your life, have you experienced an uncanny closeness to a non-human being?

13. THE GOOD PEOPLE

Although under siege from English colonizers and the Catholic Church, the "Good People"—the fairy world and invisible realms— were very much a part of 1820s Irish culture and daily life. What value did this "world of the marvelous" have for poor Irish fishermen and their families? In what ways could they be viewed as limiting and fear-based?

14. HUNGER/FOOD

Hunger, and the presence or absence of food, is as much a part of the story as are the forest medicines that Morrigan begins to learn and collect. How does this interdependent world contrast with our world today?

15. SCHOOLMASTER WINNETT

Schoolmaster Winnett seems a very *unlikable* character. Then we learn about his childhood trauma (i.e., an abusive, alcoholic father). In these days before "trauma-informed" treatment, how, if at all, does this shift your perspective of him?

16. SIR MARTIN'S ACTIONS

How can you reconcile the fact that Sir Martin cruelly banishes his wife from his daughter Mary's life and evicts villagers who cannot pay their rent, and yet has been working in Parliament for the fair treatment of animals?

17. BETHA AND DESTINY

Betha wonders if she "altered her destiny" by stealing her Grandmother Isla's parchment. Can you point to a moment in your life where one decision shifted everything?

18. GUILT

In what ways does guilt—felt guilt and true guilt—appear in the story?

19. MOTHERS AND DAUGHTERS

At one level, this is a story about mothers and daughters—Betha and Morrigan, Lady Elizabeth and Mistress Mary. Describe the complicated nature of their relationships and how it affects the characters' actions.

20. MYSTERY AND UNCERTAINTY

Morrigan is at odds with her mum. Betha has a vital need for safety, security, and certainty. Morrigan begins to let go of those necessities as she ponders her destiny and trusts in the mystery that carved a remarkable course in her life. How do you balance mystery and certainty in these uncertain times?

21. FRIENDSHIP

Mistress Mary is drawn to Morrigan against all dictates of society. Tommy says, "There is no need like the lack of a friend," and when Morrigan shares this sentiment with an ill Mary, everything shifts, and their friendship becomes deeper than the class divide that separates them. Do you find this realistic?

22. HEALING

How has this story shaped your thoughts about the nature of healing? If you were to symbolically move your hand across a parchment such as the one in the novel, which of the five cords—Body, Mind, Heart, Spirit, Terra—if any, would be "frayed," or in need of healing?

23. JOY

Morrigan learns her healing song—the words that summon The Invisibles—is *Only Joy Lives Here*. What would it look like to pursue only joy in your life?

24. BOOK TITLE

As Mistress Mary nears death, Grandmother Mamoh tells Morrigan that Isla believed "there is a moon in all things." What meaning have you drawn from the story about this phrase?

25. DESTINY

Cathleen says: "Is there one true destiny a person is fated to have? Or does a person create a destiny choice by choice?" What do you think? Is a life lived according to "the fates" or is a life lived choice by choice?

26. TOMMY AND SIR MARTIN

Morrigan's father, Tommy, learned a lesson from Morrigan in "loving your enemies" when she chose to help heal Mistress Mary despite the landowner's agents' cruelty. What lesson did Sir Martin learn from Morrigan? How is Sir Martin's story one of transformation?

27. ONE'S VILLAGE

Is one's "village" the place where one's ancestors' bones feed the soil, or is one's "village" any being one encounters?

28. INTUITION

In a dream, a turtle tells Morrigan, "[Y]ou know more than you think you know." What if we all have intuitive capacities that can be cultivated by listening deeply to our own inherent wisdom? Do you believe this to be true? How can your own intuitive capacities be cultivated?

29. FEMINISM

In what way could *A Moon in All Things* be called a feminist novel?

30. BELIEF

From the first page, the word *believe* is presented as a word heard on the winds. The concept pervades the novel—from Mistress Mary's strange pea-based curative ("Nothing will work unless you believe!") to Morrigan's healing song ("Believe believe that anything's possible if you see it differently...") to the belief that redheads like Morrigan cause the seas to churn, and the belief that counter-charms and walking in the counter-clockwise direction engender bad luck. Recent evidence from quantum scientists has supported the power of beliefs in bringing about our own reality. Even the Ted Lasso series has *Believe* as a prominent motivator for his football (in the United States, the term is *soccer*) team. Some would say beliefs have destinations, beneficial or not beneficial. What are the beliefs that enrich or inhibit your life?

31. THE DECISION

In the end, Morrigan is faced with an impossibly difficult decision—to join Finn aboard a ship to America or to remain behind to claim her role as healer in her ancestral home. Morrigan remains behind. Do you agree with her decision? Tommy reminds her she is only sixteen. In her shoes, would you have made the same decision? Is it fair to say that, in the end, both Finn and Morrigan put their calling above their love? (At least for now!)

About the Author

Jennifer Elwell Comeau was raised on Irish songs and stories. Her ancestors were woodland people, and as a certified Forest Therapy Guide, singer-songwriter, and author-speaker, her creative muse is nature. Her children's book, *The Inside of ME* (12 Willows Press, 2024), is a profound reminder of the magic that happens on the inside when we go outside. Her poems and essays have been published in anthologies: *No Ordinary Words: The Real Life Wisdom of Women* (No Ordinary Words Publishing, 2022), *A Dangerous New World: Maine Voices on the Climate Crisis* (Littoral Books, 2019), and *Sacred Stone Sacred Water* (White Cloud Press, 2019). She has produced two albums of original music—*She Flies* and *Feed the Tribe*—available on all music streaming platforms.

A former corporate executive, Comeau is an ambassador for TreeSisters.org, an international reforestation and gender equity organization, and a facilitator for OzGreen.org, in their YOUth LEADing The World program. She lives with her husband, John Comeau (Lt. Col., USMC, retired), and a spunky poodle, Bridey, in Kennebunkport, Maine, where she writes, hosts climate buoyancy workshops and sacred circles, and runs a Wild Wonder Forest Bathing business. www.jennifercomeau.com